Midnight Hour

ALSO BY C. C. HUNTER

Born at Midnight

Awake at Dawn

Taken at Dusk

Whispers at Moonrise

Chosen at Nightfall

Reborn

Eternal

Unspoken

Almost Midnight: The Novella Collection

Midnight Hour

·····◆·····

C. C. HUNTER

ST. MARTIN'S GRIFFIN ✿ NEW YORK

MIDNIGHT HOUR. Copyright © 2016 by Christie Craig. All rights reserved. Printed in the United States of America. For information, address St. Martin's Press, 175 Fifth Avenue, New York, N.Y. 10010.

www.stmartins.com

The Library of Congress Cataloging-in-Publication Data is available upon request.

ISBN 978-1-250-03588-2 (trade paperback)
ISBN 978-1-250-03587-5 (e-book)

Our books may be purchased in bulk for promotional, educational, or business use. Please contact your local bookseller or the Macmillan Corporate and Premium Sales Department at 1-800-221-7945, extension 5442, or by e-mail at MacmillanSpecialMarkets@macmillan .com.

First Edition: October 2016

10 9 8 7 6 5 4 3 2 1

To all my Shadow Falls fans who have embraced my characters as much as I have, who have loved, laughed, and cried as they read Kylie's, Della's, and Miranda's journey. To those readers who have written to tell me how these characters have touched their lives and inspired them. To those who understand, I have tears in my eyes as I write this dedication because I'm seriously going to miss these magical fictional people who have filled my imagination, my dreams, and my computer for the last six years. Thank you to all my fans and street team members who have joined me on this ride. May the spirit of Shadow Falls forever be with you.

Acknowledgments

Thank you to my editor, Rose Hilliard, and my agent, Kim Lionetti, for taking the Shadow Falls journey with me. Thank you to my friends for adding awesome craziness to my life: Lori Wilde, Susan Muller, Diane Kelly, Kathleen Adey, Jody Payne, and Tracy Goodwin. To my hubby, who reads every book I write and laughs and cries in all the right places. To my family for being the threads in the crazy tapestry that is my wacky world: To my son, Steven Craig, and Sarah Skuchko, the new, wonderful, and funny woman in his life. (You do realize when you make it into a book, you can't ever leave.) To my daughter, Nina Craig Makepeace, her husband, Jason, and that smart and beautiful little girl who completes my life when she calls me Ma Maw. Without the people in my circle, I wouldn't be who I am; I couldn't create the stories or the madcap characters who dance on the pages of my novels. So here's to all of you who have laughed with me, cried with me, given me a hand up, kicked my butt when I needed it, and added color to my world when it might have been black and white without you.

Midnight Hour

Chapter One

No sooner than the heavy door closed—*cla-thump*—did the world go vacant and black. No light. No color. No sound.

No shit! "I don't like this," Miranda Kane whispered to her sister, Tabitha, who clutched her hand. She took one small step back.

"But you're here because you love me. And you were just going to be studying."

Tabitha said it as if studying wasn't all that important. Easy for her to say. She'd already scored high enough on the SAT and she wasn't the one who was dyslexic . . .

"Please," Tabitha whispered. "I'd do this for you."

So true. "I do love you, but I—"

"Shh, she might hear you." Tabitha's shaky voice came out so low it faded into the shadows. She took a step, drawing Miranda closer. "I think we go this way."

"Think?" Miranda's heart slowed down to the eerie beat of music in a scary movie. "I thought you'd done this before?"

"I did. But for some reason it's darker in here this time." Tabitha's grip tightened with confidence, but her palm, slick with fear, told a different story. Still, she pulled Miranda into a tomb-like obscurity, a hallway perhaps, leading her to the place where an old fortune-teller waited.

Tabitha must have stopped walking, because Miranda bumped right into her. "Let's just leave." She gave Tabitha's hand a come-on tug.

Her sister tugged back. "No. I really need this."

Those words brushed against the side of Miranda's cheek. They stood that close, but her eyes hadn't adjusted and only blackness filled her vision. She blinked and finally made out her sister's silhouette. They stood at the same height. Same weight. Looked enough alike to be twins, but Tabitha, five months older, was only her half sister.

Yup, that meant their father had been a bad boy. The dirty little secret had remained buried until nine months ago. Growing up an only child had been lonely for both of them. Neither Miranda nor Tabitha had stopped resenting the missed time.

"There." Tabitha's one word tiptoed through the darkness.

Miranda blinked and saw the fire-like radiance that called them forward.

"Okay, we do this and leave. Fast." Her last word came out laced with determination. Being here felt like a bad idea. And it wasn't because they were going to be late to their dinner date.

The soft *clip clop* of their footsteps was swallowed by blackness as they inched down the hall. Soon they moved through a doorway into a glow. The air thickened with the scent of burnt herbs. Through flickering light Miranda saw the old woman, sitting at a scarred wooden table that held eight candles and one crystal ball.

She didn't move.

Didn't breathe.

Did her heart even beat?

Miranda held what little oxygen she had in her lungs. Unfocusing her gaze, she studied the woman's forehead, where patterns told one's species but were readable only by other supernaturals. Was the woman even Wiccan? Her scroll-like markings labeled her as a witch like Miranda and Tabitha. The lack of color in that design characterized her as one with questionable morals. And her overall appearance portrayed her as battier than bat shit.

Her thick gray hair stood up in knots, as if a rat had taken up residence in the unkempt mess. Her clothes, all black, hung loose and ragged as if she'd not only stopped caring, but stopped eating. Her skin, a map of wrinkles, clung to her skull.

She looked . . . older than dirt. Dirty. Dead tired. Ready to leave this world that apparently hadn't been kind to her. The question was: was she a victim or a culprit in her own demise?

"You . . ." The witch's scratchy voice clawed at the air. "You go first." Her faded gray gaze eased away from her crystal ball and stalled on Miranda.

Stalled.

Stared.

Stayed on her in a way that made Miranda's breath catch. Warning chills slithered up and down her spine and she cupped her hand to keep from sending the woman the finger. Not the middle one, where insults arose, but her pinky, from where magic and fore-warnings ensued.

"Me?

"First?

"Why?"

She almost choked on the smoky air as the shadows in the room inched closer, ready to pounce.

Miranda moved a cautionary gaze left then right. Everything felt haunted—possessed.

Heavy drapes, blood-red in color, clung to the entire back wall as if a living, breathing entity. The thick claustrophobic fabric blocked the sunlight from entering while trapping the shadowy darkness within. The room felt like a . . .

No, not just the room—the entire house—felt like a prison.

But whose?

The ambience and sinister décor was not the norm for a witch who followed the do-no-harm policy. Then again, all of this could simply be for show to entertain her human clients—clients who without eerie ambience didn't believe in magic. Still, the woman could have at least combed her hair.

Maybe even used a little moisturizer on her face.

Why in Hades had Miranda allowed Tabitha to talk her into this?

It was nuts.

Crazy.

Absurd.

"Why not you?" the old witch taunted.

Miranda stiffened her spine with false bravado. "My sister's the high priestess. She should go first." She gave Tabitha a nudge. And as soon as the fortune spilled from the old woman's lips, Miranda planned to get the hell out of here. She'd agreed to accompany her sister, not to participate.

"I know who she is," the old witch said. "I do not know who you are. And your fear feeds my curiosity." She cocked her head and continued to stare. "It isn't me you fear, is it? Are you frightened of what you will learn? Afraid my words will break your heart?"

Afraid? Hell yeah! Was Miranda the only one who understood the ol' adage: ignorance is bliss? Especially when it comes to love. And that was this witch's specialty. Supposedly humans paid big bucks for her to forecast their love lives and expose unfaithful lovers. For her fellow witches, she gave discounts. She was dubbed the reader of love, lust, and longings.

Right now, all Miranda longed to do was to get the hell out of here.

"Should I be afraid?" Miranda asked, hoping the fear rattling her soul didn't sound in her voice. But right then Miranda felt it. A new kind of fear. Her skin began to crawl, her heart felt overly heavy. This was not just fear, but a forewarning of impending doom. Was the witch causing it? This place? Or something altogether different?

Maybe the latter, since this feeling had hit yesterday as well. Impending doom didn't always mean immediate.

Miranda glanced at Tabitha. Was she feeling it, too? Was something terrible about to happen? In spite of being only half sisters, they shared the talent of premonition. Not of good things to come, mind you, just crappy stuff.

To Miranda's relief, Tabitha didn't look concerned. Which could mean that the foreboding might just be an overreaction on Miranda's part. Or was her sister not reacting because her heart remained preoccupied with Anthony Bastin?

"This was a silly idea," Miranda spoke up. They were witches for Goddess' sake. They sure as heck didn't need another witch, one who mostly did theatrical tricks for humans, to give them a look-see into their so-called love lives. Besides, she had Ernie, her real magic eight ball, to offer advice. Not that he was always reliable, but again, maybe she didn't need to know everything.

"Not silly," Tabitha said. "If she wants you to go first, just do it. Pleeeease." The last word came out soft and pulled on Miranda's heartstrings. And with that tug, the foreboding faded.

Shifting her focus away from her sister's imploring expression, Miranda caught two gold eyes staring at her—with the same look—from the shadows in the corner of the room. She wasn't sure, but those piercing eyes appeared to belong to an armadillo. Did the scaly creature live here? Was it the woman's pet? Or worse? Her prisoner? Maybe even a human turned into a rodent-like beast?

And if the latter, that could be bad. Good witches knew the penalties for imprisoning a soul. To not heed the rules could lead to dire consequences.

The animal shifted back and the slightest sound of metal on metal rattled. Blinking, Miranda spotted the small chain around the ugly creature's leg. Her breath caught. This was so not good.

She cut her eyes to her sister. "I really think we should just—"

"No. Just a few more minutes." Tabitha grabbed Miranda's

hand. "I need to know what she says about Anthony. And I don't want to do it alone."

Anthony was a French vampire she and her sister had met while in Paris. He'd come to Texas about three weeks ago and he and Tabitha had been dating secretly behind her mother's back, because her mom insisted she only date warlocks. While Miranda's mom didn't apply quite the same pressure, she often reminded Miranda how pleased she was to have her now dating someone of her own kind. "It's just easier to make a relationship work when there are no culture issues," her mom had said.

Just because something was easier, didn't mean it was right.

Nevertheless, her mom's unappreciated words of wisdom were just enough to make Miranda worry. Worry that if things didn't work out between her and Shawn she'd be disappointing her mom once again. And that seemed to be something Miranda excelled at lately.

"You promised," Tabitha pleaded.

Yeah, Miranda had promised, and letting Tabitha down felt wrong, too. They were sisters after all.

"Fine. But we're going to be late meeting Shawn and Anthony." Miranda glanced back at the witch. "Go ahead." She pushed her feelings aside, determined not to believe a damn thing the witch said.

Rising on skinny legs, the old woman reached out. Before Miranda knew her intent, her deed was done.

"Ouch!" She glared at the woman and rubbed her scalp where the old witch had yanked out her hair. The witch dropped Miranda's strawberry blond strands into an old stone bowl that looked blackened from fire.

The old sorceress slowly raised her arms. Her creaky and almost crippled body danced as if that could add power to her spell. Complete theatrics. Every witch knew all she really needed to move was her pinky.

Yet, Miranda took advantage of the woman's dog and pony show and pointed her own pinky toward the hidden animal in the shadows. The light clink of the chain falling away was barely audible but told Miranda she'd accomplished her objective.

Now to figure out how to accomplish her other objective— getting the hell out of here.

The witch stopped dancing and started to chant. "Two strands of a fair maiden's hair, a tip of a raven's feather." She picked up a feather and used the sharpened edge of a long fingernail to cut off the very end of the feather. The tiny ink-black clippings floated down, disappearing into the bowl.

She raised her gaze and her voice up, as if speaking to a greater power. "A scraping of a cat's claw, the breath of pure magic, and the fire from the devil himself!"

Okay. That last ingredient gave Miranda's nerves another hit. Was the witch well acquainted with the devil? Did she partner with evil to accomplish her magic? Or was this just part of a well-practiced act?

Pushing back the urge to panic, Miranda noted that the woman didn't look as evil as she did demented. Not that both couldn't be dangerous.

Then the witch used another fingernail, talon-like in appearance, to scratch away a few tiny particles from the feline claw. The mere specks of dust cascaded down to the bowl as if they knew their path and dared not detour. She lifted her face, pursed her lips, and breathed into the air. A plume of fire burst forth and she reached up. Catching one of the red embers between her gnarled fingers, she dropped it into the bowl.

Flames rose from the brew and the recognizable stench of burnt hair filled the room.

Miranda put her hand over her nose and cut her eyes to the door. Okay, now it looked a little more like black magic than an act. Would it be cowardly of her to run? Probably.

Did she care?

No. Not about appearing like a coward—bravery wasn't her

forte—that was Kylie and Della's cup of tea. Her roommates were badass. But Miranda did care . . . about Tabitha.

As if reading her mind, Tabitha's hand came out and gripped Miranda's arm.

Inhaling a deep gulp of singed air, she resigned herself to carry through. After all, this wasn't the first time she'd come face-to-face with black magic.

Chin held high, she turned to the woman again, the flames from the bowl flickered in the witch's eyes and made their gray color brighten to a cold hue of silver.

"Can we get this show on the road? We've got a double date to be at in fifteen minutes." Miranda forced a calm in her voice that she didn't feel.

Are you afraid of what you will learn? Afraid my words will tear your soul apart?

The witch's questions echoed inside Miranda's head and registered as truth. Her heart admitted it wasn't just the possibility of black magic that sent her pulse dancing. She was afraid of hearing she'd made a mistake. That she shouldn't have turned her back on Perry, a shape-shifter she'd loved, to turn her sights on Shawn Hanson, a hot warlock FRU agent. Maybe her heart wasn't ready.

And that next weekend might be the biggest mistake of all. Going away a few days with Shawn pretty much said they were taking the relationship up a notch. A notch that meant getting naked, getting naughty, and knocking out her whole still-a-virgin-at-almost-eighteen issue.

Not that she was ashamed of that. Face it, she could've found a volunteer to help change her status. But call her old-fashioned, she believed sex should be special, and with someone special.

Shawn was special.

She cared about him. He was . . . wonderful, kind, and patient. He had the looks that had girls staring—kisses as sweet as cotton candy. He had the attributes that not only made him hot boyfriend material, but life-mate material.

But it wasn't what he was or had that made her question her decision. It was what he wasn't and didn't have.

He didn't have that sneak-up-on-you effect that made her stop paying attention in class just to write his name over and over again. His smile, while sweet as soft rain, didn't have that melt-me quality that made her feel shaky, silly, and slightly dizzy. His presence, as fulfilling as it was when he was there, wasn't making her feel devastatingly empty when he wasn't. While his qualities were perfect life-mate material, her heart wasn't screaming soul mate.

He wasn't making her feel what a certain shape-shifter had made her feel not so long ago.

Was it because it was new? Did her feelings for Shawn just need time to grow? Was it because she was older and adult love felt less consuming? Or was she just scared to let herself care that deeply again?

She had a thousand reasons why this relationship building with Shawn would feel different from what she'd had with Perry—even more reasons to put her trust in Shawn. And that was what she had to remember.

Right?

The witch waved the smoky fumes up into her face and inhaled, then she put her hand over the bowl and smothered the flames.

"Hand me your palm." The witch's gnarled hand reached for Miranda's wrist.

"Why?" Miranda's one-word question hung in the air.

"Just do it," Tabitha said. "It won't hurt, I've had it done numerous times. This is how I knew Brady was cheating on me."

Shawn wasn't cheating on her. Miranda knew that with all her heart. He was the most loyal guy she'd ever met.

The witch looked up at Tabitha and frowned. "And if you'd come to me before you got with him, I would have warned you of him and the death of that relationship before it ever started. The guy was a weasel."

"I wanted to trust my heart," Tabitha said.

Her sister's words gave Miranda's own reservations more merit. Wasn't that what Miranda wanted? She didn't need an old witch's answer to confuse her. Her heart was confused enough.

"Never trust that fickle organ," the witch said. "It beats merely to lead you wrong, just so you feel it break and know it's there." The witch looked back at Miranda. "Now, give me your hand!"

Feeling optionless, Miranda did as ordered. The witch placed Miranda's hand on top of the bowl then turned it over. The warm ashes fell against her skin but didn't burn. Quite the opposite actually. A cold unnatural shiver ran up her arm and down her spine, leaving footprints on her very soul.

The witch continued to hold Miranda's wrist, but removed the bowl. Miranda felt it then. The power, the undeniable sensation of magic. Whatever the woman said would be the truth. Black magic or not. This woman's words would not be a lie.

And then what? Her heart thumped out the question. Would she walk away from Shawn? Would she completely give up on Perry? Was she really ready to hear this?

She glanced down. The ashes had created a pattern on her palm, almost like a henna tattoo. She watched as it spread up her wrist and midway to her forearm.

The armadillo rushed across the witch's feet, his tiny paws and overgrown claws tapping against the old wood floor. Miranda heard the old witch gasp. She dropped Miranda's hand and lurched back.

Tabitha reached for Miranda's arm. "Why did her marks spread like that and mine never have?"

The witch stumbled a few more steps back and looked first at the freed creature, then back to Miranda's arm. The white of her eyes grew larger. But from what? Fear? Shock? Anger that her armadillo was free? What was she thinking?

"You should go!" Her gravelly voice rang in the dark, followed by a sound of distant thunder.

"Go?" Tabitha asked, the single-word question punctuated with a low back-of-the-throat sound of disapproval. "Not until you read me. I need to know about Anthony. My mom hates him, but I think he might be my life mate."

"Go. Now!" The witch's gaze shot back to Miranda. Fear and something else flickered in her eyes.

Was she pissed because Miranda had freed the animal, or were . . . were Miranda's markings making the witch panic?

Before Miranda could decide which it was, encroaching thunder shattered the silence. The walls, the drapes, the table, everything in the room started trembling. The approaching storm drew closer as if something in this very room called it.

The candles on the table shook, their flames reaching up higher and higher. Miranda held out her pinky to calm the chaos, but no magic came out.

Oh, crap!

She saw Tabitha attempt and fail with the same calming spell.

The armadillo made a hissing noise. It scurried closer to the door, stopping at the threshhold. Its glowing golden eyes seemed to suggest they follow. Smart armadillo.

The sensation of a premonition restarted low in her gut and began to grow.

And grow.

"Everyone should leave." Miranda looked at the witch and knew it was true. The heart and pulse of the storm was aimed right for them. Thunder shook the foundation of the house. The smell and sting of its power filled the air.

Devastation hung seconds away. "Out everyone!" Miranda waved for the witch to move.

She didn't move. Could she not feel this? Hear this? Or was she the one causing it?

The roar of impending calamity rang louder in Miranda's ears. Lightning hit the table and the crystal ball exploded. The sizzle and crack of it sent shards of glass through the air.

Several of those shards pricked Miranda's skin. Blood trickled down her arm, streaking the marks the witch had put on her.

"We've gotta go! Come on," Miranda screamed, but the witch remained frozen in an odd kind of stillness. A few rivulets of blood snaked down the old lady's face, getting trapped in her deep wrinkles. Miranda reached for her but she jerked back as if Miranda was the evil one.

The sound of the storm screamed louder. Miranda grabbed her sister's arm and pulled her out of the room, down the dark hall, and hurried in the direction of the door. Hitting a wall, she brushed her hand around searching for . . . Finding the doorknob, she swung it open.

Sunlight blasted inside, but left her blind. She kept moving. Her clasp tightened on her sister's hand.

They'd barely escaped to the porch when the loud *ka-boom* sounded behind them. "Mother crackers!" Miranda screamed as the force of the explosion threw both her and her sister across the yard. The last thing registering in Miranda's brain was her sister's fingers sliding from her grip.

She tried to hang on.

She tried with all her heart. With all her strength. But her sister was gone. Nothing but charcoal-colored smoke filled Miranda's vision.

Everything went black.

Chapter Two

"Just do as he says and you won't be hurt." Perry Gomez's voice came out muffled from behind the Halloween mask. Through the eyeholes he watched the pretty bank teller's large hazel eyes brim with tears. His father shot his gun up in the air. Her eyes, eyes almost the same color as Miranda's, held an inexplicable foreboding that he felt in his chest, outgrowing his rib cage—pushing against his chest bone. Oddly the warning didn't seem to be only about the robbery, but about . . . Miranda.

Seconds before entering the bank, a flood of Miranda images filled his mind. Her hazel eyes, her long strawberry blond hair, her small, slightly pugged nose. One right after another, the images came.

Her laughing.

Her teasing.

Her crying.

A lot of her crying.

Not that he ever went long without thinking about her. It had been nine months and two days since he'd left Shadow Falls, and damn he missed her. But something about those last visual snapshots felt different. Like she was trying to tell him something. It felt almost like an omen. But that was stupid, because shape-shifters didn't get omens.

Not unless . . . someone had sent it to him. Shit! Had Miranda sent it to him? Was she in some kind of trouble?

"Please don't hurt me," the teller said, her voice shaking and bringing Perry back to the problem at hand. And what a handful of a problem it was. Damn it. He hated this. He'd sought out his parents hoping to find . . . something.

Love.

Acceptance.

Answers.

Answers to how someone could just abandon their child. Or maybe not answers. He knew why they'd done it. His powers as a shape-shifter had arrived way too early, and made him . . . difficult to parent. Impossible some would say.

Hell, he couldn't even put a name to the reason finding them had felt so urgent, but whatever he'd been seeking, he hadn't found it.

That empty feeling inside him hadn't disappeared. He still needed . . . something. Yet, he'd been forced to admit that their abandonment had been the best thing they'd done for him.

Right now he wished he could return the favor. Just walk away, forget everything, and not look back. He couldn't. It was too late for that.

"We're not going to hurt you." Perry met the young woman's gaze, seeing and sensing bone-deep fear. Recently, after learning to control his power, he'd tapped into sort of an extra gift. He'd heard other shape-shifters had it, he just hadn't known he did. It was the ability to read shifts in people's emotions. He made an effort to sound calm, though he knew his Frankenstein mask didn't encourage tranquility. Hopefully, she recognized the truth in his voice. He purposely kept his own gun pointing down.

He hadn't wanted to carry a shotgun, but Caleb—his dad's friend who was the boss of some secret mob-like gang—ran the show and had insisted everyone be armed: *If we're not all carrying, the FRU might suspect we aren't human.*

As powerful of a shape-shifter as Caleb was—though not quite as powerful as Perry—the asswipe had more brawn than brains. And whoever was passing down the orders was a Big Mac short of a meat patty. Because this was their second bank job this week, and Caleb let it slip that two other groups were hitting banks and even some retail stores in different towns in Texas. This wasn't just a one-man show. Nevertheless, sooner or later the fact that the robbers could disappear without being seen was going to be a red flag to officials and the FRU would be called in.

Perry saw the girl's hands tremble. "Just put the money in the bag and we'll go," Perry assured her.

Another shot rang out behind him. The girl let out a low whimper that gave Perry another wave of regret. He looked back and saw Caleb standing in the middle of the bank lobby, his gun pointing at the ceiling. "Anyone hit an alarm and the next bullet will end up in their head."

The guy, his bright gold eyes peering out of his werewolf mask, locked on Perry. Or maybe not at him, but at the girl standing behind him. And that was even worse.

"Well, well, what do we have here?" Caleb asked.

Perry's heart raced when the man started strutting over. His cold eyes turned colder.

"How did you score the pretty one?" Caleb asked, leering at the girl as if she were a toy he had the right to play with.

Emotion rose in Perry's chest. *No one is playing with anyone!*

"Put the money in the bag," Perry told the girl, motioning to the black backpack, and wanting to get out of there before things got out of hand.

She did as Perry ordered, scooping stack after stack of bills out of her drawer and dropping them in the opened backpack.

Caleb moved closer. "You are a sight for sore eyes, aren't you, sweetheart?"

The girl's gaze widened with more fear and she cut her pleading eyes to Perry as if begging him to help her.

Caleb pointed his gun at her and motioned it to the left. "Why don't you come around here and let me see all of you."

The girl made another whimper. When she didn't move, he pointed the gun at her. "Come on, be a good girl."

Perry shot forward right in front of the gun. "No. We have to go before the cops get here."

Through the mask, Perry saw the man's eyes change colors again. Anger did that to a shape-shifter. And it was never a good sign.

"This won't take long," Caleb bit out and attempted to push Perry aside. His tone, his implication was so disgusting, Perry's own anger ratcheted up a notch. His skin started to burn, a sign that his emotions were heightening to dangerous levels and if he couldn't control them, he'd shift. Shift into something bigger, meaner, and right here in front of about ten humans. And that was not acceptable. But neither was what Caleb planned to do to the girl.

Perry stood solid, staring through his own mask, and refused to budge. Through the corner of his vision, he saw the girl watching as Frankenstein and a werewolf faced off. He hoped like hell that was all she was going to see. Concentrating, he found that internal switch inside him that allowed his anger to exist without awaking an unwanted beast.

"I said no. The cops have to be on the way by now." Perry felt his eyes brighten, a sign that his switch hadn't been completely turned off.

"Since when do you call the shots, kid?" Dislike hung on the man's words, but Perry didn't give a damn. Soon the asshole would really dislike him. The plan was already set in motion.

Perry took in a noseful of air, hoping to compose himself. Finding that calm and controlling his shifts had been something he'd only mastered in the last year. And occasionally he still failed at it.

"Since I don't want to get arrested!" he told Caleb, tightening his jaw.

"What's wrong?" Perry's dad shot over holding his own back-pack filled to the max with money.

"Your kid thinks he's in charge." Caleb put his gun to Perry's chest. "Now step back before your daddy has to see you die!"

Perry's breath caught in his chest. Not so much from fear, but from waiting to see his father's reaction. Would his father defend him against his partner in crime? Silence filled the bank. The hostages seemed to hold their breath. His dad didn't speak, but Perry saw a flicker of something in his eyes. Something that told Perry he might actually give a shit.

It shouldn't have mattered. It was too late. But for some damn reason it did.

It mattered.

"I just want to leave before the cops get here," Perry said, un-sure if that flicker of emotion in his father's eyes was enough to count on. Unsure if it actually meant anything. Right then his heart took an emotional U-turn. Suddenly he wished he hadn't seen it, because it was just going to make this harder.

"And I want to spend a few minutes with our pretty new friend here," Caleb hissed and cut his eyes briefly at the girl, then back at Perry. "Don't worry, I'll give you a few minutes with her, too."

Perry's skin started to tingle with fury. How could his father befriend someone with such low morals? Perry inhaled again, and prayed he could control the beast inside him that wanted to come out and play. That wanted to come out and kill.

"Perry's right," his dad finally spit out. "We've got to leave."

Did that mean his father really gave a shit? Or was he just being logical?

"Now you, too?" Caleb hissed. "Since when do you two think . . ." Sirens echoed from outside. Behind the mask, Caleb's eyes turned black. Obviously, he hated being proved wrong.

He snatched the backpack from the counter, turned, and hauled ass to the back. Perry's and his dad's footsteps slapped the tile right behind him.

Caleb pushed open the emergency exit, no doubt to throw the cops off, allowing them a few seconds to escape. Then he darted into a small office. Perry and his dad followed on his heels.

"Police! Don't anyone move!" The door had barely clicked shut when the sound of officers entering the bank echoed from behind the closed door.

Caleb closed his eyes, and his human form quickly transformed into a mouse. His father closed his eyes at the same time. But the older shape-shifter lacked the same amount of power and his change wouldn't come so quickly. Perry waited, wanting to see his father was safe, before he morphed himself. Soon, he wouldn't be able to protect his dad from the consequences, but right now, abandoning him felt so damn wrong.

Footsteps and voices rang closer. "Police!"

Then closer.

Bubbles of leftover energy filled the air and floated off his father's weakening human form.

Finally, only a mouse stood where his father had been. Perry concentrated on his own shift into a lizard. The door slammed open at the same time as his skin stung with the shift and his own iridescent orbs of energy filled the room.

Through tiny slits of eyes, Perry watched the officer barge into the room, his gun held out, ready to fire. "Shit," he muttered and flinched when one of the bubbles hit his skin and the magical current entered his body.

Perry scurried past the policeman now staring at the emptiness of the room. Perry had only gotten a few feet when another image of Miranda flashed in his head.

She lay on a patch of grass. So still. So pale.

Miranda? Miranda? Are you okay?

The vision flashed again and it had his scales tightening along with his heart. Fear of what that vision meant made Perry's tiny lizard legs move faster.

Pain. So much pain. Breathing hurt. Her lungs refused the oxygen. Something was wrong with the air.

Something was wrong . . . with her.

Miranda? Miranda? Are you okay?

The voice echoed somewhere in the distance. A voice she knew. A voice she had one time loved. A voice of a shape-shifter who'd left her, for a second time, and hadn't contacted her in over nine months.

Perry.

Then something or someone poked at her face. Once. Twice.

The third time, she forced her eyes open. She expected Perry, to see his blue eyes and blond hair brushing across his brow. Instead she gasped when she saw the hideous pink snout and scaly body. Was that . . . Perry? She blinked, confused about everything except knowing it wasn't Perry. Somehow she just knew.

Then fragments of memory came hurling at her. She remembered. The armadillo. The fortune-teller. Her sister. Losing her sister's hand.

Oh, God! Tabitha!

Lifting her face from the grass, smoke filled her lungs. Her eyes stung. She coughed. Couldn't breathe.

The sizzle and hiss of fire had her looking up at the burning house, but the smoke was so thick she could only see flames flickering behind the wall of gray fog.

She blinked and saw bits and pieces of burning lumber littering the yard only a few feet from her. Her lungs begged for air. Clean air. She inhaled and coughed and gagged.

The armadillo started poking her with his ugly nose again.

She fought the black spots clouding her vision, and finally saw her sister lying in an unconscious heap about three feet from her.

"Tabitha?" Between gasps and hacks, Miranda screamed her

sister's name, but when she went to push up on her arm, the pain brought her back down. Moaning, she used her other arm to drag herself closer to her sister.

"Tabitha?" she said, but her sister wasn't answering. Oh, God, was she even breathing?

"Talk to me!" Blood marred Tabitha's face. *Don't you dare die.* She reached over and put her hand on her sister's neck, praying she'd feel a pulse.

Nothing. No flutter of life touched her fingertips.

"No!" Miranda screamed and called her sister's name again. "Tabitha?"

An ache burst in Miranda's heart and subsided only when she saw her sister's chest move. Miranda's next smoky breath singed her lungs and throat. She had to get them away from the smoke. Begging the Divinities for strength, she managed to stand, dizziness and wave upon wave of pain almost had her hitting the ground. But determination had her using her one good arm to drag her unconscious sister out of the line of the thick smoke.

The stabbing pain in her side finally brought her back to her knees beside her sister. Miranda's left arm hung useless at her side. But Tabitha's whole body seemed useless.

With her good hand, she pulled her phone from her jean pocket. She took her first gulp of clean air. But her lungs didn't appear to be ready. Coughing, staring at her phone, the dizziness returned full force. She barely managed to hit the first name on her contact list.

But it was a good one.

A person who could handle any crisis.

A person who would be there for her in a pinch.

She heard Burnett's deep, serious voice answer. As reassuring as his voice was, those damn black spots started encroaching again.

Closer.

Faster.

A sense of numbness descended upon her again. Struggling to stay conscious, only two words slipped from her lips. "Need help."

Chapter Three

Something stirred Miranda. Sirens, voices, people prodding her. She felt herself being pulled out of the web of darkness, but in the obscure place there was no pain. She liked it better there. More voices rang out and continued to pull her back.

"I said back up!" The commanding voice stilled the air, demanded respect.

"And I said if you don't want your face rearranged you should get out of my friggin' way!"

Miranda knew only one person who had that way with words and was willing to butt heads with authority. She forced her eyelids open. As expected, she spotted the sassy dark-haired vampire.

"Hey?" Della must have noticed the flutter of Miranda's eyes opening for the girl dropped to her knees, her expression of sheer determination fading to something softer. To the expression of a best friend who cared.

"Oh, God. Are you okay?" Della's voice almost sounded unfamiliar, because it was seldom laced with such emotion.

"Officer," the voice from earlier called out. "Can you please remove this girl?"

Della flinched and Miranda's heart did the same. Not from the scene before her, but from her memory of what had happened. She remembered her sister's bloody and unconscious body.

"No! Where's Tabitha?" Her sister's name burned her throat. Miranda tried to turn her head where her sister had been, but her head wouldn't move that far. She reached up with her good hand and felt a brace around her neck.

"Is Tabitha okay?" Her words shook as she voiced the question to Della.

"They're putting her in an ambulance now," Della said.

"Is she okay?" Miranda pushed out the question.

Della took one second too long to answer. "I . . . I'm sure she'll be fine."

Miranda's soul went straight to aching. For seventeen years, she hadn't known she had a sister, but right now Miranda couldn't imagine her life without her. They talked every day, they shared everything. Embarrassment, laughter, pain. They were . . . sisters.

She struggled to feed air to her lungs, and when she did it hurt, not that the physical pain compared to what she felt for her sister.

"How bad is she?" Miranda tried to get up.

"No, you can't move. They're taking her to the hospital." Della gently pushed Miranda back down. "And Kylie's headed there now."

Thabump, thaaabump, tha . . . bump. Miranda's heart throbbed and echoed in her ears. "Oh, God! You think Tabitha's dying? That's why you sent Kylie, isn't it? To heal her, because you think . . ." She tried to get up again.

Della pushed her down. "No, no, no." She said it three times as if hoping it would sound more believable. It sounded anything but.

Her sister was dying! Her heart, now swollen with grief, clamored against her sore rib cage.

From Miranda's prone position, she saw Della flinch and then a cop appeared, standing over her.

"You are going to have to leave!" he growled.

Della didn't look up, didn't speak. Her only acknowledgment of him was the cold angry scowl pulling at her lips. The cop went to reach down. "Don't do it," Della hissed, the sharp warning in her tone was louder than her words.

A flicker of a second before his fingers latched on to the angry vampire, something, or someone, yanked the cop out of Miranda's line of vision.

"Give us a few minutes," another deep voice said. A familiar voice, not loud in pitch, but in a tone few dared to disobey.

Miranda cut her eyes to the right to see Burnett holding out his Federal Research Unit (FRU) badge. The agency was like the FBI, but oversaw the supernaturals. Humans just considered them an offshoot of the FBI.

Della glanced up at Burnett. "She's conscious now."

The tall dark vampire knelt down. His caring gaze found Miranda's and just knowing he was there had her chest tightening with emotion.

"You okay?" he asked.

Miranda tried to shake her head, but the brace made it hard to move her neck. "No," she spit out. "Did you see Tabitha? How bad is she?"

Miranda knew Burnett well enough to know he wouldn't sugar-coat it. Della usually didn't, either. But for Miranda, she'd tried.

"They're worried." Honesty laced his voice. His eyes were bright, probably due to the smell of blood, but his words came out soft and caring. "They can't revive her."

The air in Miranda's lungs shook. Her vision clouded with emotion. "Please get Kylie to her. Tell Kylie not to let her die. Please!"

"Kylie's on her way to the hospital now." He took Miranda's hand and frowned. "I know you are hurting both physically and emotionally, but can you answer a few questions?"

Miranda attempted to nod, but the damn neck thing prevented it again. "Yes."

"Should the FRU take over this case?"

Miranda knew what he was asking. Was something supernatural behind the explosion? She answered with confidence. "Yes."

Burnett frowned. "Can you tell me what happened?"

"Tabitha wanted her fortune told." Her voice shook. "The old witch seemed half crazy, she might have been practicing black magic, but she came off more demented than evil. I wasn't all that worried and then—"

"Did the witch do this?" Burnett asked, impatient to get the answers he wanted.

Miranda tried to think. "I don't know. She was reading my fortune and she saw the armadillo and then—"

"Saw what?" Burnett's two words sounded puzzled.

"The armadillo."

"Armadillo?" Della asked, her tone matching Burnett's.

They looked at each other as if worried Miranda was out of her head.

"I'm not crazy," she blurted out. "She had an armadillo."

Burnett nodded. "Okay. But . . . what does an armadillo have to do with—"

"I don't think it was a real armadillo, but someone she cursed and imprisoned. She had it chained up. I . . . I freed it. She saw it was loose at the same time she started to read my fortune and then . . . she seemed to panic. I don't know if it was because the armadillo had been freed or because of my fortune. She told us to leave and . . . then it was like a storm raged inside."

"A storm?" he asked.

"Wind, lightning. Everything started shaking."

He nodded. "Did the witch get out?"

"I told her to. But she just stood there. I tried to grab her but she lurched back. I . . . it was getting bad, louder. So I grabbed Tabitha and ran." Miranda's throat tightened with the realization that she might have left someone to die. And that was wrong. So wrong.

"She didn't follow you?" he asked.

"No, not out the front. I don't know if there was a back door.

I should have checked, I'm sorry." Miranda tried to breathe, but it hurt.

"For what?" Della asked. "That bitch of a witch probably did it."

Miranda didn't know if she believed it. If she'd done it why would she have told them to leave?

"The armadillo got out," Miranda added. "It was what woke me when the smoke was blowing at us. It was bad. I couldn't breathe. I managed to get Tabitha and I away from the fire."

"How did you two get here?" Burnett asked.

"Tabitha's car." Miranda answered, unsure why he was asking that when she could see the car still parked on the street.

"Who was with you?" he asked.

"Just us. Why?"

Miranda saw Della and Burnett share a glance.

"You sure?" Della asked.

"Positive. What is it?"

"Nothing," Burnett said, but it didn't sound like "nothing" and he glanced at Della and then lifted his face as if to test the air.

"He was here," Della said.

"Who?" Miranda asked again.

Before either of them answered, another man, a half-fae half-were, wearing a black FRU suit, appeared beside Burnett. "The paramedics are getting pissy. They're insisting they need to take her in. And the bulldog over there wants . . ." He lifted one brow as if he was leaving some things unsaid. "They have some questions. Lots of them."

Burnett glanced at Miranda. "You did good. Try not to worry." He stood up and looked at the other agent. "I'm calling this in. We're taking over the case. I'm going to the hospital. Get some other agents here to help investigate the scene. Oh, and put out an APB." He looked at Miranda, frowned, and then refocused on the agent. "We're looking for an old witch and an armadillo."

The man's eyes widened. "You're joking?"

"When have you ever known me to joke?"

Shawn Hanson was late to a date. He didn't do late. But his mom had insisted he sit and listen to her criticism of his recent choices. So he listened, not that he actually heeded her advice. He was almost twenty. His mom didn't dictate who he dated.

Parking his car in front of the restaurant where he was supposed to meet Miranda, her sister, as well as Anthony Bastin, he got out in a hurry, hoping she wasn't upset at him.

"Hey," Shawn offered a quick hello to Anthony who stood outside the restaurant. Anthony smiled and leaned in as if to embrace him. Shawn did a quick back step, discouraging the physical contact. Not that he blamed the guy. He was . . . French, which basically meant a tad touchy-feely.

He'd met Anthony in Paris when the FRU had sent him there to protect Miranda. Anthony had met Tabitha in Paris, had liked her, and had come to live in Texas in obvious hopes of them developing a relationship. Her high-priestess title, if not her attractiveness, made her a desirable choice for a life mate.

Shawn, however, found her sister much more desirable. Miranda, a friend of his younger sister, had been on his radar for years. And it wasn't just because she was hot, it was . . . He couldn't define it, but Miranda had something . . . something sweet and so unpretentious that she stood out from all the women he'd ever met. Anthony could have Tabitha.

Or maybe not. Because unfortunately for the European traveler, Miranda had told him that Tabitha's mom was against her daughter dating anyone who wasn't a warlock.

Not that he blamed Tabitha's mom. He'd made up his own mind to marry in his own species. Not because he disliked or held any prejudices toward others, but . . .

"Ah, I forget American men shy away from physical contact."

While Anthony still carried a touch of an accent, his English had immensely improved from nine months ago. The guy had no doubt worked hard. Shawn admired him for that.

"A handshake will do." Shawn offered his hand.

They shook. "The girls not here?" Shawn asked.

"Tabitha texted me and said she and Miranda might arrive late."

"Okay," Shawn pushed away his niggling guilt for letting his mother persuade him into staying for the repeated lecture. "Did they say how late?"

"No," he said.

Right then Shawn spotted the jewelry store next door. Perfect.

"Do you mind if we walk next door while we wait for them?"

"Not at all." The bell on the door announced them. A pretty girl from behind the counter greeted them. Shawn went straight to checking her pattern.

He noted she wasn't all human, but part vampire, witch, and shape-shifter. His nod included a little extra enthusiasm to let her know he wasn't here to cause trouble.

Her widening smile told him she understood.

"You are in the market for some jewelry?" Anthony's question pulled Shawn away from the girl.

"I'm looking for something for Miranda."

"An engagement ring?" Surprise heightened his voice and his accent.

"No. Just a necklace or something." They walked to the glass countertops. "Something that shows how I feel about her."

"And what do you feel?" the store clerk asked, not at all embarrassed at eavesdropping. She smiled again and he noted the dimple in her right cheek seemed to wink at him. "If I know how you feel, I might be able to point you to the right item."

A tad uncomfortable with stating his feelings, he considered changing the subject, but why? "I like her."

The girl tilted her head to the side, sending her brown hair sweeping across her right shoulder. It looked soft and touchable. "Like?"

The question caught him off guard, or maybe it was the girl's bare shoulder. The red tank top she wore left plenty of skin visible. "Yes, I like her. A lot." A touch of guilt pulled at his gut, no doubt from appreciating the girl when he'd come here to buy something for Miranda—who had really nice shoulders as well.

"But it's not love yet?" Her soft brown eyes twinkled with tease. "Which I suppose is good news for all the single girls admiring you from afar."

His face heated slightly from embarrassment. "It's almost love." And it was, he cared about Miranda.

She chuckled, a flirty feminine giggle that pulled a smile from him even when he wished it hadn't. Then she leaned in and whispered. "Is she Wiccan?"

"Yes." The girl's soft perfume filled his air.

"I have some pieces with touches of Wicca influence. Let me pull a few."

When he realized his gaze followed her as she moved, he looked away. Since he'd started dating Miranda, he'd lived the life of a monk. Not that he was complaining. She deserved to take her time. That said, he was really looking forward to their weekend together and was thrilled that Miranda seemed to finally be ready to take things to the next level.

He wanted the weekend to go perfect. She deserved perfect.

Anthony chuckled. "I do say, the pheromones are flowing. I think she likes you, too." He looked to the door where the clerk had disappeared.

Shit! Shawn had forgotten he was with a vampire whose damn nose didn't miss anything.

"No," he denied, too quickly.

Anthony lifted one brow as if hearing the lie in Shawn's heart. "She's attractive, but she's not . . . Miranda."

He laughed. "No worries. I do not judge. The heart does not

stop the eyes from noting, it simply stops one from following their gaze."

"Right," Shawn said.

"But it is not love yet?" Anthony asked as if recalling Shawn's words to the clerk.

"It's close." Shawn frowned. "Miranda wanted to take it slow."

"Ahh," Anthony said. "But it is odd, for we French have a saying . . . 'Matters of the heart do not come with speed control.'" He chuckled. "Since I woke up to hear Tabitha's voice that day in Paris, even when her words were about letting me die, I felt the race of my pulse."

Shawn pushed away from the counter. "Well, the American way is to get one's brakes checked before hitting heartbreak head-on."

"I admit there is wisdom in that approach." Anthony frowned. "And I confess my heart is all French. So maybe I need to adapt to these American ways a little bit."

The tapping of the clerk's footsteps had them both looking up. She placed several pieces on the table. A bracelet, a ring, three necklaces, and matching earrings. "The Bacchanal Rose bracelet is my favorite." She ran her finger over the black rose centered in a scroll-like pattern.

"It is beautiful." Shawn imagined Miranda's eyes lighting up when she saw the gift. "I'll take it." He dropped his credit card.

He'd signed the receipt and she'd just come back and handed him his card and the box when his phone rang. "Excuse me." He stepped away and pulled out his cell and saw it was Burnett. "Yes," he answered, hoping his boss wasn't going to ruin his evening.

"Where are you?" Burnett asked.

"About to do lunch with Miranda. Why?"

"Something . . . something's come up." Burnett's tone sounded off, almost as if he was choosing his words carefully. And Burnett James seldom made the effort to choose his words.

"What is it?"

Burnett cleared his throat. "It's . . . It's Miranda and her sister."

* * *

Miranda had pretty much diagnosed herself before the ambulance arrived at the hospital: broken arm, bruised ribs, and a concussion. She would survive. Whether her heart would make it depended on her sister's condition. The look in Burnett's eyes when he told her about Tabitha said it was bad. It couldn't be that bad.

Miranda. Could. Not. Lose. Tabitha!

The second the nurse walked up beside the gurney, Miranda asked, "My sister, Tabitha Evans, was just brought in. Is she okay? Has anyone come to see her, another girl, about my age, a Kylie Galen?"

"I think the doctors are with your sister now."

"Is Kylie here?"

"I think we should worry about you for a few minutes. Be a good little patient." She patted Miranda's arm like she was a child.

"But if you'd just check. And if Kylie Galen is here, you have to let her—"

"Now, now, you don't want to be the patient that I have to go home and tell my husband about. Try and be an easy patient." She patted Miranda again.

Easy? Was she freaking kidding? This is life or death.

"Stop that!" She glared at the woman's hand. "And there's no taking it easy!" Even to her own ears, her tight, tantrum-like tone sounded a bit like Della. Which was okay, because the situation called for her to be a bit of a smartass. Face it, smartasses were like squeaky wheels—they got the oil. "You go find out how she's doing right now and see if Kylie is here and then we'll worry about me."

"Has she been belligerent this whole time?" the nurse asked the paramedics as if belligerent were a medical condition.

And right then Miranda's belligerentism shot up all the way to smartassism. She raised up on her good arm, to show she wasn't completely helpless. "Look, do what I say or I'm going to be your very last patient, because I'm gonna be such a pain in your ass, you'll quit after me." Natural instinct had her shooting the nurse a pinky.

The nurse stumbled back, her bright blue eyes rounded in fear. Amazingly it seemed the finger that did it. Immediately, Miranda checked the woman's pattern, and sure enough the woman had a trace of witch in her DNA. Probably only 5 percent, but enough to know the power of the pinky.

Turning around she called out to someone. "Find out about the last patient that came in, a Tabitha Evans, and see if there's someone here to see her." The nurse looked back at Miranda. "Better?" Fear paled her cheeks.

"Better." Miranda slumped back on the stretcher, eyes closed, heart breaking. She felt one tear slip from the bottom of her lashes and the heat of it stream down her cheek. Keeping her eyes shut, she prayed to God, the Goddesses, and everything holy that all of this would one day just be a bad memory and not the worst day of her life. Because if she lost Tabitha . . .

Time passed in a blur. Miranda had been x-rayed, examined, evaluated, and stripped. Instead of jeans and her favorite green flowing blouse, she wore a backless hospital gown. None of which made her happy. The news that her sister's vitals were improving was the only thing holding Miranda together. But as time crept past, the hold started weakening like reused tape.

Waiting for the doctor to set her cast, Miranda tried to relax. The shot a nurse had stuck in her rump was making her groggy.

"Feeling better?"

Miranda opened her eyes. It was the nurse from earlier, the one who had a pinch of Wicca DNA in her.

"My sister still doing okay?"

The nurse nodded. "And your . . . friends are here, too."

"Kylie?" Miranda tried to sit up.

The nurse gently rested her hand on Miranda's shoulder. "Just relax." She paused. "Is she the blonde?"

"Yes." Knowing the cavalry had arrived made emotion hug her chest, and she fought the need for tears.

The nurse leaned in. "What is she?"

Miranda hadn't known if the woman, with so little supernatural DNA, could read patterns or not. But obviously she could.

"A chameleon."

The woman's round eyes blinked in surprise. "I've heard of them, but I've never seen one. Can they really go invisible?"

Miranda nodded. "Has she visited with my sister?"

"Not yet. At least not that I've seen, but if she can . . ."

"She needs to," Miranda said. "She's a healer. You have to make sure—"

"Shh." The woman nodded. "I'll see to it. But your sister is doing much better now. She came out of the coma. She still has a little swelling in the brain, but she's conscious. And she's just as worried about you as you are her."

"Can I see her?" Miranda's throat tightened.

"Not yet. When your arm is set." She paused. "The others . . . the two vampires . . ." The nurse's tone grew hushed. She glanced over her shoulder as if she thought someone might sneak in. "They're your friends, too?" Disbelief widened her eyes and fear dilated her pupils.

Miranda nodded. The fact that the world could be so prejudiced against certain supernatural species still shocked her. Of course, that was why Shadow Falls existed. To help supernaturals realize that different didn't mean deadly. Good and bad existed in each and every species.

"Burnett James works for the FRU? He's the best—"

"Yes, I know, he showed me his badge. He's still scary if you ask me."

"I didn't ask." A protective tone deepened Miranda's voice.

"I didn't mean . . . He told me about the camp. I'd heard there was one, but I'm new in Texas and didn't know it was here in Fallen."

"It's okay." Miranda closed her eyes and reminded herself that before she'd started going to Shadow Falls, she'd pretty much been afraid of other supernaturals as well. Thank God her mom had enough insight to know change needed to happen and sent her to be educated at the camp. God help her, but she couldn't imagine her life without her friends at Shadow Falls. Kylie and Della, though they shared no blood, were as close to her as Tabitha.

The thoughts of her mom had Miranda recalling her parents were in Colorado at one of her father's boutique hotels. Had Burnett called her parents? Had Tabitha's mom been notified? Miranda's heart squeezed at them learning of her sister's condition.

"I really need to see my sister." Miranda started to get up. The nurse put her hand on Miranda's shoulder.

"You can't just yet," the nurse said. This time something in her voice made Miranda suspicious.

"You're lying to me. She's not okay!" She drew in a shuttered breath, her emotions becoming a lump of pain in her chest.

"No, I'm not lying. She's in room six and she's doing well." She looked over her shoulder again.

"I don't believe you!" Miranda held her pinky up. "I want to see Burnett James. Now!"

The nurse's frown deepened. "They won't let them come back just yet."

"Who won't let them?" Miranda asked.

"The police."

The two words bounced around her sore head. "The police? Wh . . . why?"

She leaned closer. "They want to question you and your sister before they let anyone back to see you. And the doctor won't let them question you until your arm is set."

"Why do they want to question us?"

She hesitated as if she'd been given orders to keep her mouth shut, then she finally spoke. "The drugs."

Chapter Four

"What?" Miranda asked.

"In the house," the nurse responded.

"What house?"

"The house that blew up was a . . . drug house. They think you and your sister are involved somehow."

"Drug house? They think . . ." Miranda shook her head. "No. An old witch lived there. She read fortunes. She wasn't . . . And I'm not . . ." *Oh hell!!!*

"I'm not saying I believe them, I'm just saying . . . that's what's going on. Mr. James is super pissed. It's chaos out there right now. It's probably just a big mistake."

It had to be. Miranda closed her eyes. "This doesn't make sense."

"I'm sorry." She sounded sincere. "Now, I need to clean your arm so we can give you some shots to numb you. Unfortunately, I'm assuming the alcohol might mess up your henna tattoo."

That had Miranda opening her eyes. She'd forgotten all about that. Lifting her head, she glanced at her arm, and a little gasp caught in her throat. The limb was swollen, slightly purple. The tattoo, a pale grayish pink, came halfway up to her elbow. It was bigger. Wasn't it? Then again, it had happened so fast.

She couldn't help but wonder what it meant. Did it tell her if

Shawn was the right man for her? Did she even want to know? No. Yes. Maybe. "Where's my phone?"

"With your clothes, why?"

"I'd like to take a picture of it." Maybe later, she'd have the courage to see if anyone could tell her what it said, what it meant. If it meant anything.

The old witch might have been pulling a hoax. Miranda really didn't believe that now, but she wanted to. Her heart grew heavy again, realizing the witch might be dead. Sure, Miranda had tried to get her to leave, but she could have tried harder.

She couldn't help but wonder if the death angels, the angels overseeing the supernaturals, were going to hold Miranda accountable.

The nurse found her phone and snapped a few shots of the pattern on her arm. Then she gently went to rubbing Miranda's arm with astringent-scented wipes. Just the slightest touch set the bone to aching and Miranda closed her eyes and repeated a calming mantra.

"Maybe I didn't need to take a picture of it," the nurse said. "It's not coming off."

Miranda tilted her head and stared at the tattoo. "It has to." Her mom did not like tattoos.

"Oh!" The nurse's touch jerked away from Miranda's arm, fear rounded her eyes.

"What?" Miranda asked.

"Your tattoo is climbing your arm and down your fingers."

"Oh, friggin' frack!" Miranda lifted her head and watched as the squirrely lines snaked up to her elbow and down to her knuckles.

How long was this thing going to be visible?

She racked her brain to recall a curse or a significance to the pattern but came up empty.

Was she going to be covered in this crap? The inky pattern moved another inch before it stopped.

Stopped, but for how long?

What the hell did this mean?

Panic pulled at her chest and then she remembered that Tabitha had gone to the fortune reader before, and she didn't walk around with a permanent tattoo. Surely it would fade.

"Okay." A white-coated pale-faced doctor walked into the room with fake cheeriness. "Why don't we get you put in a cast, so the cops and your friends out there will calm down? The mouthy brunette out there, I swear if she could, she'd wring my neck."

Little did the doctor know—if the brunette who he referred to was Della—she'd have no trouble wringing his neck. Not that this was Miranda's biggest concern. She had a moving tattoo, a semiconscious sister, and possibly some drug charges to get out of.

The doctor's neck was his own problem.

"Don't you ever question my orders again!" Caleb, morphing from bird to man, screamed at Perry as the three of them landed behind a wooded lot at the side of the three-bedroom house they'd rented while doing jobs in the Dallas area.

Caleb shot forward and slammed both of his palms on Perry's chest. Perry didn't budge. In the last year, he'd spent hours making his human form as powerful as he could. It would take someone more than this asswipe to knock him down.

He stood square and firm, and fought the urge to get in the man's face. The temptation to morph and give the jerk a real fight shot adrenaline into his blood. But the intensity didn't compare to what it had been at the bank when Caleb threatened an innocent girl. A girl who had reminded him of Miranda.

For that low-life action, Perry had a bone to pick with this guy, a freaking big one, but everything in his gut said "not now." In part because he didn't need to be tossed out of the group just yet—his objective wasn't complete—but mostly because at this second he had something else to do.

His heart demanded it.

He had to check on Miranda. That feeling, the image of her lying lifeless hadn't stopped digging at his soul. Would she even answer his call? Probably not.

He'd have to call someone else.

"Did you hear me!" Caleb lurched forward as if to come at him again.

Perry held up one hand and promised himself that soon, soon he'd teach this guy a lesson he wouldn't forget. "I heard you. But if we hadn't left we probably would've been arrested."

"Hell no! We could have turned at any time and left them scratching their asses!"

"And bring the FRU down on us?" Perry tossed out. From the corner of Perry's eye, he saw his father had completed his turn.

"Perry's right!" his father, running his hand through hair that was still as blond as Perry's, added his two-cents' worth. The fact that those two cents were on Perry's side felt better than it should.

"We had to get out of there!" The frustration in his father's bright eyes echoed in his posture.

Was his father's anger because he felt something for Perry or simply because Perry was right? Not that it mattered anymore. He couldn't change this now.

The image of Miranda flashed again. Perry started walking away, but his father's next words brought his steps to a halt.

"We get made as supernaturals, and it's over. How many times has Jax said that?"

Who was Jax? Perry turned around.

His father, looking ready to morph into something badass, stared daggers at Caleb. "Are you friggin' forgetting his rules?"

Jax? Rules? Perry stored the name. So his father *did* know who was really behind this? The realization landed with a thump against the sore spot in Perry's heart. How many times had his father told Perry he knew nothing? And damn it, but Perry had wanted to believe it. Wanted to believe that his father wasn't in so deep that the price would be too high.

"Don't start with me old man," Caleb yelled, his eyes now glowing yellow. "You don't have what it takes to do this job."

"I'm doing just fine," his father barked back. "It's you that's screwing up, taking too many chances. You and you alone are going to bring the FRU down on our asses! The human police we can outsmart, the FRU, not so much."

Perry didn't move, listening, hoping to hear something else, but then his wounded soul rushed right back to Miranda. Was she really hurt?

He walked away from the side yard to a patio where he might have some privacy.

Pulling out his phone, he glanced back to confirm he wasn't being monitored. Caleb watched him like a hawk—always suspicious. And for good reason. They hadn't stayed off the FRU's radar without being careful. But they hadn't been careful enough.

Perry was going to bring them down. The whole damn gang, his parents included, just as soon as he knew who the whole gang included.

He pushed his phone's contact button then remembered he'd deleted all his numbers as soon as he'd learned his dad's job included robbing banks. Not the end of the world, he knew the numbers by heart. The ones that mattered anyway!

He dialed.

The phone rang once, twice, then three times. What the hell? Burnett James always answered his phone. Especially when he had a beef with you. And right now Burnett had a big one with Perry. He'd ordered Perry to return to Shadow Falls. The man was just too protective. And not just as a camp leader or a training agent with the FRU.

Perry and Burnett had been in the same foster home for about six years. When Burnett turned eighteen and left the home, he'd pretty much left everyone behind, everyone but Perry. He would come to see him at least twice a month. It had been Burnett who had arranged for him to go to camp Shadow Falls.

Perry knew Burnett was letting their relationship cloud his judgment. And Perry hadn't even told him everything that was going on, just that there was some criminal activity happening. Burnett still had ordered Perry to back away, telling him he was too close to it because of his parents.

But Perry wasn't walking away. This might be his one chance to really prove himself to Burnett. To the FRU. And maybe even to himself.

The call went to voicemail. "Leave a message," Burnett's recording said.

Something had to be wrong. Bad wrong.

He inhaled and fought the urge to take flight toward Fallen, Texas, to see if his stupid vision was just his mind playing tricks on him, or if . . . if something had really happened to Miranda.

He hung up, his finger lingering over the keypad to punch in the next number. His heart said to go right to the source, to call Miranda, but his heart wasn't running on logic. He'd screwed up with her. Royally.

It wasn't fair for him to go to her. She had his number—if she'd found it in her heart to forgive him, she'd call.

She hadn't called.

But not once since he'd left had he stopped hoping she would. Like a lovesick little boy he'd slept with his phone close to his bed. Anytime his phone had been out of hearing range, even for a few seconds, he came back, holding his breath checking for missed messages.

She hadn't called.

He knew she was dating Shawn Hanson, a warlock, someone of her own kind, someone more deserving of a girl like Miranda. But damn it, he'd worked his ass off this last year to try to be the type of person to deserve her, too. And at times, he actually felt he'd accomplished that feat, but then he'd mess something up, fail to meet up to his own expectations. And he'd start questioning it all over again. Questioning if he could ever be deserving of her.

Oh, she thought less of herself because she was dyslexic, but he didn't care about her powers. Or that she occasionally made goofs. He loved her, goofs and all.

She was so much more than she gave herself credit for. She could just look at him and make him smile. She could touch him and make him feel more alive. She could stand beside him and he wanted to be a better person for her. Because she believed in him, he wanted to believe in himself.

She loved people. Loved them unconditionally.

Even when they weren't deserving.

And he didn't want to be that—didn't want to be another person in her life she had to sacrifice for because she loved them. He wanted to be the person she needed. The person she could lean on. Count on.

But . . . She hadn't called.

Exhaling, he punched in another number.

"Perry?" Holiday James, Burnett's wife and owner of the Shadow Falls Academy, answered immediately. While he'd always looked up to Burnett like a big brother—Holiday had taken on a different role.

Emotion swelled in his chest from hearing her voice. She'd been the closest thing to a mother he'd ever had. Like Miranda, she infused in others the need to be the best they could be. No one wanted to let Holiday down.

He suddenly felt stupid for panicking—as if his crazy thoughts could actual mean something. "Hey . . . I just . . . wanted to talk to someone from home. I tried to call Burnett and it went to voice-mail. That's strange, right?"

She didn't offer up reassurance like she always did. That was kind of strange, too. He glanced back again, to confirm it was safe to talk. His heart did another lap around his chest, thoughts of Miranda driving its speed.

"Holiday?" he asked.

"Uh . . . he's in the middle of something. I'm sure he'll call you back. He told me you were supposed to be back here yesterday. He stayed up late last night waiting on you. He's been worried and didn't want to call you in case . . . it caused trouble."

"I told him not to worry. What's he in the middle of?" Perry went to rake a hand through his hair, then dropped it when he recalled seeing his dad do the same. If there was a man he wanted to emulate it was Burnett. Not his real father.

"He said what you were doing could be dangerous, Perry. You need to step away."

"I can't leave just yet. But I didn't call about that. Is Miranda okay?"

"How did you . . . Who called you?" she asked.

"No one. I just . . . I had a feeling. What is it?"

"What kind of feeling?" she asked.

"Is something wrong? Is she okay?" *Please be okay, Miranda. Please!*

The sound of a twig snapping sounded behind him, pulling his heart from one problem to another. Someone was there. He racked his brain to remember if he'd said anything terribly incriminating.

"Who the hell are you talking to?" The voice, angry and tight, sounded behind him.

"Please be okay, Miranda."

A hand touched her good arm stirring her awake, but the voice she heard seemed to come from somewhere else.

Miranda tried to open her eyes, but they felt so heavy. Probably the drugs. When setting her arm, the doctor, after Miranda had let out a good moan, had given her a pill to help her relax.

"Tell me you're okay?" The tone whispered tenderness and something so genuine that her soul trembled. Sometimes just knowing someone cared that much could almost hurt.

She worked to identify the deep male voice. Perry. Had he come here? Had he heard she was hurt and come running home for the first time in months?

Her chest felt like it opened up in a way that it hadn't since he left. Something like relief, a special kind of joy, a Perry kind of joy filled her heart.

"You came." She finally opened her eyes.

"Of course I did."

Miranda blinked. Once. Twice.

On the third time the face came into focus. And so did her heart.

Not Perry.

Shawn.

Sweet. Warm. Kind. All of it defined Shawn.

"You couldn't keep me away." He leaned down and pressed a soft and gentle kiss to her lips. One that spoke of just the kind of guy he was. When he pulled back, the emotions in his eyes echoed the same sentiment and told her how much he cared.

And she cared back. She did. She really did. Pushing thoughts of Perry from her mind, she felt her chest tighten.

"You scared me to death!" He looked at her cast and winced as if her pain was his. "Are you hurting?"

"No, not now." She looked around, unsure how long she'd been asleep. "Have you heard anything about Tabitha?"

"No. I came right to your room."

"Where's Burnett?"

"He's arguing with police about something. I just got here. I don't know what's going on, but I talked your nurse into letting me sneak back."

"They think I'm a drug dealer."

"What?" Shock filled his blue eyes.

"The house that blew up—"

"A house blew up?" His mouth hung open. "What house?"

"The witch's house." She tried to sit up but her ribs still hurt, so she slumped back on the bed.

"What witch?" His brow tightened in puzzlement.

"The fortune-teller with the armadillo."

He stared at her, his eyes filling with a new kind of worry. "Are . . . you okay?"

And by okay, she was pretty sure he meant mentally. "Burnett didn't tell you?"

He still hesitated before answering. "He said you and Tabitha were in an accident. I thought car."

"Not a car," she said.

He blinked and frowned. "A house blew up?"

She nodded.

His eyes widened again. "Wait. Did you say armadillo?"

"Yeah. I know it sounds crazy, but it was there. And it was being held against its will. And when the storm came inside—"

"Storm?" he asked.

"Yeah."

"At a witch's house?" By his tone she couldn't tell if he came closer to believing her or believing she was a few fries short of a Happy Meal. But she suspected the latter.

Frowning, she found her bed control and raised up a few inches. As her head raised, she flinched slightly as the new position hurt, but the pain wasn't nearly as bad as before.

She looked up. "I'm not hallucinating. This happened."

"Okay." He paused again. "But what . . . what were you doing there?"

"The witch was a fortune-teller."

He frowned. "What kind of magic was she practicing?"

Miranda shifted, the question reminding her that this whole thing could have been prevented if only she'd been more assertive with Tabitha. Oddly, while Tabitha was the eldest, and high priestess, she wasn't always the wisest.

"It might have been black, but . . . but she didn't seem evil. Tabitha wanted . . . She'd gone to her before. She was worried about dating Anthony. Her mom doesn't want her to, but she has feelings and she wanted to know if it might really be love."

The soft caring look in his eyes shifted to frustration. He leaned in and his tone lowered. "You know better than to play around with black magic. And please, you don't go to someone to tell you how you feel. You feel it or you don't!"

She wasn't sure if it was his words or if it was his tone that annoyed her the most. She attempted to push the itch of anger aside, because down deep she knew he was right. At least about black magic, but . . . about feelings? No, he wasn't right about that.

Her feelings for him were a prime example.

Stiffening her shoulders, she met his eyes. "So you've never questioned how you felt about someone?"

His brow tightened. "Not enough to toy with evil. You could have been—"

"I told you, she didn't come off as malicious." Miranda's emotions must have sounded in her voice, because before he even opened his mouth, she heard his apology.

"I'm sorry, I just . . . hate seeing you hurt. The thought of what more could have happened scares the hell out of me."

Before Miranda could respond, before she even decided what the ping-ponging emotions meant, the door to her room whooshed open.

A man, potbellied, so much so that his extended gut entered the room before he did, charged into the room. From his body shape and jowls to his demeanor, he reminded Miranda of a bulldog—one who didn't like backing up from his food bowl.

The man glared at Shawn, then turned to look at the nurse who'd followed him. "I told you no visitors until I spoke with her!"

The nurse flinched.

The bulldog turned his attention away from the nurse to Shawn. "I snuck in," Shawn insisted.

"Who the hell are you?"

Shawn's shoulders tensed, not at all intimidated by the man. "I'm an agent with the FRU."

The man growled, yes, growled just like a dog. "As I was telling the other agent out there, I don't give a damn who you are. This is our case. Back off before I get your asses arrested."

"Excuse me!" Burnett charged into the room. When he was angry the vampire looked bigger. And right now he appeared seven feet tall.

Miranda noted his normal brown eyes held a golden, pissed-off hue. Then again, they were in the hospital where no doubt the smell of blood lingered. He held out his phone to Mr. Bulldog. "Someone wants to speak to you."

"Who?" The cop stared at the phone as if he debated taking it.

"Take it," Burnett said. "He's not someone you want to keep waiting."

"You got my sergeant?" the cop asked, suspicious and maybe worried.

"No," Burnett answered, his voice a low rumble that sounded dead serious. "Your sergeant wasn't available. Neither was his boss. It's the police commissioner. Take it!" He shoved his phone into the man's hand, but Miranda could tell Burnett would rather have just broken the man's neck.

The bulldog, looking unsure, took the phone. "Yes."

The man's face, already a pissed-off shade of red, got redder. "I understand sir, but we have evidence leading us to believe—" His frown deepened all the way into his jowls. "I understand."

He shoved the phone back into Burnett's hand. Now looking embarrassed as well as furious, he growled again. "This isn't over by a long shot."

"I'd say it is," Shawn added.

Burnett stared down at the police officer. And considering he stood almost a foot above him, it was apparent that he made the cop feel small.

"You can go now." Burnett motioned him out.

As soon as he left, Miranda met Burnett's gaze. "Thank you."

He frowned. "Don't thank me yet. We still have to prove you didn't have anything to do with the drugs."

"So it was really a drug house?" Miranda winced.

"I'm afraid so."

"That doesn't make sense," Shawn said. "Why would a witch be working out of a drug house?"

"We don't know," Burnett said, his frown punctuating his statement.

"The witch?" Miranda asked. "Did you find . . ." She couldn't say it, but heaven help her, she couldn't say it. Had she left the elderly witch in the house to die?

"So far no human or non-human remains have been found. It appears she got out. No sight of the armadillo, either."

"Burnett?" The voice came from the door. Holiday stood there. Miranda immediately picked up on her frown. Then Holiday's faded gray aura, that usually meant worry, caught Miranda's attention. Because Holiday was a mother and shouldered the responsibility for all her students at Shadow Falls, worry always tinted her aura, but this . . . this was stronger than usual.

Fearing the worst, Miranda's sister's name slipped from her heart and then from her lips. "Tabitha?"

Holiday walked in, her caring gaze stayed on Miranda and she smiled but it came off more as a mask. "She's fine. You gave us all a scare." She pressed her hand on Miranda's shoulder.

The calm of a fae's touch eased some of Miranda's fears. Everyone had assured her Tabitha was okay, so why did she not want to believe it? "I'm sorry."

"Nothing to apologize for," Holiday said. "I spoke to your parents. They'd tried to call you, but you didn't answer. I assured them you were okay and told them you were probably asleep. They should be here in about four hours."

"And Tabitha's mom?" Miranda asked.

"She was in Galveston. She's on her way, too. She and your father did speak with Tabitha."

Holiday's gaze slipped back to Burnett and her stressed aura got stronger. "Can I see you a minute?"

"What's wrong?" Miranda asked.

"We'll be back," Burnett said, his tone deepening as if he too sensed something was wrong. Something that Holiday hadn't wanted Miranda to hear. And that just worried her more.

Burnett and Holiday walked out of the room. Shawn sat down on the foot of her bed. After several silent moments, Shawn blurted out, "I'm sorry I upset you. I was scared."

She nodded. He moved up to the front of the bed and leaned down. His kiss was soft and it told her how much he cared.

When he pulled back, he brushed a strand of hair from her cheek. "It's going to be okay."

"I hope so," she said, but that feeling kept brewing in her gut. The feeling that said it might not be okay.

Five minutes later, after casual chitchat, Shawn's phone rang. He slipped it out of his pocket and looked at the screen. "Burnett," he said, meaning he had to take the call. Very few people would ignore Burnett.

"Yeah?" Shawn answered and paused. "Now?"

Miranda studied Shawn, wondering if Burnett's call was about her.

Shawn frowned as if whatever Burnett said didn't sit well with him. "Yeah, but can't you find someone else? I know, but I kind of wanted to be assigned to Miranda's case." His frown deepened.

Miranda could hear Burnett's voice, but couldn't distinguish his words.

"Fine," Shawn said. "Where's it at?"

She watched frustration fill his eyes, and then those baby blues widened.

"I was just there," he said. "No, it's beside the restaurant where I was meeting Miranda and Tabitha." Pause. "Yeah, Anthony and I walked into the store." Pause. "I'm not sure. I'd just gotten there, so about ten minutes. Yeah, he came with me. Why?"

Miranda sat up a bit, now even more curious.

"Fine. Was . . . anyone hurt?" Shawn asked.

Concern filled Shawn's expression. "Who? Yeah, well, no. I met the clerk." His frowned deepened. "Yes. A mix-breed." Pause. "Okay. I'll call you as soon as I got something." He hung up and sent her an apologetic look.

"What?" she asked.

"The jewelry store beside Maxi's Burgers was robbed. Anthony and I walked in while we were waiting on you two."

"Is it an FRU case?"

"Could be. He wants me to go check it out."

"Was someone hurt?" she asked.

"He said there were injuries, but no causalities." His frown deepened.

Miranda recalled other questions she had from her little eavesdropping. "Who did you say came with you?"

"Anthony."

"Why was Burnett asking about him?"

"He didn't say." His gaze softened. "You sure you're okay?"

"I'm fine. Go."

Alone, Miranda sat for two seconds, wanting to believe the nagging feeling of doom was simply leftover from the chaos. But doubt ate at her sanity.

"Oh, hell." She tossed off her covers. She wanted to see Tabitha. Buttscooting to the edge of the thin mattress, she dropped her feet down and stood up. The cast felt heavy. She felt a little dizzy. But she'd waited long enough. The worry for her sister hung in her chest like a lead weight.

Grabbing the back of her gown with her good hand, she went in search of room six and her sister.

Chapter Five

Perry hesitated before facing his father, trying to chase any glimpse of guilt from his expression.

"I asked who you were talking to?" his father repeated.

As Perry turned around, his mind raced into recall mode. Exactly what had his father heard? How far up shit creek without a paddle had he traveled? When he replayed his words in his head, the tension in his gut slackened. He hadn't said anything completely incriminating—that he remembered. But at times like this, Perry's memory wasn't its best.

To reassure himself, he tried to read his father's body language. He got nothing.

In spite of Perry's natural ability to read emotional shifts in others, his father was often unreadable. Or was he too close to his dad to read the man correctly?

Probably for that reason, Burnett had insisted Perry pull out. Not an option. Especially knowing what Caleb was capable of doing.

His dad had said they hadn't brought anyone new into the gang in a year. That meant no one had a better chance at stopping this than Perry. And no one had more of a reason to do it. Not that he completely understood those reasons, or the reason he'd felt compelled to find his parents, but something drove him to be the one to make this right.

"A girl. I was talking to a girl. Why?"

"You got a girl?" The edge in his voice was gone.

"Sort of."

"You banging her?" his father asked.

The crude question ran over every nerve Perry had. It sounded like Caleb. "That's none of your damn business!"

"Of course it is. I'm your father."

And I'd never have seen you again if I hadn't come found you. And soon you're going to wish I hadn't. He couldn't help but wonder if his father would feel half as betrayed by him as Perry had by his abandonment.

When Perry didn't have a comeback, his father spoke up again. "Just don't sneak off to make calls."

"Since when do I need my calls monitored?"

His father frowned. "Since Caleb's got it out for you. Don't give him a reason to suspect you're up to something."

"I don't give a damn what he suspects," Perry lied. One of the many untruths he'd told his father. In the beginning, Perry kept his link with Shadow Falls a secret because of the FRU's association with the school. He knew unregistered supernaturals like his parents feared all things FRU. Then Perry learned other reasons to keep it to himself.

His father glanced over his shoulder, as if making sure they were alone, then refocused on Perry. "You need to take your attitude down a notch. For now. Caleb's gonna screw up. Jax already has him on his radar."

Jax again. "You said you didn't know who was running this show."

"Maybe I know more than I said. But you've got to trust me."

Trust. It hit then. A whole knot of hurt, like tightly wound rubber bands, unfurling in his chest—each one snapping free and leaving an emotional welt.

He stepped closer to his father, now just inches from the man's face. "Trust you? You friggin' abandoned me when I was three years old. Left me in a damn mall. I almost killed someone." It was the first time Perry had brought it up. Not that he hadn't wanted to. It was the damn elephant in the room.

But pointing out the elephant wouldn't accomplish anything. So why had he spilled his guts now? Because he wasn't thinking straight—his concern over Miranda had pushed him over the edge.

Suddenly, he didn't just want to talk to someone about her over the phone. He wanted to see Miranda—in person. He needed a break from this, from his father and the scum he hung out with.

He needed it now. His eyes stung with heightened emotions. He inhaled once, then twice, hoping to rein it in before he morphed into something big and angry.

Before he said something he shouldn't.

Before his father guessed that he wasn't here to rekindle their lost relationship.

"You were impossible to handle. Your mom was going to leave me if I . . ." Was that regret in his old man's eyes?

Nothing like a mother's love. Perry had figured out that it had been his mom's idea to abandon him. The memories of his early years were not of him clinging to his mom, but to his dad. Even at two he'd sensed her lack of love.

Maybe that was why this was so hard. Because while his dad was the one committing the crimes, Perry knew it was his mom's idea.

"Hey, you're the one who looked us up," his father said. "And if you came just to give us some crap, then pack your shit and leave. If you came to see how we might be able to help each other, then forget the past. And start listening to me."

He paused. "We can help each other, Perry. With your power and your mom's and my connections, we can be rich. We can make things right."

Perry could only nod. Because right then another vision of
Miranda hit. She was lying very still in what looked like a hospital bed.

His father exhaled. "When you meet Jax, you can show him
what you can do. He's gonna be impressed. We're gonna be running
this team in no time. You and me. We'll make your mama so
proud." He slapped his hand on Perry's shoulder.

"Yeah." He moved away from his father's touch. "I need to go
check on my girl." If he left right now, he could be there and back
before eight in the morning when Caleb held his mandatory morning meetings. And if he didn't make it. Screw Caleb. Miranda
needed him.

"You can't go anywhere," his father snapped. "If Caleb finds out
he'll get all up in arms. He might fill Jax's head with a reason not
to like you."

"Then it's your job to make sure Caleb doesn't find out." Perry
started his morph into a falcon.

"Damn it! Where are you going?"

"Houston," he said, remembering that's where his father thought
he'd lived before. His form changed. Spreading his wings, he flew
up. Before he found a good momentum, he saw Caleb walking to
the back toward his dad.

Perry didn't turn back. If there were consequences, he'd pay
them later.

"Is she trying to escape the hospital?"

Miranda had just stepped out of the hospital-room door and
turned down the hall when she heard the familiar sassy voice. She
turned to see her two best friends in the world hurrying toward her.
Kylie, blond, perky, and pretty, and Della, almost black hair, ex-
otic looking, and generally grumpy.

"Are you okay?" Kylie hugged her cautiously.

"Fine."

"You scared us!" Kylie said.

"Do you know what's going on?" Miranda asked.

"You don't remember?" Della asked. "You were almost blown up in a drug house. How hard did you hit your head?"

Miranda rolled her eyes. "There's nothing wrong with my head. I meant what's wrong with Holiday. She snatched Burnett out of my room as if something was wrong."

Della looked over her shoulder. "They walked outside. They didn't say anything was wrong."

"Well, it is. Holiday's aura was clouded with worry. Are you sure my sister's okay? Where's room six?"

"Six?" Della asked.

"That's where Tabitha—"

"I'm right here." The voice came from behind her.

Miranda swung around to see the nurse—the part-witch nurse—wheeling Tabitha down the hall in a wheelchair.

"You can't walk?" Miranda ran toward her sister, who sported a bandage on her forehead.

"I can." Her sister looked at the nurse. "She won't let me."

"Doctor's orders." The nurse took a step back.

Miranda knelt down. "Thank God you're okay."

"Me?" Tabitha said. "I just banged my head. You broke an arm."

"Heads are more important." Miranda hugged her sister, hugged her tight. Her chest ached from the thought that she could have lost her.

"You're cutting off my air," Tabitha said.

"See, I'm not the only one who thinks that," Della said moving with Kylie.

Tabitha glanced up at them. "The FRU thinks I'm a drug dealer?"

"They really don't believe that," Miranda said, even if she'd worried about it herself.

"Yeah, they do," Della said.

Miranda pretty much accepted Della's outspokenness, but

occasionally it still scraped across some raw nerves. "Not really." Miranda graced Della with a don't-go-there expression.

"Yeah, really." Obviously, Della didn't read the look. "They were ready to arrest your asses."

Miranda cleared her throat in a way that said, Shut the crap up!

The vamp's eyes widened as if she finally got it. "Not us. We don't believe it. The police . . . think it. Burnett had to call the big dogs to stop it from happening."

"And Burnett's going to clear this up," Kylie added. "We're just glad you're both okay. Right?" Kylie, forever the peacekeeper, directed the question at Della.

"Duh, that goes without saying." The vamp looked at Tabitha. "We'll get to the bottom of this. We've got your backs."

The honesty in Della's voice had Miranda pushing aside her aggravation. The vamp meant well.

"Burnett's already assigned Lucas and Chase to the case," Kylie said.

Della frowned. "He said I was too close to you, but Chase will keep me updated."

Tabitha squirmed in the wheelchair. "Do you know why they took Anthony down for questioning?"

"They took Anthony down?" Miranda remembered bits and pieces of Shawn's conversation.

Tabitha sighed. "They said they wanted to question him."

"About the jewelry store robbery?" Miranda asked.

"What jewelry store?" Della asked. "It was a drug house." She looked at the nurse, still standing behind Tabitha. "Have you done x-rays on her head?"

"I'm fine," Miranda snapped. "Burnett called Shawn about a robbery at the jewelry store next to where we were meeting for lunch."

"Oh," the vamp said. "I don't know about that."

Tabitha looked at Della. "What do you know?"

Della got the deer-in-the-headlights look. "I . . ."

"What's going on?" Miranda asked.

Della gave her a don't-blame-me shrug. "I might as well tell you. When I arrived at the drug house, or what was left of the house, I picked up a bunch of supernatural traces. I recognized one. Anthony's."

Hearing the name of her boyfriend caused Tabitha's mouth to fall open. "His scent was on me."

"Nope. It wasn't a secondary trace," Della said.

"This has to be a mistake." Miranda focused on the vamp. "Anthony wasn't with us."

Della shrugged again. "Which is exactly why he's being questioned."

Her sister looked slapped. "You think Anthony has something to do with the drugs? He doesn't do drugs!"

"Then he doesn't have anything to worry about," Della said.

"I'm sure it's going to get cleared up." Kylie moved in and touched Tabitha—probably offering a touch of calm.

Her sister glanced up and her brow wrinkled. "Were you in my room earlier?"

"Yeah. I saw both of you." Kylie looked at Miranda. "Your rib better?"

"Yes. I don't remember you . . ." Miranda paused.

"You just didn't see me." Kylie's expression insinuated that she'd been invisible. Something that only chameleons could do. Not that it was all they could do, she was also a healer, plus she could shift into different types of supernaturals.

"Can we . . . move into a room before they tell you to leave." The nurse's voice shook. As soon as she pushed Tabitha's wheelchair into the room, she rushed out.

Della stared after her. "I didn't even growl at her."

"I don't think it's you as much as Kylie," Miranda said.

"I scared her? I'm not scary," Kylie said.

"Yeah, you are," Della said. "You scared the piss out of me when I first met you."

Kylie laughed. "Ditto." Then she glanced back at the closed door. "Now that we're alone . . . What happened?"

Miranda sat on the edge of the bed and started repeating her story. When she got to the part where the armadillo got loose, Tabitha spoke up. "Your fortune. It grew up your arm. I still don't get that."

Miranda looked down at her arm, checking to see if the crazy tattoo had faded yet. She couldn't see it extending from the cast, so maybe it had.

"What grew up your arm?" Della asked.

"The ashes," Tabitha answered. "When the witch does her spell, she places the bowl upside down on your palm and it creates a pattern on your palm. She reads your love fortune from the pattern. For some reason Miranda's grew larger than mine, and mine was always bigger than anyone else's."

Della looked at Miranda. "What did she tell you? Are you going to get hot and heavy with Shawn now?"

"She didn't tell me anything. That's when everything went crazy." Miranda felt a light tickle and glanced again at the edge of her cast. And damn if she didn't see a sliver of a swirl peek out.

Her gaze shot to her sister. "How long until it goes away?"

"What goes away?" Tabitha asked.

"The tattoo."

"It's gone as soon as she reads it."

Miranda gave her arm another quick peek and sure as hell, it was there, and inching up another fourth of an inch. "What if she doesn't read it? How long am I going to have this?" She looked at the tattoo.

"Huh?" Tabitha moved closer.

Della and Kylie did the same. "Oh, that's freaky." Della stepped back.

Kylie nodded in agreement. Tabitha's eyes rounded. "I . . ."

"What?" Miranda asked her sister. "Does it mean something?"

"I . . . I don't know," Tabitha sputtered.

"What do you mean you don't know?" Della looked from Miranda to Tabitha. "You two are witches and this is witch crap. How could you not know?"

"We don't know everything!" Tabitha said. "Especially . . ."

"Especially what?" Della snapped.

Tabitha looked at Miranda with fear in her eyes. "Black magic."

Miranda felt the tattoo crawl up her arm. What the hell was happening to her? Would it ever stop growing? Was she marked for life?

"Did you show that to Holiday?" Kylie worried aloud.

"No, I thought it went away."

"Well it hasn't," Della said. "That shit's climbing up your arm now."

"I'm getting Holiday." Kylie yanked out her phone. She hadn't touched one button when her phone rang.

Kylie looked at the screen and up. "It's her."

Miranda got that feeling again. Like something was wrong, or something was about to go wrong. Her gaze shifted to Tabitha. "Do you feel that?"

Her sister nodded.

Kylie took the call. "Hello?" Her gaze shifted to Della. "Yeah. What's wrong?" Pause. "Okay, we'll be right there. But . . . you need to come see Miranda." Pause. "She's got a . . . thing growing up her arm." Pause. "No, not a rash."

"What was that about?" Della asked the second Kylie hung up.

"Burnett needs to see us."

"What's wrong?" Miranda asked.

Kylie hesitated, but then just said it. "It's Perry."

"What about him?" Doom and gloom crowded Miranda's lungs.

Concern filled Kylie's eyes. She wasn't good at hiding things. "All she said was . . . Burnett wants us to check on him."

Miranda felt another pang of doom. "Is he in some kind of trouble?"

Before Kylie answered, a big scream, followed by some loud crashes and bangs, echoed outside the hospital room's door.

"Shit!" Della bolted toward the door, but it swung open.

The nurse stuck her head in.

"Are you doing okay?" Her gaze shifted to Kylie and then Della.

"What happened out there?" Della asked.

The nurse almost flinched. "Uh, one of the nurses thought she saw uh . . . an armadillo. I'm sure she just imagined—"

"Call Burnett." Della shot toward the door. The nurse ran as if Della were after her.

Miranda dialed Burnett's number for the second time that day.

Chapter Six

Shawn arrived at the jewelry store as an ambulance pulled out. Sirens filled the cloudy sky. He watched the vehicle with red lights flaring pull away. The moon, missing only a sliver, already hung in the sky. Walking through the door, he smelled the coppery scent of blood. His chest tightened remembering the pretty clerk. Was she the victim?

"You can't come in here." An officer shot in front of him.

Shawn flashed his badge.

"What the hell is FRU?" the officer said.

Another officer, larger in stature, who was standing behind the counter speaking to an elderly woman, turned around. "Let him in. He's from a special crime unit, an offshoot of the FBI. They're looking into cases similar to this one."

Shawn nodded at the officer, checking his forehead for his pattern. Half vampire. The FRU assigned many supernaturals to work with emergency public service jobs so they could keep the FRU informed of any suspicious cases.

They exchanged a knowing nod. The petite elderly woman next to the officer was human. Shawn's focus shifted back to the blood on the floor. He recalled the girl again.

The half-vampire officer walked over and extended his hand. "Officer Johnson."

"Agent Hanson." Shawn didn't waste any time. "Whose blood is this?"

"Mr. Crow's. He and his wife own the store," the officer answered. "He walked in during the robbery and tried to stop it. They took him to the hospital."

"How bad is he?" Shawn asked.

"The paramedics thought he was going to make it." Johnson paused. "Where's Agent James?"

"On another case. I work under him." Shawn glanced back at the woman. "Any other employees present?"

"She hasn't mentioned anyone." He lifted his nose in the air. "I get were, witch, shape-shifter, and traces of vampire."

Shawn glanced back at the blood. With the exception of the were trace, those scents could be explained by the employee he'd met, along with his and Anthony's earlier presence. That said, the FRU wasn't called out just because of scent.

Still sniffing the air, Johnson looked suddenly puzzled. "Is that your scent?"

"Yeah. I was here earlier. Along with a vampire. There was an employee, a mix-breed. Vampire, part witch and fae. But no were."

"But I'm picking up more than one shape-shifter."

Shawn started trying to connect the dots. "Besides the scent is there another reason you called?"

The man moved in to make sure they weren't overheard. "According to Mrs. Crow, a couple walking past saw the fight and rushed inside to help. The three assailants took off to the back. She assumed they'd run out the back door, but Mrs. Crow realized the door was locked. She even has the key around her neck. With the scents of shape-shifter, I assumed—"

"Sounds like a good call." Shawn paused. "Is that Mrs. Crow over there?"

Johnson nodded and Shawn walked over to the woman. "Can you tell me what happened?"

She frowned. "I already told the story three times, and I'd really like to get to the hospital."

Shawn, knowing you could get more flies with honey, smiled. Normally, his smile alone could put people at ease, but when her expression didn't relax, he cast a minuscule spell, settling the woman's nerves.

"I totally understand, Mrs. Crow. And I promise to be quick. Do you have an office? Maybe you'd like to sit down."

She nodded. "But quick."

"I promise." A minute later, he had the elderly woman settled behind her desk. She spotted a photo that held an image of her and a man. Concern filled her eyes. She touched the frame and appeared to say a silent prayer.

Shawn got her a drink of water and dropped into the chair across the desk.

Between sips of water, she told him what occurred. Honesty resonated from her voice. Or it had until she answered his question of who all had been working in the store at the time of the robbery.

That's when her tone shot up an octave higher, and she glanced away from him to the left.

Shawn, envious of his fellow vampire agents' ability to detect a lie, had made a mission of studying human behavior to recognize a mistruth. While his method wasn't as reliable as hearing someone's heart rate, he seldom missed a falsehood. Why was this old lady lying?

"Can I go now?" She stared back at the picture.

"Mrs. Crow. Look at me." Her eyes met his. "I'll let you go as soon as you tell me why you're lying to me."

Holiday, the school leader, came walking into the hospital room at the same time Della shot out. Miranda hadn't even set her phone down after calling Burnett and telling him about the armadillo when Holiday started asking questions.

"What's the deal with the armadillo?" Holiday pressed. The redhead was soft-spoken and caring, but when she asked something, she wanted answers.

"The witch had one chained up. Miranda freed it," Tabitha answered.

Another crease of worry etched in Holiday's forehead.

"I don't think it wants to hurt us," Miranda blurted out.

"We don't know that for sure," Tabitha said.

"I do. Kind of," Miranda added. "It was the armadillo who woke me up when the smoke was coming right at us. And when things started happening in the room, the armadillo scurried to the door and then just stood there, like . . . trying to say we needed to go."

"So you don't think it was a real armadillo?" Tabitha asked.

"Why would she chain a real armadillo?" Miranda asked.

"To keep it from running away," Tabitha offered, but her tone said she didn't believe it.

"What do you think the armadillo wants?" Holiday asked Miranda.

"I don't know," Miranda said.

The room went silent. Miranda's thoughts traveled back to Perry . . . in danger. She looked at Holiday. "What's going on with Perry?"

The fae frowned. "I . . . I don't know . . ." Guilt pulled at her expression. "Everything."

"What do you know? Is he hurt?"

Holiday twisted her hair as if considering her answer. "I don't know if I'm allowed . . . You should ask Burnett."

That made it sound bad. "Is he on a mission or something? Burnett told me Perry was with his parents."

The fae's expression flinched. "He was."

"Then why would Kylie and Della need to check on him?"

The door slammed open. Burnett walked in.

"Did you find it?" Tabitha asked.

"No." Frustration tightened the man's eyes. "We've checked everywhere. It got away." He groaned. "You didn't see it in here at all?"

"No," Miranda and Tabitha said at the same time.

"How could it have gotten away without being seen?" Holiday asked.

"Hell if I know," Burnett answered. "There're three exits out of the hospital and we had them covered immediately. Armadillos aren't what you would call fast!"

"Maybe it's a shape-shifter," Tabitha said, then stiffened a little as if Burnett's presence scared her. Miranda understood. Burnett, tall, dark, and slightly gruff, could be intimidating—if you didn't know him.

The vampire stood like a rock, as if considering her statement. His presence seemed too loud for the small room. He finally let go of a low growl. Holiday walked to her husband and offered him a touch, no doubt to calm him.

He turned his focus on Miranda. "If it was a shifter how could it have been imprisoned at that house like you thought it was?"

"A curse maybe?" Tabitha offered the obvious that wouldn't be obvious to a vampire.

Burnett swiped a hand over his eyes, eyes bright gold with frustration. "But if it could shift to get out of here, why not shift into something less noticeable while it was here walking around the hospital?"

Miranda looked at Tabitha to see if she might offer some insight. Her sister appeared as clueless as Miranda felt.

Burnett let go of a puff of air.

Holiday spoke up again. "Miranda thinks it's possible that the armadillo saved their lives. She doesn't think it's trying to hurt them."

"I know," Burnett said. "But until I know that for sure, I'm not taking that chance."

"Good. I'm glad you don't jump to conclusions." Fear leaked from Tabitha's words. "While I don't know anything about the arma-dillo, I do know Anthony isn't involved in it. You can't blame him."

Burnett took a step toward Tabitha. Her sister shrank into the chair.

"Why would Anthony have been at that house?" he asked.

She hesitated, but finally spoke. "I told Della that she had to be wrong. She just smelled him on me."

Burnett didn't flinch. "Vampires know the difference."

Her sister's posture tightened, frustration won over fear. "He's not into drugs if that's what you're insinuating."

"He wouldn't have to do drugs to be involved."

"Involved how?" Tabitha asked. "Just because he's French you think—"

"I don't care if he's half chimpanzee. If he's not guilty, he'll walk away." Burnett's eyes brightened. He looked at Holiday. "Now, what's this tattoo thing about?"

Miranda glanced at her arm. "It's gone," she said hoping to take a notch out of the tension in the room. "But I took a picture of it." She picked up her phone, found the photograph, and passed it to Holiday.

"I'm sending it to my phone," said Holiday. "I'll look into it."

Burnett stared over Holiday's shoulder at the screen then at Miranda and her sister. "Being witches, you don't have a clue what this could be?"

"No," they said in unison.

He stood completely still as if mentally taking some tally. "Here's what we're going to do. The doctor just informed me that Miranda can go home." He motioned to Tabitha. "They're keeping you over-night. I'll put a guard—"

"No," Miranda said. The thought of leaving her sister did not sit well. "I don't think that's a good idea. Not with the feeling I got. Let me stay so . . . if something crazy happens, we'll be together." She looked at her sister. "We can do blood magic if we had to."

Burnett shot forward. "Feeling? Do you . . . you think some shit's going down, like before?" Burnett asked. "A premonition? Do you feel that?"

Burnett's and Holiday's auras darkened, and they stood there staring.

"Just"—Miranda held up her hand and posed her fingers less than a half an inch apart—"a little bit." She glanced at Tabitha, curious if she agreed.

As if reading Miranda's mind, her sister nodded. "It's small."

Burnett looked flabbergasted, and that wasn't a good look for him. "Are you saying that you're just getting a little bit of premonition, or that the shit coming is small? Tell me."

Tabitha's face paled. "Wh . . . which one do you want me to say?"

He frowned. "Small shit. If I get a preference, I want small shit." No sooner had his words echoed in the tiny white room than he looked over his shoulder and cringed.

The door swung open. The doctor looked at Burnett. "You got a problem with constipation?"

The fact that the doctor looked so serious shattered the tension and had everyone laughing.

Everyone but Burnett.

Shawn parked in front of the address Mrs. Crow had given him for Lily Chambers—the employee she'd finally admitted was there at the time of the robbery. The woman's excuse for not mentioning her earlier was that the girl was hiding from her family. The story went that Lily, at sixteen, had been placed in foster care with Mrs. Crow's niece. A human foster home from what Shawn assumed. Assumed, because it wasn't a question he could ask.

But if so, that surprised Shawn. The FRU had its own foster care and had people working that system just as the police did. Why wouldn't Lily have been placed in a supernatural's home?

According to Mrs. Crow, six months after Lily's placement, her family showed up to get her. She refused to leave. While they didn't take Lily, they'd beat Mrs. Crow's niece pretty badly. After Lily had gotten her foster mom help, she'd run away—leaving a note saying she didn't want anyone else to get hurt.

Six months later, the Crows had run into Lily while visiting Houston. She'd been living on the streets. The Crows had offered her a job and a place to live. Only when they agreed not to tell anyone who she was did she agree.

"She's a good girl," Mrs. Crow had insisted. "We just didn't want to put her in the spotlight so her family could find her again."

Perry asked if Lily had seemed to recognize the robbers, and she insisted that the girl had been in the office getting a deposit together and had barely seen them. But, since Officer Johnson was convinced that there were several different traces of shape-shifters in the store, Shawn couldn't help but wonder if Lily's family, also shape-shifters, wasn't behind the robbery. And considering that the girl was part vampire she might have the gift of scent. So she didn't have to see the robbers to recognize them.

Or was there more to this? Could she be behind the robbery?

He hated thinking that because . . . because she'd had such kind, pretty eyes. But Shawn wasn't stupid. Pretty didn't equal innocent. And when Mrs. Crow had admitted it had been Lily's idea not to mention her, it made Shawn even more suspicious.

For all he knew, Lily's family might be here right now, counting the booty they'd stolen.

He got a flash image of her in the store, looking soft and feminine. He hoped his suspicions were wrong.

He got out of his car. In the distance he heard thunder. One of the sudden summer storms was rolling in, he smelled it. The sky had gone dark. There were no lights on in the house, but Lily didn't live in the house. His footsteps tapped quietly as he moved to the back of the house where there was a garage apartment.

As Shawn moved away from the streetlights, the storm seemed to close in on him. The sky had turned to a deep dark gray.

Slowing down, he reached back to confirm he'd brought his cuffs. Not so much for Lily, the girl probably didn't weigh a hundred pounds soaking wet, but for any company she might keep.

He cut the corner around the house, staying on grass instead of concrete, hoping to silence his steps. There were a few lights on in the apartment. He spotted movement through one of the windows. Just Lily? Or did she have company.

A blast of wind stirred his hair—moving past him and hopefully making it harder for other supernaturals to pick up on his scent. Still, he reached inside his shirt and drew out his gun from his shoulder strap.

Heavy in his hand, the weapon had been designed to look like a regular Glock.

It wasn't.

It had two settings: to stun, and to kill. The first setting sent out a minuscule dart with enough drugs to stop an elephant. The second shot a bullet with enough power to take out any lunar-enhanced were or ticked-off shape-shifter.

Right now it was on stun, but, with a flick of his thumb, he could change that.

Chapter Seven

Shawn neared the porch. Someone moved past the front window. The door opened. He darted to the side of the building.

Careful not to breathe, he leaned forward to see who'd walked out. The long dark hair swaying from shoulder to shoulder told him it was Lily.

He stared as she moved almost seductively in a pair of red high heels. The roll and grind sound of the large suitcase she pulled behind her echoed in the dark. The tapping of her heels bounced on the concrete walkway. A large backpack hanging over one of her shoulders swayed back and forth.

Suitcase?

So Lily Chambers was skipping town, huh? Generally, only the guilty run.

Disappointing, since he'd wanted to believe Mrs. Crow. He waited to see if anyone else walked out. When they didn't, he lowered his guard and eased away from the house.

She stopped as if she'd heard him.

She lifted her nose up. No doubt, to catch his scent.

So the girl did have the gift of sensitive hearing and scent. But probably not like a full vampire, or she'd have detected him earlier.

"What are you doing here?" she asked without looking back.

"You going somewhere?" he asked.

She turned around on her heels and faced him. At first she looked baffled, but then her gaze shot straight to the gun. Fear filled her eyes.

She gasped. "You're with Jax!" she screeched.

He didn't have a friggin' clue who Jax was, and while he hadn't known how she'd react, he hadn't expected the suitcase that came hurling at him.

She took off in a dead run. Too late for him to duck, the damn case, weighing a ton, slammed into his gut—knocked him on his butt.

The gun flew from his hand.

Bolting to his feet, not even taking the time to snatch his gun, he hauled ass after her. "FRU, stop!" he yelled but she never looked back.

She ran fast. He was faster. He caught up with her around the front of the house.

Taking one hard flying leap, he tackled her. She went down with a soft whoosh, and he went down on top of her.

One side of his brain, the male side of it, reminded him that it had been a while since he'd been on top of a girl. The other side of his brain, the FRU-trained side, rolled off her, flipped her on her back, yanked out a pair of you-ain't-going-anywhere cuffs and had them on her before she caught her breath.

Unfortunately, before he caught his, she'd flipped back over.

"Don't try to run," he said. "Because—"

Before he could state the handcuff warning, before he put up his proper guard, she kicked him right in the face with the toe of her red shoe.

He fell back—again—tasted blood, and ran a hand over his busted mouth. "I wouldn't run," he screamed. "The cuffs are charged." He patted his right eye—*which felt swollen*—and checked to see if any of his teeth were missing. Then he waited.

Patiently.

Miss Lily Chambers wouldn't go far.

He heard her yelp and watched her hit the ground.

Whoever had invented those handcuffs should get a silver star.

Shawn wiped the blood from his lips, stood up, and walked over to where she was lying face up on the ground. The electric shock, set to go off if a perp got more than ten feet from the agent, wasn't strong enough to kill, but it hurt like hell. He knew. Burnett's policy was that an agent had to experience it before they were allowed to carry the cuffs.

Seeing her on the ground, still jerking, brought on a guilty frown.

"Take deep breaths." The pain in her face sent him deeper into guilt mode. But then he saw the backpack she'd carried over her shoulder lay tossed on the ground and its contents spilled out. An unzipped deposit bag and money, lots of it, littered the ground. He immediately recalled Mrs. Crow telling him that Lily had been in the office preparing a bank deposit.

"Preparing it" all right!

He thought of all Mr. Crow's blood at the crime scene. No need to feel guilty for this gal. She'd brought it on herself.

His chest still felt heavy. "If you'd listened you'd have known what could happen. But you didn't. Bet you touched the stove when your mama told you not to, didn't you?"

"Who the hell are you?" she gritted out.

"I am the FRU agent who is taking your ass in for robbery." He motioned to the money fluttering in the breeze around her and ignored his throbbing lip. "And let's just hope Mr. Crow makes it, or you'll be going down for murder."

"What?" She sat up. "The paramedics said it wasn't bad. Tell me he's going to be okay!"

When he didn't answer, she got to her feet.

She still twitched, but the fact that she could move this soon after 100 milliamps of electricity ran through her impressed the hell out of him. He checked her pattern to make sure she wasn't full vampire.

No surprises. Definitely a mixed-breed. With a high tolerance for pain.

"Take me to the hospital now!"

"Hurts, doesn't it?" he asked, his side and face throbbing.

"Not for me, you idiot! For Mr. Crow." She stomped her foot like an angry child.

Shawn stared, the taste of blood still lingering on his tongue. She'd already made a fool of him twice. He wasn't going for a third.

"The only place you're going is a cell. And if you don't want to get zapped again, you'd better stay within ten feet of me at all times." Shifting out of kick range, he knelt down and collected the bills and shoved them back into the bag. Throwing it over his shoulder, he walked back to collect his gun and her suitcase.

He heard her dogging his steps. So the girl could learn.

"How bad is Mr. Crow?" The question came out with all kinds of emotion: fury, frustration, and fear. "Answer me!"

No sooner had the door swished shut, leaving Miranda alone with her sister, than Tabitha blurted out, "I'm so sorry."

"About what?" Miranda asked.

"This. All of this. You didn't want to go." Tears formed in Tabitha's eyes. "And look what happened. I brought this on you and Anthony."

"You didn't have a clue anything like this would happen." Miranda reached over with her uncasted arm and gave her sister's hand a squeeze.

Tabitha squeezed back. "I swear I didn't. I've been there twice. It never happened before. I just wanted to find out about Anthony. I needed something to keep my mom off my back about dating him. Now she's going to refuse to let me see him. Our dad and your mom are blaming me. Not to mention your friends have more of a reason to hate me."

"No one hates you," Miranda said.

"Please, Mr. Scary-as-Shit FRU Agent can't stand me. And he's taking that out on Anthony."

"No. Burnett's firm but he's always fair. He comes across grizzly sometimes, but he's . . . not. He let me hug him once. And not because he needed it, because I did. And if you ever see him with his baby girl, Hannah, he's talking sweet to her and making funny faces. He's more teddy bear than grizzly."

"I hope to the Goddesses that you are right. Because . . . I really think I'm in love with him."

Miranda's mind started scrambling. "You're in love with Burnett?"

"No! With Anthony."

Miranda considered her sister's confession. "It's kind of soon for that, isn't it?"

"Isn't that what love's like?" Tabitha asked. "It hits and you know it."

"It's not always like that." Miranda wished she could suck the words back in. If her sister put two and two together . . .

"So that's the problem?" Damn Tabitha was good in math.

"What problem?" The skirted lie gave Miranda's voice an unnatural pitch.

Tabitha eyeballed her.

"I'm just saying sometimes it takes a while."

Tabitha leaned closer. "You don't love Shawn, do you?"

"I didn't say that."

"No, but . . ."

"I care about him." Miranda held up her fingers. "I'm . . . this close to falling in love with him."

"That close, huh?" Her sister's brow narrowed and she got that you-ain't-gonna-like-what-I'm-about-to-say expression. "How close are you to falling out of love with Perry?"

The question bounced around Miranda's bruised conscience where she'd been kicking the question around herself for the last few weeks. She wanted to deny it.

"Close," she offered in truth. Or at least what she'd thought was the truth until she'd started thinking about taking that first-time step with Shawn, the one she'd almost taken with Perry. Thinking and wondering why she'd felt so ready then, and not so ready now.

Tabitha's shoulder came against Miranda's. "If you need to talk. I'll listen."

"I know," Miranda said. "But to talk about something you need to at least have a handle on how you feel. I'm handleless! Part of me still cares about Perry, and part of me hasn't forgiven him. I loved him and he completely blindsided me by breaking it off."

Tabitha's brows narrowed. "Yeah, but you said he broke things off because he thought you deserved better."

"It still hurt. And I would have taken him back when he admitted it to me, but he didn't give me a chance before running out of my life again."

"Well, when he came back and you were paying attention to Shawn, Perry probably thought you had made your mind up."

"Shawn was in the hospital, I wasn't seeing him as a girlfriend."

"I'm not saying you did anything wrong, just that it sent the wrong message to Perry."

Miranda took in a big gulp of air that tasted like guilt. "I hate it when people do that."

"Do what?" Tabitha asked.

"Use logic. Kylie does it all the time." Miranda exhaled. "I'm so screwed up."

Tabitha gave Miranda's shoulder another I'm-here-for-you bump. "Not screwed up, but you do need to shit or get off the pot."

"How? I'm emotionally constipated." She eyed her sister. "First you sounded like Kylie and now you're beginning to sound like Della."

Tabitha grinned. "Probably the word 'shit.' Shit seems to be an essential part of a vampire's vocabulary. Anthony says it all the time." She almost smiled. "Not that I mind. Everything he says in that French accent sounds like poetry."

Tabitha dropped her head on Miranda's shoulder. They sat there in the mostly-white room with nothing but white noise. Miranda's mind went to Perry. She suspected her sister's stayed on Anthony.

Tabitha's phone dinged with a text. Her sister shifted and picked up her cell from the bedside table. After reading it, she let out a moan of frustration and her posture went from relaxed to rock hard. "I can't fracking believe this!"

"Your mom?" Miranda asked, knowing Tabitha's mom was the leading cause of her sister's frustrations.

"No. It's Anthony. He says they're blaming him. And his English isn't that good and he feels like he can't defend himself."

Miranda breathed in some of her sister's frustration. "Burnett won't let that happen."

"Well, so far he's not stopping it. They threatened to have him deported."

"If he's innocent, Burnett—"

"If?" Her voice echoed. "You think he did this? You think he has something to do with the house blowing up?"

"No," Miranda said. "I meant that there has to be a logical reason why Della picked up his scent. Maybe you told him about the fortune-teller . . ."

"I didn't." The two words tripped off her lips in anger.

"Then maybe he followed us there and left before—"

"No." Her sister's eyes narrowed. "I told you, his scent was on me."

Miranda hated conflict and never liked telling someone they were wrong, especially when it was someone she loved. Her heart crumpled up like used aluminum foil. She pushed the words off her lips with caution. "But it's like Burnett said, vampires know the difference between a scent carried by someone and a scent of someone who's been there."

Tabitha's mouth thinned, and her rose-colored lips turned white. "His scent was all over me." The pain in her voice hung in the air. "Like all over me! We had sex before I came to pick you up."

Miranda frowned, thinking that was way too fast, but she shelved that problem for later. "It's still a—"

"Stop!" Tabitha sat up on the bed, straight up. "I can't believe this. You're going to put this on him, too. Here I am trying to support you in your romantic chaos and you accuse my boyfriend of being a drug addict and trying to blow us up."

"I didn't say . . ."

Tabitha shot off the bed and out of the room. Loud voices echoed behind the door. Miranda did the one-arm scramble out of bed to follow, but a black-suited FRU agent blocked her exit.

"No, you stay here!" His brown eyes, glowing with green, told Miranda he was a vampire.

Still posed in the doorway, he pulled out his phone. "The sister is going back to her room." He paused. "You think I didn't try? She threatened me with her pinky. Just get there. Agent James will have my balls if something happens to either one of these girls!"

Chapter Eight

Miranda shut the door, shot back inside, found her phone, and texted her sister.

Come back, pleeeeease! She paused, trying to think what to write, something that would bring her sister back. *I don't think Anthony did anything. Just come back and let's figure it out!*

She hit send and waited. Staring, praying that the three little dots would pop up on the screen.

They didn't pop. "Don't do this!" she muttered aloud and typed: *You're my sister. You can't be mad at me!*

Finally the three dots flickered on the screen. Miranda took air into her lungs, waiting . . . Words finally appeared.

Need to be alone. Anthony on his way here. Going down for another MRI scan. Later. Love you.

The last two words lifted the lumpy emotion from Miranda's chest, then she read her own text, and a few lumps grew back. *I don't think Anthony did anything.* Why did that read like a lie? She didn't think . . . did she? No, she liked Anthony, but . . . why didn't he just tell the FRU why he'd been to the witch's house?

The only reason he wouldn't tell would be if . . . if he had something to hide.

Doubt tugged at her mind.

What if her sister was falling in love with someone mixed up in . . . drugs? And she'd already had sex with him.

"No." Miranda couldn't think that. She had to support Tabitha in this. Had to. But Anthony had better start explaining things and quick. Burnett's patience was only so long.

She dropped her phone on the bed and hurried into the bathroom. Reaching down to lower her panties, she discovered she wasn't wearing any.

Awkward!

Bladder emptied, and not accustomed to hospital attire, she realized the lower tie had been swimming in the toilet.

She'd probably peed all over it, too. Remembering seeing another gown in the closet, she held the wet fabric away from her backside and dashed out. The cool air humming through the ceiling vent hit her bare butt.

She opened the cabinet and found some of the hospital's finest lingerie—which was so far from fine. Before the cabinet door shut, she spotted her pink panties folded on top of her jeans. No reason to go around commando when you didn't have to.

Then, not wanting to give anyone a peep show, and because the door didn't lock, she yanked the curtain between the bed and the hospital room's door. Eyes on the flimsy wall of privacy, she quickly reached back with her right hand, untied the top of her gown and let the whole thing drop to the floor.

Dressing in a hurry, one-handed, was no easy task. She stepped into her panties and slid them up her legs. Fitting her cast through the snapped arm holes proved to be an even bigger challenge.

On the third missed attempt she muttered, "Crap."

"Uh . . . need some help?" The voice came from behind her.

Behind her! Where her ass had just been shining.

The screech climbed up her throat, but then the deep tenor of that voice rang some familiar bells.

With only one arm in the gown, the flimsy piece of cotton clutched to her chest, she swung around to face . . .

Perry. He sat in the chair backed to the wall.

The shock of someone being in the room gave way to the shock of *him* being in the room. A breath whispered from her lips, her lungs opened and pulled in air that tasted sweet, like birthday cake, like . . . broken promises.

No one else had made her laugh so much, love so much. Hurt so much.

She should so be over him, and yet here she was, not over anything, caught in his soft blue gaze, breathing sweet air, and remembering everything. She couldn't look away. She felt trapped. But not at all eager to free herself.

He stood up, and took one step toward her as if to hug her, or just touch her.

She blinked and fought to rein in her runaway pulse.

Not easy when inch by inch she continued to take in the details, Perry details. There were differences from the boy nine months ago to the one who stood in front of her. He looked taller, not just one inch. Maybe two. And his arms and shoulders were far more broad and muscular than they'd been. He looked . . . older. But more than just older. He looked grown up. The peach fuzz on his cheeks was now a blond five o'clock shadow. His jawline looked a little more chiseled. His eyes, a little more worldly. His hair, the color of morning sunshine, had darkened to a bolder hue of gold.

He needed a haircut.

Or maybe he didn't.

She'd always liked his hair a little long, how it felt slipping through her fingers.

The strands part curly, part straight, hung past his ears, flipping up on the ends. The tips of her fingers tingled with the need to touch. Her gaze whispered past his facial features down to his body, which looked bulkier. Lifting her gaze, she realized he'd been doing the same thing. Taking inventory of her. Did he see changes in her?

Her hair longer. Her breasts a bit larger. Her heart a lot more broken.

Did he even regret leaving her?

She drew in a sobering breath that still tasted sweet, Perry sweet. She cleared her throat.

Guilt flashed in his eyes and reminded her of the complete inappropriateness of this situation.

"What are . . . How . . . ?" Careful not to expose herself any more than she already had, she slipped her cast in the arm hole and finally managed to push a full sentence from her lips. "What are you doing here?"

"I came in while you were . . . in the bathroom. And then you came out and . . . you didn't see me."

"And *you* just sat there, didn't say anything, and let me take my clothes off!"

"I . . . was going to say something, but then you . . . I saw . . . and I couldn't talk." His eyes brightened, the corners tightened, and she waited, almost certain he was about to . . .

His lips quivered and then finally gave way to a smile, part nervous, part shameless bad boy.

That's all it took to set the butterflies chasing rainbows in her stomach.

He tried to pull the smile back, but didn't succeed. Then he gave up. A noise, a pulled back chuckle, escaped his mouth. "It's not like I haven't seen it all before."

She pressed her palm against her fluttering abdomen. His words were like brushstrokes that painted memories in her head.

Memories of them skinny-dipping. She remembered that night—and not just now but a thousand times—always late, right before she gave in to the sleep, right when her guard was down, her heart vulnerable.

He'd dared her to do it. *Come on. I'm going to.* And he did it. Under the silver shadows of the moon he took his clothes off . . . slowly. Not a touch of embarrassment filled his eyes, and she'd been just as comfortable removing hers. They had stood there in front of each other and just stared. What should have been awkward and uncomfortable was sweet, special, and so right.

The water had been just cold enough. His skin just warm enough. She remembered in painful detail how close they'd come to going all the way.

Less than three weeks later, he broke up with her and left for Paris. Left her to pick up the pieces of her heart. Left her to try to figure out how something could feel so right and have been so wrong.

"That was a long time ago." The words left her mouth dry, her chest open, her heart cracked.

"Nine months, two weeks, and three days. I could tell you the exact hours if you told me the time." Honesty gave his words a deeper tone, and something almost sad flashed in his eyes. The mirror image of what she had seen in his baby blues echoed inside her chest.

How many times had she regretted that night? Not because of how far they went, but because they hadn't gone any further. Kylie and Della kept talking about the first time and how it needed to be special. She'd never experienced special like that since.

Crazy as it seemed, while they hadn't had sex, it felt as if they'd somehow made love.

"I'll never forget it," he said.

Neither will I? Pride, that ugly emotion she wished she didn't have, kept her from saying it. But how could she not be a little smug? He'd been her everything. Her reason she got up every day. Her reason to laugh. Then he'd become her reason to cry.

He shuffled his feet amidst the obvious tension. "Are you hurting?" He motioned to her arm.

Yeah. And you caused it. "I'm fine." She paused. "What are you doing here?"

"I thought you called me."

She glanced at her phone. "No, I . . . I didn't."

He lifted one shoulder in a half shrug. "Not on the phone, but . . . in your head."

"What?" she asked.

"You know, telepathically."

"No. I can't." Suddenly not wanting to think, she started talking. "Well, I could but it would take hours working on a spell, and even then clairvoyant spells usually need to be blessed by a mystic Wiccan."

"A what?"

"A mystic. They're powerful in different ways. Telepathically talented. But they aren't tied to the Wicca Council. There aren't a lot of them around."

He lifted his other shoulder this time. "Then maybe it was like dreamscaping. You know, like Kylie can do."

"Witches can't dreamscape."

"Well, all I know is that I . . . saw you and you were crying and lying on the grass, bleeding. And you called my name. Then later I had another image of you on a stretcher. And since—"

"That's odd." Especially when she . . .

"What's odd?" he asked.

"I . . . heard. Well, I thought I heard you talking to me a couple times. But I was injured."

"Then you must have contacted me?"

"No, like I said, I can't do that." Realizing she was still not completely dressed, she reached back to attempt to tie the gown strings. Unfortunately, one-handed it was impossible.

"Well, I'm less likely to be able to do it, so it had to be you."

She bit down on her lip. "Maybe it was just . . . a fluke?" She reached back again.

"Odd that it happened to both of us." He took a step closer. "Let me help you."

She offered him her signature eye roll. "I think you've seen enough."

He grinned. "Not really. But I was going to tie it facing you so I wouldn't . . . see anything else."

"Oh." Her face flushed.

He moved in close, close enough that his natural scent—a little musky, a little like wind—filled her airways. Her skin tingled as if just his scent could heighten her awareness of being a girl. A girl close to a boy. Close to a boy who made her heart sing and cry at the same time.

He reached around her neck to find the two strings. His fingertips touched the curve of her neck and her first instinct was to lean into him. To bury her face on that soft spot of his shoulder, to beg him to hold her, to pretend that he'd never left. That he hadn't taken her heart with him.

She closed her eyes. Her sinuses stung.

"One down. One to go." His voice sounded as jittery as she felt.

He lowered his hands down, reached around her waist to get the other ties. As he searched for the strings, his palms brushed against her lower back. Each soft touch sent another chill slow dancing up her spine.

His soft breath came against her neck. His chest came against her breasts. She became aware of every inch of her body and where it came to his.

"Done." He pulled his arms from around her and inched back. Not far, they were almost as close as two people could be without touching. And yet it felt as if they still were . . . touching.

Swallowing a lump of raw nerves down her throat, she glanced up. She had a thousand things she should ask him, but she couldn't think of one.

She forced herself to step back. Finally able to breathe, the air still birthday-cake sweet, she formed one of the questions. "What kind of trouble are you in?"

His brows tightened. "What do you mean?"

"Burnett sent Della and Kylie to check on you."

"Oh, it's nothing," he said, but she could swear she heard a hint of a mistruth in his voice. "I ran into them, halfway here. Everything's okay."

"I thought you were with your parents?" She moved over to her bed and pulled herself up.

"I am."

"Then why were Burnett and Holiday worried?"

His hesitation told her she hadn't imagined his white lie. The corners of his eyes tightened with a barely-there frown.

"I . . . stumbled on something happening that Burnett needed to know about. And as soon as I figure it out, I'll hand it over to him."

"What kind of something?"

He didn't answer.

"Is it illegal?"

He nodded.

"Is it dangerous?"

"Nothing I can't handle."

"You sure?" She didn't ask if it involved his parents. She knew. It was the look, the lost-little-boy look he got whenever he talked about them. The dull pain in his eyes said what he wouldn't. He was hurting. Even more now than before.

Hadn't they hurt him enough already? Anger swelled inside her. She almost reached to hug him.

"I'm fine," he said. His eyes widened. "They were right?"

"What?"

"The tattoo on your arm. Della told me about it."

She glanced down. It was back. Even bigger. "It'll go away. It did before." *She hoped.*

"You don't know what it means?"

She watched as the swirl pattern moved higher, past-her-elbow high. "No. I'm clueless."

"Do you think the witch could have put a curse on you?" he asked.

"I've never heard of a tattoo curse." She looked up and their gazes met, locked, and it started hurting again. He'd left her and just within a few minutes she felt it all again. All the things he'd meant to her.

"Why are you here?" she asked.

"I told you. I thought you were hurt really bad and you called me."

"So the only reason you came is because you thought I was dying?" She regretted the words, and the attitude in which she'd said them, the nanosecond they spilled from her lips. But damn it. He'd hurt her.

"It's not the only reason." He glanced at his feet, shuffled them around as if hoping they'd kick up some words he could use. Finally, he looked up. "I know you're seeing Shawn and I'm not asking you to . . . to break up."

Was he really saying this? "You left me. You left me twice."

"I know. Look . . . what I'm asking is if we can . . . be friends."

"Friends?"

"Yeah. Could I come back and see you sometimes? I wouldn't try anything." His lips fluttered again, forecasting a smile. "Next time you walk into a room and start taking your clothes off, I'll try really hard to speak up."

His humor was lost on her.

"I promise to keep my hands to myself. We can just talk. We used to talk all the time. I miss that. I'd come back every week or so. What do you think?"

He shuffled his feet again. "What? Shawn won't let you?"

"Shawn doesn't tell me what to do." Then what he'd said earlier hit another chord. A painful one. "So all you want to be is friends?"

"Hell no! But I figure it's a start. How else am I going to convince you that you should be with me and not him? Give me a second chance, Miranda."

"I was giving you a second chance when you came back from Paris and then you . . . left. Again." She remembered what her sister had said about him leaving because she'd been going to the hospital to see Shawn. Part of her knew that was true. Maybe she'd even done it because he'd hurt her. She'd wanted him to fight for her. He hadn't fought.

"Okay, a third chance." He ran a hand through his hair. His

blond strands landed in almost the same position—giving a wind-blown bad-boy surfer appearance.

He swallowed as if struggling for words. "Look, I know I shouldn't have left like that, but I had to . . . I needed to work through things with my parents. And . . . you were seeing Shawn. I didn't think . . . I could compete with him."

"I told you I wasn't seeing him as a girlfriend. Maybe I—"

"I know . . . but it hurt. I already needed to prove something to myself about my parents. So I . . . decided to go."

"What did you need to prove?"

"Just . . . stuff." He grinned. "You know, if I came by these good looks naturally."

That smile. That laugh was as transparent as thin glass.

"Stop," she said.

"Stop what?" he asked.

"Trying to cover up how you really feel by joking. I see through that every time."

He shrugged again, this time deeper, as if trying to loosen the pain in his heart.

She looked him dead in the eyes. "Just say you don't want to talk about it. Don't play those games with me."

He blinked. "Okay, no games. I don't want to . . ." He stopped, the hurt in his eyes brighter. "I'm still figuring things out. Give me some time. When I understand, I'll talk to you about it. I always talked to you about things. Didn't I?"

"Yeah." She flinched. His pain echoed inside her.

His phone dinged with a text. He pulled it out of his jean pocket and frowned. "It's Burnett. He's upset that I didn't go straight to see him." He met her eyes. "I should probably go before he sends someone to get me."

He slipped the phone into his back pocket. "If I finish in time, can I swing by before I leave?"

It was a simple yes or no question. Why did it feel so big? She nodded.

"And later, every week or so, I'll come home. Just to talk?"

Before she even realized she was doing it, she nodded again.

He smiled, a real it's-Christmas-morning kind of smile—the sadness about his parents gone. His expression was so beautiful, her ribs hugged her heart and the air went back to tasting like birthday cake.

He started to reach for her, but caught himself. "No touching. See? I remember."

He moved to the door, reached for the knob, and hesitated. He glanced back—that sweet smile still on his lips. "Thank you."

She gave him another beyond-her-control nod.

He left.

She inhaled. No sugary, birthday-cake smell anymore. No fresh wind-and-hot-boy scent. Just the astringent odor of the hospital, and the bitter smell of a startling realization. A cold, oh-shit realization.

She had just agreed to start seeing Perry again. "Only as friends," she whispered aloud, but it left her tongue like a lie.

For Goddess' sakes, what have I done? But there was no taking it back.

Nope. It was done. She was going to be spending time with Perry.

How in hell was she going to explain this to Shawn?

Perry left the hospital, his smile still in place, and did one leap of joy and a fist pump in the night air. She'd agreed to see him. Just see him, but that was a start. A really, really good start.

For one second his mind churned on how Miranda was going to explain this to Shawn. Hopefully the warlock would finally see that Miranda still had feelings for him and back off. He could hope. Not that he would blame the guy if he didn't give up without a fight. Miranda was that special. But she was Perry's special someone.

He'd known it from the first time he'd laid eyes on her over three years ago, the first time he'd met her at the summer camp.

He hadn't even spoken to her the first year. But he'd spent time shape-shifting into every kind of animal there was, just so he could hang around her. The second year, he started teasing her a little. The third, they finally became more than friends.

Happy for the first time in months and feeling light on his feet, he jogged to the back of the hospital behind a brick wall and the garbage Dumpster to turn. Right before he stopped, his phone rang. Probably Burnett. The guy could be relentless.

Certain it was Burnett, he answered before checking the number. "I'm on my way." He hoped Burnett couldn't hear the sheer happiness in his tone, but then again, he didn't care. He wanted to shout this feeling to the world.

"On your way where?" The voice wasn't Burnett's. Immediately it felt as if someone had stuck a pin in his happy balloon. Even the buoyancy in his steps changed.

"To see my girl, like I told you," he said. "I thought you were her."

"Where are you?" his father asked, and Perry listened to see if he heard suspicion in his old man's voice, but didn't get it.

"I told you. In Houston."

"Where about in Houston?" he asked.

"Why?" Perry asked, hearing suspicion in his own voice. All these years of being a shape-shifter, he should be an expert at putting up fronts, but for some reason with his dad it was hard.

"Because your mom and I are in Houston. I thought we might drop by and meet your girl."

Shit! "Not happening," he said.

"Why?"

You mean besides the fact that I'm not there? "Not happening," he repeated.

"You ashamed of your parents?"

Yeah. He was. And the fact that his dad had to ask that was almost funny. "We're just starting. It's not time to meet the parents." And it would never be that time.

"Okay. But when you're done tapping some girl's ass, meet us at the bar, 2323 Handle Street. We got a room not too far away, but your mom wants to get a buzz on and she hears they serve the best wines in town."

So not happening! He could almost tolerate his dad's presence, but his mom when sober was difficult, when drunk, impossible. "Why don't I just get back to Dallas in the morning?"

"Because we're not working in Dallas anymore."

"Why aren't we working in Dallas?"

"Jax called. He's sending us somewhere else."

"What for?"

"A job."

"So we're going to be in Houston?"

"He hasn't said where. Just that he needs a face-to-face. He really wants to meet you. I told you he was getting tired of Caleb's screwups."

"So Caleb's out?" Perry asked.

"Not completely. But he will be after I chat with Jax."

"Who is this Jax guy anyway?" Perry asked.

"You'll learn soon enough, son. Just do what your daddy says and I'm gonna make you a rich man and you'll be able to snag you a fine woman like your mom."

Oh, yeah, that's what Perry wanted. To find a woman who would abandon her own son and push her husband into a life of crime so she could drink expensive wine and dress like she was twenty. What was sad was his dad honestly loved the woman. "It will be late," he said.

"Then come to our room. You can crash here. We got two beds. It's the Marriott Hotel right off Main and Fifth in downtown."

"I'll see you in the morning." He started to hang up.

"Fine," his father snapped. "But be here early. We're supposed to be at Jax's place by nine."

Interesting. "So Jax lives in Houston?"

"Yeah."

"Where?"

"Just be here by eight. And stop asking questions. It makes you sound like you have ulterior motives."

I do. "What kind of motives could I have? I just don't like being told what to do."

"I'm your father. I can tell you what to do and I deserve respect."

"Not really." Perry flinched when he realized he'd said that aloud. He'd been around his father for a month and had managed to keep his mouth shut. Why was it getting harder?

"Just get your ass here by eight! Prove to me that my son is worth a damn." His dad hung up.

Perry kicked at a discarded beer can. It clanked against the Dumpster and rang out in the night. A night that until just a few minutes ago had held promise.

He stood there, the smell of garbage thickening the air. He blew out a cloud of frustration, angry he'd allowed his dad to chase away his joy at seeing Miranda. Angry that with one conversation he felt it again. The emptiness. He needed something. Something he couldn't even name.

Maybe it was all in his head.

Hadn't he felt complete when he'd been with Miranda? Wasn't that enough?

The temptation to tell Burnett everything he knew and just back off swelled in his chest. Burnett was probably going to insist on it.

His dad's words echoed in his head. *Prove to me that my son is worth a damn.*

The muscles in Perry's shoulders tightened.

He couldn't.

He wouldn't back off.

He didn't care what Burnett said.

His dad was right. He needed to prove his something. Maybe his worth. But not to his father.

Not to Burnett.

Not even to Miranda.

But to himself.

Was it that easy? Perry wondered. Was that all he needed? His gut said no. There was something more. Until he had it, he wasn't walking away.

Chapter Nine

Shawn stared through the two-way mirror watching Lily Chambers fidget in the adjacent interrogation room. Occasionally, she'd get up and pace the room like a trapped lion. Right now, she squirmed in the chair, worry marring her pretty face. Not that he felt bad—well, a little about her getting shocked—but she needed to fret. He ran his tongue over his swollen lip and watched her lift her restrained hands and set them on the table. She let out a deep exhale of frustration then dropped her forehead on her locked, fisted hands.

He'd deactivated the cuffs but hadn't removed them. He already had two blows from her, three if you counted the chip off his pride.

How had he let the girl who barely weighed a hundred pounds get the upper hand on him? He could understand it if she were full vampire. She wasn't.

He heard her first soft sob, and his chest tightened. Why the hell was he feeling sorry for her? She'd brought this down on herself.

The door behind Shawn swung open. Burnett, Chase, and Lucas all walked in. Chase, a vampire, and Lucas, a werewolf, were the boyfriends of Miranda's two roommates, and both of them worked for the FRU. So Shawn spent a lot of time with them, even considered them friends.

"Damn it!" Lily Chambers muttered, rubbing her tears off her cheek with her shoulder.

"Whatcha got?" Burnett's gaze lingered on the girl behind the glass. He frowned as if seeing the girl cry didn't suit him, either. It made Shawn feel a little better.

Then Burnett looked at Shawn's face. "What the hell happened to you?"

"It's nothing." Shawn touched his busted lip. He hadn't taken the time to look at it yet. Was it that noticeable?

"Nothing? Half your friggin' face is blue."

Shawn pointed to the two-way mirror. "She got me with her foot."

"You got beat up by a girl?" Chase snickered. Lucas did the same. Shawn could swear he even heard Burnett hold back a chuckle.

"She's tougher than she looks. She tried to run after I put the cuffs on her and got herself zapped. It barely fazed her."

"You shocked . . . *her?*" Lucas asked, his blue eyes widening.

"I didn't do it. She kicked me in the face and ran." Shawn pushed away his annoyance, his thoughts turning to Miranda. "Have you got anything about who blew the house up?"

"Nothing other than proof the cops are right," Chase answered. "We found all kinds of drugs in what was left of the house. Meth, cocaine, marijuana."

"And Anthony?" Shawn asked. "Did you figure out why he was there?"

"No," Burnett answered this time. "I had another agent question him. Someone who doesn't know him."

"And?" Shawn asked, not wanting to believe Anthony had any involvement, but if he was wrong, he'd personally like to teach his new French friend a lesson.

"He told the truth on most things."

"Most things?" Shawn asked.

"That he's not dealing drugs and wouldn't hurt Tabitha."

"But?" Shawn asked.

"He's hiding something. He'd answer the question about why his trace was there with another question."

"But you got his trace there for sure, right?" Shawn asked.

"I didn't," Burnett said. "Della did. She got to the scene before I did."

"Could she be wrong?" Shawn asked.

"Not Della," Chase said, quick to defend his girlfriend.

Burnett nodded. "If she says she got it, she got it. The boy's hiding something."

"What could he be hiding?" Shawn searched his mind for clues that told him Anthony was dirty.

"I think he's protecting someone," Burnett answered.

"Protecting who?" Shawn asked. "He's been here less than a month. He spends all his time with Tabitha."

"I know, but he's living with an uncle. And he has two cousins. As soon as I'm done here, I'm going to go see his family."

"You want me to question Anthony?" Shawn asked. "He might—"

"No. I let him go," Burnett focused again on the two-way mirror.

"You what?" Shawn asked, certain he'd misunderstood.

Burnett looked back at him. "I'm having him followed. If my instincts are right, he'll lead us to someone who knows something more than he does."

"Who do you have on him?" Shawn asked.

"Agent Brown," he said. "They've never met so his trace won't be familiar. And Brown just texted me. Anthony went back to the hospital."

"I've met the guy several times," Lucas said. "He seems to care about Tabitha."

"I liked him," Chase said. "I can't believe he's up to no good."

"I know," Burnett said. "I don't believe he's behind this, but he knows more than he's telling."

"Is he our only lead right now?" Shawn directed the question to Lucas, knowing he'd been working the case.

"Right now, yes," Lucas said. "I've got a meeting in an hour to speak to the landlord of the drug house. Chase is going to canvas the neighborhood."

Burnett motioned back to the two-way mirror. "So she's tied to the jewelry store robbery?"

"Yeah," Shawn said.

"Is she the one you met earlier at the store? The employee?"

"Yeah." Shawn's gaze shifted to Lily, and again he felt a tinge of guilt.

"Why do you think she's in on it?" Burnett asked.

Shawn heard Burnett's doubt. "She did this, didn't she?" He motioned to his face with one hand and his bruised ribs with the other.

"She kicked you in the side, too?" Burnett asked, sounding more like a worried parent, than a boss.

"No. She threw a suitcase at me."

Lucas and Chase grinned. Shawn scowled at them.

"Do you need to be checked by a doctor?" Burnett asked.

"I'm fine," Shawn insisted.

Burnett gave Lily another glance. "Any evidence other than her being combative?"

Shawn accepted Burnett wasn't really doubting him. Every good agent gathered facts and asked questions. It still burned. "How much evidence you want? She had her suitcases packed, leaving town with the store's deposit."

"Busted," Chase said.

"And she still hasn't confessed?" Lucas's surprise mirrored what Shawn felt.

"She's lying through her teeth," Shawn said. "At first she claimed she was just going away for a few days. Oh, and she was dropping the deposit by the bank on her way. Then I checked her phone, I found a text to her landlord saying she was moving out."

Everyone looked back at the two-way mirror.

Burnett sighed. "Let's go get to the bottom of this."

"Hey," Chase said, as Shawn started out. "Don't worry, Burnett won't let her hurt you again."

Shawn shot the young vampire agent the third-finger salute.

Chase returned the favor.

Lucas let go of a hoarse chuckle.

Burnett continued out of the room, leaving a parting jab in his wake. "Ya'll make me so proud."

Ten minutes later, Perry, his attitude adjusted to the best of his ability, walked into the FRU headquarters.

The receptionist on duty, who always reminded Perry of a Mrs. Claus, let out a squeal, jumped from her chair, and grabbed him around his middle. Her head, covered in coarse gray hair, barely came to his chest.

He'd met Mrs. Conner eight years ago. Burnett, who'd been Perry's older foster brother and the only one Perry had ever gotten close to, had already moved out of the foster home, but he'd regularly pick up Perry and bring him to work with him. It was one of the safe places a shifter, who might morph accidently, could go. Hell, it was practically his second home.

Considering how much affection Mrs. Conner doled out, Perry was pretty sure that Burnett had told her about his past. Not that Perry minded. He'd been ten and had pretended she was his grandmother. It didn't matter that she was 100 percent were.

When the rounder-than-she-was-tall woman released him, she stepped back and took inventory. "Just look at you. When did you turn into a man? Oh, my, if I were seventy years younger you'd have to beat me off of you."

Perry laughed. "I could never beat you. How's your family?"

"Always causing drama."

Perry just laughed. "I think Burnett's waiting for me."

"Okay, I'll let you go." She walked to her desk and pushed a button allowing him to enter. "But don't you dare leave without giving me another hug. And you're coming to my house for dinner soon."

"Deal." He almost left, then remembered. "Oh, I brought you a little something." He pulled out one of those miniature spoons. The word "Dallas" was engraved in the handle. She'd asked him to bring her one from Paris, and he had. A couple of weeks ago, he saw this one at a gas station and picked it up.

"You brought me a gift?" She clutched the spoon to her chest like it was some prized possession. Who'd have guessed five dollars could make someone so happy?

She waved to the door. "Go before you see me cry."

"You take the lead," Burnett said to Shawn.

Shawn nodded, and sensed this was a test. If he was weak in any area as an agent, interrogation was it. Burnett followed him into the small room where Lily Chambers waited.

Her gaze found Shawn's first then shot to Burnett. "Tell me you're not as big of an idiot as this dirt bag. I've seen opossums with more intelligence."

Okay, maybe Shawn should have let Burnett take the lead on this one?

Shawn looked at Burnett. "Told you she had a mouth on her." And for one second his gaze went to her mouth. It would be pretty if it didn't spout so many lies.

Burnett dropped into the chair across from the little spitfire. "You know the thing with my agents is that when they're attacked, they don't seem to show their best sides."

His calm voice and relaxed posture struck Shawn as odd. Usually at the first sign of disrespect Burnett came back all barrels loaded. Then again, this was the first time he'd seen his boss interrogate a girl. How many times had he heard Della complain that he was a male chauvinist? Maybe Della wasn't just whistling Dixie.

"That's just it," Lily said. "I wouldn't have attacked him if he hadn't snuck up on me."

"I didn't sneak up on you," Shawn said, proud his voice sounded calm.

"Pleeeease! You're lying because you know you were wrong. Your exact words were, 'Going somewhere?' You didn't say, 'I'm the FRU,' or anything official. I turned and found you holding a gun on me. I panicked."

"I was about to tell you I was FRU when you tossed your suitcase at me." His tone came out edgy, but still controlled.

"But when you came in the store earlier you neglected to tell me you were FRU. So I thought you were some freak following me."

He stepped closer. "I wasn't on FRU business when I was at the store."

"You expect me to believe that?" she snapped.

"It's the truth," he replied.

"Right." She focused back on Burnett. "He shocked the piss out of me with these!" She held up her hands.

Her words struck a nerve. "*I* didn't shock you! They go off if a perp runs! You ran."

"You hadn't informed me you were the FRU! As far as I knew I was running from a serial killer!"

"I said it when you were running away." Her accusation hit another nerve and bruised his conscience.

He tightened his shoulders to come across as the aggressor, but purposely kept his expression from showing tension. He'd seen Burnett do it a thousand times. "I was telling you again when you kicked me in the mouth."

She glared up at him with her maple-brown eyes. "Then you need to learn to talk faster!" Her gaze shot back to a very silent Burnett.

She started again. "I want to go to the hospital to check on Mr. Crow! Release me now and I won't file charges against him."

"Charges against me?" Shawn spilled out, his calm façade slipping.

"Give me the key?" Burnett held out his hand to Shawn.

He instantly realized this was probably Burnett playing good cop bad cop. Normally, Shawn played the good cop better than the bad. But he'd give it a shot.

"Tell me you aren't releasing her."

"Nope." Burnett plucked the key from his hand. "Just removing the cuffs so we can talk calmly."

"Remember she did this!" He pointed to his face.

Burnett nodded. Lily held out her hands. The handcuffs clanked against the table.

Shawn saw the red burn marks on her wrists and had to remind himself again that he'd done his job. Nothing more. Nothing less.

"Now," Burnett said. "I want you to answer some questions, in a calm manner. Got it?"

She settled back in her chair, evidence of the flies-to-honey theory. One Shawn might have tried if she hadn't beat the shit out of him.

Burnett rested his hand on the table, close to hers, and adjusted his posture to resemble hers. Nothing Burnett did was accidental. The man could get a rock to talk.

He leaned forward ever so slightly. "Yes or no. Did you have anything to do with the robbery at the jewelry store?"

The girl, her dark hair curling against her slim shoulders, didn't flinch. "No." After two beats of silence, she continued, "I would never do that to the Crows. They've been like parents to me. And I need to see Mr. Crow." She bit down on her lip, her soft brown eyes sparkling with gumption. "I heard one of the paramedics say he was going to be fine. But this . . . brute here," she pointed to Shawn, "said he might die."

"No," Shawn corrected her in a tone a smidgen too tense. "I said you'd better hope he doesn't die."

"Same thing!" She looked back at Burnett. "Any more questions before I walk out of here? Ask me. Ask me anything. I know you can tell if I'm lying."

Burnett cut his eyes to Shawn. He read the look to mean the girl wasn't lying. And yeah, he'd already figured out she was a good liar—maybe better than good if she could control her heart. Few people could control their heart rate. Chase Tallman being one of them, but for the most part, only sociopaths or truly crazy people mastered it. Like really crazy.

"What about the evidence?" Shawn asked. Making the point to Burnett as well as her.

"What evidence?" She looked up at him as innocent as a Girl Scout selling Thin Mints. And that lead him to the inevitable conclusion.

Lily Chambers was as looney as Saturday morning cartoons.

Perry was greeted by about five more people before he was told Burnett was interviewing someone. Then he was told Lucas and Chase were watching the interview now.

Eager to see Lucas, and even Chase, he hurried down the hall.

The room, just like the interrogation room, was all white and held only a metal table and chairs. The large two-way mirror gave a nice view of the ongoing interrogation. Speakers piped in the voices. Air from the interrogation room flowed through the vents, carrying with it the scents of the suspect, helpful to some supernaturals when identifying a suspect.

The two guys turned around when he opened the door. Lucas stepped forward and gave him a man hug, a thump on his shoulder. Men didn't hug. Well, not each other. Girls? That was another matter. It hit him then that Miranda, who'd been dubbed a serial hugger, hadn't embraced him. He pushed the thought away, reminding himself to take things slow.

"Burnett's been worried about you," Lucas said. "What kind of trouble have you gotten yourself into?"

"Nothing I can't handle," Perry said. "Della and Kylie said you two are working on Miranda's case. You got anything?"

"Not much," Lucas said.

"Just some leads that we're following in a couple of hours," Chase said.

Perry turned toward Chase and offered his hand. He'd never disliked the vampire. And he seemed to make Della happy. Perry hoped they could be friends.

Chase pumped his hand. "Good to see you again." His tone rang honest.

"You, too." Perry's gaze went to the two-way mirror.

He saw Burnett talking to a young woman. He squinted to see what she was. A mixed-breed. "What's going on?" Perry's attention shifted away from the girl to Shawn. The guy looked uncomfortable and a little roughed up.

"A jewelry store robbery," Chase said. "The chick works there. Shawn thinks she's behind it."

"What happened to his face?" Perry asked.

"She kicked him." A touch of humor sounded in Chase's voice.

Perry let out a chuckle. "He got beat up by a girl?"

Lucas grinned. "We said the same thing."

"Stop!" the girl being interrogated said loud enough to pull Perry's eyes back to the window. "I'm going to say this one more time. I had the money because I was making a deposit!" She glared up at Shawn.

Shawn moved closer to the table. "You were leaving town. You told your landlord you were moving out. Give it up."

The girl slapped both hands on the table. "What does moving have to do with making the deposit?"

"Do you think we're that stupid?" Shawn growled.

She tilted up her chin and met his eyes directly. "This guy?" She pointed to Burnett. "No, I don't think he's stupid. You, however . . . The Almighty obviously gave you a double dose of looks because you are dumber than dirt."

Chase, Lucas, and Perry all laughed. "She doesn't like him!" Perry said.

"Actually"—Chase lifted a nose in the air—"she does."

Lucas took a sniff of air. Perry didn't bother, shape-shifters didn't have the gift of scent.

"You're right," Lucas said.

"And that's not just *her* pheromones," Chase said.

Lucas chuckled. "That girl better watch out. Miranda will get jealous and might turn her into a kangaroo with . . ." Lucas's words dropped short. He gazed at Perry. "Sorry. I didn't mean to . . ."

"No problem." But the heaviness in Perry's chest implied it was. How serious had Miranda and Shawn gotten? Had she ever skinny-dipped with him? Perry swallowed the thought down, but it tasted like sour milk.

He studied Shawn again and realized the guy being attracted to someone might be a good thing. Maybe he wasn't so in love with Miranda as Perry feared.

Perry glanced back at the possible jewelry thief. The brunette with long hair and big brown eyes was hot enough that most guys might let out a little pheromone. It didn't mean Shawn would act on it. And it didn't mean he was a jerk—just a normal guy.

Still Perry couldn't help but find a little comfort in it. When he'd been with Miranda he'd barely noticed other girls.

"Enough!" Burnett's voice echoed over the sound system. Perry watched as Burnett stood up. "Look, Miss Chambers, if you could take a break from tossing out insults and explain what was really going on, then maybe you could be on your way."

She drummed her fingers on the table as if finally nervous. "What is it you want me to say?"

"See," Shawn spoke up. "That look, that's what I saw earlier. She's lying."

Yeah, she was, Perry thought. Being able to cue in so close to emotional shifts wasn't as reliable as hearing someone's heartbeat, but it was close.

"He's right," Burnett said. "What are you not telling us?"

Perry and the other two in the room stood silent, watching this play out.

"I'm not lying."

"But you are hiding something. What is it?" Burnett cleared his throat. A small sound that sounded big. Tension filled the room. "If you expect us to believe you weren't stealing the money, explain why the sudden rush out of town?"

Lily shrank back into her chair. "Can't a person decide to move?"

"Sure you can. But not with four thousand dollars of cash that doesn't belong to you," Shawn added.

"How many times do I have to tell you? I was going to deposit that money! I would never steal from the Crows."

She didn't show any outward signs of lying that time, Perry realized.

"Why were you running out of town?" Impatience deepened Burnett's voice.

Her fingers started dancing on the table again. Even through the speakers, Perry heard them tap-tapping on the metal top.

"Come on," Chase said. "Just spill it."

Perry waited.

She finally lifted her eyes. Her fingers stopped dancing. Silence hung for a good thirty seconds.

"Did you see the people who robbed the store?" Burnett asked.

She blinked. Dark, almost black lashes, fluttered against the pale skin beneath her eyes. "Barely. And they . . . they were wearing masks."

Her voice lacked the ring of confidence she'd had earlier.

"But you're part vampire," Burnett said. "Don't have the gift of scent?"

"No," she said, then her lips shut tightly as if regretting it.

"Now she's lying," Chase said. And Perry concluded he was right.

"See, she's lying," Shawn said to Burnett. Then the warlock

moved closer to the table. "You caught my scent before you ever saw me tonight."

Lily folded her arms on the table and dropped her head down.

"Start talking," Lucas said at the same time Burnett did, but Burnett's came out as a severe warning.

Lily raised her head. Her eyes said she was about to spill.

"I had nothing to do with the robbery."

The girl's lips quivered ever so slightly.

"Then why didn't you try to stop them from hurting him?" Shawn put out there.

The girl twisted her head, fury showed in her eyes. "I was in the back, by the time I got up to help they'd stopped."

Burnett leaned back in his chair. "You aren't guilty," he said. "But you know who is. Don't you?"

She didn't say anything and the chair seemed bigger as she shrank down deeper.

"Jax," Shawn said. "It was Jax?"

Jax? Perry edged closer to the mirror. A coincidence. But Jax wasn't a common name.

"Who's Jax?" Burnett asked Shawn.

"I don't know," the warlock answered, "but I just remembered she asked me if Jax had sent me. I think that's why she was afraid." He faced the girl again. "Who is he, Lily? Why are you afraid of him?"

Perry looked back at Lucas and Chase. "Are there shape-shifters involved in this?"

Chase nodded. "Yeah, that's why they were called out there. The three guys who robbed the place ran into the back and somehow escaped through a locked door. Why?"

Perry's mind still tried to deny it, but . . .

Shit. It really could be the same Jax!

"Who is Jax?" Burnett demanded.

"I'll tell you who he is!" Lily spurted out. "He's someone I never want to see again!"

Chapter Ten

"It's just a broken arm, Mom," Miranda repeated into the phone for the fifth time. Her parents' plane had landed in Houston, and they were on their way to the hospital. Her mom sounded like a mess, all nerves.

Sort of how Miranda felt. Between a growing tattoo, a sister who might be in love with a French scoundrel, a possible drug conviction, and now the whole Perry problem, Miranda could use a break. And that wasn't even mentioning her school problems, or rather her dyslexia problems.

She'd studied ten times more than Kylie and Della for the SAT test and even had an assistant read the test to help her. Both her roommates had scored high. Miranda hadn't met the school's score requirements.

Holiday knew someone who knew someone who knew the dean of the school, and they were allowing her time to retest, in spite of it being past the cut-off date. The thought that she might not make it into the school of her choice was a life changer. She had plans with Della and Kylie. They were all going to the same college.

She had to pass!

"Are you listening?" her mom asked.

No. "Yes."

Her mom let out a deep gulping sigh. "So I guess you'll have some answers for us when we get there."

"Answers?" Miranda asked, noting her mom's voice had gone from worried mom to disciplinarian mom.

Had Holiday told her mom she'd failed to get the school's required score?

"Like why a DEA agent left a message and informed us that they are looking at you and Tabitha for drug trafficking."

For a second, Miranda wished it had been about her SAT score after all. "You know me better than that."

"I don't know Tabitha!"

Miranda sighed. "Didn't Burnett or Holiday explain things?"

"All they said on the voicemail was that you and Tabitha were in the hospital due to some explosion. When I called back, the reception at the airport was terrible, but I'm pretty sure I'd've heard if they told me the part about it being a drug house."

Miranda searched for the right thing to say. Truth be told, she didn't know how to explain anything, because it didn't make a lick of sense. Not anything! She glared down where her tattoo had been dancing up and down since she answered the phone.

"Tell me you aren't selling drugs, young lady!"

"Mom!"

"Every time you turn around Tabitha is getting you into trouble."

"What has she done?" Miranda thought she heard footsteps outside her door. No one came in. They'd moved Miranda to a double room an hour ago. Her sister had yet to show up.

How freaking long did an MRI take?

"That girl is a bad influence on you," her mom said.

Her mom couldn't accept that Miranda had become friends with her half sister. But that was just tough.

In the background, Miranda heard her father's graveled voice defending his other daughter.

"Neither of the girls is on drugs!" her father's raised voice came through the line.

Stop it. Stop it. Stop it. Miranda slammed back onto her pillow. Bad enough she had to hear them fight when she went home, she refused to have to listen to this over the phone.

The arguing continued. Miranda closed her eyes. Her mom had known about Tabitha and Mary Esther even before Miranda was born. But since the secret had been yanked out of the closet, her mom had turned into a bitch on mud-slinging wheels and a revved-up engine.

It took everything Miranda had not to remind her mom that *she* was the other woman, not Tabitha's mom!

Not that her mom was the only one misbehaving. Now that things were out, Tabitha's mom regularly called her dad to discuss issues about their daughter.

Last month when Miranda had gone home for the weekend, Mary Esther had called three times. And each time she called, she'd kept Miranda's father on the line a little longer. Her mom flipped. She'd come close to flipping her father a pinky and turning him into something unpleasant. Miranda had nightmares about the last baboon incident.

Not that Miranda felt all that sorry for him. He'd caused this monster of a problem nineteen years ago by having an affair with her mom. Oh sure, according to him the marriage to Mary Esther had been over, but why hadn't he told her mom? Then again, her mom had practically admitted she'd suspected her father was hiding something when they started dating.

Who was wrong?

Everyone.

Everyone except who it was hurting the most. Miranda and Tabitha.

"Are you listening to me, young lady?" Her mom's voice dragged Miranda back to the call.

I'm trying not to. "Can we talk later? My arm's hurting."

"Fine, but you'd better have your facts straight when we arrive." Her mom hung up.

Facts? Miranda had no facts. She was factless!

Frustrated, she dialed Holiday's number.

"Hey sweetie, you okay?" the woman asked in a soft, caring tone that nearly brought tears to Miranda's eyes. Love emanated from Holiday—even through the phone lines.

"Yeah, I just . . . my mom and dad are about an hour away and the DEA agent left a message and told them that Tabitha and I are into drug trafficking."

"Oh! Burnett thought he took care of that. I'll let him know."

"Can you or Burnett be here when they arrive because I don't even know where to start?"

"Sure. I'll touch base with Burnett. I can't come until Jenny shows up to watch Hannah, but I was wanting to come up. I thought I'd bring your books so maybe you could study."

Miranda collapsed back on her pillows. Holiday knew how much Miranda wanted to get into the college. The fae kept assuring Miranda that if she applied herself, really applied herself, she'd make it. Was Miranda going to disappoint Holiday?

Miranda scratched her arm where the tattoo caused her skin to tingle and itch. "Yeah, bring them." She closed her eyes.

Holiday started telling her a cute baby Hannah story. Normally, Miranda loved cute baby Hannah stories. But right now all of Miranda's problems swam around her head and splashed over to her chest like it was high tide. But she couldn't let any of this keep her from making the needed score.

Why was it her life always felt like a test?

Then again, the SAT might not be an issue if she was convicted for drug trafficking. At least she wouldn't have to get a jailhouse tattoo, because she already had a doozy.

"Did you find anything out about the tattoo?" Miranda asked, cringing when she realized she'd interrupted Holiday's story.

"No, I haven't gone through all of my Wiccan books, but so far I've found nothing. I've got a call in to an old professor of mine who is an expert on everything Wiccan. But she hasn't called me back."

"Did you tell my parents?"

"No, I wasn't aware of it when I spoke with them."

"Holy crap! What am I going to tell them?"

"You could go with the truth," Holiday said.

"I don't know the truth."

"Then that's what you tell them. I know it's hard, but maybe telling them is the best thing. Your mom was a high priestess, so maybe she'll have heard of this."

"Believe me, my mom has told me everything she knows about being a high priestess. She's never mentioned a tattoo. I hate my life," Miranda moaned.

"No you don't," Holiday said.

"Yes, I do. Perry came to see me," Miranda tossed out the words like a confession.

"And that's got you upset?" Holiday asked.

"I don't know what to do." She closed her eyes a second, wishing Della and Kylie were here. Not that talking to Holiday wasn't good, but Kylie and Della were her touchstones. A talk with them always made her feel better.

"You'll figure it out," Holiday said, as if it wasn't a big deal. As if it was easy.

Nothing felt easy!

She recalled her almost argument about Anthony with her sister. "Has Burnett said anything about Anthony?"

Her question met silence. Silence was never good.

Perry moved closer to the two-way mirror, staring into the interrogation room, waiting for Burnett to pull more information out of Lily. Could it really be that it was the same Jax?

Chase and Lucas moved in a bit as well.

Lily closed her eyes. "I told you, I don't—"

"Okay, he's a badass, but that still doesn't tell us who he is," Shawn spoke up.

"Was Jax the one who committed the robbery?" Burnett went with a direct question. The man never beat around the bush.

She shook her head. "No, not him. It was one of his friends . . . one of his 'boys' he called him."

"Who is Jax to you? Does he have a last name?" Burnett asked.

She looked down at her hands and ran one finger over her wrist that looked inflamed. "If he thinks I'm the one who gave up his friend, my ass is grass. He'll come after me—"

"I won't let him get to you," Burnett said.

She lifted her eyes. But didn't answer.

"I need you to tell me what you know," Burnett said.

She stared at the wall.

"Now," Burnett growled.

"He's my stepbrother. Jax Bowen."

Perry filed that name away.

"Is he a gang leader?" Burnett asked. "Is that what you mean by his boys?"

Her shoulders slumped. "I guess you'd call it that. He always had people doing things for him. He wouldn't rob a convenience store, or beat someone up. He'd get someone else to do it."

"Where does he live?" Burnett asked next.

She hesitated again as if answering might cost her. "The last I heard he was in Houston."

Houston? Perry's suspicions grew.

"Do you know the name of the gang?" Burnett asked.

She shook her head.

"Is Jax supernatural?" Burnett leaned in closer.

She nodded.

"What kind?" The question hung in the air unanswered.

A cracking bang shattered the silence as Burnett hit the table with his fist. Not really hard, but hard enough to make a scared girl jump.

Hard enough that Perry saw regret in Burnett's eyes.

"Shape-shifter," she said, her voice thin.

"It has to be him," Perry muttered.

"What?" Lucas asked.

"Just thinking out loud." Perry looked back at the two-way mirror.

"You don't understand," Lily spoke. "He . . . he already . . ." She glanced away. Her words pulled back in with what looked like fear.

"Is Jax the one who hurt Mrs. Crow's niece?" Shawn asked.

The girl's gaze shot up at the warlock. "How did you know about that?"

"Mrs. Crow told me." Something about Shawn's tone had changed. As if he no longer looked at Lily as the enemy, but maybe a victim.

Lily's shoulders pulled back with a snap. "You talked to her? You didn't tell her I was part of this, did you? Because I'm not. I would never hurt them." Desperation gave her words power.

Remorse filled Shawn's blue eyes. "You were leaving because you were worried they'd hurt Mr. and Mrs. Crow, weren't you?"

"He'd hurt them for helping me. He already hurt Mrs. Crow's niece. I had to leave."

"Shit," Shawn muttered.

"Comeuppance is hard to swallow," Chase said and let out something a little less than a chuckle.

"Yup," Lucas said. "Especially when it's handed to you by a pretty girl you zapped with enough volts of electricity to kill a small cow."

Perry didn't talk. He didn't want to miss anything Lily said.

She sat up a little straighter. Burnett adjusted his chair, preventing Perry from seeing the girl and reading her body language.

"They didn't deserve to be mixed up in this. The only way to protect them was to leave."

Burnett's posture was no longer intimidating. "This friend of your stepbrother that you recognized. Was he also shape-shifter? And do you know his name?"

"Only part. He's also were. The only name I know him by is Chuckie."

"Did this guy recognize you?" Burnett asked.

"I don't know."

"What does Chuckie look like?" Burnett asked.

"It's been years since I've seen him."

"What did he look like?" Burnett asked.

"Tall, around six feet. Dark hair, green eyes. He's older than Jax. Old. Like your age." She faced Burnett.

Burnett's shoulders tightened ever so slightly at the insult.

"Yikes!" Chase chuckled.

"Yeah," Lucas said. "If one of us told him that, he'd probably break our arm."

Shawn moved in closer to the table, now completely destroying Perry's view. The warlock spoke up. "So you took the money to get away."

"No," she snapped. "You are completely dense. I told you, I was dropping the deposit off like I was supposed to do."

Burnett spoke up next. "Lily, if you were taking it to get away . . ."

"Now you, too? I'm not a thief! Wait. I can prove it!" She stood up. "Get my backpack. You'll find the deposit slip in the bag. All the money is there except for four hundred and sixty dollars. I took that out because that's what my check was supposed to be. It's in my wallet. Get it. You'll see."

Burnett looked toward the two-way mirror. "Someone bring in her backpack from the evidence room."

"I'll do it." Perry took off. He snagged the backpack, then hesitated. What was he going to tell Burnett? The man already wanted to pull Perry out of investigating his parents' crimes—and Perry hadn't even told him what he suspected. That this wasn't just his father and a few old friends getting together to pull off a few robberies for extra cash. It went deeper.

Underground deep—where badass gangs wreaked their havoc.

He'd heard Burnett say that underground gangs were like supernatural terrorists.

His parents were involved with terrorists.

If Burnett knew, he'd yank Perry off the case. Not just because he worried Perry might not be in control of his powers. Burnett looked at him as a brother—a baby brother. The vamp had been protecting Perry since he was five. He wasn't stopping now.

And neither was Perry.

Exhaling to the point of blowing his hair from his brow, he tried to think. He needed to pick and choose what he said, and not lie. Burnett could smell a lie a mile away.

Miranda stared at the two food trays on the bedside table, stinking up the room with a canned soup smell. It was late. The nurse had graciously brought them a late dinner. Miranda didn't think she could eat. Where was Tabitha? She'd texted her twice in the last fifteen minutes. No answer.

Was she still avoiding Miranda? Or had they found something in the MRI?

Voices echoed on the other side of the door. Miranda sat up a little.

"I can walk," she heard her sister's less-than-happy tone.

Remembering her sister had left mad, Miranda jumped up and met her the second she stepped into the room. Her sister's aura was muddy. Unhappy.

Miranda wished she were fae and could offer a dose of calm. A hug would have to do.

Tabitha didn't fight the embrace, but Miranda had barely wrapped her arms around her when her sister spoke up. "You really have a hugging fixation."

"Hugs are happiness," Miranda said. Tabitha ended the hug way too short. "I don't want you to be mad."

"I'm not mad." Tabitha paused. "At you," she said. "Your friends, however, are pissing me off."

Miranda pulled in a short gulp of air. She didn't need to ask why. Considering what Holiday had told her—that Anthony had denied ever being at the witch's house and that Burnett, in spite of the fact that he liked Anthony, was suspicious.

"I'm sorry," Miranda said, and she was. She liked Anthony, too. But something was amiss here, and Miranda didn't think it was Della.

"It's not your fault." Tabitha climbed into one of the two beds in the room, kicking the covers off with gusto. "I got a call from our dad," her sister said. "He and your mom are almost here. And my mom is due to arrive at the same time. Which means, we get front row seats to World War Ten! I'm not ready to deal with them."

"Me, either." Miranda pulled the curtain that stood between the two beds all the way back and then climbed into her bed.

Tabitha sighed. "Everything is crazy."

"I know." Miranda almost told her about Perry, but decided her sister had enough on her plate.

"You might be able to help." Tabitha looked at her with one of those pleading gazes. The same gaze that had led Miranda to the witch's house earlier.

"How?" Miranda asked.

"Do you think if you asked Della to . . . to say she might have been mistaken about Anthony's scent at the house, do you think that she'd do it? I mean, I know she wouldn't do it for me, but . . . You're her best friend."

Miranda's mind went on hyperalert. She wasn't just asking Miranda to do something, she was asking Miranda to ask someone else to do something. "I think Della's pretty sure it wasn't a mistake—"

"But couldn't she just fudge a little. Would it kill her to . . ."

"Lie?" Emotions played a game of bumper cars in Miranda's chest. "That's wrong, Tabitha."

"And Anthony getting sent back to Paris, or going to jail, isn't wrong?" Tabitha asked. "He didn't do anything!"

Miranda chased a few words around her brain, trying to find something to say that wouldn't make her sister mad. Then something suddenly dawned on her. Tabitha's argument had changed. She no longer claimed Anthony wasn't at the house. Why?

"He told you he was there, didn't he? He was at the house?"

"If he was, he wasn't doing anything wrong . . . I told you he's a good guy."

"Then why can't he just tell the truth? If he tells Burnett what happened then—"

"This isn't a perfect world." Tabitha clenched her hands.

"But lying is wrong. If he was there—"

"I didn't say he was there!" Tabitha snagged the pillow from behind her back and crammed it in her lap.

She didn't have to say it. It was implied. For Goddess' sakes! What had Anthony gotten himself into? As much as Miranda liked Anthony, her main concern was for her sister.

Tabitha hugged the pillow so tight the stuffing appeared about to explode. "I don't know what to do."

"About what?" Miranda attempted to choose her words carefully.

"You know what she's going to say, don't you?"

"What who's gonna say?" Miranda felt lost in the conversation.

"My mom. I can hear her. 'You are high priestess and you can't do this.' Do you know how many times I've heard her say that? She tells me I have an image to maintain. My hair has to be perfect. I can't wear a tight skirt. What would the Wicca Council think? Now I'm tied to a drug house."

"You didn't do anything for them to get mad about." Miranda wanted to go to her sister but wasn't sure if she should crowd her right now.

Tabitha tossed the pillow across the room. It landed with a soft thud against the wall. "Well, I can't be high priestess if I'm not here."

"Why would you not . . . be here?"

Tabitha bent her legs, hugged her knees, and then buried her face on top of them. She spoke without looking up. "I'm sorry, I just can't. I shouldn't hold the rank anyway. You're the special one. And I can't . . . can't do it anymore."

Miranda crawled off the bed and went to stand beside her sister's bed. She put her hand on her sister's shoulder. "What's going on, Tabitha?"

Her sister lifted her face but stared at the ceiling. One tear spilled from her lashes and slipped down her cheek. Then she met Miranda's gaze.

Tabitha appeared ready to say something, maybe even confess, but her eyes widened with fear. "Crap."

"What?" Miranda asked, slightly exasperated with her sister's crazy conversation.

"Your tattoo. It's . . . it's crawling up your neck."

Miranda felt the spider-on-you kind of tickle on her neck and slapped at it, as if she could knock it off.

Swinging around, she ran into the bathroom. Stopping in front of the mirror, she grasped onto the sink with both hands.

The first thing she spotted were her eyes. Wide and round with fear. How could she not be afraid, when she didn't have a freaking clue what was happening? Slowly, she forced herself to look at her neck.

"Oh, damn!" The swirly pattern was crawling up to the arch of her neck—almost to her ear.

"What's happening to me?" Miranda squealed.

"I'm sorry. All of this is my fault. You and Anthony. It's on me."

Miranda's gaze, still locked on the mirror, shifted to her sister behind her. She looked truly remorseful.

The sound of the hospital-room door swooshing open echoed. Voices followed, but Miranda's focus stayed on the tattoo moving past her ear.

A gulp of air filled her lungs. One vine-like tendril of the tattoo worked its way over her jaw bone, to her cheek. "No. Not my face. Not. My. Face."

She put her hand over it as if that could stop it.

Voices echoed behind her.

"Daddy," Tabitha said, her voice sounding splintered.

"Where's Miranda?" her mom's voice called out.

"As if my daughter is chopped liver?" Tabitha's mom commented next.

"Are you okay, Tabitha?" she heard her father ask.

"Can you stop hugging her long enough to find out where your other daughter is?" her mother screeched.

Then her mom and Tabitha's mom started talking over each other, their voices growing louder. Louder.

"Don't start this," her father's voice boomed.

Miranda looked at the tattoo, the dusty pink vine-like pattern crawling up her temple to her forehead. "Go away!"

"Miranda," her mom yelled.

Miranda's shoulders slumped. "Oh, mother cracker."

Chapter Eleven

Burnett's gaze was the first thing Perry saw when he opened the door. The vampire offered a barely-there duck of his head. Relief and concern flashed in his eyes. No one looking would even catch it. Perry did. It was a sign of affection.

He turned toward Shawn to acknowledge him. The warlock nodded, but the look in his eyes was anything but welcoming. Not that Perry expected Shawn to be overjoyed with his return. Yet the dislike seemed stronger than before. As if Shawn saw Perry as a threat to his relationship with Miranda.

Good.

The guy could consider himself prewarned.

Perry had every intention of winning Miranda back.

Moving in, Perry nodded at the girl and handed Burnett the backpack. He opened it, set the money and deposit slips aside, and pulled out her wallet. No one said a word as he counted the money.

Only after replacing everything back in her bag, did Burnett look up at Lily. "It's apparent you're telling the truth."

She cut a quick scowl toward Shawn. "I knew this guy was smarter than you. Not that it takes much."

Perry sucked in his cheeks to keep from smiling.

If the twitch in Shawn's injured eye meant anything, Lily's jab hit a nerve. "If you hadn't turned into the Kung Fu Panda, I—"

"Oh, how cute. The twerp watches cartoons!"

Embarrassment filled Shawn's eyes. After inhaling, he started again. "If you'd told me about the money in your wallet, I'd've counted it, and—"

"Can I go now?" Lily interrupted Shawn to ask Burnett. Yup, Perry had to agree with Lucas and Chase. Something besides simple animosity existed between these two.

"Not quite." Burnett glanced between Shawn and Lily as if he picked up on the pheromones, too. "We need help finding out who robbed the store and hurt Mr. Crow."

"But I . . ." Fear clouded her eyes again.

Burnett continued, "Look, if you recognized Chuckie's scent, whom you've told us is part were, then he recognized yours. You can connect your stepbrother to the robbery. And if your stepbrother is the person you've made him out to be, he won't let that happen and he won't stop just because you ran away. He'll go after the Crows. If you care about them, and it sounds like you do, you have to help us."

Her shoulders dropped back against the chair. The sigh she let out told Perry she'd cratered.

Her brown eyes filled with a slow kind of unselfish fear and the finest mist of tears. "I'll do anything. But seriously, I've told you what I know."

Burnett leaned in. "Let's go over exactly what happened. And I'll ask questions as you do."

She nodded and a tear slipped from her dark lashes. "Please don't let him get to them. He'll kill them. He's that warped."

Miranda flinched when Tabitha slammed the bathroom door. No doubt offering her a few more seconds to figure out how to explain this. Problem was a few seconds wasn't enough.

Then even those seconds were cut short when the door slammed back open. "What are you doing?" her mom asked.

Miranda, a palm pressed against her cheek, stared into the mirror, right into her mom's eyes.

"She was trying to use the restroom. Can you let her be?" Tabitha snapped, still trying to help.

But too late.

Miranda froze. Still facing the mirror. Still locked on the reflection. Still zeroed in on her mother's eyes. Still about to pee in her panties.

The next instant she realized the look of horror she'd expected to see on her mom's face wasn't there. Miranda shifted focus to the reflection of her face, prepared to see . . . Her heart skipped a beat. What . . . ? How . . . ?

No tattoo.

She moved her hand from her cheek, where the vine-like image had been less than a second before, but now wasn't. Dropping her gaze down to her arm, expecting to see . . . Nope. Gone.

"You okay?" her mom asked.

Miranda, shell shocked, nodded. Why had the tattoo hidden itself? Had she made it go away?

"Miranda? Talk to me." Her mom's worried high-pitched tone seemed to bounce off the white walls. "Something's wrong with our daughter," her mom yelled at her father.

"I'm fine." Miranda forced the words over the lump of shock in her throat and turned around.

"It's my fault," her sister blurted out, obviously standing right behind her mom. "She'd never have gotten it—"

"It's nobody's fault." Miranda hurried past her mom where her sister would see her.

Their gazes met. Her sister's eyes widened.

"I told you it was her fault," Miranda's mom said to her dad. "She's nothing but trouble!"

"It wasn't her fault," Miranda said, but her words were lost in Mary Esther's booming response.

"Control your two-bit hussy," Mary Esther shouted at her dad.

Her dad, face red, arms waving about in anger, exchanged words with each woman. Which only made them scream louder.

Pinkies appeared. Threats bounced around the room. Her dad kept yelling.

The noise level shook the room.

Miranda met Tabitha's gaze and she mouthed the words "I'm sorry."

Tabitha mouthed back, "No, I'm sorry."

The door slammed open with a loud whack. The nurse stood in the doorway. Sweet silence fell in the tiny room. "This is a hospital. It's almost nine at night. We have sick people trying to rest!"

The guard assigned to her door, cowering behind the nurse, looked terrified.

Her father looked embarrassed.

Her mom looked angry.

Mary Esther's expression held a mix of both.

"Can I leave now?" the nurse asked.

Everyone nodded. Even she and Tabitha. Not that they'd been a part of the chaos. Nope. It was just the adults showing their asses.

As soon as the door closed, Miranda's mom pulled her into her arms. "I've been worried sick."

Tabitha's mom did the same with her. Miranda's father stood there in the middle of the two hug-locked groups as if afraid to move in either direction for fear it would cause another outburst.

Sad thing was, he was probably right.

Perry stood back, listening to Lily Chambers go over her story for what felt like the fifth time. Burnett would occasionally stop her to ask questions. Sometimes it was the same question he'd asked before, but worded differently hoping to jiggle something loose in the girl's memory.

"Okay, one more time," Burnett said. "What all can you remember about the guys."

"I told you already," Lily whined. "I barely saw them when they ran past the office door. They all had gloves and masks. Other than Chuckie, I don't know what color hair, eyes, or skin."

"Close your eyes this time, and try to see them."

She did as Burnett requested and again Perry noticed something, a slight tilt of her head. It was as if she was trying to remember something but couldn't grasp it.

"Chuckie was the tall one. The other two were smaller. One of them was thin and the other not so thin."

"Who seemed to be in charge?" Burnett asked.

"Chuckie. He spouted out the orders."

"Anything else, Lily?" Burnett asked.

"No." She opened her eyes, but Perry saw something in her brown gaze. Not a lie, just uncertainty, as if she still couldn't recall something.

Perry racked his mind for anything Burnett hadn't asked.

"Okay," Burnett said.

Lily went to stand.

"Did they say anything?" Perry moved to the table. "The other guys, did they ever speak?"

The girl's eyes widened. "That's it. I knew there was something. One of the guys answered Chuckie and he had an accent."

"An accent?" Burnett cut Perry a good-job glance. "What kind of accent."

"Not Spanish." She looked at Shawn. "Like the guy who came in with you earlier."

"French?" Shawn asked.

"Yes, that's it."

Burnett raked a hand through his hair as if trying to put a mental puzzle together. "And you got the scent of a vampire?"

"Yeah. But it couldn't have been that guy. Because this guy was definitely part shape-shifter, because they shifted."

Burnett scratched his five o'clock shadow. "You know for certain no one got out through a back door?"

"Yeah," Lily said.

"Anthony's all vampire," Shawn said.

"I know," Burnett said. "But his uncle is married to a shape-shifter." Burnett paused again. "Didn't Anthony go with you to the hospital?"

"Yes," Shawn answered.

"Did he stay there the whole time?" Burnett asked.

"I . . . He walked off with Kylie and Della to get coffee. They came back without him. I didn't see him again for at least an hour."

"And the restaurant where you guys were meeting for lunch is right next to the jewelry store, right?" Burnett asked.

Shawn nodded.

Lily fidgeted as if ready to leave, Perry stood listening, trying to follow. "You think Anthony was involved in what happened at the drug house *and* this thing with Jax?"

Burnett's brow wrinkled as if trying to put a puzzle together that didn't fit. "Well, we know Anthony was at the drug house. We know his cousins are French, and they're vampire and shape-shifter. If he picked the restaurant . . ."

Burnett pulled out his phone and dialed. After a second, he said, "Miranda. Who picked the restaurant that you guys were going to eat at for lunch?" He paused. "I'll explain later. Thanks." He hung up. "Anthony picked it. He supposedly had gone there the day before with his cousin."

"So you think his cousin was casing the store?" Perry tried to piece it together.

Shawn spoke next, "You just told me that you believed Anthony when he said he didn't have anything to do with the drug house."

"I've been wrong before." Burnett frowned and blew out a mouthful of frustrated air. "Nothing makes sense."

"Hey, you Sherlocks. While you solve the crime, can I go?" Lily asked.

Burnett focused back on her, but didn't speak.

"I want to go see Mr. Crow," Lily said, a bit unnerved.

Burnett looked to Shawn. "Take her to the hospital and then . . ." His gaze went back to Lily. "We'll put you up in a safe house for a few days until—"

"What about the Crows?" Lily asked.

"They're not supernatural. But I could have an agent do run-bys to—"

"Then no," she said. "I'd rather stay with them."

Burnett's lips thinned. "I can't guarantee your safety if . . ."

"I'm not leaving them." Her chin lifted at a stubborn angle.

"Fine. Someone should be checking in every hour or so."

"Not him." She pointed to Shawn. "And I can call Uber to get me to the hospital."

Frustration wrinkled Burnett's brow. "The agent I assign won't stay with you. He'll just make passes by the place to assure—"

"Not him!" She jabbed her finger toward Shawn.

Shawn followed Burnett and Perry out of the interrogation room. Shawn's chest tightened. He was ticked at Lily Chambers. But more ticked at himself. He'd screwed up. Though for the life of him, he couldn't pinpoint exactly where he'd gone wrong. Hadn't he fol-lowed protocol? Okay, maybe he should have announced himself as an FRU agent sooner, but . . .

Burnett came to a dead halt in the middle of the hallway and swung around to face Shawn. Air caught between his tonsils. Was Burnett about to dish him up a ration of shit?

Probably. Shawn might even deserve it. Then again, he'd followed his gut. And one of Burnett's rules was to always follow your instincts.

All the evidence had pointed to . . . Who was he kidding? It didn't matter where it pointed. The girl wasn't guilty.

Meeting Burnett's gaze, he prepared himself for a reprimand. But then he saw Perry. Surely Burnett wouldn't tear him a new asshole in anyone else's presence.

Had Perry returned for good? More importantly, was the guy thinking he would pick up where he'd left off with Miranda?

If so, the shifter had better like disappointment.

Shawn wasn't about to be pushed aside. The shot of confidence gave his backbone an extra inch but he lost it just as quickly. The decision wasn't all his, but Miranda's. Yet, Perry had already hurt Miranda. Surely, she wouldn't go back for round two.

Instantly realizing that Burnett stood there, eyes on him, Shawn motioned to Burnett's office. "Can we step into—"

Burnett didn't wait for him to finish. "Get Uber's last name and run a check on him before she leaves with him."

"Uber?" Shawn saw Perry bite back a grin, but he didn't jump in to correct Burnett. No, he left that to Shawn, and no one liked correcting Burnett.

"Uber isn't a person," Shawn said.

Burnett's brow tightened. "She said she was calling him to give her a ride to the hospital."

"It's a cab service."

"Then why didn't she just say she'd call a cab?"

"It's a new kind of cab service," Shawn said.

The crease between his brows deepened. "Just drive her to the hospital and—"

"Me?" Shawn asked.

"And stay with her until she goes home. I'll have to assign someone for the night shift to keep an eye on the Crows' house."

"But . . . you heard her," Shawn offered. "She—"

"Stop." Burnett glanced at Perry. "Wait in my office," he told the shape-shifter.

Okay, *now* Shawn was going to get shit.

Shawn watched Perry walk away before continuing. "I think she'd prefer another agent."

"Probably because you nearly fried her ass," Burnett said, not quite a reprimand, but definitely a jab.

Shawn knew he deserved it, but . . . "I didn't mean—"

Burnett held up his hand. "Not your fault. Sounds as if the situation just got out of hand. But it is your problem. Agents have to deal with all kinds of people and situations, even the difficult ones. Oh, and Miss Chambers doesn't get to pick who works her case. I do that."

Shawn should shut up, but he wasn't one to always do what he should. "Don't you think it would be easier if you assigned Chase or Lucas to her? I could work Miranda's case—"

"My gut says it might be the same case," Burnett said in a firm tone. "Go do your job. And whatever shit she dishes out to you is a lesson on how you'll approach the next difficult suspect."

Shawn turned and found the "lesson" waiting outside the interrogation room door.

Perry moved away from the door where he'd eavesdropped on the conversation. It seemed odd that Burnett had assigned Shawn to Lily Chambers when the girl had been so adamant. Not that Perry didn't like it. Maybe the warlock would fall for Lily and leave Miranda free and clear. Could Burnett actually be doing it to . . . help Perry out?

No, Burnett wouldn't play matchmaker.

Hearing footsteps down the hall, Perry moved all the way over to Burnett's desk. He picked up a picture of Hannah, Burnett and Holiday's daughter.

The baby had grown. Before he'd left, she'd squealed every time he walked into the room. Would she even recognize Perry now? He kind of fancied himself as the girl's uncle. Setting the picture down, he vowed to make up for lost time when he got back for good.

"Good call in there . . . with your question about hearing the other guys speak." Burnett stepped into the room. "I missed that one."

"Thanks." The praise brought a smile to Perry's lips. Living in the foster home, without a father, Perry had found a role model in his older foster brother. Burnett had never let him down.

"Now," the vampire said. "Explain why you took your sweet-ass time getting here."

Perry leaned against the desk. "I went to check on Miranda. Della said she'd tell you."

"She did." Burnett shut his door, the thud echoed in the office. "I wasn't talking about now. I told you two days ago to get your butt back here."

"And I told you I wanted to finish this."

Frustration tightened the angles of Burnett's face. "And did you . . . finish it? That's why you're back?"

"No. I had a vision or something like that of Miranda in trouble. I just needed to see she was okay. I'm heading back in just a bit."

Burnett stared at him for a long second, disappointment flashing in his eyes. "Perry, I don't know what it is you're trying to prove. But—"

"Me, neither." The hurt he'd carried around like an anchor leaked into his voice. He cleared his throat. "That's my biggest problem, not knowing exactly what I'm trying to prove." The truth rolled out without asking permission.

Perry looked back at the picture of Hannah. "Is she talking?"

Burnett took a few steps closer. "Your parents abandoned you, and that hurt you. Now you want to hurt them back. But I'm not sure—"

"No." Perry continued to stare at Hannah's photo without really seeing it. "It's not that simple. I'm not even looking forward to . . ."

"Then don't. Let me put someone on them. When they pull the next stunt, we'll bring them in."

"No." Perry met the man's stern gaze. "I have to do this, Burnett. Even if it pisses you off."

Burnett's lips tightened. "At least tell me what's really going down."

He considered it again, at least telling him about the Jax connection, but damn it, he knew Burnett, he'd pull Perry out for sure then. He didn't understand it, but he needed to be the one to stop his parents. "I told you."

"All you said was that they're up to no good. Doing something illegal for fast cash."

And this was where Perry needed to tread lightly. "As soon as I know who all is behind this crap, I'll hand it over." The case would be closed. His past permanently put behind him.

"What kind of crap are we talking about?" The vampire, now only a few inches taller than Perry, clenched and unclenched his right hand hanging at his side. When Perry didn't respond in the limited microseconds Burnett's patience allowed, he continued. "Don't tell me this is tied to the two Dallas-area bank robberies."

A little air caught in Perry's lungs as he worked to snatch an answer from his brain without lying. "How did—"

"I'm not an idiot. I've been looking at all the local crimes in the Dallas area since you told me." Now both of Burnett's hands fisted. "Tell me you didn't participate."

More treading was needed, but he was treadless. "I had to or—"

"Damn it!" Burnett said. "You could have been shot and killed."

"I can handle—"

"The hell you can! You might be one hell of a shifter and can morph faster than most, but you aren't faster than a bullet. You have to pull out of this now!"

"If I was working a case for the FRU, they could easily have had me working undercover doing this same thing."

"But you're not undercover! If something goes wrong, you aren't legally working for the FRU. That means you'd be held accountable. I'd have to arrest your ass."

"Then assign me the case."

Burnett frowned. "I can't authorize a junior agent to work on his own, on a case we haven't even looked into."

See, he knew he was right, Burnett would have pulled him. "Then I'll do this my way."

Burnett let go of a gulp of air. "Whether you give a shit for yourself, don't do this to me or Holiday! How do you think we'd feel if . . ." He stopped talking and clenched his jaw.

Burnett's concern had Perry's chest aching.

"I've got a meeting tomorrow to meet the lead guy. If I get what I need, I'll turn it over."

Burnett's eyes brightened with anger. "You are not robbing another—"

"I'm just meeting the guy."

"I'll send someone with you," Burnett added.

"No." A pound of frustration resounded in his voice. "They won't accept anyone. The only reason I'm in is because of my father."

"And your father could get your ass killed."

"Have a little faith in me," Perry said, and like it or not, old insecurities rose. Did Burnett's protectiveness stem from affection or a lack of confidence? "I haven't lost control and shifted in public in a while."

"It's not that. I—" His phone rang and he took the call. "What's wrong?" His biting tone spoke of his anger. "Where?" Pause. "Shit. Call the men watching Miranda and Tabitha and give them a warning. Tell them if he shows up to hold him. Don't treat him as a complete hostile, but do not let him leave! I'll come help you search. And I'll have Chase meet us." He hung up.

"What?" Perry asked.

Burnett answered while he dialed another number. "Anthony must have made the agent I put on him. He got away."

"Do you want me to go back to the hospital?" Perry asked.

Burnett appeared to consider it.

"Please," Perry snapped. "Sooner or later you've got to cut the apron strings!"

The man growled. "Fine. Go."

Shawn drove to the hospital. Lily sat in the passenger seat giving him the silent treatment. After the bombardment of insults she'd slammed on Shawn during the interview, he couldn't say he minded. Or he didn't for the first half of the ride. The second half it started to get annoying.

He saw her rubbing her wrist.

He recalled he'd had burns when he'd tried out the cuffs. He also recalled how much it had hurt. Knowing he'd put an innocent through that sat like a fat frog on his conscience.

"Your wrists okay?" The words slipped out.

She looked out the window. They went under a streetlight, and with her hands stilled he saw the welts on her wrists.

That frog put on a few pounds. "I'm sorry. It wasn't my intent to hurt you."

She never even looked at him. Her silence was really starting to annoy him. Or was that his conscience.

He spotted a drugstore ahead and pulled in. He cut off the engine. "Can you come in with me?" he asked in a patient tone.

She didn't look at him. Didn't move. Didn't speak.

"Come on. I want to get something for the burns." He opened the door and waited for her to do the same. She didn't.

Frustrated, he shut his door again. "I said I was sorry, okay. Can we just start over?" Still nothing. "This is silly," he snapped. "Get out, please."

She reached for the door handle and muttered, "I can't believe I thought I liked you. I'm an idiot." She scrambled out of the car.

He shot out to catch up. Hoping to find new ground with her, he attempted humor. "You're not an idiot. I'm actually quite likable."

"Some people like pains in the asses, I guess."

"That's not nice."

"I don't have to be nice. I'm teaching you a lesson, remember?" she snapped, reminding him she'd heard Burnett take him down a notch.

"But can you not enjoy it so much," he snapped back. The muscles in his shoulders knotted. Right then he realized she'd stopped walking.

He turned around. The first thing he noted were her eyes. Vampire bright. Surely she wasn't going to try to run. Or try to kick him again.

"Come on."

"He's here." Her words came out like a whisper.

"Who's—" A car shot past and a spray of bullets started bouncing off the concrete parking lot.

Shawn hit the ground, rolled over and grabbed his gun. He got off one shot before the car squealed away. Jumping to his feet, he stared at the car, trying to get a license number, when it passed under a streetlight.

He got shit. Well, not shit. Two letters. CV and the type and make of the car.

"Let's go," he yelled at Lily, and started sprinting toward his car before they decided to come back.

He only got a few feet when he realized she wasn't following.

He turned back.

She lay stretched out in the parking lot.

"Damn it!" He sprinted over to her. Her eyes were closed. "Lily, look at me!"

She didn't look. Didn't move. Didn't speak.

This silent treatment hurt ten times more than the last.

He saw blood pooling around her body.

He went to pick her up. She flinched. Her eyes, vampire neon green, shot open and were filled with pain.

"I got you." He scooped her up in his arms and pulled her soft weight against him.

"You . . ." she said, her voice weak as a newborn kitten. "You sure do know how to show a girl a good time." She passed out.

Chapter Twelve

Perry was told Miranda had been moved to a new room. As he got off the elevator on the new floor, the hospital scents filled the air, but the thrill of seeing Miranda chased away the bad aroma. A few nurses sat typing at movable work desks. He spotted Agent Jankowski standing in the hall, his phone to his ear, a scowl on his lips.

"What is it?" Perry asked.

He hung up. "They took Tabitha Evans up for an emergency MRI on the sixth floor about ten minutes ago. Agent Farrell went with her. The nurse came by and I asked how long it would take. She didn't think one was ordered. She's checking on it. But Farrell isn't answering his phone. Reception is shit here, but I don't like it."

"Me, neither." Perry's gaze shifted to the door. "You sure Miranda's okay?" He took a step toward the door.

"Yeah, her parents are still here."

He stopped. Mr. and Mrs. Kane weren't Perry fans.

"I'll check on Farrell," Perry said.

He got off the elevator on the sixth floor. Empty silence greeted him. The lights were dim. Was anyone even on the floor?

Moving with caution, he heard a faint noise. A moan. Considering he was in the hospital, it shouldn't alarm him. It did.

This floor didn't seem to be used for patient rooms—just offices and labs.

His first instinct was to prepare himself to shift. Problem was that shifting in a public place should be a last resort. Breathing in deeply, he cut his eyes left then right, listening.

Only the silence rained down.

A sign marked RADIOLOGY DEPARTMENT pointed down the empty hall. He continued that way, following another sign and turning, purposely keeping his footfalls as quiet as possible.

The moan came again. He tracked the sound to a waiting room. An empty gurney was left in the middle of the room, the sheet dangled off the mattress to the floor. Had they brought Tabitha down on that?

On the counter, a note hung: PLEASE SIGN IN.

He edged over and looked at the clipboard. No one was signed in.

A door led the way to the back. Another note hung there. PLEASE WAIT TO BE CALLED BACK.

He couldn't wait.

He pushed his way in, the door creaked, as if needing a squirt of oil. Then it swooshed closed. Darkness rushed at him. He blinked to help his vision adjust.

Pausing, he felt it again. Something was wrong.

A dangerous kind of wrong.

He reached for his phone, but he heard another sound. The distinctive moan of someone hurting.

Someone needing help.

His next step was met with a fist to his face. Slammed against a wall, pain exploded behind his right eye. Unable to stop it, his blood started to fizz. The need to morph, to protect himself, made his skin tingle. He inhaled deeply. The vision of a lion, strong, hungry, and mad, filled his mind. He gritted his teeth to stop the shift from happening.

Stiffening his shoulders, he forced himself to rely on his physical strength. Something he'd worked on. Something he should be able to count on.

He heard movement and spotted a figure coming at him.

He swung his fist, made contact, and heard the person hit the ground. He didn't stay down long, but after he sprung to his feet, he collapsed against the wall.

"Kinda hurts, doesn't it?" Perry said. Ready for round two, he fisted his hands, ignoring that his knuckles now throbbed in rhythm with his eye.

Trying to focus on the shadowy figure, he took another step. Time to end this. But Perry tripped over something . . . or someone. Someone lying dead still on the floor. He pushed up, his palms slid on a thick substance on the floor. The coppery scent of blood filled his nose.

Another moan told Perry his reason for falling was still alive. The door he'd seconds ago entered whooshed open and closed. Perry bounced up to give chase, but the person losing blood caught Perry's ankle and yanked him back. The slick sticky blood on the ground added to his second fall.

"Let go!" Perry demanded, not knowing if the person was friend or foe.

When the demand wasn't met and he could hear the jerk who'd hit him running away, Perry kicked his foot to lose the hold. The shoe connected with something solid. Another moan escaped. If he was friend not foe, Perry would apologize, but not now.

He bolted up and shot out the door.

The need to shift rose again. He fought it.

He shot through the waiting room, his heart thump-thumping against his chest, then stopped. Looking both left and right, he saw no one. The elevator down the hall to his right dinged as if opening. He started toward it, but then a whoosh of another door closing echoed down the hall to the left.

He shot left, guessing that someone escaping would choose a faster route than the elevator.

At the end of the hall was a door, still shifting back and forth. He entered another black room. Only this time the sound of traffic below filled the darkness. His gaze darted around. Seeing no one, he walked to the window. His feet crunched on shards of glass.

Someone had broken the window. Had they jumped out? Perry hadn't heard it break. Perhaps it had been broken earlier.

He recalled he was on the sixth floor. No human could jump.

Unsure, he shifted his gaze up, down, left, right. Only empty shadows hid in the corners. He blinked, his right eye throbbed, and his hand hurt like a mother. Moving to the window, he looked down to the dark parking lot. No one was on the ground. The perp was either a vampire, or a . . . Right then he felt it. A minuscule sting hit his arm. He felt it pop.

An orb. An orb left by a shape-shifter who'd just morphed.

He considered changing and giving flight, but to chase what? He couldn't see anything in the dark sky.

Instead, he ran to see who he'd left bleeding—and kicked—in the other dark room.

As he went, he saw bloody footprints. One pair belonging to him, one not.

He snagged his phone and dialed Burnett. The call was answered before it rang. "We got a problem at the hospital! Sixth floor." He never heard Burnett speak. Hanging up, he pushed open the door, not knowing if the guy he'd left was trouble. Or if he owed someone an apology for kicking the shit out of him.

Perry pushed open the door. The figure lay still on the floor.

Perry ran his hand on the side of the wall, looking for a light switch.

He found it. Light chased away the darkness.

Looking down at the unconscious heap on the floor, Perry's breath caught at the official black FRU suit. Agent Farrell. He knelt, felt for a pulse, and whispered, "I'm sorry."

. . .

Miranda sat on the bed, her knees pulled up to her chest, her heart gripping. Ignoring the arguing adults. She'd started having the oh-shit feeling five minutes ago, but hadn't said anything. Then Burnett had stormed into the room, his demeanor and aura told Miranda that her oh-shit premonition hadn't been a ruse.

Tabitha was missing.

"We've searched the hospital," Burnett said. "She's not here."

"I don't understand," Miranda's father screamed at Burnett. "She went down for an MRI. How could she be missing?"

"We're trying to figure that out, Mr. Kane," Burnett said.

"Are you saying someone took her?" Mary Esther asked. She stared at the vampire as if he'd done something wrong, her panic palpable in her expression.

Burnett's empathy-filled gaze met Miranda's briefly, before focusing on Tabitha's mother. "We're investigating it."

Raw panic pulled at Miranda's mind.

"No you're not investigating, you're here talking to us," her father snapped. "Go find my daughter!"

Burnett didn't flinch. "I understand you're upset."

Miranda looked back down at her phone. It had dinged with a text thirty seconds after Tabitha had been wheeled away. The message hadn't made sense.

He's innocent. Don't have a choice. Sorry.

Was her sister saying . . .

The door swung open. Perry, followed by Shawn, walked into the room. Miranda's gaze shot from one guy to the other and her heart did a complete stop, drop, and roll.

Blood.

Both were covered in it.

Both sported black eyes. What the hell had happened?

Burnett's gaze, bright probably from the blood, went to Perry first. "And?"

"He's going to be fine," Perry said.

Burnett looked at Shawn.

"She's in surgery."

"Who's fine? Who's in surgery?" Miranda asked.

"What does this have to do with my daughter?" Mary Esther asked.

"We've had a couple of incidents," Burnett said.

"What incidents?" Miranda asked.

"Agent Farrell, who went with Tabitha, was found injured."

Her father, her mom, and Mary Esther all started talking at once. At first their angry words were directed at Burnett, then to each other.

"Quiet." Burnett's stern but considerate plea went ignored. Voices bounced off the white walls.

"Stop," Miranda said, but her voice got lost in the sea of sound.

"Silence!" Miranda lost her cool. The mind-numbing chatter stopped like magic. Completely stopped. Like real . . . magic. One second she was grateful, the next she saw that their mouths were still moving. Moving, but not a sound leaked out.

Crap! Had she done that? She shot a look at the only spell-wielding person in the room, Shawn. He understood her unasked question and shook his head.

Then she felt it. The tingle on the tip of her pinky.

She'd done it. Mother crackers, she'd done it. But could she undo it?

She shot up a prayer to everything holy to make it so.

"I'm fixing it," she muttered.

Their mouths stopped moving. Her father's and her mom's wide-eyed, oh-you-are-so-grounded stares shifted to her. Mary Esther's look was more glare than stare.

"But let . . . let him talk." Her backbone weak, she twitched her finger. Relief hit when she heard them gasp. She hadn't rendered them mute for forever. But witch's hell, she really needed to stop doing shit like that when she wasn't sure she could undo it.

Mind to pinky spells were difficult to do, but more difficult to undo.

"You did that?" Pride rang in her mom's voice.

"You twit!" Mary Esther screeched.

Unfortunately that unleashed her mom's fury on Mary Esther. The women commenced name-calling, her dad commenced screaming. Mary Esther lifted her hand, her pinky held in warning.

Burnett looked at Miranda as if asking her to silence them again. She shook her head in an oh-hell-no way.

He shot forward, smack dab in the middle of the arguing threesome. He closed his eyes. When he opened them, they were lime green. "Stop!" Burnett's voice shook the walls.

Silence became golden again.

He did a full circle, looking from her mom to her dad to Mary Esther. "I understand this is hard, but I have questions. The sooner you answer them, the sooner I can start looking for Tabitha. Clear?"

They nodded. Mary Esther let out a heartfelt sigh of a mother in panic mode.

"Sit." Burnett pointed to the three chairs flanking the two beds.

"Who do you think took my daughter?" Her dad's tone wobbled and so did Miranda's heart.

She looked down at her phone again. *He's innocent. Don't have a choice. Sorry.*

Her sister's text accompanied by her earlier statement about how she couldn't be high priestess if she wasn't here had a big heavy lump of hurt forming in Miranda's stomach.

She didn't want to think it. She didn't want to say it. Because then Tabitha would be in more trouble. Especially with Agent Farrell being hurt. Then logic intervened. Tabitha would never hurt anyone.

She was kind.

She was gentle.

She was . . . in love. And that could make you do crazy things. What was Miranda to do?

"You agree, Miranda?" Burnett asked.

She didn't have a clue what she should or shouldn't be agreeing to.

She opened her mouth to say . . . what? Logic said she had to tell them, loyalty to her sister said . . .

More logic intervened. Anthony might not be dealing or doing drugs, but he was doing something he couldn't share with Burnett. She didn't know what it was, but it couldn't be good. And Tabitha was just enough in love with the guy to be blinded by this.

"Uh . . . I don't think . . . I don't think Tabitha was taken."

"What do you mean?" Mary Esther asked.

Miranda's father and mother looked puzzled. Mary Esther looked angry. Burnett and Shawn looked baffled. Perry managed to look at her with empathy. As if he sensed this was eating her up inside.

She didn't have time to let his concern soothe her. "I think Tabitha might have left with Anthony."

Chapter Thirteen

Miranda explained everything.

Or tried to.

"And you didn't try to stop her!" Mary Esther snarled.

"I didn't know she was going to do it," she explained, telling them again how Tabitha's conversation had been convoluted and how the text never said she was leaving.

It didn't help. Everyone blamed her. Or seemed to. Or maybe she just blamed herself.

"I'm sorry," Miranda finally said.

"You'd better be!" Mary Esther snapped.

"It's not Miranda's fault," Perry defended first.

Burnett came in a close second. "It's no one's fault. I'll talk to you later," he told Miranda. Then he glanced from Shawn to Perry and nodded to the door.

Burnett started out, Shawn followed.

Perry turned to leave then stopped. He came over to the bed. Before she knew his intent, he wrapped his arms around her. It wasn't a sexy-boy kind of hug. Just a worried-about-you hug. It didn't help, or maybe it did.

When he released her, she saw Shawn standing at the door, watching them. She bent her legs, hugged her knees, and watched the three of them leave. Frankly, she was too anxious about her sister to worry about Shawn.

Perry followed the two other guys out. He didn't miss the warning in Shawn's eyes. He just didn't give a damn. Miranda had needed a hug. He gave her one.

He planned on doing that a hell of a lot more, too.

"Watch it," Shawn said, seething at Perry the second the door closed.

Perry stopped and faced him.

"No!" Burnett swung around at them.

The vampire was right. Now wasn't the time.

Burnett looked back at Agent Jankowski. "Don't let Miranda out of your sight. Don't let anyone, anything, in. Not a mouse, a fly, or a speck of dirt. I've got someone watching her window on the outside." Then Burnett looked at Perry and Shawn "Come on."

Burnett stormed down the hall. Then turned on a dime and shot into a patient's room.

It was empty, of course. Burnett's sensitive hearing had deciphered that.

The man stood, locked his hands behind his neck, and groaned. "None of this makes a lick of sense." He took a deep breath and faced Shawn. "Tell me again what happened. Every detail."

Shawn explained how he'd stopped at the drugstore to get something for the burns on Lily's wrists and how they'd been overtaken by gunshots. His last words were, "I shouldn't have stopped."

"No," Burnett said. "The mistake wasn't stopping, it was not watching to see if you were followed—obviously they followed you from her place to the offices and then again when you were driving her to the hospital."

Burnett stared at the ceiling and then back at Shawn, who looked filled with self-hate. "I might not have had my own guard up, either. But we all should." He squeezed his hands behind his neck again. "Did you get the license plate?"

"Just the first two letters. I called in what I had. We've got regular police and agents looking now." He frowned. "I should have gotten more."

"It was dark." Perry wasn't sure why he felt compelled to ease the guy's blow.

Burnett continued. "And Lily's in surgery?"

Shawn nodded.

"Who's doing it?" Burnett asked.

"Dr. Lynch. He's warlock. Because she's part human I thought I'd better bring her here."

"Good call." Burnett's frown deepened. "Does he think she's going to make it?"

"Yeah," Shawn said. "The bullet hit her shoulder. She lost a lot of blood. With her being part vampire he expects she'll heal quickly. As long as no infection sets in."

"When she's out, she's going into protective custody!" Burnett rolled his shoulders as if to throw off stress. "I don't give a shit if she likes it or not."

The vamp stuck his hands into his pockets then pulled them out. "Have you heard how Mr. Crow from the jewelry store is doing?"

"Lily wouldn't go into surgery until I found out. Just a concussion. They're keeping him overnight."

Burnett stilled. "The way I see it is this Jax knows that she can connect him to the robbery." He stood there in silence for several seconds. "I'm running out of agents, but text the office and tell them I said to put one on Mr. Crow, and his wife. If they came after Lily, they might go after the Crows." He paused. "Wait. Just ask for one. I'll get Della to cover one of them."

"Got it." Shawn started texting.

Burnett turned to Perry. He didn't say anything, but it was clear it was Perry's turn to spill.

He started from the beginning, how he'd heard moans and had gone into the dark room to check.

"You sure it was a shape-shifter?" Burnett asked when he finished.

"Positive. He left an orb around after he jumped out the window. And . . . Farrell's injuries were more consistent with a bear than . . . anything else."

Burnett ground his teeth as if chewing on the information. "You said he was going to be okay. You sure?"

"Yeah." Perry held up his wrist, exposing two small puncture wounds. "I gave him blood right away. When Chase got there he was able to get him out and took him to see Dr. Whitman. Chase texted me and said he's good. Good enough to be pissed because I broke his nose."

"You broke his nose?" Burnett asked.

"It was dark, I'd fought with the shape-shifter and then tripped over Farrell. The perp ran and Farrell woke up enough and grabbed me, I shook my foot to get loose. His face was in the way. He can't be mad at me. I gave the guy my blood."

Burnett stood there as if everything ran laps around his mind. "Someone's working the scene now?"

"Yeah."

"Did it appear that anyone else besides Farrell was hurt?"

"There was blood in the room with the broken glass, but not much."

Burnett clamped down on his jaw again. "When Chase got there, did he get any traces of who'd been there earlier?"

Perry nodded. "An unidentified shape-shifter and Anthony and Tabitha."

"Damn it!" Burnett seethed. "I still don't get it. Did Tabitha get taken or did she go willingly with Anthony? And how the hell is Anthony involved with shape-shifters?"

"It has to be the drug house," Shawn said. "The gang running it must also have their hand in pulling off robberies."

"But that means it involves witches, shape-shifters, and vampires." Burnett breathed deeply. "Is this a non-specific species gang?"

"It has to be," Shawn said.

Burnett clenched his fist. "Do you know how much havoc a gang of different supernaturals could raise? Each have their strengths and weaknesses, but if they come together . . . Shit!"

"We'll stop them," Perry said, thinking he had the best lead.

Burnett started again. "It would make more sense if they were half-breeds, but Lily said this Jax is all shape-shifter and Anthony is full vampire. What are they doing working together? Was the explosion an accident? Or was it supposed to hurt Miranda or Tabitha?"

"We've gotta stop them," Perry said. The thought that someone might be after Miranda, or her sister for that matter, had his protective instincts standing at attention.

At least tomorrow morning he'd be meeting with Jax. He considered again telling Burnett what he knew. But in big-brother mode, Burnett would never let him go.

"Nothing makes sense," Burnett continued. "If Anthony is in on it, does that mean Tabitha is? But no," he surmised aloud. "Why would she risk being in an explosion?"

"Maybe Anthony has Tabitha fooled?" Perry offered.

"That would mean he has a lot of people fooled," Shawn said. "I could be wrong, but I still don't think Anthony is a killer. He's more of a hugger." The warlock paused. "Maybe he was trying to make some cash selling drugs. No, I don't even believe that, either."

"Me, neither," Burnett spit out. "Shit! Damn! Shit! I can't fit one friggin' piece of this puzzle together."

He started pacing laps around the hospital room. Thankfully the room didn't have a bed in it and allowed him space. Even then, both Perry and Shawn backed up.

After making five tight circles, he stopped and faced Shawn. "Check in with the office and Fallen PD to see if they've got anything on the BOLO. Then go back to the drugstore and see if anyone in the area spotted something. When Lily's out of surgery I'll have someone talk to her again."

"Do you think she's hiding something?" Shawn asked.

"Do you?" Burnett asked.

Shawn seemed to consider it. "I don't think so."

"Thinking doesn't prove anything!" Burnett frowned. "Go. But don't stay out too late. I need you in early tomorrow."

Shawn left.

Burnett grabbed his phone and dialed. "Perry said you got a trace where you found Farrell?" Pause. "Good. Is he still doing okay?" Pause. "Are you sure? Shit! Come back to the hospital and comb the area and see if you can get another scent and follow it. And call Della and tell her to meet me at the hospital."

Burnett hung up and focused on Perry. "Get this. A 911 call was made from a cell phone, saying someone was hurt on the sixth floor. They had a French accent."

"So Anthony isn't all bad," Perry said.

Burnett just groaned. "Is there any chance you could stay here and help out?"

Perry didn't answer.

"Not even for Miranda?" Burnett asked.

Perry emotionally flinched. Burnett would have to put it like that, wouldn't he? "I have to go. Hopefully, I can return quickly." *With something that will help blow this case open.*

Burnett continued to stare. "Why do I get the feeling there's some shit going on that you aren't telling me?"

He couldn't lie, so he went with the truth—a truth that wouldn't open up the can of worms. "I have to do this. Please understand."

"Even when you don't?" Burnett asked. "You told me you didn't understand."

"Yeah, even then." Perry looked down.

Burnett rested his hand on Perry's shoulder. "I know all about wanting answers about your parents. I just don't want those answers to hurt you more than you've already been hurt."

Perry shuffled his feet and thoughts before looking back up. "Aren't you the one who told me that sometimes doing the right thing can hurt, but it's still right?"

"You are never supposed to use my own words against me." He sounded only half serious.

Perry smiled. "Then stop dropping your wisdom bombs."

"Promise me you'll be careful?"

"I promise," Perry said.

"Call me after this meeting tomorrow. And no more robberies! Got it?" Burnett squeezed his shoulder tighter. A vampire's hug.

"Got it," Perry said, hoping he wouldn't have to break that promise. They walked out. "I'm going to go say good-bye to Miranda."

"Do it quick. I'm taking her back to the camp. It's a hell of a lot safer than here."

Perry's gut tightened. "Don't let anything—"

"I won't," Burnett said.

Perry glanced down the hall and saw Miranda's mom giving Agent Jankowski a come-to-Jesus talk about God only knew what. "Will her parents let you take her back?"

"Her dad will listen to reason. Her mom is going to be a problem. She always is."

Burnett looked at Perry. "You and Miranda . . . back?"

"Not completely, but . . . she's agreed to talk with me." Perry couldn't keep from smiling. Then the smile faded a notch. "I'm not sure she's forgiven me. I did her pretty shitty."

"Yeah, you did." Burnett paused. "And Shawn. He knows that she's agreed to . . . talk to you?"

"He'll figure it out," Perry said.

"I don't want trouble."

"Is that why you kept him on the Lily Chambers case?" Perry asked. "There were sparks flying in there. The romantic kind."

"That played no part in my decision." But damn if the vampire's left brow didn't twitch. So the big bad vampire did have a little matchmaker in him.

Not that Perry minded. He wasn't too proud to accept any help he could get.

"Thank you," Perry said.

"I didn't say . . ."

Perry walked off.

"You need to calm down," Miranda's father told her mom when she stepped back in the room after giving the agent hell. Miranda didn't have a clue what it was about, but it didn't matter. Even if her mom was right, her approach wasn't.

At least Mary Esther had left. Miranda felt sorry for her.

Her witch of a mom had turned into a bitch of a mom. And Miranda had a front-row seat. She didn't want to see this. Didn't want to hear this.

"Someone tried to kill my daughter," her mom snapped. "How can I calm down?"

In bed, Miranda's castless arm wrapped around her legs, she tried to think of something to say that would stop this.

"We are all upset, but your attitude isn't helping," her dad said.

So not a good thing to say, Miranda thought and felt the air crackle with tension.

"If you want to go be with her, why don't you just go?" her mom hissed.

Her father looked slapped. "I've made a lot of mistakes, but I told you, Mary Esther and I are co-parents and nothing more. How many times do I have to—"

"You hugged her!" her mom accused.

"She's Tabitha's mom and our daughter is missing!"

"What about our daughter?" her mom spit out.

"Enough. This is child abuse," Miranda said.

They looked at her as if they'd forgotten she was there. Then her father focused on her mom. His shoulders dropped. His aura faded. Miranda couldn't remember him looking so exhausted, exasperated, emotionally perplexed. He always held it together.

"I can't do this anymore." He walked away. The door whooshed shut.

Miranda felt the foundation of her life crack, right along with her heart. Had she just witnessed the end of her mom and dad's relationship?

Her mom gazed back at Miranda. "I can't believe he just left!"

And I can't believe he stayed as long as he did!

A knock sounded. Perry stuck his head in the door. His hug from earlier replayed in her mind. That safe feeling of being in his arms. She needed to feel it again.

"What is it?" her mom snapped.

He flinched. "I wanted to say good-bye to Miranda."

"It's not a good time, Peter," her mom said.

It happened then. Miranda's patience snapped like a broken pencil.

"Perry," Miranda corrected her mom. "His name is Perry."

"It doesn't matter. It's not a good time."

It did matter! *I can't do this anymore.* Her dad's words rang in her head. "Yes it is a good time. Give us some privacy."

"Young lady. You're with Shawn."

"Go." Miranda swallowed really hard to keep the tears back.

With a light exhale of angry air, her mom stalked out. Perry gave her a wide berth at the door before he walked in and shut the door behind him.

Chapter Fourteen

"Sorry," Perry said as if he'd caused the trouble.

"Don't be," Miranda pushed the two words out, her vision growing watery. She lowered her legs to the side of the bed, her breath shook and her insides trembled.

He wrapped his arms around her.

She dropped her face on his shoulder and did what she'd been wanting to do since Burnett told her Tabitha had disappeared. She cried. Big Texas-sized tears.

She cried for her sister and the trouble she was in.

She cried over her parents' relationship.

She cried because nothing made sense and nothing felt right.

Nothing but the guy with his arms around her. That felt . . . it felt like home felt when you'd been away for a long time. It felt safe.

After several long minutes, her face still against his warm chest, she opened her eyes. She spotted the stains on his shirt that looked like blood and the safe feeling leaked out of her like helium out of a balloon.

She pulled back. "What happened?" She flinched when she saw his black eye. "How did you get hurt?"

He blinked, and his eyes widened, or at least one of them did. "I uh . . . Are you . . . ? Your tattoo is . . . uh, all over you."

"Crap." She held out her arms. "Go away." She watched as the vine-like pattern seemed to chase itself as it escaped under her cast.

"That's weird," he said, but he wasn't stepping away as if scared.

"I know." She stared down at her arms. "And I don't have a freaking clue what it means."

She pressed a palm to her cheek. "Was it on my face?"

He nodded.

"Is it off my face now?" Panic tinted her voice.

"Completely." He ran the tips of his fingers down her cheek. It was an easy soft touch that seemed intentionally given to calm her. "It doesn't hurt, does it?"

"No. It's like a ladybug walking across your arm. It's just . . . It's freaking me out."

"But it left when you told it to," he offered, as if to put a positive spin on it.

"Yeah, but it doesn't wait to be invited. It just shows up."

"Is that why your mom's so upset?"

His question led her to more questions. "That's odd," she muttered.

"What?" He ran a palm down her forearm.

"It didn't show up in front of my parents."

"Do you think that means something?"

She bit down on her lip. "I don't know. Maybe."

"Didn't Kylie say Holiday was trying to figure it out?"

"Yeah, but the last time I talked to Holiday, she didn't know anything." She drew in a breath. "She said she was coming up."

"I saw her getting out of the elevator when I walked in here. She's talking to Burnett."

Miranda's heart reminded her she had bigger problems. "Any news on Tabitha?"

"Not much." He said the words gently, as if it might hurt less. "Chase got her and Anthony's trace on the sixth floor."

"What's on the sixth floor?"

"Where . . ." He hesitated as if choosing his words. Choosing them for her, because . . . because he cared. Her chest filled with a sweet ache.

"Where they do MRIs and where I found Agent Farrell."

The whooshing sound in her ears was her heart. She felt the fluttering of her pulse at the base of her neck. "Do they think Tabitha and Anthony had something to do with that?"

Perry sat down on the bed beside her. "They don't know. There was a shape-shifter, and Agent Farrell's wounds looked like he was hurt by a bear."

"So they didn't do it?" Relief came and went. "Is he going to live?"

"Yeah."

Her mind reeled. Her pulse raced. Her heart wanted to revolt. It couldn't take any more. "You don't think Tabitha or Anthony were hurt, do you?"

"It didn't appear that way."

She blinked and gazed at his bruised face. "How did you get hurt?"

"The shape-shifter."

"You fought a bear?" she asked.

"No, I think he'd just changed back when I got there."

"So you caught him?"

"No, he got away."

She heard the ding in his pride, but her mind jumped back and forth. "I don't understand. What does any of this have to do with the explosion at the drug house? Is it connected?"

"Don't know," Perry said. "It's driving Burnett crazy."

Her gaze caught on the blood on Perry's shirt again and she remembered Shawn's shirt and eye. "Did Shawn fight with the shape-shifter, too?"

Until the words were out of her mouth, she didn't think it might be awkward asking her ex-boyfriend—who was beginning to feel less like an ex—what happened to her new boyfriend—who was feeling less like a new boyfriend. Oh, hell she was so mixed up.

"No." He almost smiled. "He got beat up by a girl."

"What?"

"A jewelry store was robbed. He went to question the girl who worked there and supposedly she didn't know he was FRU and she kicked him." He shrugged and the humor vanished. "Then someone shot her."

"What?" Miranda's mind couldn't keep up.

"She's going to be fine."

"Is Shawn okay?"

A frown tightened the corners of Perry's eyes. "You saw him. He's fine."

Her thoughts continued to spin. "But the jewelry store robbery has nothing to do with the explosion?"

"It might," Perry said. "One of the robbers sounded French."

Trying to input more information into her what-the-hell-is-happening file, she remembered Burnett asking about who had picked the lunch spot. "They think Anthony robbed the jewelry store?" Her sister was with a drug-selling, jewelry-thieving vampire?

"Not him. Maybe his cousin." Perry took her hand. "It's going to be okay."

"It doesn't feel like it." She sighed. "My sister's missing, people are getting shot and mauled by bears, my mom's a bitch, my parents are going to get divorced before they ever really get married." *And my ex-boyfriend feels more like my boyfriend.*

"What?" Perry asked.

"They are fighting all the time. He said he couldn't do it anymore and left."

"He probably didn't mean it." Perry leaned closer, his forearm came against hers and sent a jolt of warm emotion.

"I hope not." She dropped her head on his shoulder. It felt good. Sitting there, close, leaning on him. She missed leaning on him. Had she ever leaned on Shawn?

She lifted her head. "Are you still leaving?" Until she asked it, she hadn't realized how badly she wanted him to stay.

"Yeah, but now I don't think I'll be gone that long."

"What's changed?"

"What?" he asked.

"Earlier you said you would come back every week or two."

"Yeah . . ." He paused. "Now, I don't think it's going to take that long."

A vagueness clung to his words as if . . . as if hiding something.

She recalled asking him earlier if his issue with his parents was dangerous. His answer, "Nothing I can't handle," didn't sound convincing.

"Does Burnett know about this?" she asked.

"Most of it."

"Most?"

"It's nothing."

She peered up at him through her lashes. "You suck at lying."

A smile brushed across his lips. "I don't want you to worry, but knowing you do makes me happy."

He dipped his head. His mouth was a breath away from hers. She could practically taste his lips. Feel them.

It would have been so easy to let it happen. But it wasn't right. Not until she talked to Shawn. Oh, hell, not before she decided what she planned to talk to Shawn about.

She'd only agreed to meet with Perry. Not pick up where they'd left off. And that was a big fat lie she'd told herself, too. With all the shit falling on her right now, was it wrong not to want to think about it? But she couldn't start something here, without ending it there. Here being Perry, there being Shawn.

She pulled back, making Perry's lips less tempting.

Disappointment flashed in his eyes. The same feeling resonated in her chest.

"I should go," he said.

This time he leaned in, all the way, but not to her lips. He pressed a soft kiss on her forehead.

It wasn't altogether wrong, but how it made her feel might have been. Because now she really wanted to feel his lips on hers. She wanted to curl into him and ask him to hold her again. She didn't want him to leave.

He pulled back, his smile still in place. "I'll call you."

Voices rang out on the other side of the door. And not just any voice. Her mom's.

"Why should I trust you to protect her? You already lost her sister."

"Shit," Miranda muttered. The door slammed open. Perry stood up, her soft grip on his hand slowly falling loose. For some crazy reason, that loss of connection hurt. The feeling almost as devastating as when she'd lost her grip on Tabitha's hand after the explosion. He looked down at her and whispered the word "Bye."

Her mom stormed in, followed by a bright-eyed, tense Burnett.

Perry moved past her mom, nodded at Burnett, and stepped out. He glanced back one more time, and in some ways, seeing him leave hurt more than when her dad had left.

"She's safest at Shadow Falls!" A vein jumped on Burnett's temple.

"I'm not convinced of that," her mom shot back.

"Her father just told me he felt it was best."

"Well, her father didn't tell me that." Her mom came and stood by Miranda.

"Then call him." Burnett charged through the door. The rest of his words left in his wake. "As soon as I get her paperwork, we're leaving."

Her mom let out an angry squeal. "That man needs to learn some manners."

As do you. The words rested on her tongue begging to be set free.

"And I don't know what you were doing cuddling up with Peter—"

She heard it then. Literally heard it. A pop. Her patience cracking, completely broken. "Perry!" Miranda said, her voice louder than she intended. "And I wasn't—"

"I saw you. He was holding your hand and you are practically engaged to Shawn."

A warning signal flashed in her head. "We're not engaged."

"You should be. He's your own kind."

She saw it then, numbers flashed in her mind like a countdown to a bomb. Ten, nine . . .

Her mom glared back at the door. "That vampire thinks—"

"That vampire has a name," Miranda said, proud her voice sounded even. But it almost sounded too calm. "It's Burnett. And he's right. With the security alarm, Shadow Falls is the safest place." Eight, seven . . .

"No. When your dad knows you're at home, he'll—"

Six, five . . . "Didn't you hear him? He can't do this anymore."

"He will if you call him and ask him to come home."

Four . . . "Instead of using me, why don't you just apologize?"

Her mom brought out her finger. Not her pinky, but the index one, the one she used to discipline.

"You may have gone to school there young lady, but I am still your mother! And what I say goes!"

Three . . . "No," Miranda said. Just no.

"Respect me, young lady," her mother snapped.

One. Kaboom! "If you want my respect, earn it!" Miranda seethed.

Her mom's gasp added another layer of tension to the air.

"You're not behaving rationally," Miranda continued. "We're all worried about Tabitha and all you can do is be bitter and angry. You got freaked because Dad consoled Mary Esther. I was here, and it wasn't like he said he loved her. She was hurting and Tabitha's their child. And Tabitha's my sister. If I wasn't so damn worried about you ripping her head off, I'd've hugged Mary Esther."

"I can't believe you're siding with your dad and that—"

"Don't say it!" Miranda's ability to censor her words grew

weaker. "I'm not siding with dad. He deserves to be punished for cheating on Mary Esther."

"They were separated," her mother defended him, or was she defending herself? "And that woman is a bitch."

Kaboom! Another explosion happened. Without a countdown this time.

"Maybe she's a bitch because you took her husband. What's your excuse?"

Miranda slid off the bed. A voice deep inside her said she should shut up, but there was no stopping her now. "You're right. He deserves to be punished for not telling you. But maybe he's been punished enough. And maybe it's someone else's turn."

Her mom just stared. Her expression was a mix of hurt, shock, anger. But Miranda wasn't finished yet.

"Don't pretend you didn't know! You told me that you had your suspicions about Daddy when you met him. Maybe you should have asked a few more questions before you got naked and pregnant!" Kaboom. Kaboom. "And . . . with morals like that, you don't have a right to say anything about me and Perry! And I said Perry! P. E. R. R. Y!"

One look at her mom cowering against the white wall almost brought Miranda down to her knees. Mother cracker, she'd gone too far! "I . . ." *Was she sorry? Could she lie?*

"You just . . ."

"I think you've said enough!" Her mom's voice shook. "Go with Burnett. I'll . . . call later." A heartfelt sob escaped her mother's lips. She pressed a hand to her mouth. Tears shimmered in her hazel eyes. Her mom never cried.

Grabbing her Gucci purse, she started out, leaving Miranda in a cloud of regret.

"Wait," Miranda pleaded, but her mom didn't wait. *I'm sorry.* The two words rested on Miranda's lips, but she still couldn't push them out. Hadn't she meant every word? But it had hurt her mom. And hurting people just wasn't Miranda's thing.

She almost went after her, but she knew her mom well enough to know that she didn't forgive easily.

Standing alone, heart aching, Miranda pushed the words out. "I'm sorry I hurt you." She could've, should've said that.

She went back to her bed and gave in to another round of tears.

Chapter Fifteen

It was almost eleven when Burnett pulled into the Shadow Falls parking lot. Miranda, a lump of hurt with a cast, sat in the passenger seat. They hadn't talked on the ride, but with Burnett, chit-chat was optional.

To busy herself, she went through her unanswered texts. She'd checked her phone every ding, hoping it would be Tabitha. It hadn't been. She had seven in total. Several from Della, apologizing for not being there because she'd been given an FRU assignment. Three from Kylie, checking in and saying she'd come up to see her, but when she'd heard Miranda's parents shouting, she decided not to interfere.

She had one from Shawn. *Call me when you get a chance.*

She'd have to do that tomorrow. But what the hell was she going to say to him?

About to put her phone away, she saw a text she hadn't heard come in. Not from Tabitha.

Perry.

Miss you already.

Her heart spasmed and sent jolts of wish-you-were-here-now emotion. She flipped back to Shawn's message. Read it. Reread it. No jolts.

Not wanting to go there, she looked down at her school books that Holiday had brought up. The fae had stayed at the hospital for almost an hour, offering calming touches.

Unfortunately, she hadn't come bearing good news. She still hadn't gotten anywhere on finding out what the tattoo could mean. Then again, it hadn't shown back up. Maybe it was gone for good. It would be one less thing to worry about.

Burnett turned the car's engine off. Miranda got out, snatching her backpack from the floorboard. The moon, a day away from being full, added a silver hue that reflected off the concrete parking lot. A light breeze, smelling like rain, stirred the air, offering slight relief from the Texas temperature. But not much.

Then maybe it was the hurt in her heart and not the heat that had Miranda feeling uncomfortable in her own skin. She'd tried to call her mom, even texted, but her mom had yet to reply. Needing some parental connection, she'd called her dad. He'd answered on the first ring—concern and love in his voice.

She'd asked him where he was, and he'd tried to waffle out of telling her, but finally confessed, "In a hotel. I can't handle your mom and worrying about Tabitha."

She hadn't told him about the blowup. It didn't feel right adding something for him to stress about.

Burnett hit the clicker and the car beeped as it locked. He came and snagged her backpack from her shoulder.

"I still have one good arm," she said.

He shook his head and walked on. He stopped at the gate, waiting until the low click sounded. A small light on the gate turned from red to green. Shadow Falls' security system was probably the best out there.

Burnett glanced at her. "You know until we figure this out, you can't be leaving alone."

"You really think someone is after me?" she asked.

"I don't know, but I'll err on the side of caution if you don't mind."

She heard frustration in his tone. They walked through the gate.

"Thanks for everything," Miranda said, following him. "I'm sorry all this happened."

"You didn't cause any of this." His honest empathy rang into the darkness.

His sentiment sent a shot of emotion to her chest. "I really don't think Tabitha did, either."

While they had waited for the release papers, Burnett had her go over everything Tabitha had said. He also told her that they had tried to track her sister's and Anthony's phones, but they had both been turned off.

Miranda knew that made Tabitha look guilty, but Miranda refused to believe it. She knew her sister inside and out.

"I don't think Tabitha is a bad person," he said. "I'm just not clear how she plays into all this."

"She thinks she's in love with Anthony, and maybe she's blinded to some things, but I can't see her involved with robbing a jewelry store. She'd never hurt Agent Farrell, and even Anthony's not like that."

"I know," Burnett said. "Nothing makes sense. It's chewing on my sanity right now."

They neared the path that lead to her cabin and she reached for her backpack.

Burnett pulled it back. "I'll walk you there."

She rolled her eyes.

"Humor me," he said.

She fell in step beside him. The trees lining the path seemed to close in and sway in the still air. A bird called out in the night, and Miranda's thoughts went to Perry, to the almost kiss, to the way his hand had felt slipping out of hers. To one of the saddest goodbyes she'd ever experienced.

"Do you know what's going on with Perry?" she asked, her words seemed to hang in the muggy night. A mosquito buzzed close to her ear.

Burnett's jaw clenched, then unclenched. "What has he told you?"

They continued walking. The sound of their footsteps on the moist graveled path played like music in the humidity. "He said his parents are up to something that's 'not right' and that he's got to figure it out before he can hand it over to you."

"He told me the same thing." But the vampire's tight tone had Miranda's apprehension growing.

"It's hurting him. I can feel it, see it in his eyes. I hear it in his voice."

Burnett inhaled. "I know. I tried talking him out of it."

"Is he in danger?" She put the question out there, just as another bird called out.

Slow air came from Burnett's lungs. "He swears he can handle it."

"And you're a vampire. Was he lying?" An achy sensation filled her chest.

"No. He thinks he can handle it." The doubt slipping and sliding on his words echoed in Miranda's chest.

"What do you think?"

Burnett hesitated. "I've tried to find out information on his parents before, but they aren't registered and have stayed off the FRU radar, which could mean they aren't hardened criminals. Petty stuff seldom gets reported to the FRU. Or they're smart hardened criminals. Because Perry's not telling me much, I can't say if he's bullshitting himself about handling this."

She took a few more steps. The sound of insects singing in the distance filled the air. "Something changed with whatever is going on with him," she said.

"What do you mean?" Burnett slowed his steps.

"Earlier today Perry told me he was leaving and would try to see me every few weeks. Then this afternoon, he said he wouldn't be gone long. Like he'd be back in less than a week."

Burnett seemed to consider her words. "Maybe he's just . . . worried about you."

"Maybe," she said, but didn't buy it. "Couldn't you just send someone to watch over him?"

Burnett looked off into the trees.

"He'd be really pissed if I did."

"That's never stopped you with anyone else," she said.

Burnett didn't answer. Miranda found the tiniest bit of hope that it meant Burnett had sent someone.

Her first instinct was to push him to confirm it, but pushing Burnett never worked out. Not for Miranda. Della seemed good at it though.

They got to the turn in the path where she could spot her cabin through a line of trees. The golden rays of light flowing from the windows seemed to call her name. Were Kylie and Della still awake? Or had they just left the light on for her?

For all she knew both Della and Kylie might be hanging with their boyfriends. They did that quite often.

She increased her pace, needing, wanting a little girlfriend time, but then Burnett cleared his throat. She looked back.

He handed her the backpack. "You care, don't you?"

"Care?" she asked.

"Perry?"

"Of course." She sensed he was talking about . . . romance. But on second thought, no, not Burnett.

"It's none of my business, but . . ." He reached back and squeezed the back of his neck. "I know Perry hurt you when he left. My wife reminds me that he did it to you twice. She's also said that if it had been anyone else, I'd kick you for giving him another chance, but . . ." He inhaled again. "He's not just anyone else."

Miranda realized that Burnett might not care about romance, but he did care about Perry.

She recalled thinking Burnett wasn't all that happy about her seeing Shawn, but when he never spoke up she just assumed she'd imagined it.

Burnett scuffed his feet on the gravel, reminding her of Perry's nervous habit. Of course, Burnett had probably influenced Perry during their time in the foster home. She'd always known that Perry carried a soft spot for Burnett. She knew Burnett felt the same, but she'd never seen it more than right now.

The vampire looked down and then up. "Sometimes, when you don't have a great home life, it makes you feel . . . like damaged goods. Both times Perry screwed up, it was never about you. It was about him."

"I kind of know that," she said. *What I don't know is . . . what's stopping him from doing it again?*

Perry walked into the bar. The lighting was low, the music live. The walls shook from the beat and so did his eardrums. Thankfully the bar catered mostly to supernaturals so the bouncer checked out his forehead and didn't bother to check his ID.

Standing a few feet inside, he waited for his eyes to adjust. Because he'd lived in the shadows of the human world most of his life, the bar scene still felt awkward, and a little dangerous.

The smell of alcohol—malty beer, vinegar-scented wine, and fruity drinks—scented the air. He'd tried beer a few times, and learned that alcohol inhibited his ability to control his shifts. Considering he struggled with this stone sober, it was a good thing he hadn't acquired a taste for the stuff.

If he needed a mood enhancer, he'd take to flying. The only thing that topped flying was being with Miranda. Just the time he'd spent with her today had sent his mood soaring.

To his right was the dance floor. Couples moved, bumped and grinded to the music. Immediately, he recalled Miranda teaching him to dance. The memory of her laughing as he'd copied her moves brought on a smile. "Don't try to imitate me, listen to the beat and move."

"But I'm good at imitating. Not so good at being original."

"Yeah, but the way you do it, it looks . . . too sexy." She'd giggled.

"Then I must be doing it right," he'd teased, "because you look hot doing it, too."

Yup, emulating was both a gift and a curse of being a shape-shifter. Because when you could be anything, sometimes you had trouble just being yourself. Or maybe it wasn't something all shape-shifters dealt with, maybe it had something to do with how he was raised, or not raised.

He took a few more steps inside; the band ended their music, said their good-byes, and promoted the sale of their CDs out front. Perry continued to check out the patrons, most were supernatural. He spotted his mom walking out of the bathroom. Her blond hair hung in soft waves around her shoulders. The tight red dress, better suited for a woman ten years younger, was low on the top and short on the bottom.

Lifting his left shoulder, he rubbed it against the side of his neck, as if to wipe off the feeling being around his mom brought on. There wasn't one memory that caused it. It was all of them. Being a shape-shifter, his mind retained memories from as young as a year old.

She hadn't hit him. He hadn't gone hungry.

She just . . . hadn't wanted him—funny how someone that young could pick up on that. True, considering his ability to shift at that early age, he'd been a pretty big undertaking. But—

"Perry!" someone called out. His father stood next to a table occupied by two other men. As Perry drew closer, he noticed the empty glasses littering their table.

Perry hadn't planned on coming here. Yet, now knowing that Jax could be mixed up with what happened to Miranda and her sister made him even that more determined. It wasn't just about him or justice anymore, it was about protecting the girl he loved.

For that, he'd deal with his mom.

"There's my son," his mom said, arriving at the table the same time he did. She hugged him. Her embrace felt plastic. Who the hell was she trying to impress? She pulled back. "Your dad said you've got a girlfriend!"

"Dad talks too much," Perry said.

His mom touched her dad's elbow. "Paul, go get your son a whiskey. He's a man now."

"I don't want—"

"Sure you do." She motioned for his father to go. He didn't argue. He never did. Not even when she'd told him to take their son to the mall and leave him there.

His mom looked back at the two guys sharing the table. "Meet our new friends. Charles and Mark, this is my oh-so-powerful son." The two men nodded, thoroughly unimpressed.

Perry checked their patterns. Charles's pattern showed mixed blood, part were and shape-shifter. The other was all shape-shifter. Their glassy-eyed expressions said most of the empty glasses belonged to them.

"What happened to your eye?" his mom asked. She grinned as if a black eye made him a more deserving son.

"I ran into a fist," he said.

"Whose fist?" she asked. "Your girlfriend's?"

"No."

"He can't be your son," Charles said, his green gaze raking over his mom. "You're not old enough to have a boy that old."

"Well, aren't you a prince. Prince Charles." She leaned down and kissed the guy. Just on the cheek, but Prince Charles gaped at his mom's cleavage. Obviously liking what he saw, he fit his palm on Perry's mom's ass.

An unnamed emotion swelled inside him. Then he recognized it: shame.

Not for his mom.

For his dad.

Perry considered grabbing the guy's hand and breaking a few fingers. But if she didn't want the guy fondling her ass, shouldn't she stop it?

Yet, unable to stop himself, he cleared his throat in warning. Charles lifted his eyes and his hand from Perry's mom's butt.

Standing, she inched in as if to sit down in the chair beside the horny prince. Perry flopped his ass down first. She cut him a that-was-rude frown.

He smiled. "I'm sure you want to sit next to your husband."

Her lips tightened.

The shape-shifter, Mark, took a sip of his beer. "If your girl's here, why didn't you bring her with you?" The question, suspicious in tone, had Perry mentally backtracking. He'd thought these two men were just bar patrons. Had he thought wrong?

Could they be mixed up with Jax? The suspect behind the robberies and possibly even the drug house?

He took another look at Prince Charles, recalling the interrogation with Lily Chambers. Yup, the dark-haired, green-eyed mixed-blood with loose hands looked more like a Chuckie than a prince.

Right then Perry realized a potential disaster. What if the shape-shifter he'd fought with at the hospital had shown up, too? He glanced at Mark's and Chuckie's faces, searching for bruises.

Perry had hit that guy as hard if not harder than he'd been hit. They were bruise-free. And their stature didn't match, either.

Then it hit Perry. Caleb was about the right size.

Holy shit! Had he fought Caleb?

"His dad thinks he's keeping her away because he's ashamed of us," his mom added.

"Go figure," Mark said.

"Now why would I be ashamed of you?" Sarcasm dripped from Perry's words. If anything, his mom's behavior just gave him a good defense for not bringing a girlfriend.

"Well if it isn't the prodigal son?" A voice rang out behind him. Palms came down on each of his shoulders and squeezed. Hard.

He didn't have to look back to know who stood behind him.

Caleb's voice struck all kinds of nerves. But more important than his voice was his face. Was the lowlife sporting a bruise?

Perry's instinct to shift pulsed through his blood. He fought it.

Reaching back with one hand, he caught one of Caleb's wrists. "Enough," Perry ground out.

His skin around his eyes tightened, his natural instinct, begging to morph. If it was Caleb who Perry fought, Caleb would see the bruise and know. Or maybe Caleb already knew.

Deciding better sooner than later, he looked back, checking Caleb's face for bruises.

None.

"Can't handle a little pressure, kid?" Caleb pulled away, but his bullying tone scraped across Perry's nerves. He hated bullies.

Caleb looked at his mom. "Someone hit your boy, mama."

Perry inhaled through his nose, bringing air in only through his right nostril, and out his left, a trick he'd learned in Paris to help garner control. Why had his father forgotten to tell him his friends would be joining them tonight? He wasn't prepared for this. Wasn't completely sure what his dad had told Caleb about his leaving this morning.

Or had his dad told him what these goons thought. That he'd come to Houston to see a girl?

To use one of Miranda's sayings, *mother cracker*. He'd better be ready to up his game.

His father moved in. Perry saw his father's tight stare go to Caleb, who was still standing behind him.

"Looks like daddy wants to protect you," Caleb said.

His father dropped the two glasses of whiskey down, his eyes glowing yellow. "I don't have to protect him."

Caleb laughed, not believing it. "I've seen your boy shift, ol' man. He's not that fast."

The speed of a shape-shifter's shift generally marked their power. During shifts, both in and out, was the most vulnerable time for a shifter. Even a shifter's human strength was compromised.

Perry would admit that Caleb's powers were impressive. What Caleb didn't know was Perry had never shown his cards. Not that it made Perry invincible, but a hell of a lot less invincible than Caleb assumed.

"You don't know what he can do," his father said. "If he wanted to."

Perry didn't know what he fought off the hardest, his need to prove his dad right, or the need to deny his father was actually standing up for him.

"Sorry," Caleb said. "I haven't seen it ol' man."

His father reached for one of the drinks. "I get a feeling that one of these days he's gonna show you how wrong you are." He pushed the other drink to Perry. "Right, son?"

"One of these days," Perry repeated his dad's words. Problem was he planned to show everyone at the table, even the one defending him, how wrong they were.

Caleb pulled a chair over between his mom and dad. "Aren't you looking hot tonight, Sophie."

"Thank you." She ran her tongue over her bottom lip.

His father's eyes grew brighter. Was that why his father didn't like Caleb? Did his dad not care that the man was an all-around bastard?

"How did you get the shiner, boy?" Caleb asked, now focusing on Perry's face instead of his mom's lips.

"He ran into someone's fist." Mark chuckled.

"How did the other guy look?" Caleb asked.

"About the same," Perry said.

Caleb made a belittling laugh and looked at Perry's dad. "And you say he's all-powerful. If someone did that to my face, they wouldn't be breathing." Smirking, he pushed the glass Perry's dad had brought over to Perry. "Drink up, kid. Or are you a wuss? You need me to order you a Shirley Temple?"

A low growl hung in his throat. Even his fingernails ached to turn. After the breathing trick didn't work, he conjured up an image of Miranda. That was always his last resort.

"Drink!" Caleb bullied.

Somehow knowing the man wouldn't let this go, he picked up the drink and downed it. The amber liquid burned going down his throat. Burned when it hit his stomach. The need to cough clawed at his throat. He swallowed that need.

He never flinched. Never blinked.

Dropping the glass back on the table with a clank, he leaned back in his chair, hoping he didn't have anything else to prove.

Chapter Sixteen

Miranda watched Burnett leave then she turned to go inside. When she saw both Della and Kylie sitting at the kitchen table with three diet sodas, waiting for their round table meetup, Miranda's chest swelled with warm gooey emotion.

"You waited up," she said, biting down on her lip.

"Duh, you thought we wouldn't? We're just wondering what took you so long," Della said. "Can I open my drink now?"

"Yes." Miranda moved in. She dropped in her chair and opened her own soda. The two cats, Socks and Chester, came running up, both doing figure eights around her ankles.

"What did your parents say?" Kylie asked.

"What didn't they say?" she said, unsure she could talk about this without crying again.

Kylie continued. "I went there, but I heard your parents arguing. I texted Holiday. She said you two had spoken and you were . . . hanging in there."

"By a thin thread." Miranda listened to her soda fizzing. She looked up at her two friends. "Do you two know anything about what's happening that I don't?"

"What did Burnett tell you?" Della asked.

Miranda repeated everything she knew. About them suspecting

that Anthony and her sister had participated in the attack. About how they now suspected Anthony was somehow involved with a robbery.

Both Della and Kylie said that's all they had. But then Della glanced briefly at Kylie, almost as if they knew something they couldn't share.

"What?" Miranda asked.

"Nothing," Kylie insisted.

Della spoke up this time. "Burnett is putting a shadow on the girl who worked at the jewelry store and the wife of the owner. I did an earlier shift and I've got to be there at four in the morning."

Miranda thought they were still holding back, but maybe she was just being paranoid. She took a big sip of Diet Coke, finding solace in the bubbly tingle sliding down her throat. "When did everything in my life go bat-shit crazy?"

"Probably when the drug house exploded." Della snickered.

When the fizzy soda hit Miranda's empty stomach she remembered she hadn't eaten. "I'm starved."

"I've got some blood I'll share," Della said.

Miranda frowned.

"Just joking. Why don't you zap us some pizza?" Della asked.

Miranda collapsed back in her chair. "Too tired to zap." And after uncontrollably zapping her parents and Mary Esther mute, Miranda worried something might go wonky if she wasn't in tip-top shape.

The vamp jumped up at super speed and opened the fridge. She looked over her shoulder. "Cheese and semi-stale cold Oreos. What's your poison?"

"Both." Miranda stood.

"No," Kylie said. "You just relax."

In a few minutes, they set a plate of cold cookies and cubes of cheddar cheese down in front of her.

Miranda went for the cheese first.

They watched her eat. "So?" Della finally asked.

Miranda reached for a cold cookie. "Who put the cookies in the fridge?"

"Forget the cookies," Della said. "I need details on the rest of the bat shit."

"You know everything about the case."

"But not about Perry," Kylie said.

"And about the tattoo," Della said.

Miranda looked at her arm where the cast ended to see if it had appeared again. It hadn't. "I hope it's gone."

"Perry came to see you, right?" Kylie asked.

"Yeah." Propping her cast on the table, she grabbed ahold of a cookie and twisted it with her good hand until the two chocolate wafers came apart, then she looked up. "What am I going to do?"

"What do you want to do?" Kylie asked.

"If I knew I wouldn't be asking you," Miranda said.

"Okay, let's make this easy," Della said. "Look at your cookie. It has two sides. One of them is Shawn, one is Perry. You're the white stuff in the middle. Which one are you stuck to?"

"That's a stupid analogy." Miranda suddenly didn't want to eat either one of the cookies.

"She's right," Kylie said. "That's stupid."

Miranda put the cookie pieces back on the plate.

"Not really," Della said. "I've been the white stuff. There was Steve and then there was Chase. It wasn't easy, and it took me a while to see it, I finally realized it came down to where I wanted to be."

Miranda looked at the broken cookie.

"You can't compare them against the other." Della grabbed a cookie herself. "Each side of the cookie is good. But when under pressure"—she twisted the cookie—"you always stick to one side." She dropped the two pieces of cookie, one with icing and one without.

"What if half of you sticks to one, and half of you to the other," Miranda asked.

"Good question," Kylie said.

"That doesn't happen," Della said.

"Yes it does." Miranda grabbed another cookie, twisted without care, hoping to prove her point. Again, all the white stuff ended up on one side.

"I'm with Miranda." Kylie snatched one up and twisted it. Hers all ended up on one side, too.

Della pumped her hands up in the air. "My cookie analogy stands proven."

They all laughed.

Della swiped a half-of-cookie with icing from the plate.

"I used to love these." The vampire took a bite.

"You're chewing on my ass." Miranda chuckled.

"Yuck," Della said. "But the question is, who else's ass am I tasting?" Her tongue dipped out to catch a crumb on the corner of her mouth. "Is that shifter, or warlock? I think it tastes like a shape-shifter."

Miranda laughed, but was Della right? Was she still stuck on Perry?

Suddenly the specific, nauseating, scratchy sound of a cat hacking up a hairball filled the air.

"Oh, that's disgusting," Della said.

"What? The sound? Or the taste of shape-shifter?" Kylie giggled.

"Both." Della bolted up and spit the cookie in the sink. Swinging around, her gaze went to Kylie. "I'm not cleaning that hairball up. This morning, I picked up two the size of a small cat."

"You know the rule." Laughter shook Kylie's words. "You see it, you clean it."

Della slapped a palm over her eyes. "I swear I'm blind."

They laughed. Laughed hard. Laughed like good friends do over silly things.

Somewhere with that release something else in Miranda broke free. Her lungs shook. Her heart broke. Her vision became a watery mess. Not just silent tears, but loud ones.

"What's wrong?" Kylie asked.

Miranda couldn't talk. She stood, brushed the tears from her cheeks, and tried to pull up her big-girl panties. She couldn't find them.

Kylie and Della shot around the table.

"It can't be that bad," the chameleon said.

"It is," Miranda said. "One minute I'm sure I'm the white icing stuck to Perry, but then I think about Shawn and I remember how sweet he is. How he's never done anything to hurt me, and Perry has." Her voice trembled. "I'm not even sure Perry isn't just going to hurt me again. But forget boy problems. My sister has run away. I still might go to jail for drugs, and my dad and mom are probably going to divorce. Or they would if they were married. I don't know if I'm going to get to go to college with you, and . . . and I called my mom a bitch and a slut."

"Ouch!" Kylie said.

Della set a hand on her hip, striking her sassy pose. "It's about time."

Miranda's next breath trembled all the way down. "Honestly, I didn't . . . really call her a slut, I insinuated it."

"There, see," Kylie said. "It's not as bad as you thought it was."

Della stepped back. "On second thought."

The vamp's oh-shit expression accompanied with Kylie's empathic stare told Miranda what was up.

"My tattoo's back, right?"

They nodded, making "sorry" eyes.

"It's a . . . little bigger than before," Kylie said.

"A little," Della snapped. "Don't sugarcoat it. She needs to know." Della glanced back at Miranda. "You're covered in swirly crap."

Kylie glared at Della. "But we love you anyway. Group hug." The chameleon put one arm around Miranda's shoulder and held out her other to Della.

Della studied Miranda. "It's not contagious, is it?"

"Don't be silly," Kylie said to the vampire.

They wrapped their arms around Miranda, tattoos and all.

Miranda drew comfort from her two best friends, then she felt bad. "It could be?"

"What?" Kylie asked.

"It could be contagious."

"Mo fo!" Della shot back so fast she fell on her butt. No sooner had she landed did she let go of a gagging sound. Closing her eyes, she lifted her hand out. On her left palm clung something dark, hairy, and gooey.

"Tell me it's not a hair ball! And if it is, I didn't see it." Della gagged again.

Kylie and Miranda fell on the sofa from laughing so hard.

"Yuck. Yuck. Yuck!" Della jumped up and ran to the garbage.

His dad bought Perry another whiskey. Perry knew better than to drink it. Already he felt a crack in his resolve.

He didn't want to be here. Didn't want to see his mom flirt, the men ogle her like a piece of meat. Didn't want to see his dad's eyes grow brighter, his pride smaller.

Reminding himself why he was here, Perry tried to bring up the new job. Caleb slapped a lid on that conversation.

Music, not as loud as the band, piped into the room through speakers. Men moved about the room, on the hunt, preying on women, hoping not to go home alone.

"Why can't I dance with him?" his mom ground out to his dad.

"I'll dance with you." His father stared at Caleb who'd issued the invitation.

Caleb, appearing content with the trouble he'd started, laughed and moved to the table to their right, where he plopped his butt down next to a brunette.

She cut her eyes to Perry, and it wasn't the first time, either. She looked familiar, too. He checked her forehead. Vampire.

"It's not fun to dance with the same guy," his mom bitched.

His dad dragged his wife to the dance floor. The wine and whiskey added a different gait to their steps.

His mom's arguing played like background music.

It wasn't a matter of if the shit was gonna hit the fan, it was when. And how Perry intended to handle it.

A waitress, a pretty sandy-haired vampire with a nametag that read BELL, swung by to drop off beers. She purposely didn't get close to Chuckie or Mark. She'd shown her canines twice when they'd gotten touchy-feely.

Chuckie reached for her again. Perry started to intervene, but Bell swung around so fast she became a blur. "Touch me again and I'm going to rip your carotid artery open and offer free shots to all my vampire friends here tonight."

Chuckie and Mark laughed. Bell didn't. Perry couldn't say he believed her, but he wouldn't chance it. And supposedly neither would Chuckie or Mark.

Once again, Perry realized the favor his mom had done by abandoning him. If raised by them, he might have grown up to be an asswipe.

"Did you need anything?" The waitress moved next to Perry.

"I need something," Mark said.

"I'm fine." Perry ignored Mark. "Thanks."

"You new in town?" Bell picked up a few dirty glasses.

The word "yes" almost slipped out. Then he recalled his dad believed he'd lived here. Which meant Mark and Chuckie probably thought it, too.

His brain sought a diversion. And found one. The button with a picture of her and a baby on it pinned to her apron. "That your baby?" She looked too young, but . . .

Pride filled her eyes. "Yeah." Then she added, "His daddy left us."

Not knowing how to respond, Perry offered. "He's cute."

Bell laughed. "And you just lied. But don't worry, I know he's ugly. The doctor promises me he'll grow out of it." She hesitated. "You should come in more often."

"Yeah." He was flattered, but he had his girl.

"She wants to dirty up the sheets with you." Mark's comment echoed and earned some laughter from neighboring tables.

The girl, rightfully offended, let out her canines again. Perry backed her up with a low growl.

"What the hell," Chuckie said. "You're going after this kid when you got two real men here."

"I only see one man at this table, grandpa." She sashayed off.

Chuckie stared after her. "Bitch. She ain't even got big tits."

Perry waited for the tension to defuse, for his own anger to weaken, before bringing up Jax again.

"So you two worked for Jax long?" Perry asked.

"Jax and I go way back," Chuckie said.

Mark, eyeing the red-haired woman at a table to their right, didn't answer.

Chuckie leaned in. "I'm shocked the boss let you in just by the word of your old man."

"He must like my dad." Perry brought the glass to his lips and pretended to take a sip. Even the smell burned his sinuses.

"Is it true what your dad says? That you're stronger than you seem."

"I surprise a few people." Perry purposely hadn't shown his cards. Hell, his father hadn't seen all he could do. Burnett, who was a reborn vampire with super strength, had warned Perry against it early on. *If people think you're the best, or better than most, it makes you a target. Show them just enough to get their respect, but not enough to make them want to bring you down.*

"Do you know what this new job is here in Houston?" Perry folded his drink napkin so he wouldn't appear too interested.

"It's not in Houston," Chuckie said.

"So are we heading back to Dallas?" Perry looked up.

Before Chuckie answered, his phone rang. He pulled it out, turned the phone off, and staggered to his feet.

"Hey." He nudged Mark, who now sat with the red-haired woman.

"Jax called. I'll be back."

Jax?

Chuckie walked toward the exit. Perry checked the room. Mark continued chatting up the woman. Caleb was lost in conversation with the brunette. His parents danced without arguing.

Perry rose up. Following Chuckie could be risky, but it could also be worth it.

Perry hadn't taken one step when Caleb fixed Perry with a glare.

"Gotta drain the lizard."

He found the bathroom empty.

He yanked a bunch of paper towels from the dispenser and shoved them at the base of the door. Wasting no time, he darted into the stall and shifted into a small mouse.

Skirting out of the bathroom, he had to dodge drunken feet to make his way to the door. A man and a woman, arms wrapped around each other, walked out and he escaped with them. Staying in the shadows, Perry followed the building around to find Chuckie. The man wasn't on the right side, so Perry headed left.

Gotcha! Chuckie leaned against the old redbrick structure, phone to his ear. Perry scurried in the shadow of the building. He needed to be in hearing distance, but not too close to be stomped on by the bozo's fat feet.

Not that it would kill him, but it would hurt like hell.

"I was in a bar," Chuckie argued. "I wouldn't have been able to hear you." He paused. "What? I shot that bitch at a drugstore. I saw her go down."

So Chuckie not only robbed the store, he shot Lily Chambers? Damn, Perry knew he didn't like this guy. He wished he'd broken the guy's hand when he'd touched his mom's ass.

"I can't help it if she didn't die," Chuckie exhaled. He raked a hand over his face as if trying to wipe off the drunken haze.

Perry's tiny brain flashed a large image of pretty Lily Chambers sitting in the interrogation room. Then he flashed an image of the girl's blood on Shawn's shirt. Perry's rodent skin started to burn with the need to morph into something vicious to teach this jerk a lesson.

He couldn't. Not in public. Not until he had enough to bring this gang down.

"Now?" Chuckie continued. "I just got here a few hours ago. And I had a few beers. It's illegal. I could kill someone on the road."

Seriously? The absurdity of his statement made Perry's brain roll.

"Can't you get someone else?" Chuckie hesitated. "She's not going to connect you to the robbery, besides it was me she recognized, not you." He kicked at the gravel. "I know the rule, no loose ends. Fine. I'll go! I'll take care of her."

Chuckie stormed into the bar.

Perry stayed hidden in the shadows forming a plan. He had to warn Burnett. Which meant Burnett would know what Perry was up against and try to pull him out. But not telling Burnett would put Lily Chambers in more danger. Perry needed to call Burnett. And when the big bad vampire, who wasn't really all that bad, insisted Perry come in, Perry would just have to insist harder that he had to stay.

Realizing he might be missing something when Chuckie told the others, he almost morphed to go in. But nope, he needed to go in the same way he came out. He'd call Burnett later. He took off. Fast. As fast as his tiny feet would go around the building to the front door.

Almost there, he saw the dark-haired vampire, the one Caleb had been hitting on, standing in the door. She really looked familiar.

He knew her. From where? She looked around. Searching. For what?

Or who? The earlier urgency filled his chest. One mystery at a time.

He ran right between her two black pumps and through the door before it closed.

He darted under a few tables, heading to the bathroom to shift, but he spotted Mark walking out.

"He's not in there," Mark shouted to Caleb standing at the table with his mom and dad.

Perry needed a new plan. He eased closer to the table to find out how much trouble he was in.

"Did he follow you outside to eavesdrop?" Caleb spit out to Chuckie.

"Don't go accusing him of anything!" his father bellowed.

"Shut the hell up!" Caleb poked his dad in the chest with his index finger.

His dad's eyes went bright. "I'm tired of you . . ."

"Don't fight." His mom touched his dad's arm. Wow, she could do the right thing.

Caleb looked back at Chuckie. "Did he follow you out?"

Doubt flashed in the man's eyes. "I don't think so."

"Damn it, Chuckie!" Caleb's expression hardened.

"Why would he need to eavesdrop? He works for Jax, too."

"He doesn't know everything. And if I have anything to say about it, he won't." Caleb looked at his dad. "I don't trust your boy. He's up to something."

His father scowled.

Caleb looked around the bar, then back at Chuckie. "Did he know you were talking to Jax?"

Chuckie's brows squeezed together. "I told Mark who it was."

Caleb scowled. "Find that little shit."

Okay, now the "little shit's" mind raced. Perry needed an alibi. A good one. And fast.

Chapter Seventeen

The midnight hour had come and gone when Miranda, now tattoo-free, collected one-armed good-night hugs from her two best friends in the world and ambled into her bedroom where her worries hid out in every dark corner.

Dropping on the bed, she closed her eyes and her thoughts shifted first to her sister. Where the hell was she?

Was she okay?

Where had Anthony taken her?

Propping up on a pillow, she stared at her phone, as if that would make a magical text appear.

Then to make herself feel better, she sent another text to Tabitha. *Call me.*

Staring at the screen, Miranda remembered the phone conversation with her father. Desperation had dripped from his voice. She couldn't recall ever hearing her father sound so broken. No doubt, his shattered heart stemmed both from concern for his daughter and from his fight with her mom.

"I love you, Miranda. Please don't think like your mom. Just because I love Tabitha, it doesn't mean I love you any less."

"I know. I love Tabitha, too." Her anger toward her mom for being so selfish bubbled up in her heart.

Her father's breath caught.

Miranda had wanted to hug him. She almost wanted to forgive him. Forgive him for the lies he'd told her mom about not being married, forgive him for keeping Tabitha and her apart for all these years.

Right then another hurt found a spot in her heart. Would her mom and dad really split up?

Bending her knees and hugging them, she recalled Kylie hurting when her parents had divorced. Was that what Miranda had to look forward to? Her world, the one she'd always known, would be ripped apart.

And what about them? Wouldn't they be miserable without each other? But hadn't they been miserable together these last few months?

Damn it, she knew her parents both still loved each other.

But was love enough?

The question brought on a swarm of questions. About Shawn. About Perry. About what the hell she planned on doing. Or was that her problem? She didn't have a plan.

Mentally, she added "Get Plan" to her list of to-dos.

She recalled that Shawn's text asked her to call him. She hadn't. Because it was late, because . . . she was white icing and stuck to a chocolate wafer named Perry.

Setting her phone on the nightstand, she saw Ernie, her magic eight ball.

Picking him up, she ran her thumb over the little window where words of wisdom appeared—if he decided to be wise.

Closing her eyes, she asked the question. "What do I need to do?"

She gave the black ball a shake. One word started floating to the tiny window's surface.

Listen.

Her breath hung in her throat. Nine times out of ten, Ernie's answers were the same: *You'll have to wait and see* or *You know the answer to that.*

"Listen to what?" She turned the ball over then anxiously waited for his reply to float to the surface. "And don't say my heart because that fickle organ has gone on strike!"

When no word appeared, she gave it another shake. Finally a message appeared.

Look under your . . .

"Under what?" She pulled her knees a little closer. Her legs were covered in tattoos again. She jiggled Ernie again.

"Under what?"

Bed.

"This isn't funny." Her words echoed in the darkness followed by a rustle . . . coming from . . . under her bed.

A hiccup of fear slipped out of her mouth as chills danced across her tattooed skin. She considered screaming. Kylie and Della would come running. Before the cry for help escaped, a realization hit. One that was way overdue.

She needed to learn to take care of herself.

Inhaling air all the way down to her belly button, she hoped it contained courage. She slipped out of bed, and stretched out on the cold wood floor. She reached for the bed ruffle. Fear left an almost metallic taste on her tongue.

She lifted the thin cotton material up. At first she saw nothing. And then she saw . . . everything. Saw it like a movie in her head.

Perry kissing some other girl.

Shawn holding a bouquet of flowers.

Her sister crying.

Then the ugliest image of all flashed. A girl sprawled out on a scarred wooden floor, her neck ripped open, a puddle of blood widening around her.

Miranda went to scream, only to have the sound trapped by her gasp when she saw the next vision. This image, not in her head, consisted of what she really had hidden under her bed.

• • •

Perry stayed concealed under the bar table in the darkest shadows, watching and listening.

"Where's your son?" Caleb questioned his father.

"He's probably off tapping that waitress," Chuckie said. "She was all over him."

The words made Perry's whiskers twitch.

Good one. Remind me to thank you later, Chuckie!

He scurried under another table. Staring up, through several pairs of jean-covered legs, he saw Bell move through swinging doors behind the bar.

He shot through a pair of dirty tennis shoes and a dangerous pair of red spiky high heels, hoping not to be impaled.

Behind him he heard Chuckie say, "The waitress . . . she just went into the back room."

Perry shot forward. Footsteps sounded behind him. *Don't be Caleb!*

Perry glanced back. Caleb.

Racing forward, Perry focused on the swinging doors.

To get there first he'd have to shoot across the floor in plain sight. If seen, his plan would be ruined.

Perry ducked his head, tucked his whiskers and gave it all he had. Luckily a group of people blocked Caleb's way. Perry scurried through another maze of shoes, finally entering the back room.

Bell had her back to him, a phone held to her ear. "I had eight when I dropped him off. How many times can a three-month-old go pee?" Frustration eked out of her. "Yeah I made some, but the rent's due tomorrow."

"Get the hell out of my way!" Caleb's voice sounded right outside the door.

Perry morphed. Fast.

He heard people shuffling, arguing. Crap! He needed it to appear as if he'd been in here a while.

"Bell?" Perry said.

She turned.

Footsteps behind the swinging door drew nearer.

Knowing his time was out, he kissed her.

She didn't fight. Not at all. She leaned into him. The feel of a soft female made it hard to think. The fact that it wasn't the female he loved made it feel wrong.

Her tongue slipped into his mouth. He heard a chuckle at the door. Caleb's chuckle. Bell must have heard him, too, because she waved a hand for him to leave.

Caleb walked off.

The kiss ended.

"Saved by the Bell." Perry flinched when he realized he'd said it out loud.

Bell tilted her head to the side, looking a little shy. "And I didn't think you liked me."

"I do. I mean, I don't. I do, just not . . ." Okay that made a lot of sense. How in snowy hell was he going to explain?

Her eyes twinkled with anticipation. "You want to hang out tonight? I have to pick up my son, but he usually sleeps and we can just have a beer and . . . talk."

"Thanks, but . . . I'm seeing someone."

Her brows tightened and her eyes brightened to the color of a ticked-off vampire. "And that kiss?"

He needed an answer that made sense and didn't include trying to get his parents arrested or stopping a murder.

Bell pursed her lips tight. "It was a bet, wasn't it? You bet your asshole friends that you could score a kiss? And I had you pegged for a decent guy. I suck at picking out guys!"

"No. I didn't . . . I am decent."

She cocked her head, listening for a lie.

"Then why . . . ?"

"It's complicated."

Frustration shone in her eyes. "Fine, but . . . you owe me twenty bucks."

"I do?"

"Yeah, I don't kiss for free!" She frowned as if her words tasted bad on her lips.

He remembered her phone conversation. It hit him then. Here was a mother, unlike his own, who was doing everything she could to take care of her kid.

Pulling out his wallet, he took out three twenty dollar bills and placed them in her hand.

She stared at the money. Something like shame took over her expression. "I said a twenty." She held out the other two bills. Then closing her eyes as if dealing with some internal argument, she added the last one to the others.

"Sorry. That was wrong. Take it all back."

"No, keep it. Please." He slipped his wallet into his back pocket. "You helped me out."

"I'm not a prostitute."

"I know. You're a mother taking care of your kid."

She almost smiled. "You really are decent, aren't you?"

He turned to leave. Before he made it out the door, he heard it. The roar of a lion. Someone had pissed off a shape-shifter. Perry had a sneaking suspicion who it might be.

Darting out, Bell on his heels, he came to an abrupt halt. Two lions fought on the dance floor. Blood dripped from their jowls. Vampires in the room looked at the scene, their eyes bright green from hunger. Weres and half-weres, at full lunar strength, stared on with orange gazes.

Perry cut his eyes left, then right. Caleb and his father were no longer at the table. Perry's focus shot back to the lions, and instinctively he knew the smaller one, the one losing the battle, was his father.

Bell shot forward. Perry grabbed her elbow. "It's dangerous."

"It's my job." She jerked loose. "I'm waitress and security."

"I'll take care of it!" Before he could stop her, she jumped on his father's back, latched on to his mane.

"Stop fighting!" she yelled.

His dad's head swiveled as if to latch his teeth on to her. "No!" Perry shot forward, stopping only a foot from the fight.

His father roared but turned to look at him. Caleb lunged, teeth exposed, and snatched Bell from his father's back and shook.

And shook.

Blood. Bell's blood, splattered all over Perry.

Shock. Rage. Hot emotion burned Perry's skin. The option to morph or not was no longer an option.

His blood pulsed. His skin crawled.

"No!" someone screamed.

Bell's limp body was slung through the air. Caleb in pure lion form charged at Perry. Half morphed, Perry was helpless. The scent of lion breath filled his air, then Perry felt himself being lifted from the dance floor.

Caleb stood on his hind legs, swatting his large paws. Perry's father attacked, his jowls sinking into the shape-shifter's soft underbelly.

Struggling to free himself, Perry saw the face of his abductor, the brunette, the one who'd looked familiar. He tried again to fight. She head-butted him.

He slid into unconsciousness.

Adrenaline, pulsing and pumping through Perry's veins, brought him out of the darkness. Flashes of memory ripped through his mind. Not knowing if it had been hours or minutes since he'd been swooped up by the vampire, he bolted to his feet. His lungs begged for air. Unsure of his location, he turned left, then right. He recognized the brick wall behind the bar where he'd followed Chuckie. Remembering Bell had Perry racing for the entrance.

Panicked voices littered the air. He met bar patrons tripping over everyone as they sought escape. The vision of Bell in the lion's mouth raced through his mind. He knew vampires could live through a lot, but . . . Oh, hell!

He pummeled his way through the crowd. Silence—a dead silence—filled the bar that had recently hummed with noise.

His gaze shot from one corner of the room to the other. He finally saw her. Bell lay—still, too still—in the middle of the dance floor. He ran to her, ready to offer her his blood. Her wide eyes stared up. Stared at nothing.

"No." He knelt, still praying he'd find a pulse.

Chapter Eighteen

With the scream trapped in her throat, Miranda gaped at the gold armadillo eyes staring back at her.

Do not fear me. The words echoed in her head.

And that alone was a reason to be afraid. Who the hell, or what the hell, could talk to her telepathically? Besides a . . . mystic Wiccan. Was this creature . . . ?

I'm here to help.

"Help? I think freeing you is what caused the house to explode."

No, freeing me is what saved you. Don't you remember I told you to leave?

"You didn't tell . . ." Miranda remembered back to the drug house, the armadillo looking at her as if prodding her to leave. Or had he actually told her to leave, telepathically, and she just hadn't realized it. "What are you?"

I'm . . . The creature tilted its head to the side as if hearing something. *If you want me to help find your sister, you can't tell anyone or—*

Just like that Miranda found herself staring at cat-hair dust bunnies. No gold eyes. No ugly pink snout. She blinked once. Twice. "Or what?"

A knock sounded on her bedroom door.

"Miranda?" Della called. "You okay?"

Was she okay?

Hell no, she wasn't okay.

If you want me to help find your sister, you can't tell anyone or . . .

Popping up as fast as a one-armed girl could, Miranda hadn't gotten to her feet when the door opened.

"What are you doing?" Della asked.

Miranda stood. Unsure if she should . . . "I was . . . checking under my bed." It was the truth. She couldn't get a lie past a vampire.

"For what?"

"Monsters." Another truth.

Della tilted her head to the side. "And?"

"And what?" Miranda plopped her butt on the mattress.

"Is there a monster under your bed?" The vamp lifted her face and sniffed the air as if to detect any monster scent.

Shit! Miranda hoped the armadillo was scentless. "Just a couple of scary-looking dust bunnies." Her heart skipped a beat.

Della, now looking doubtful, moved into the room, studying Miranda as if she were a suspicious speck of something floating in her drink. "You're acting weird."

"You act this way when your life's gone to shit."

"That's part of what's weird. You're always nauseatingly positive. All rainbows and unicorns. What's up with that?"

"I fell off my unicorn, and my rainbow crapped in my pot of gold. Good night."

The vamp's gaze shifted to Miranda's phone on the bedside table. "Who were you talking to?"

"I'm tired. Please leave."

Della stared harder. "You need a hug?"

"No," Miranda snapped.

"Now I know something's wrong. You never turn down a hug."

"I want to sleep!" She held up her pinky. "Go before I turn you into a goon."

Della gave her the pissed-off vamp look.

Miranda countered with the bug-off witchy eye roll.

"Is it the tattoo doing it? Because you're covered again."

"At least I don't drink blood." Miranda tossed out the insult purposely, hoping it'd send the vamp packing.

Della gave the door a good slam on her way out.

Lumpy emotion tightened Miranda's throat. She stared down at her tattooed arm.

She waited for a good twenty seconds, then quietly, she got back down on her knees and picked up the bed skirt. No armadillo. But those damn dust bunnies must have done the Humpty Dance and had babies, because she saw four now.

When she got up, she recalled the crazy visions. Her heart started pounding.

Perry kissing someone else. Ouch.

Shawn with a bouquet of flowers. Probably for her, and that brought on a guilty ouch.

Tabitha looking scared and upset.

And last, but so not least—the dead girl.

Miranda didn't have a clue who she was. Yet everything in her gut said it was true. Somewhere out there, a girl had died. Perry had kissed someone. Shawn had bought her flowers. Miranda had seen it.

What the hell did all of it mean?

Rage had every animal inside of Perry begging to come out. It multiplied when he saw what the girl had gripped in her hand. The button of her and her son. "I'm so sorry," he whispered.

"You should go." The voice came from the bar's door.

He shot to his feet. Felt his morph start.

"Burnett sent me." The dark-haired vampire stepped back. "He was worried."

Perry stopped the shift. The FRU, that's where he knew her

from. The realization didn't stop the onslaught of emotions. He wanted to tell her that Burnett hadn't needed to send someone, but . . .

He'd messed up.

A girl, a young mother, was dead. He probably would have been too if this vampire hadn't saved him.

His eyes stung. His heart stilled. Guilt swelled inside his chest.

She must have spotted it. "It wasn't your fault. You tried to stop her. You almost died trying to stop her."

"I should have tried harder." He looked back at Bell.

"Do you know that Caleb guy's last name? Where we can find him?"

Perry looked up. "I should have dealt with him earlier."

She moved in. "His name?"

"I don't know. I don't know where he is now. But I'll find him."

"No. Go back to Shadow Falls. I'll get him."

Her lack of confidence in him hurt, but he couldn't blame her. Not when he blamed himself. "I screwed up once. I won't screw up again!"

"You didn't . . ." She looked over her shoulder. "You have to go before the local FRU get here. Burnett won't want you mixed up in this."

Perry clenched his fist. "I'll take care of Caleb."

"You can't . . ."

He would.

A phone rang behind the bar. They both looked back. Perry remembered Bell putting her phone down.

Someone needed to tell the babysitter that Bell wasn't coming to pick up her baby. That she'd never be back.

"They're almost here! Leave. Call Burnett!"

"You call him," Perry said. "Tell him that Chuckie is the one who shot Lily Chambers and he's headed back to Fallen to finish the job."

Perry darted past the bar into the back room, where he'd kissed the same girl who now lay dead. He snatched up her ringing phone. The back door was ajar. No doubt the owners of the bar had escaped because the place wasn't registered with the FRU.

Voices echoed from behind him. Perry morphed and took off.

"Miranda, I need some help."

Miranda's eyes popped open. She'd heard the voice. Perry's voice. Heard it as clear as day.

Blinking, she cut her gaze around to confirm he wasn't there. Nope. Then she glanced toward her bedroom window that faced the east. Darkness greeted her with only the slightest hue of purple.

A dream. Wasn't it?

She slumped back on her pillow. Had she even slept an hour? Right then her cell beeped with a text.

Tabitha? Miranda rolled over so fast to get her phone that she almost fell off the bed. Looking at the screen, she saw Perry's number. She read the message.

Miranda, I need some help.

Her breath caught when she realized she'd dreamed, or somehow heard, those same words.

She typed in. *What's wrong?*

The three dots appeared. Then his text flashed across the screen.

Meet me at our spot by creek. The one beside the fence. Alone . . . if possible.

Alone? Right. As soon as Miranda got up, Della would be asking questions. Heck, the beep of the text probably already roused her.

Then Miranda recalled the vamp had said she had shadowing duty. She noted the time. Della should've already left.

If Kylie wasn't in vampire mode, with sensitive hearing, Miranda might . . .

Curiosity almost had her typing questions back to Perry, but the urgency she sensed had her typing in two letters: *ok.*

Easing out of bed, she decided changing clothes might be too noisy. So holding her phone, wearing her Batwoman pj's, and her Mickey Mouse house slippers, she eased out of her room, out of her cabin, and into the darkness.

Once away from the cabin, worry almost choking her, she started speed walking as fast as her Mickeys could go.

The Texas morning air felt fresher, but still muggy. A small drop of sweat eased down between her breasts.

Before entering the cove of woods, she saw the moon, a sliver from being full, hanging low. In the eastern sky, the slow-to-rise sun had painted strips of color on the horizon.

It wasn't until she felt the darkness of the trees close in on her that Miranda stopped and thought about being alone.

Or rather about not being alone. She felt . . . watched.

She searched the dark shadows for the armadillo. No gold eyes peered back at her.

She paused. All she could hear was her heartbeat swishing in her ears. Silence was wrong. The night always sang, unless something startled it.

Or someone.

Looking at the trees surrounding her, she got the eeriest sensation as if they'd leaned closer.

What if . . . this wasn't Perry? But a trick? She pulled her phone up to make sure it had really been Perry's number sending the text.

It was.

Of course, just because it was his phone, didn't mean it was him texting. In the corner of her eye, she saw a tree branch dip down.

Sure it was only paranoia. She kept walking, ignoring the feeling that the trees were reaching for her.

Right then her mind flashed the scary image from earlier. The girl. Dead.

Then she heard it. A cry.

Not too loud.

Not too low.

But a profound sound that echoed with such emotional cadence that even the leaves on the trees seemed to quake.

Following the sound, came a breeze. Cold. Ghostly cold.

The sun hadn't risen when Shawn walked into the hospital. He'd stayed out past midnight trying to find anyone who'd witnessed the shooting. And failed.

Now, with less than two hours of sleep, he felt empty. Empty from all but the raw guilt over Lily. First he'd allowed her to be zapped by the cuffs, then he'd made her target practice for some asshole by stopping at the drugstore.

He'd made mistakes in the past, but never any that resulted in real harm to an innocent. Anger coursing through his muscles, he gripped tighter on the stems of the semi-wilted flowers he'd picked up for her last night. Then Burnett had given him assignments. When he'd finally gotten home last night, he'd almost tossed them away, but guilt had him sticking them into a jelly jar with water. Guilt also had him calling the hospital to check on her.

She'd skated through surgery. Doctors expected a full recovery. Not that Shawn doubted it. She was too much of a spitfire to stay down. Chances were that spitfire held him responsible. Chances were he was about to get an earful.

He deserved it, but God, he hated listening to angry women. Which was one reason he liked Miranda. She seldom got mad. Not that she was a pushover, but she held her temper in check.

Stepping out of the elevator, a few nurses moved around the dimly lit floor. He spotted Chase Tallman talking to someone in a waiting room. Chase acknowledged him with a nod, but Shawn kept walking. He stopped right in front of her door, suddenly concerned. Just because he couldn't sleep, didn't mean Lily shouldn't.

The door swung open and a nurse walked out. Startled, she glanced down the hall to the waiting room.

"Have . . . have you been cleared to enter?" she asked. "The last time I allowed someone inside I was given hell by someone else wearing a black suit."

"I'm FRU." He showed her his badge.

She glanced at his wilted bouquet. "Nice," the nurse said.

Shawn nodded, half ashamed of the droopy peace offering. "Is she awake?"

"Yes. I just gave her another injection for the pain. Shoulder surgery is the worst."

He grimaced. The nurse left, leaving the door open. Her footsteps echoed in the sleepy-morning ambience of the hospital.

Inhaling, preparing himself for an ass-chewing from a pissed-off girl in pain, he walked into the room.

Her eyes were closed. He let himself study her. And like the first time he'd seen her in the jewelry store, he noted how pretty she was. She was . . . feminine without being fancy, pretty without being gorgeous. He stood there, unsure if he shouldn't leave his peace offering and go.

He looked at the bedside table debating where to leave the flowers.

"What are you doing here?"

Startled, he looked at her face. Her eyes remained closed.

"Just wanted to check in."

"I wish you wouldn't. I barely know you and already you and pain are synonymous in my mind."

He flinched. "I brought you flowers."

She lifted her head an inch off the pillow and studied him. "So you fry my ass, get me interrogated, accuse me of robbing people I love, get me shot, and you think bringing me a"—her eyes went to his offering—"a bouquet of flowers that you picked up on the clearance rack will make it okay?"

"I'm sorry, but—"

"Stop right there! An apology should never come with a 'but'! You're either sorry, or you're not."

He exhaled. "I'm sorry." *But I was just trying to do my job.*

"Good, now leave." Her head dropped back on the pillow.

He turned to do as she requested, then frustration had him turning back. "Are you always this easy to get along with?"

She lifted up again. "When someone gets me shot. Yes. Now go." Her gaze shifted beside him. "And . . . take that pink kangaroo with you."

"Kangaroo?"

She dropped her head. "Every time they give me a pain shot she pops in. And she can't sing or dance worth a flip."

Shawn chuckled. "Can I put your flowers in water before I go?"

"Yeah. I think I saw a urinal in the cabinet."

He went to the cabinet to see if he could find anything, besides a urinal, to put the flowers in. "I didn't buy them on the clearance rack. I picked them up last night, but had to investigate your shooting first."

"Did you find Chuckie?"

"No. But we will."

Her soft brown eyes tightened. "Someone's watching the Crows, right?"

"We've got it. Nothing's going to happen to them."

"Excuse me if I don't trust you."

"How many times do I have to say I'm sorry?" He found a plastic cup that would work as a vase.

"Maybe a dozen."

He smiled, even though he wasn't sure she meant it to be funny. Adding water to the plastic cup, he sat the arrangement on her bedside table.

When he looked up, she was staring at him.

"What?" he asked.

"Your eye's a very pretty purple color."

He touched his shiner. "Yeah, you did that. I assume you don't think you owe me an apology."

"Nope." She giggled. It sounded pain-med induced, but still nice.

Their gazes locked.

She glanced away. "Did your girlfriend like her bracelet?"

"I haven't given it to her yet."

The room went silent. The emotion crowding him felt too big. "I should go."

She nodded.

He started to turn away, when she spoke up. "Wait."

"What?" Their gazes locked again. Something in her eyes drew him closer.

Chapter Nineteen

Shawn waited for her to say something.

"I remembered something else . . . about Jax."

"Yeah?" He moved closer.

"I got a text from an old friend of mine a few months ago. She said something about a rumor that Jax was going to be a daddy. I didn't answer her 'cause . . . I didn't want contact with anyone who had contact with him. But if she heard rumors, she might know where he lives."

Thrilled he'd gotten something to report back to Burnett, he asked, "Do you still have her number?"

"Yeah." She reached for her phone and flinched in pain.

"Let me." He handed her the cell. Their fingers touched and Shawn felt the spark. And apparently so had she, because she glanced up.

After swiping the screen, she said, "Here." She called out the information and he typed it into his phone.

"Thanks," he said.

"Do everything you did to me, to him okay?"

He smiled. "You're kidding? I went easy on you."

Her gaze went to her side table. "Thanks for the flowers. Even half dead, they're pretty."

"I could say the same about you," he said and flinched because it sounded, too . . .

He turned to leave but stopped when he saw Della Tsang perched in the doorway.

He wasn't . . . doing anything wrong, but his last comment rang in his head. He walked out. She followed.

"She gave me a lead," he said, hoping that explained it.

"Good." One word and it didn't sound friendly.

"I should go let Burnett know."

"Yeah." Her second word sounded downright pissy. He got about two steps away when she added, "She's fine, by the way."

He glanced back.

"I'm sure you wanted to ask about Miranda." The vamp put a hand on her hip.

I texted her to call me and she didn't! And I think it has to do with a damn shape-shifter showing up. He almost defended himself, but didn't.

"Thanks." He walked off, pretending he'd missed her real meaning.

The odd mew-like cry faded in and out several times. The closer she got to the creek the louder the sound of water, rushing, splashing. The only thing that had her putting one foot in front of the other was . . . Perry.

The peculiar chill hung on and created a fog rising from the dew-covered ground. She kept walking, pinky ready. Her gaze shifted left then right, searching for the gold eyes of the armadillo.

No eyes—just dark shadows playing peek-a-boo through the mist.

Above, through the leaf-filled branches, slivers of sky grew lighter, but beneath the umbrella of the forest, the blackness clung to the misty gray fog. And suddenly it felt colder.

She'd felt this before. This kind of chill. Death?

No! She was wrong. This happened to Kylie and Della. Not her.

She considered running the way she'd come, diving back in bed and covering up her head. The consideration died a quick death. Perry was in trouble. She felt it.

Only when she moved to the edge of the property where the trees thinned, did the moon add a silvery light. Light was good but it only made the fog more pronounced.

Relief washed over her when she spotted Perry standing on the other side of the fence, partially hidden in a wall of fog. She edged closer, the fog lifted, and before he saw her, she saw him. His expression. His black eye was now more pronounced. His shirt was ripped open with stains that looked like . . . blood.

"You okay?" She ran those last steps, wrapping her arms around herself to fight the cold.

"Thank God." He turned. "Thank you for coming."

"What's happening?" Then she saw what he cradled in his arms. "Is that a . . . ?"

The soft cry came again.

"A baby? I need you to take him to Holiday. He keeps crying and I don't know what's wrong. He could be sick or—"

"Sometimes babies just . . . cry." Miranda inched closer to the fence and stared at the red-faced infant, who looked more like a little old man. "Sometimes they miss their parents." She tightened her eyes and saw it was half vampire and . . . *mother cracker* . . . half shape-shifter.

Lifting her eyes she froze, her heart swelled. "Is it . . . yours?"

"Like my kid?" He looked insulted. "No. I went to see the sitter to explain . . . She gave him to me and wouldn't take it back."

"Why would she do that?"

"The mom . . . she . . ." He closed his eyes as if searching for words.

"You know the mom?" Miranda asked and the air grew colder.

"Yeah. Not really. Barely."

He wasn't making sense. Nothing did. Yet for reasons she

couldn't explain, part of the puzzle started coming together. "You kissed her? The mom?"

He blinked. "I did." His eyes widened. "Not because I wanted to. And that's not important."

"Really?" The one word slipped out. Her heart felt scratched.

The baby's cry leaked out into the dark. Perry rearranged the loose blanket around the tiny being and he juggled it in his arms. "I only kissed her because I needed an alibi." His words came out jolted with his movements to comfort the child. "I was out eaves-dropping, hoping to hear news about your sister. They suspected I'd been there. I needed it to look like I hadn't."

His words, the raw panic in his tone, ran laps around Miranda's brain, almost making her dizzy. Finally she latched on to one thing he'd said.

"You know something about my sister?" she asked. "I thought you were trying to figure out what your parents were up to."

"I am, but . . . I don't have time to explain everything, but it's connected . . . The guy who my dad is taking orders from is mixed up with everything else." The baby stopped crying. He looked down with relief and concern.

The sight of Perry, bruised and hurting, holding the baby so protectively against his bare abdomen sent emotion right to her heart.

"I need to go before I miss a meeting."

"Why isn't the mom taking care of the baby?"

He closed his eyes tight. "She's dead."

The image of the dead girl flashed in Miranda's mind. Once. Twice. Three times.

He grimaced. "It's my fault. I should have—"

"No." Miranda heard his pain. Her need to console him suddenly came stronger than her confusion. "I don't know what happened, but I know you'd never . . ."

"I didn't do it, but I didn't stop it."

He tried.

The two words echoed, but she didn't know if they'd come from within or from the patchy fog.

Oh, crap! The armadillo?

Startled, she glanced around. Saw nothing. No one.

No one except Perry. Pain and guilt bright in his eyes. The voice felt less important.

"I'm sure you tried—"

"It's not important now."

Yet Miranda instinctively knew it was. He blamed himself for someone's death. She knew Perry, knew his moral compass, knew this was killing him.

"Look," Perry continued. "As far as I know there's no one to take the baby. The babysitter refused to keep him. Tell Burnett to please not put him in foster care. Find him a home." He motioned to the fence. "It's loose at the bottom. Come out then take the baby around to the front."

"Why . . ." Right then something else didn't make sense. "Why don't you take the baby to Holiday?"

"Burnett won't let me leave again. I have a meeting with Jax this morning. I'm hoping I'll get answers that'll help find your sister. Then I can take care of the piece of shit who killed this baby's mama."

"But . . ."

"Please, come get the baby. I'd come in, but Burnett would be here in seconds."

Her brain snatched the words, trying to understand but . . . One thought eked out. "The alarm works both ways. Burnett will know—"

"Yeah, but because it's close to a full moon he'll think it's a were. He accepts they refuse to be caged up this close to a full moon. This is where they leave from. Pleeease. I'm running out of time."

She knelt, pulled up the fence, and crawled under it. The moist, gritty dirt, somehow hotter than the air, clung to her palms. Standing, wiping her hands on her pajama bottoms, she got a close-up view of the anguish in Perry's eyes.

"Perry, if he doesn't want you going it's because it's too dangerous."

"I know, but I have to do this."

Fear for his safety and anger that he cared so little about it, curled her toes in her house shoes and pushed Mickey's face into the dirt. "What if he's right?"

Perry held the baby out to her. "Miranda, I'm begging you. I need someone to believe in me right now. No, not just someone. I need you to believe in me."

He moved the baby closer. Using her casted limb, she cradled the infant in the crook of her arm. When it wiggled, she pulled it closer. It felt warm. But the air around them seemed to get colder.

She looked up at Perry. "I do believe in you, but . . . if something happened to you, I'd die."

"Nothing's going to happen! Part of the reason I'm doing this is to make sure you don't die." He ducked his head down and kissed her. A fast, but emotionally charged kiss.

Tears filled her eyes. "Promise you'll be careful."

"I promise." He ran a finger over her lips, still wet from his kiss. "Damn, I miss kissing you." He kissed her again, this one just as sweet. Just as short. Just as powerful.

"I gotta go." He morphed into his favorite prehistoric bird. His wings whooshed open, the breadth of their span more than six feet. Before she knew what he meant to do, he'd wrapped her and the infant in a warm hug. His feathers were soft as down and felt like a security blanket. A place nothing bad or evil could ever touch her.

It ended before Miranda wanted it to. His wings whooshed open. He bounced up into the air, and just before he took flight he said, "I'll watch you until you're in the gate. I love you. And . . . I love your Batwoman pajamas."

The baby started to cry again and so did her heart. She held the infant close and watched Perry's ascent. Tears filled her eyes. "I love you, too," she whispered. And never until right now had she known it to be truer.

She was the gooey icing stuck to a wafer who bore the name Perry Gomez.

And that was wrong. Wrong to feel this way about one side of the cookie when you had the other side thinking you felt that way about him. Now all she had to figure out was how to break this news to Shawn without breaking his heart.

Yet, as high as this matter marked on her problem card, she took a second to reevaluate. The little problem she held in her arms took top priority.

How the hell was she going to explain the baby to Holiday and the quick-to-anger vampire?

She neared the gate. She looked up and saw the skyscape made up of blue, purple, and streaks of orange. In the forefront was a majestic creature soaring on the paint strokes of the sunrise.

She hesitated, giving him time to get away before she walked up to the gate. Pulling the child and his loose baby blanket closer, she looked at the camera, waiting for the ding of the gate to open.

She'd barely gotten a foot past the gate when the office door shot open.

Burnett blasted off the porch, becoming nothing but a blur until he stopped in front of her. Feet slightly apart, a frown on his lips, his eyes bright, he stared at her. "What are you . . . ?"

The baby cried. The cold got colder. Burnett gaped at the wiggling infant.

"What the hell's going on, Miranda?"

Footsteps sounded behind them. Holiday stopped beside her husband, her eyes widened.

"Who is she?" Holiday's words created a cloud of steam that hung in the air.

"I think it's a he?" Miranda pulled the blanket around the baby.

Holiday glanced at the child. "No, not the baby," she said. "The ghost?"

Chapter Twenty

"Why didn't you contact me as soon as you got the text?" Burnett had demanded.

"Because Perry asked me to come alone." Whoever said the truth could set you free had never been asked questions by an angry vampire.

After an hour of drilling her, he'd told her she could go. Hand on the doorknob, she shamefully realized she hadn't asked about her sister.

Miranda looked back. "Anything on Tabitha?"

He grimaced. "Not from a lack of trying, but Shawn got another lead. I'll let you know when we hear something. Meanwhile, don't keep things from me, got it?"

She rushed out before she was tempted to tell him everything. Oh, she'd shared everything Perry had said, and even about her crazy visions. The armadillo, however, she kept to herself.

Listen up. If you want me to help find your sister, you can't tell anyone or . . .

But damn it, she didn't know what to do. To tell, not to tell. Nothing made sense. Not a thing.

She took off in a dead run. Fearing . . . ghosts and . . . trees.

Flying into her cabin, she fought to catch her breath. Even her

Mickey Mouses looked out of air. Chills ran down her back, but she no longer knew if they were from fear or from the presence of the ghost.

Holiday had surmised that the ghost was the baby's mother— surmised because the spirit had never spoken before vanishing into the chill of the morning air.

"Is she gone for good?" Miranda had asked.

"We don't know," Holiday said. "Call me if you feel anything. And don't worry."

Right!

Shutting her cabin door, doing a visual of the room, she felt swallowed up by the silence. She puffed out air testing to see if steam rose. No steam.

How reliable was the steam test?

Frozen in one spot, she flinched when she spotted movement in the kitchen.

She almost screamed but recognized Chester attacking a dust bunny. A slight creak echoed from Kylie's bedroom.

It was all the invitation Miranda needed.

Bolting into the room, she ran into the arms of a naked Lucas— with the exception of a tight pair of boxers—who looked totally embarrassed. Doing a high-speed U-turn, she barged right out. "Sorry." She slammed the door.

The door swung right back open. "You okay?"

Miranda faced Kylie. "No. Is she here?"

"Who?" Kylie asked.

"I felt her earlier and didn't know what I felt. I suspected because I felt it with you guys, but my mind wouldn't let me go there. Now I don't know if I feel it or if I think I feel it."

"Stop!" Kylie held up a hand to silence her. "Slow down. Breathe."

Miranda did.

Kylie moved closer. "Now. Are you okay?"

"You already asked me that." She looked around again. "Is she here?"

"If you mean Della, no. Burnett sent her—"

"Not Della. The ghost."

Kylie's mouth dropped open and seemed to note Miranda's pj's. "You had a nightmare?"

"I wish." Miranda moved and dropped on the sofa. "So, no ghost?"

Kylie looked around the room. "I don't feel anything."

Miranda sighed.

Kylie, being Kylie, came and sat down beside her. "Did you dream about ghosts?"

Miranda lifted her face. "No. She was real."

"You saw a ghost?" The question had doubt wrapped around it.

"I never saw her . . . as a ghost. I just . . . felt her." She shivered from the memory. "I think I heard her. I think she thought . . . Do I look like a person who would hurt a baby?"

"No." Kylie's eyes tightened. "You're confusing me again. What baby?"

"Perry . . . he gave it to me," Miranda said.

"You and Perry have a baby?" she asked.

Miranda's mind ran so fast. "I gave it to Holiday. What's crazy is that I saw it."

Kylie took her hand. "Saw what?"

"I saw him kissing a girl. Then I saw her dead. I didn't know it was the same girl. But she wasn't a ghost when I saw her. It's like I had a . . . front seat to a freaky slide show."

Then Miranda remembered. "I saw Shawn with flowers."

"So you dreamed that you and Perry had a baby and Shawn brought you flowers?"

"It wasn't a dream!" Miranda said.

Kylie touched Miranda's forehead as if checking her for fever. "We should call Holiday. This may be because of your accident."

"Don't call Holiday. She's taking care of the baby."

"That's it!" Kylie said, sounding scared, and she stood up. "You and Perry do not have a baby."

"I never said the baby was Perry's or mine." She frowned remembering. "I did think it might be his for a few seconds."

Kylie's eyes tightened.

"Don't look at me like that. I'm just trying to figure it out."

"If you have a concussion, it could be dangerous."

"I don't have a concussion. Sit down, please."

Kylie did as Miranda requested, her weight had the sofa sighing. "So it was a dream."

"It wasn't a dream. Just listen." She racked her brain to find a way to explain things in a way that didn't sound crazy. It didn't exist. It was crazy.

Taking one more deep breath, Miranda told Kylie everything. Well . . . she told her everything she'd told Burnett and Holiday. Again, the armadillo was her secret.

When she finished spilling her guts, Kylie sat there looking dumbfounded. Pretty much how Miranda felt.

"What did Holiday say about the visions?" Kylie asked.

"She said it could be related to the tattoo. But they weren't really visions. Not like you and Della have. I'm not living it like you two say you do. There were images. Like a picture explodes in my mind. Then it's gone."

Their cabin door swung open. Swung so hard, it banged against the wall.

Della swooped inside and put her breaks on when she saw Kylie and Miranda on the sofa.

Della exhaled. "Did you tell her?" Della asked Kylie.

"Tell me what?" Miranda asked.

Kylie shook her head.

Della placed a hand on her hip. "Girlfriends don't lie to each other."

"Lie about what?" Miranda asked.

"Can't do it," Della said to Kylie. "He's calling her pretty and bringing her flowers."

"What?" Miranda asked.

Della focused on Miranda. "Look, I just hope the wafer you're stuck on is Perry, because the other side of that cookie is flirting his ass off with another glob of icing."

Perry flew hard and fast. He couldn't miss the meeting. Most of the way, he flew as his favorite prehistoric bird, something close to a pterodactyl, but faster and better looking.

Realizing it was getting light, he started morphing into a per-egrine falcon while flying. Then he noticed the thick brush that probably held thorns below and remembered what he needed to do. He landed.

His next stop was behind the Marriott Hotel where his father had rented a room. He morphed and checked the time. Five min-utes after eight.

Damn. They might have left.

He noticed he had ten messages from his father, all wanting to know if he was okay. He hit redial.

"Perry? Tell me this is you, son," his father answered.

"It's me," Perry said.

"He's alive. Our son is alive!" his father's voice piped through the phone.

The emotion he heard in his dad's voice tugged at Perry's heart. The silence from his mom, added a different kind of tug.

"Why didn't you return our calls? We've been worried sick."

He'd prepared for this question.

"That vampire nearly killed me. Luckily I was half morphed and it didn't completely do me in. But I was no good for hours. I made it to my girlfriend's place. I told her to text you, but she forgot."

"You're alive," his father said. "That's what matters. We'll hunt that vampire bitch down later."

"Yeah," he said, not having planned for that. "What room are you in? I'm at the hotel. We're going to Jax's, right?"

"We left the hotel already. Why don't you just lay low? I'll explain it to Jax."

Perry clenched his fist. "No. I want to do this."

"You sure you're up to it?" he asked. "He's gonna want to see you at your best."

"I'm up for it."

"Okay, we're at the diner about six blocks over on Jackson Street. But hurry, we're supposed to be there at nine and Jax doesn't tolerate tardiness."

"I'm on my way!"

Less than three minutes later, Perry walked through the restaurant door. He braced himself to see Caleb—knowing when he saw him, he'd want to kill the bastard. Right then. Right there. Even in a restaurant filled with witnesses.

He couldn't do it. Nope.

If he wanted justice he had to be patient. But Caleb's time would come. Perry had never taken a life, but this time might be different.

Still wearing the ripped and bloodstained shirt, mostly because he needed to carry off the story, he walked into the diner. The smell of bacon, eggs, and cinnamon French toast flavored the air and reminded him he'd skipped too many meals. He spotted his dad and mom in a booth. Alone.

How had he gotten so lucky?

Avoiding eye contact with worried customers, he went and sat in the booth across from his parents.

"You have no idea how good it is to see you." His dad smiled. So did his mom. But it looked as fake as the pink stuff she was sprinkling in her coffee.

"Do you need to eat something? We've got about fifteen minutes before we have to leave," his dad said.

The waitress came by carrying a cup of coffee. "Coffee?" She stared at his shirt.

"Motor oil," Perry said, but he wasn't sure it looked convincing with his battered face. "And yes, I'll take the coffee. Thank you." Caffeine wasn't his friend, but he needed something.

Perry ordered the fastest thing on the menu, and she walked off. He focused back on his parents. "Where's the other guys?"

Pride beamed from his father's eyes. "Jax sent Chuckie and Mark to finish something. Caleb no longer works for Jax."

Perry's mind scrambled to take it all in. Mark had gone with Chuckie. Perry needed to let Burnett know. Trying to play it cool about the Caleb information, Perry sipped the bitter coffee. "What happened with Caleb?"

"I talked to Jax," his father said.

"That's not the only reason." The sound of his mother's voice said she drew pleasure from chipping at her husband's pride.

"Maybe not all of it." His father frowned and focused back on Perry. "But when he found out the FRU had been called because a girl was dead, he was livid. He told Caleb to pack his shit and run because he was sending guys after him."

Perry set his cup down.

His mom spoke up. "Jax doesn't take shit from anyone." She looked right at Perry, almost as if she was warning him.

Two thoughts hit and not about the warning. One: Perry hoped Jax did him the favor of killing Caleb, but then how would Perry know for sure? He personally needed to know that Caleb paid for killing Bell. Two: How was it his mother seemed to know Jax so well? Perry had assumed his father was the one with the connections. Had he assumed wrong?

His father forked another bite of his French toast. "It made things worse that the girl Caleb killed was Jax's ex-girlfriend."

His father's words bounced around Perry's head. Shit. Was Jax the father of Bell's baby? And if so, would he go looking for him?

His father picked up his fork and went in for another bite of his French toast. His mom pushed his dad's plate back. "You're gonna get fat. And I have to see you naked." She snatched his fork from his hands.

Perry waited, hoping his dad would tell her where she could put the fork.

He didn't.

His mom nudged her hardly touched plate of French toast away. "She wasn't Jax's girlfriend, just some slut he'd screwed. And she was stupid to jump into a fight with shape-shifters."

Her words were like a hot poker hitting every nerve Perry owned. "She was the security. It was her job."

"Then she was an idiot taking the job. Everyone knows vampires can't control shifters."

Perry took in a deep breath. "She's dead. It's disrespectful to speak ill of her."

"I only said the truth." She smiled as if annoying Perry made her happy.

He swallowed the emotions clogging his throat. After several beats of silence he spoke up again. "You sound like you know Jax well." Faking calm he didn't feel, he turned his coffee cup.

She looked at his father. "You haven't told him?"

His father shrugged. "Not yet."

"What?" Perry picked up the cup, staring at them over the cup's lip as he took a sip.

"Jax is your half brother," his mom said.

Perry choked on the hot liquid sliding down his throat.

He set his cup down a little hard and the hot liquid sloshed over the mug's lips.

"You're joking." He grabbed a napkin to soak up the mess.

"No," his mom said. "I had a baby a year before I met your dad."

Perry took in air. "I don't remember a brother."

"His dad kept him," his mom said as if that didn't reflect badly on her at all.

What? Your first child's daddy refused to abandon this one?

Cynicism filled Perry's chest. At his mom. At his dad. Then came a realization—equally disturbing.

Not only was Perry going to put his mom and dad away, he'd be taking down his half brother. Damn it! Any more family members to destroy?

Then another thing occurred to him. The baby, Bell's baby, could be Perry's nephew.

The waitress dropped Perry's pancakes down. He took a few bites, but noted the blood on his shirt again, and his appetite went south.

"Should we get going?" he asked his father.

"Eat, he just lives two blocks down Jackson."

His mom's phone rang. She looked at the screen. "Speak of the devil. Hi son." She looked at Perry as if he would be jealous. "We're on our way."

She frowned. "Why not?"

Perry could hear Jax talking, but couldn't distinguish his words.

"I wouldn't worry about it," his mom said. "You didn't think it was yours anyway."

Oh, hell! Was Jax trying to find the baby?

"Okay," his mom said. "Why?"

Why what?

"What time?" She paused. "Fine, call me with details."

She hung up. "Jax can't make it today. He wants us to meet him tomorrow. He's going to let us know where and when later."

Perry took another sip of his coffee, his mind racing. First order of business was losing his parents.

"If we're not meeting him, I'm going back to my girlfriend's."

"You don't want to try to find that vampire?"

Perry had to think fast. "I already went back there, turned wolf and caught no scent."

"But if we both went . . ."

"It wouldn't help. Right now I want a bath and to get out of these bloody clothes."

His mom stared at him as if suspicious. She leaned in, her hand snaking across the table at him.

He jerked back. He suffered from her touch last night, he didn't want to do it again. "What?"

"Show me where the vampire bit you?"

"Why?" he asked.

"A mother's concern." She smirked. "Show me."

He sat back. "You're not worried about me. You think I'm lying, don't you?"

Her eyes went cold. "Yeah. And so did Caleb. So open your shirt and prove to me you aren't here to start trouble."

Chapter Twenty-one

Miranda had slept the rest of the morning. Thank the Godesses she woke up ghostless, tattooless, and armadilloless. She'd checked the temperature. She'd checked her arm. And she'd checked under her bed.

On second thought, she wished the armadillo would show up and help her find Tabitha. Lying there, staring at the ceiling, she talked to the creature in her mind. Since it had spoken telepathically to her, maybe it could hear her, too.

No answer came back.

Rolling over, she grabbed her phone to make sure she hadn't missed a text or call. Maybe one from her mom. Tabitha. Maybe Perry telling her he was okay.

But nope. Nothing.

Sitting up, she considered calling Shawn. But to say what? The whole thing about him flirting with some girl messed with Miranda's mind.

Her mind, but not her heart. Her heart was with Perry.

Still, she felt . . . betrayed.

Her phone rang. She answered it before she checked the screen. "Hello?" She waited to hear the caller's voice.

"How are you feeling?" Holiday's caring tone ran through the line.

Miranda inhaled. "Fine. You got news? About Tabitha or the tattoo?" She'd take either, but preferred sister news.

"No, an old professor of mine, half witch, who has studied everything Wiccan, still hasn't called back. I just called to . . . check in."

"And ask if I've seen a ghost?" Miranda said.

"That, too." Guilt colored her voice. "Have you?"

"I just woke up. It's not cold." She pushed her leg out from the covers, retesting the temperature. Ghostless. "How's the baby?"

"He's fine. Such a cute little guy."

"Really," Miranda asked. "He looked like a grumpy ol' man without his teeth."

"Burnett said the same thing. That's just a stage." Humor filled Holiday's voice.

"What are you going to do with him?" Miranda asked.

The silence filled the line and it seemed to mean something. Miranda just didn't know what. "You're not handing him over to a foster home, are you? Perry said—"

"No. Burnett's checking to see if his mom had family." She paused. "Another reason I called is . . . I know you've got a ton of stuff to worry about, but . . . next Monday you are going to have to retake the SAT. The cutoff for this has come and gone. I've begged for this retake. I don't think they'll give you any more time."

Miranda balled the sheet up in her hand. "I know."

"If you want I can get you a tutor—"

"No, I got it." She bit into her lip. She knew how hopeless this was. "As a matter of fact, I should go study now."

Hanging up, she swallowed a knot of frustration. The reality of her situation rolled over her like a cement truck. She wasn't going to college with Della and Kylie.

She tossed her pillow to the ground. "I hate being stupid."

. . .

Less than an hour later, nose in an SAT study guide, Miranda read the same paragraph three times. Why wasn't any of this sticking? Why was she even trying?

A knock came at her bedroom door.

"Yeah?" Miranda asked.

The door whooshed open. Della stood there, dressed in don't-mess-with-me black.

"What?" Miranda snapped.

"Are you studying?" The vamp's surprised tone hit Miranda in her sore spot.

"No, I'm dancing. What does it look like I'm doing?" A lump of pain swelled in her chest. Her two best friends were going to move on with their lives and Miranda wasn't.

The vamp frowned. "Still mad at me about—?"

"I'm not mad!"

"Don't shoot the messenger," Della said. "It's Shawn who—"

"I've got so much crap on me right now, I don't care about Shawn!" That wasn't altogether true, but in the big scheme of things, Shawn didn't rate.

Della smirked. "When are you gonna learn you can't lie to vampires."

"Go away." She couldn't handle this right now.

Della didn't move. "I was going to offer to help you study."

"I don't want your help." Miranda clutched a handful of sheet.

"Don't be silly!" Della struck a pose against the door frame. She always looked badass. Smart and strong. Couldn't Miranda be just one of those?

Miranda tossed her extra pillow at her. "Go. Away. Go bump uglies with Chase." Miranda held up her pinky, the only badass move she had.

Della didn't go. "I can't."

"Why?"

"Because Burnett thinks if Perry contacts you, you'll try to sneak off without telling him again."

Burnett didn't trust her. That hurt. Then again, she was keeping the armadillo from him. "Then just leave my room!"

"Why don't you let me help you study? I'm good at it."

"And I'm not! Is that what you're saying?" Feeling small, inadequate, she did the only thing she could . . . she got mad. "Have you ever had a rude, hurtful thought in that blood-sucking brain of yours that you kept to yourself in lieu of offending someone?"

Della stood there staring, her mouth dropped open. "Yeah. Right now." She swung around and shot off.

Tears filled Miranda's eyes. She was gonna lose her two best friends. Was that why she seemed to be purposely pushing them away? So it wouldn't hurt so much later?

Before Miranda could blink away the tears, Della shot back in. "I wasn't trying to offend you! Believe it or not, I care."

She shot out again.

Miranda took in another shaky breath. The vampire shot back in.

"That's why I offered to help you study and that's why I told you about Shawn! And I know it hurts, but if you found out that I knew this and hadn't told you, you'd be pissed at me. Hiding things like a cheating boyfriend goes against the girlfriend code of ethics. So can we just . . . hug and make up?"

The lump of pain in Miranda's chest liquefied, and she wanted to cry. Della hated hugging. The fact that she'd do it for Miranda said how much the vampire cared.

Miranda brushed a tear from her cheek. "I'm sorry. I'm . . . I'm not mad at you for telling me about Shawn. And yeah, you're right, I do care. And that's crazy, because . . . because you were right last night, too."

A smile filled Della's eyes. "I'm always right, but . . . what was I right about last night?"

"Your cookie analogy. I'm stuck on Perry and I'm going to break up with Shawn—somehow—but knowing he's buying someone else flowers still hurts. I'm terrible, aren't I?"

Della dropped on the bed. "Not terrible. Just a little sadistic." She chuckled.

When Miranda didn't laugh, Della continued. "Look, it hurt when I thought Steve was seeing someone, too. And I was stuck on Chase, so it's not just you. Just because we don't love them, doesn't mean we don't want them to love us. It's not right, but . . . look at us, how could anyone not love us?"

This time Miranda laughed.

Della picked up one of Miranda's books. "Let me help you."

"I don't think anyone can help. Nothing's sticking!" She palm-butted her head.

"We could sing," Della said.

"Sing?"

"Yeah, you know, make up songs about whatever you're learning. My mom did that to help me. Like that poem song . . ." She started singing. "In fourteen ninety-two Columbus sailed the ocean blue." She hesitated then started again. "Derivatives, derivatives." She snapped her fingers and wiggled her butt with absolutely no rhythm. "It's so fun, it's one prime two plus two prime one."

Miranda fell back on her pillow, laughing harder. "You can't sing worth a flip. I finally found something that Della Tsang sucks at."

Della put her hand over her heart. "What, are you saying my dream of a musical career isn't going to work out?"

When the laugher ended, she looked at Della. "Did Burnett really tell you to shadow me?"

Della nodded. "But don't be mad. It's his peculiar way of saying he loves you. He's worried for your safety."

"Why does everyone treat me like I'm helpless? I helped save Tabitha in Paris, didn't I?"

Della stood from the bed as if arguing required standing. "Yeah, but that was almost like an accident."

"An accident?" That stung like fire ants. "So anytime I do something right, it's an accident?"

Della hesitated before speaking, something the vampire seldom did. "I didn't mean . . . What I meant was that . . . sometimes you goof."

"So now I'm a goofer. For your information, I'm goofing less and less." Miranda recalled what she'd done in the hospital room to her father and mom, and Tabitha's mom. And right then she realized how true her statement was. With a little work, she might even be badass. She might never understand calculus, or get a high score on the damn SAT, but maybe she'd overcome her dyslexia where her powers were concerned. It would be really nice to know she didn't suck at everything.

Della frowned, not so much a pissed-off frown, as a guilty one. "I didn't call you a goofer." Standing in the middle of Miranda's room, she held up her hands. "And yes. You are getting better, but if someone popped into this room to hurt you—"

"I'd do this!" Miranda wiggled her pinky and a cage suddenly appeared around Della.

The thrill of success made Miranda's chest feel lighter. The fact that she'd done it so effortlessly surprised even her. Not to mention the caged vampire.

Della frowned and with tight lips and bright eyes, she pulled the bars apart, stuck her head out, and glared at Miranda. "Now what?"

Feeling extra confident, she wiggled her pinky and another cage fell, this one made of heavier metal.

Della growled and yanked the first set of those bars farther apart, slipped out, and was about to start on the second.

"Wait for it." Miranda smirked and held up her pinky.

"Don't do it!" Della hissed.

The door to the cabin opened. Della sniffed the air. "Kylie, you're right," Della called out. "Miranda's losing it."

"What? Did she say I was losing it?" Miranda asked.

Kylie appeared at the door and saw Della prying her way out of the cage. "Oh, crappers. I'm scared to ask."

"Did you say I was losing it?" Miranda spit out.

Guilt clouded the chameleon's expression. "I said I was worried you were losing it when you thought you had a ghost attached." She looked back at Della. "What's this?"

"I'm just proving a point," Miranda said. "And I'm not losing it. Thank you very much." Or was she? Maybe she *had* to lose it before she found a way to make things right.

"What point?" Kylie asked.

"That I'm not helpless." Miranda frowned. "I could maybe even help you guys find Tabitha." The second the words left her lips, she knew how much she wanted that. She was so damn tired of waiting on the sidelines. She wanted to do something, not sit like a knot on a log and wait for someone to feed her information.

"You want to work for the FRU?" Della asked, making it sound like a joke.

"Maybe." Miranda glared at her. It sure as hell didn't seem like college was an option.

"Seriously?" Kylie said.

"You two don't think I could do it, do you?" Their lack of faith hurt. "I could. I could be good at it."

Della exhaled. "You might be able to zap a cage, but what if someone grabbed you. What if there's more than one and they come at you. You can't say, please don't stab me with that knife while I work up a spell. And you don't know how to fight."

They were right. But . . . "Then teach me."

Della shook her head. "I don't know if . . ."

"Kylie was taught," Miranda interrupted her, looking at the chameleon, hoping she'd take Miranda's side. "You never thought you'd be able to fight, but you learned. Burnett even takes you on missions."

"I kind of did learn." Doubt still clung to Kylie's words.

"See," Miranda said, ignoring the doubt.

Della shot Kylie a wide-eyed gape. "Don't encourage this."

"Pleeeease!" Miranda said. "Kylie knows I'm making perfect

sense." When Della didn't look convinced, Miranda added, "What would it hurt?" And just like that, Miranda latched on to her new goal. She was going to learn to fight.

"If it's the ghost you're afraid of, then fighting isn't going to help," Della said.

"It's not that. Look, even if I don't ever work as an agent, I should be able to protect myself. I'm tired of feeling"—*less than*—"afraid."

Kylie looked at Della. "She's right."

Della's expression softened and Miranda let out a yelp. "When do we start?"

The vampire didn't appear too thrilled. "You've got a broken arm."

"I can still learn. And besides, it should be off in a few days."

"You just got it."

"Witches heal fast, too," Miranda informed her.

"Okay," Della said. "We can do this, but—"

"I don't like buts," Miranda said.

"Well, you are going to have to deal with this one." Della spoke with sass.

Miranda sent the girl the stink eye.

The vamp and chameleon looked at each other as if they were on the same mutual mental wavelength. One Miranda hadn't been invited to join. Probably because the only ones accepted were smart people.

"What's the 'but'?" Miranda asked.

Chapter Twenty-two

"Just tell me already," Miranda demanded.

Kylie spoke up. "For every thirty minutes you spend learning to fight, you spend twice as many studying."

Miranda's backbone stiffened. Were they trying to murder her newfound dream?

"I like it," Della said.

While Miranda had pretty much accepted she wouldn't be going to college, saying it hurt like a zit on her nose. "Look, I don't think this is going to be a shock to you." Her throat tightened. "As a matter of fact, I'll bet the reason you're both doing this is because Holiday told you I wasn't going to make the grade. But I just don't think I have what it takes to . . . make the grade."

"Now that's a bowl of rainbow-colored shit!" Della said.

"It's not." Miranda's sinuses stung with the need to cry.

"Della's right," Kylie added. "Although I don't know about rainbow-colored, but it is shit. You can do this."

Miranda felt one tear slip from her lashes to her cheek—a little wet, a little warm, and a lot woeful. Swallowing, she said what had to be said. "I've tried, guys. You think I want to be left behind? You think I like being . . . stupid?" More tears slipped. "I can't do it." Now her nose started running. Using the sleeve of her pajamas, she wiped it. Her breath shook, but she looked up. "I barely scored thirty percent on the first test." She fist bumped her head. "It's not here."

"You are not going to be left behind." Della's eyes brightened to a vampire pissed-off green.

Kylie agreed and wiped a few tears off her own cheeks.

"I've tried." Miranda appealed to them.

"No, you've quit trying," Della snapped. "You just said you don't think you're going to make it."

"What do you think I'm doing with these books on my bed? Having sex with them?"

"If you are, you're faking it." Della grabbed one of the books. "You just refused to let me help you study. Why? Because you've already thrown in the towel. Who is it that said, if you think you can, you can, and if you think you can't you might as well shit in your cheerios."

"I don't think that's what they said." Kylie, still teary-eyed but now almost snickering, dropped on the bed and took Miranda's hand. "But Della's right."

"I'm always right," Della said.

"You aren't," Kylie said to the vamp. "But I admit you've got a lucky streak going." She looked back at Miranda. "You've kind of thrown in the towel. I understand how hard it is, but if you want this, you've got to fight for it."

"We'll help you," Della said. "I'll teach you songs."

Miranda wiped her tears away again, but more fell. She glanced at Kylie and pointed at the vampire. "She can't sing worth a crap."

Kylie laughed. Della laughed. And Miranda finally followed in.

A few minutes later, they all three lay crossways on the bed, and Miranda had agreed to their terms—agreed to retrieve the towel she'd thrown in the proverbial dirty clothes hamper of her life, the one containing all her other failures.

Time spent learning to fight would equal double study time.

Did she really believe she could do it?

She didn't know, but they were right. Mentally, she'd given up. And that made her a failure even before she failed.

"When I talk, you listen," Della said sounding badass again.

Miranda, Kylie, and Della had walked down by the lake to carry out Miranda's first "fight" lesson.

"I heard you," Miranda said, but in earnest she hadn't been paying close attention. She'd seen a bird flying and her heart and mind went to Perry. It couldn't be him, could it?

"One more time," Della said, "and there will be a test. First you need to know that there are three parts of your attacker's body that are most vulnerable."

She pulled Miranda close, stood a bit to the side and raised her knee, lightly tapping her between her legs. "His boys."

She lowered her leg. "His eyes." She caught Miranda by her temples and lightly pushed her thumbs into her eyes.

"Ouch!" Miranda said.

Della rolled her eyes. "And the throat." Her right palm thrust up and stopped right before smashing Miranda's larynx.

"Got it?" Della asked.

Miranda nodded. "Yeah. Balls, eyes, throat."

"Right." Della sounded proud. "Now did you notice when I busted your balls—"

"Miranda's got balls?" Kylie chuckled.

Della cleared her throat. "This is serious, guys."

"Serious." Miranda wiped the smile off her face.

"Did you notice that when I hit you, I was standing to the side?"

"No," Miranda said. "I didn't notice."

"Well, you'd better. Because if I hit you in the balls, standing right in front of you, you'd probably fall right on top of me and prevent me from escaping."

"I thought they just went like this." Miranda cupped herself and bent her knees down a bit and moaned. "That's what Perry did when I accidently got him."

"No," Della said. "If you'd hit him in the gonads hard enough, and he didn't have balls of steel, he'd've gone down. And a real attacker is gonna be pissed so you don't want to be close to them right then. So for God's sake don't hang around to apologize for doing it or offer them a hug to make 'em feel better."

Miranda glared at Della. "I'm not an idiot."

"No, but you got that soft heart going against you. I've seen you try to doctor a grasshopper you stepped on."

"The grasshopper wasn't attacking me. And Kylie's heart is softer than mine and she manages just fine."

Kylie, now sitting in the grass, checking her phone, looked up with empathy. "My heart's toughened up some."

Della nodded as if her point was proven. "When you go for the eyes, don't go halfway. I showed you how to do it with your thumbs, but if that's not possible use whatever you can. Use your nails. Gouge their eyeballs out."

"But that would blind them, wouldn't it?" Miranda asked.

"Oh, I forgot. That wouldn't be nice, would it?" Della said in mock empathy. "Look! I'm not teaching you how to defend yourself on a kindergarten playground. This is the real McCoy. Someone is trying to kill you, and if you're not willing to kill them first, then just stay a coward."

Della could be so mean! "So you never just try to wound someone instead of killing them?"

Della frowned tighter. "My point is that I don't think about it. If I spent one second trying to figure out how to hurt them less, it's one second of advantage they have to kill me. You understand that, right?"

Miranda nodded. But understanding and liking something were two different things. Not that she was throwing in the towel, but it was something else for her to chew on. Could she really kill someone?

"Now if someone grabs you from behind—"

Della had her arms around her when Miranda's phone rang. Miranda jerked free and yanked her cell out of her back pocket. She'd tried to call her mother again, and got nothing back. Not a peep out of Tabitha, either. Or Perry. It had to be one of them.

Glancing at the cell, she felt her heart sink. Holiday. Probably checking in about ghosts.

"Where are you?" Holiday asked as soon as Miranda hit accept.

"By the lake with Della and Kylie."

"Can you come back to your cabin? I'm here now."

"What's wrong? Do you have bad news?"

Della and Kylie moved closer, no doubt to listen to Holiday's answer with their vampire hearing. When Holiday didn't assure Miranda that everything was right with the world, she knew it wasn't.

She tightened her grip on her phone. "What's wrong?"

Perry spotted Miranda with Della and Kylie by the lake, but before he went to see her, he needed to check in with Burnett.

He'd landed in the thick of the forest, close to the front. He morphed and called Burnett. He'd already texted him earlier and told him that two men were trying to take out Lily Chambers, but now he had to see the man face-to-face.

"Where the hell are you?" Burnett answered.

"Let me talk." Perry started the spiel he'd practiced. "I have news. We need to meet. But I'll only do so if you give me your word you won't try to stop me or put another shadow on me."

He could actually hear the growl of frustration from the vampire's chest. The man literally rattled when upset. "You were almost killed!"

"But I wasn't. Do I have your word or not?"

The silence that followed didn't mean the answer was no, just that Burnett took the question seriously. He never gave his word on a whim because he never went back on it. "Fine. How long before you get here?"

"I'm walking in now."

"I still may kick your ass!" Burnett muttered right before he hung up.

"No you won't." Perry slipped his phone away. "At least I hope not." He'd never pushed Burnett this far.

He hurried around to the gate. Glancing down at his shirt, he considered changing. Surely some of his things were still in his old cabin. But the office door swung open. Burnett, looking completely pissed at forty feet away, stepped out on the porch.

It was show time.

Perry hadn't gotten to the porch when Burnett's eyes brightened, probably due to his . . .

"How bad is it?" He motioned to Perry's shirt. "I'll call Dr. Whitman." He turned as if to make the call.

"No, I'm okay." Perry followed him inside, all the way into Holiday's study. He tugged on the shirt. "Most of this isn't mine." His gut tightened with thoughts of lions and senseless death. "And what is mine, I put there on purpose."

"Why would you . . . ?"

"The agent you sent swooped me out of the bar last night. I had to make it look like she tried to suck me dry." He pulled back his shirt collar and showed off the two puncture wounds he'd made with thorns.

Burnett's lips tightened until they turned white. "Perry, you aren't ready to handle this kind of case."

"I am. What happened at the bar won't happen again."

Burnett raked a hand through his hair and squeezed his neck—a sure sign of stress. Perry continued, "Tell me you haven't come close a couple of times?" He saw the tiny blanket on Holiday's desk and thought of Bell, the waitress. "The baby?" he asked.

"Jenny and Derek are watching Hannah and the little guy at our cabin. How did you end up with him?"

Perry told Burnett about grabbing Bell's phone, calling the babysitter, and then going to give her the news.

Burnett frowned, but didn't tell Perry he'd been wrong. "I've got someone searching for any of Bell Stephens's relatives. Or family to the baby."

Perry dropped his hands in his jeans. "I think you're looking at one."

Burnett's eyes widened. "He's yours?"

"No," Perry said. "I just found out that Jax is my mom's son from another guy. Bell was his ex-girlfriend. That would make the kid my nephew. And it sounds as if Jax is looking for him."

Burnett's shoulders tightened. "Will he be able to trace the kid here?"

Perry, proud of what he'd done, spoke up. "No."

"But the babysitter saw you. You probably even told her your name. You don't think she isn't going to tell Jax if he finds her?"

"Yes, I gave her my name, but not where I was bringing the baby."

"Then you can't go back—"

"Hear me out," Perry said. "I called her as soon as I found this out. She admitted that she knew who the father was and was terrified he'd come looking for her. She thought if a stranger took the baby then Jax wouldn't be able to find him. When I spoke to her this morning, she was about to catch a plane back to Mexico."

Perry reached into his pocket. "Here's Bell's phone. It has the babysitter's number and a Jaxon Bowen's, too."

Perry could tell that Burnett was impressed. He stood there as if filing away everything. He took the phone and nodded. "Miranda said you were meeting with Jax this morning."

"I was, but he called my mom and postponed it until tomorrow. I think he's looking for the baby."

"And you're certain no one else knows you have the baby."

"I'd swear on it," Perry said. "But . . . there's more."

"What?"

"I met my parents at the diner in Houston. Dad told me Jax lived a couple blocks up Jackson Street. I combed the area. I think I've got it narrowed down to five or six houses."

Burnett's shoulders dropped as if the news lightened the baggage he carried. "I'll put a crew together. Depending how close everyone is, it might take an hour. Stay here and you can go with us."

Perry nodded. Knowing that Burnett wasn't trying to push him out sparked a feeling of pride.

The vamp, eyes still bright, grabbed his phone. "Go clean up."

Miranda didn't normally fidget, but sitting still now felt impossible.

Holiday had summoned her back to the cabin because her old professor, the half-witch half-human, who was an all-things-Wiccan expert, had just shown up. She'd told Holiday, "It's imperative I see Miranda."

Miranda sat on her sofa, while Kylie and Della sat at the kitchen table. Holiday had taken the chair. Ms. Wales, who, oddly enough, talked, dressed, and sort of looked like the Queen of England, stood in the middle of the living room, staring down at Miranda through her granny glasses as if she might sprout a second head.

"And the tattoo really goes away when you request it to?"

Miranda nodded. "It has so far."

"Does it pain you?"

"No. It tickles like a bug walking on your skin."

"That must be bloody frightening," the woman said.

"A little," Miranda admitted.

"Can I examine your arm?"

"I have a cast, but sure," Miranda said. The woman sat on the sofa. Miranda held out her arm.

She spent a good thirty silent seconds staring up close and personal at Miranda's arm. Miranda could feel the woman's breath whispering across her skin.

Finally she glanced up. "Miss James has explained about the fortune reader. Have you recalled anything more that she said?"

"No," Miranda answered. "I told Holiday everything."

"So your sister claimed she's gotten the tattoo before, but it faded as soon as the fortune was read?"

"Yes. That's why I think this is somehow due to the fact that she never finished reading mine."

"Puzzling." She stood up and pulled out a photo from her briefcase. Miranda saw that it was an eight-by-ten a printout of her tattoo. The woman studied the image then focused on Miranda.

"Did your sister say the tattoo was exactly like hers?"

"Not exactly. She said mine climbed higher on my arm."

The woman pursed her lips. "Did the fortune-teller react to this?"

"I . . . don't know, that's when everything went crazy. A storm filled the room and the armadillo got loose."

"Armadillo?" The old woman tapped her index finger to her lips as if thinking. "Odd."

"I mentioned that in my message," Holiday said.

"Yes, I am just digesting it." She continued digesting, tapping her lips before focusing again on Holiday. "You said your husband was attempting to find the fortune-teller. Has he had any luck?"

"No," Holiday answered. "But he's not giving up."

Ms. Wales refocused on Miranda. "When the tattoo appears, is it in reaction to anything? Are you experiencing distress or . . . pleasure?"

The way she said pleasure with her English accent made it sound naughty. "Nooo." Miranda heard Della smother a laugh.

Miranda gave the woman's question another consideration. "Wait. It does seems to appear when I'm upset or overwhelmed. But . . ."

"But what?" She leaned in as if holding on to every word Miranda said.

"It's kind of strange that it hasn't appeared with just anyone."

"I'm intrigued. Tell me more."

"It's only shown up in front of my sister, my two close friends, and Perry. When my parents came to the hospital I was afraid they'd see it. That's when I . . . kind of said, 'go away,' and it did. They were there for hours. It didn't come back." Her mind raced. "Oh, but wait, there was the nurse in the hospital. And I didn't know her. So I guess it's not about who's there."

"Still interesting," Ms. Wales said. "Perhaps you trusted this nurse since she was taking care of you."

"Maybe."

The woman went back to digesting. "Have you attempted to ask the tattoo to appear?"

Miranda bit down on her lip. "Why would I? I mean, I'd like it to go away and never come back."

"So you associate the tattoo as a bad thing?" she asked as if puzzled.

"I . . . I associate it as being freaking weird," Miranda spoke honestly.

"I suppose it is a bit peculiar." Ms. Wales paused. "But for the sake of unraveling the mystery, would you be willing to try?"

Miranda looked at Holiday. Holiday looked at Ms. Wales. "Is there a chance it could be harmful?"

"It has not hurt her thus far."

Holiday exhaled. "It's completely up to you, Miranda."

Miranda considered it. While the woman seemed a little off her rocker, she might be the only person to understand what was happening.

"How should I say it?" Miranda asked.

"Politely, I would assume."

Della coughed again.

Miranda, feeling a little stupid and a lot frightened, held out her arm. "Tattoo, come back."

Everyone held their breath. Nothing appeared.

"I don't think it works."

"Very disappointing." The woman went back to tapping her lips. Then she looked up. "Would you mind disrobing?"

"What?" Della and Holiday spoke up at the same time.

Miranda's mind choked on the idea and left her speechless. She was not taking her clothes off.

"Oh, my." The woman glanced at Holiday. "I simply . . . I'm wondering if the tattoo has relocated elsewhere on your body. You may keep your underclothing on."

Miranda met Holiday's befuddled gaze.

Holiday stood up. "Ms. Wales, it's not that I don't trust you, but . . . is there a reason for this? I'm aware that I contacted you, but you didn't answer my call and then you drove all this way as if you know . . . something. Maybe if you explained—"

"Yes, I suppose I should enlighten you." Her thick gray brows tightened. "It might be easier to just show you." She dropped the photos on the sofa and started unbuttoning her blouse.

Miranda's mouth fell open. When she saw the woman's leopard-print Victoria's Secret bra, she almost covered her eyes. Della let out another stifled snicker.

Holiday stood up. But then the old woman pulled her blouse off her shoulder and exposed her upper back and Miranda saw it. Air caught in her throat.

Kylie, Della, and Holiday moved in.

"It's identical," Kylie said.

"No shit, Sherlock," Della said.

Miranda just stared at the swirly, almost vine-like pattern on Ms. Wales's back. "You didn't get that put on there?"

"No, dear. I was told that it appeared when I was only a few months old. My mother, the Goddesses rest her soul, was a mystic witch as was her mother before her. My grandmother died shortly after I was born, so I never knew her. Normally, mystic talent isn't hereditary. And being half human, my gifts are nowhere near that of a mystic witch. That said, it was viewed as extremely odd that the gift was passed on to my mother. Adding to the mystery is that I'm told my grandmother occasionally wore the same tattoo. It came and went, apparently emotionally charged, and at times it covered her from head to toe. Growing up I always assumed the marking was related to my mystic heritage."

"But I'm not . . ." Doubt buzzed like bumble bees in her head. A faint tickle, like a butterfly's breath, moved under her cast. She glanced down fearing the tattoo had returned. It hadn't. Only goosebumps lifted the fine hair on her arms. "I couldn't . . ."

"What dear?" the woman asked, refastening her blouse.

"It's . . . it's probably nothing, but . . ." She looked at Holiday. "Perry said it was as if I called him and he knew I was hurt. And I could swear I heard him, too."

"He told me the same thing," Holiday said.

Miranda glanced back at the older woman. "So . . . you think I'm a mystic?"

The woman's expression was apologetic. "I . . . I didn't mean to insinuate that. I know you would like answers. Unfortunately, I've sought them for the last forty years of my life, unsuccessfully. I've traveled the world and spoken with at least a hundred mystic witches. None have carried these markings." She looked back at Miranda. "To be frank, I've never seen this pattern on anyone other than myself. And now . . . you. That is, if indeed you still have them."

Chapter Twenty-three

Miranda had relented. She'd pulled her shirt up and her pants down. No tattoos were found.

Ms. Wales had left with promises that they would stay in touch and inform each other if anything changed. Holiday walked her out.

Miranda moved to the kitchen table with Kylie and Della, all of them eerily quiet.

And that made Miranda think . . . "She's not here, the ghost's not here, is she?"

"I don't feel her," Kylie said.

"Me, either," Della said. "She probably passed over."

They got quiet again.

"So what the hell is a mystic witch, anyway?" Della asked.

Miranda looked at her. "I'm not a mystic witch." The fact that she'd even considered it was insane. Whatever happened with Perry was . . . a fluke.

"I asked what they are. I didn't say you were one."

"They're powerful in different ways. They can communicate with their minds, no spells required. Telepathic spells are extremely difficult for normal witches."

Kylie popped up and got out three Diet Cokes. "Before I knew

I was chameleon and was exhibiting some witch-related powers, I read a few books on Wiccan traditions. I remember reading about how mystic powers were somehow connected to witches in Salem, right?"

"You mean that witch hunt in 1692?" Della asked.

Miranda took the soda Kylie handed her. "Yeah, legend has it that mystic witches arose from the need to communicate silently during that time. But you heard Ms. Wales, the tattoo isn't related to being mystic."

"True," Kylie popped the top off her soda. "But . . . the tattoo connects you to her, and she comes from a mystic."

"And you have some of that ESP crap going," Della added. "You get those premonitions. That's telepathic."

"No, not really. It's not communicating."

Della opened her drink. "I disagree. When someone tells you bad shit is about to happen, it's communicating."

"I'm not mystic." Miranda said.

Della looked puzzled. "Do you not want to be a mystic witch? Is it bad?"

"It's just silly to even think it. Mystics are powerful. But yes, they are a little weird."

"Then that seals the deal." Della chuckled. "You're weirder than neon-blue shit."

Miranda scowled. "What's your thing with colored shit lately?"

Della shrugged. "I was joking. Kind of. I mean you're kind of powerful. You zapped those cages like bam. And I didn't want to admit it, but that was—" Della tilted her head to the side, sniffed, then smiled. "Your wafer's here."

"Perry?" Miranda asked.

"Oh my." Kylie appeared startled.

"Isn't that just bloody interesting," Della said in a mock English accent. "Maybe the Queen of England was right. Those tattoos are associated with pleaaaasure. Because just after saying his name you're covered in them."

Miranda looked down at her arms. Yup, covered.

Not that it mattered. Perry had seen them. And right now, she wanted to see Perry. Voices echoed from outside.

She didn't mind if Perry saw them but she did mind if anyone else did.

Miranda jumped up. "Send him in my bedroom! Just him."

Perry spoke with Derek and Jenny as they walked past Miranda's cabin. They were a real item now. Perry envied that. He wanted that with Miranda. He turned to her door and knocked. His stomach felt fluttery and light—in a good way.

The last time he'd seen Miranda, he'd kissed her twice. But the whole meeting had been super tense and maybe she'd simply let down her guard.

He really hoped it hadn't been a onetime thing—because she was the one good thing he had going in his mixed-up life.

The door swung open. It wasn't Miranda. Della curtseyed. And Della was so not the curtseying kind. She waved her arm for him to enter as if she were playing a part in a play. "She waits for you in her bedchambers, my dear."

Okay, she wasn't just acting strange, she was talking strange. He grinned. "You're weird."

She looked back at Kylie. "Just like my friend, Miranda." Accent hanging on, she waved an arm toward Miranda's bedroom door. "Go. You have been summoned."

Kylie laughed.

"What?" He sensed he'd missed part of a joke. Or was the joke on him? He recalled Miranda somehow knowing he'd kissed Bell. This morning, she'd seemed to believe him about only kissing her for an alibi, but maybe now . . .

"Everything is bloody fine." Della laughed. "Your girl is just covered in pleeeaasure tattoos. For your eyes only."

Perry didn't follow, but . . . "Her tattoos are back?"

Kylie nodded.

Was that freaking Miranda out? It would him.

He started toward her door, then remembered and turned around. "Burnett wants you and Kylie in the office. Now."

"Trouble?" Della lost her accent.

"He'll explain."

Miranda's door swung open. Hungry for the sight of her, he turned. And what a sight. She stood there in running shorts and a pink tank top. Every inch of bare skin was covered in pale tattoos. He'd never thought of himself as a tattoo-loving guy, but that could change. It had changed. She looked . . . hot.

Before he could stop himself, he envisioned her naked and with the pink swirly pattern painting her curves.

"Hey." He wanted to move in for a kiss, but hesitated. Miranda didn't like to be pushed. Nudged, maybe. Pushed, no. But there was a fine line between those two.

"You okay?" she asked.

"Yeah. I promised I would be, didn't I?"

She stared at him. Just being in the same room somehow lightened the weight he'd flown here with.

"We'll go," Della said.

Perry had completely forgotten they were still there.

"The room reeks of pheromones." Della chuckled.

"Drop it," Miranda snapped.

"Come on." Kylie used her "bad Della" tone and she caught the vampire's elbow and pulled her out.

Just before Kylie shut the door, Della called back. "Hey, bird boy, you can thank me later."

Perry looked back at Miranda. "What do I need to thank her for?"

Miranda rolled her eyes. "With Della? Who knows?" She glanced away quickly as if it wasn't altogether true. But that was okay. Girls kept secrets.

Realizing they stood in silence and were completely alone, he let his gaze move over her again, taking in every painted inch. Like a canvas, her body was covered. "So they're back."

"Yup."

"I'd say they kind of look hot, but I'm not sure you want to hear that."

"I don't." She frowned. "They freak me out."

"Can you still make them go away?"

"Don't know." She looked down at her feet in flip-flops. "Go away."

A spot of bare skin appeared on the top of her feet and chased the tattoos up her legs leaving clear skin. In a few seconds, the tattoos were off her arms and face.

"Have you learned anything about them yet?" he asked.

She frowned. "One of Holiday's old college professors, an Englishwoman, was here, but she didn't have answers, just more questions." Miranda told him about the woman's tattoo and what she said about her mother and grandmother being mystic witchs.

"That explains Della's accent?" He grinned.

"She can be such a twit."

He considered what else Miranda had told him. "I still say you called me when you were hurt. So maybe—"

"It was a fluke."

He remembered her knowing about the kiss, and wondered if that was a fluke, too. He started to mention it, but bringing up the kiss didn't seem smart.

Then when he least expected it, she stepped closer. Closer was good. Perry wished she'd walk into his arms. Let him pull her against him. He needed it as much as he sensed she did. But again, he didn't want to push.

Flipping her hair off her shoulder, he shifted his gaze to the curve of her neck. Everywhere he looked at her she had curves and he longed to explore each and every dip and valley. The earlier image he created flashed in his mind. So beautiful, so naked.

"Perry?"

"What?" He realized she'd been talking while he'd been enjoying . . .

"I asked if you found anything out."

"Yeah. I—"

"Tabitha? Did you find anything out about her?" Desperation sounded in her voice.

He wished he had news on that. He wanted to be her hero.

"No. But I think I have a location on the guy who's behind the robberies. We're about to go there now."

Worry filled her eyes. "I've texted her like five times today. She hasn't answered. Do you still think Tabitha's with Anthony?"

"There's no reason not to believe it," he offered. And with everything he had, he hoped it was true.

She nodded. "Are you really okay?"

He considered telling her about his newly found family member, but she had enough to worry about.

"I feel better just seeing you." He smiled.

He moved in another few inches. When she didn't back up he brushed her reddish-blond hair off her shoulder and let his hand linger against the soft curve of her neck "Are you okay? Between your sister and the tattoo stuff, it can't be easy on you."

"It's not," she said. "But I'm not cratering. As a matter of fact, I've talked Della and Kylie into teaching me to fight."

"Fight, fight?" he asked.

"Yeah, and don't look as if you don't think I can do it."

"No, it's not . . . You just never seemed interested in that kind of stuff."

"Well, I'm interested now. I think it might be hard to kill someone, but at least I'll be able to protect myself."

He grinned. "With your tattoos, you'll really look like a badass."

His phone chirped with a text. "I'm sure that's Burnett. I should go." He inched back to the door.

She came a little closer. "Are you coming back with Burnett?"

"It depends on what happens."

She glanced up. He glanced down. Her lips looked so fresh, so sweet. "I really wish you'd just come back with him."

Her request brought part pleasure, part pain. "I really like that you want me to. But I can't come home until this is finished. I need you to understand that."

She nipped at her lip. Holy hell, he wanted to kiss her. He dipped his head.

She did one slight shuffle back.

Damn that hurt. "Are we . . . still good?"

The second it took for her to answer felt long, empty, and it left a hole in life's plans.

She finally nodded. "Yeah."

"Can I kiss you?" He didn't like the insecurity in his voice, but that slight shuffle away had seemed intentional.

"A hug," she said. "Before we . . . I need to . . . I . . . soon."

She hadn't made a lick of sense, but "soon" sounded promising.

"I'll take a hug." He moved closer, didn't stop until his tennis shoe bumped the toe of her pink flip-flop. He folded her into his arms. She melted against him.

Soft where he felt hard.

Warm where he felt cold.

Whole where he felt incomplete.

Perfect where he felt broken.

He buried his face into her hair and inhaled. She smelled like flowers, vanilla, and berries rolled into one. She'd smelled like that the first summer camp when he'd met her. He was pretty certain he'd been in love with her since then.

She stirred slightly in his arms.

He didn't want to let her go. Ever.

Yet before he played the forever card, he had to fix what felt broken inside him. Only then could he truly be someone she deserved.

· · ·

Alone, Miranda had studied longer than her agreement required. She'd even made up a jingle about algebra to help her remember. Crazy as it was, singing helped. Della was going to love hearing that.

Then she walked around the cabin checking under beds and behind furniture, calling, "Here armadillo, armadillo, armadillo." Chester and Socks kept circling her, probably confused by her come-here-kitty voice.

Not that the voice helped. She never found the armadillo. Unfortunately, she did find a few mummified hairballs.

Kylie had texted to say she and Della had gone with Burnett and wouldn't be home until real late. This was why Miranda wanted to learn to fight. She wanted to help, too.

Then she remembered . . . She texted Kylie back asking if Shawn was with them.

He hadn't been. Which meant Miranda had a job to do. A job that was . . . even less desirable than removing crusty hairballs.

Miranda had only done the breaking up thing with one guy in her entire life. Herold Hanker. He'd been devastated, which made her devastated. How could she not be when he'd gone on a hunger strike, claiming he'd die of starvation if she didn't take him back? And yes, he'd skipped lunch but then their kindergarten teacher had passed out Girl Scout cookies. Obviously, Herold loved Thin Mints more than he did her.

Still, she hated the thought of making someone feel as if they weren't good enough. It hurt. She knew. She'd lived with that feeling for as long as she could remember.

Knowing Shawn was hot on the chase of another girl should have eased her guilt. It didn't.

His interest in another girl made her mad.

The thought of breaking up with him made her feel bad.

One sentiment didn't nullify or lessen the other. Guilt and anger didn't play well together.

What was she going to say? *I'm so sorry I don't want you in my life, but how dare you want someone else in your life before I walked out of yours.*

Well, that wouldn't work.

Postponing it wouldn't make it any easier, so she wrote him a text. Then deleted it. Deleted the next three. She'd even written one just calling things off. Then deleted it.

Text breakups were tacky. Tempting, but tacky. She finally wrote one and hit send: *What time do you get off?*

The three dots appeared on her phone, dancing on the screen. Dancing. Dancing. Dancing. The text finally appeared.

Ten.

Why had that taken ten minutes to type one word? It hit then. Did he know that she intended to break up with him?

Before she chickened out, she sent: *Can you come by?*

The dots started dancing again. His reply finally came.

Ok.

Della must have said something to Shawn about the flowers. Frankly, now that she considered it, she'd be surprised if the vampire hadn't said something.

Shawn had to know Della would tell Miranda.

Was he sweating bullets? Miranda, the Angry Miranda thought, good. Guilty Miranda thought he shouldn't feel bad because she was going to make him feel worse.

Guilty Miranda also reminded her that she'd kissed Perry twice while being with Shawn.

Angry Miranda reminded her that she hadn't bought Perry anything and . . . Why hadn't Shawn bought Miranda flowers when she'd been in the hospital?

Coward Miranda—yeah she had that side of her, too—actually considered just telling him it was over and letting him assume it was all on him.

Honest Miranda—she wasn't all bad—knew she couldn't do that. He deserved the truth.

Not that she believed the old adage that the truth would set you free.

Sometimes the truth was sharp and jagged and could gut you.

Take her mom and Miranda's argument for example.

With that thought, she pushed Shawn concerns aside and tried to call her mom again. Still no answer. No text this time, either.

Miranda kept hearing the spiteful words she'd tossed out. She kept seeing the look on her mom's face when they made a direct hit right to her pride, to her heart.

Yes, those words had been true, but . . . Miranda had used the truth as a weapon. And that wasn't right.

Anxious now about her mom, she called her dad. Not to dump her problems on him, but to assure herself she still had one parent who loved her.

They commiserated over their concern for Tabitha. When she went to tell him the new information, he informed her he already knew. Burnett had been calling him with updates every few hours. No doubt her father had demanded it. And Burnett had indulged him—probably because Burnett was a father, too.

Still, she'd have to thank Burnett later—indulging people wasn't the vampire's norm.

"How's your mom?" her dad asked, opening up the can of worms she'd tried to cap.

Guilt had her heart swelling up in her throat. "Uh, I called her several times and all I got was a text saying she'd call later."

"That's not like her." Concern rang in his voice.

Don't tell him. Don't tell him. "She's mad at me. She hates me." The words fell out.

"No, hon', she's mad at me."

"No, I'm pretty sure I'm on her shit list, too." Miranda gave him the short version.

"Miranda! How could you say that? You have no right to—"

Her chest ached with regret. "I know . . . I was angry."

With his next breath, her father said, "I'm sorry. I didn't mean to blame you. It's not your fault. Your mom . . . can be difficult. But you know, I never told her I was married. I lied. I did this to her. I should have handled things differently. From the very beginning, I . . . screwed up."

Her father's quick defense of her mom spoke volumes and even eased the parents-breaking-up heaviness in her chest.

Maybe her parents weren't finished. Then she wondered . . . would it be fair to help things along? It wouldn't take much. She could probably do it with just . . .

It fell out. "Should you call her or better yet go check on her? I mean, I hurt her and she's alone and . . . I'm worried." It wasn't a lie, but she recognized a ploy when she played one.

Was that wrong?

Maybe? Probably. Hadn't she gotten angry at her mom for wanting to do the same thing? She waited for the you've-done-wrong feeling to hit.

No hit.

Heck, with everything so wrong in her life, maybe her moral compass was on the fritz. Nothing felt right.

Except Perry.

He was the one thing that felt right.

"Bloody hell. I'm sorry," his father said, bringing Miranda out of her mental stupor. "My business phone is ringing. Let me go. I'll call you after I see your mom."

He hung up.

And his last words hung in the air. *Bloody hell. Bloody hell.* She stood there with the phone in her hand, connecting some mental dots that should've connected immediately.

Her father was from England. Ms. Wales was from England. Could they . . . somehow come from the same family lineage?

Chapter Twenty-four

Perry pulled out his phone to check the time. It was almost nine when Burnett parked the large white utility van in front of the yellow Victorian house on Jackson Street. They weren't completely sure it was Jax's house, but when Burnett went through city records and discovered it was owned by a corporation, he'd decided to move forward.

Perry looked out the window in the back of the van. The gated neighborhood had no streetlights. Night had settled in. The golden hue of tungsten lights spilled from the home's windows. The scene looked like a page out of a fairytale book—a happy place where children played, laughed, and were loved.

Perry saw through it. Knew it for what it was. A façade. A mask to hide evil.

Burnett swiveled in his seat and commenced with outlining his plan.

"Why can't I just shift and go in?" Perry asked. "I can give you a count of how many are in there."

He really thought Burnett was making this more complicated than it should be. Dressed in orange jumpsuits with the gas company's emblem on them, seven of them were in the van: Burnett, Kylie, Della, Hayden Yates—a chameleon and teacher at the school—Chase, Perry, and Stephanie Tobler, the vampire agent who saved his ass at the bar.

Their objective wasn't to go in with guns blazing.

Not that they didn't have guns. At least the official agents were armed.

Burnett made it clear that until they knew for sure that this was Jaxon's home, and exactly what they were up against, they weren't storming the house. If there were more than four perps, Burnett was calling for backup from Houston FRU.

While Perry had been cleaning up and visiting with Miranda, Burnett ran his half brother through the system. Burnett wasn't happy with what the system turned up.

Jaxon Bowen was on the most-wanted list of the FRU. Only twenty-two years old, he had more felony offenses than he had years. He'd been the leader of three unscrupulous gangs in the Houston and Dallas areas that the FRU had managed to shut down. Jax had ultimately escaped all three times. And whatever he was involved in now, Burnett suspected it was equally devious.

No one said it, but everyone thought it. If Anthony and Tabitha were somehow mixed up with Jax, chances were the only thing they'd be bringing home were their bodies. Perry couldn't imagine how much that would hurt Miranda.

"I could be in and out in no time," Perry continued.

"But Kylie and Hayden can go in invisible," Burnett said.

"I'm practically invisible when I shift."

Burnett's jaw tightened. "Jax is a shifter, and a damn good one. The first thing he'll look for is another shifter. Everyone else," Burnett said, "will stay in the van, unless I call you. Got it?"

Perry nodded. It made sense, but he didn't like being put on standby when he'd been the one to give them the lead. It fed his insecurity. Burnett still didn't trust him.

Burnett continued. "There's a pipeline easement in the back of the house. About five minutes ago, someone called and let the residents know that there was a report of a gas leak in the area, and that we'll be out checking. I'll ask whoever opens the door to let me into their backyard. Kylie and Hayden, invisible, will search the house while I'm out back. I'll give them a few minutes and then I'll knock and let the homeowners know all is well, Hayden and Kylie will come out with a report. They'll never know we were there." He slipped a baseball hat on his head. His pattern now hidden.

"And what if there's another vamp or were inside and they get your scent?" Perry asked, now turning into the one with concerns.

"Houston has a large vampire population in the city. Just being a vampire shouldn't set off any red flags. If trouble strikes, I'll call."

Kylie and Hayden went invisible. Burnett walked out, leaving the door open long enough for them to follow.

Perry gazed back to the window. The curtain in one of the downstairs rooms fluttered. "They know we're here. They're watching. Should we . . . ?"

"We wait until he calls us," Agent Tobler said.

The door to the house opened and Burnett disappeared inside.

"I don't like this." Perry's gut said something wasn't right. He held a gulp of oxygen in his lungs. Before he let it out, a blast of gunfire exploded in the night.

Miranda was almost to Holiday's cabin when her phone beeped with a text. Tabitha? Snatching it out of her pocket, she felt her hopes die when she saw Holiday's number.

Can you come over?

Instead of texting back, she bolted up the steps and knocked.

The sound of a baby's cry reached Miranda's ears. The door to the cabin swung open.

"That was fast," Holiday said.

"I was coming to see you."

Holiday nodded. "Can you take him?" She handed Miranda the baby. "Dealing with two kids is a job."

Using her casted arm, Miranda pulled the wiggling baby close. Holiday went to get a whimpering Hannah out of her high chair.

Miranda pushed the door closed, but not before noticing how the trees seemed to move in the breezeless night. She'd been aware of them all the way over here. When had she gotten paranoid of trees?

Holiday pulled Hannah into her arms. "It's okay," she whispered and then looked back at Miranda. "I texted you because I remembered something that could link you to Ms. Wales."

"That's why I came here, too." Miranda sat down in Holiday's rocker and pulled the unhappy baby closer. "I don't know why I didn't think about it immediately."

"How would you know . . . Wait, what do you see as a link?" Holiday asked.

Miranda ran a finger over the baby's soft cheek. "That Ms. Wales is from England and so is my dad. We could be . . . related somehow."

Holiday sat on the sofa, holding a very sleepy Hannah. "I didn't think about that, either."

"Then what did you come up with?" Miranda asked.

"When I was taking her class in college, Ms. Wales mentioned that she was dyslexic."

"And she's a professor?" Miranda asked a little shocked.

"I told you just because you are dyslexic doesn't mean you aren't—"

"Smart. I know," Miranda said, she just found it hard to believe. "I guess it is weird both of us being dyslexic."

"Right. It could mean nothing. But . . ." Holiday paused. "Because dyslexia can be hereditary, it gives your assumption that you two could be distant relatives more credibility."

"Yeah, I guess." Miranda looked down at the baby in her arms. He'd quieted and now looked up at her with wide light-gray eyes. "He's not as ugly as I thought he was."

"I think I see Perry in him," Holiday said.

Miranda nearly choked on air. "Perry?" Hadn't he completely dismissed her crazy assumption that—

"He didn't tell you?" Holiday asked.

Perry had a baby? "No."

"He's pretty sure that the baby's father is his half brother."

Her words floated around Miranda's head a few seconds before she deciphered them. "I wasn't even aware he had a half brother."

"He just found out. Jax, the one behind all this, is his mother's son from an earlier marriage."

Miranda nodded, but didn't like that she was learning things about Perry that he should've told her. She recalled their quick visit. He'd spent most of the time worrying over her. He probably hadn't told her because he hadn't wanted to toss his own problems on her. Didn't he know she wanted him to toss them on her?

"Let me put Hannah down." The fae disappeared into a bedroom.

Miranda stared at the baby that did kind of look like Perry. She wondered if one day she'd hold Perry's baby. While having a baby was several years away, she wanted to have children.

And if what she felt for Perry was real, and she felt pretty damn certain it was, he truly might be her life mate.

An image of him with pain in his eyes flashed in her head. Her life mate had to be hurting. She considered how her argument with her mom stung, how her lingering hurt toward her dad ate at her conscience. She could not fathom how it would feel to know your parents and now a half brother were criminals. How would it feel to be the one sending them to prison?

Holiday walked back in.

Miranda looked up. "I'm worried about Perry being caught up in all this."

Holiday sank into a chair. "We're all worried. But Burnett tried everything to get him to pull back."

The room fell silent. The baby in her arms suddenly felt warmer.

"Has your father done your family tree?" Holiday asked.

Miranda looked up from the sleeping child. Her question had her train of thought doing U-turns. "I . . . I don't know. Up until I found out Tabitha was my sister, I didn't even know his real name was . . . Evans." Just saying it stirred up some of her still present resentment.

"Would you be okay if I asked Ms. Wales if she has any Evans lineage in her family? I don't know if she's done her family tree, but I get a feeling she would have."

"That'd be fine," Miranda said. "And . . . I'll ask my dad if he has one."

Holiday's gaze shifted to the baby. "You seem to have the right touch with him. He didn't fall asleep for me."

"He's probably just exhausted." But Miranda liked the idea of her having a knack with babies.

"She doesn't seem worried about you anymore, either."

Miranda looked up. "She?" Right then Miranda felt the bone-deep cold that could only mean one thing—a ghost was present.

The gunshot hadn't stopped ringing in Perry's head when Agent Tobler bolted up. "Perry, Chase take the back. Della and I are taking the front."

Perry didn't hesitate. But no way in hell could he keep up with a reborn vampire. By the time Perry got to the fence, Chase was on the other side.

He started to leap over the fence when he heard yelling.

"Move and I'll fill your friend with enough lead he'll glow."

Floodlights brightened the backyard. "Who the hell are you two?" a dangerous voice asked.

Perry backed against the house. Heart slamming against his ribs, he peered through the fence. He saw three guys holding guns. No, not just guns. AK-47 rifles. All were aimed at Burnett. Air locked in his chest, making breathing impossible. His need to morph, to protect the man who'd been a brother to him, singed his veins. His skin crawled.

He held back. One wrong move could get Burnett killed. He gathered every ounce of willpower he had, held on to it with an iron fist.

He recalled the number one rule Burnett had taught him when he'd been working with him last summer. *Assess before acting.*

He leaned in again, peered through the fence slats. He checked the armed guys' patterns. Human? What the hell?

He'd take human over supernatural, but those assault rifles could be just as deadly as a rogue.

"Who are you?" one of the jerks spoke up again. When no one answered, he put his gun to Burnett's head.

Damn! Perry needed to do something. Fast. "Who sent you?" One of the other guys asked Chase. "You with the Bloods?"

"We're here to check on the gas line." Chase glanced left and right as if looking for a way to take the three down before they filled Burnett with holes. Then his eye cut to the fence. He knew Perry was there.

He recalled another piece of advice Burnett had given him. *If you have to morph—and I mean dire circumstances—make it something no one in their right mind would ever believe if the story gets repeated.*

Voices erupted from inside the house; the three men looked back. Perry morphed. A fraction of a second later, he marched his pink polka dotted elephant ass through the fence.

All three guys turned their guns on him. Not that it surprised Perry. He knew going in he'd be shot.

Loud pops sounded and chunks of dirt flew up. Perry took one, two, three bullets. Two in his front right leg. One in his face. That one hurt. Hurt all the way into his tusks. Not that he regretted his decision.

The second they took to shoot at his pink butt was all the distraction Chase and Burnett needed. They unarmed and tossed the three men to the ground—none too softly. Then Burnett pulled out his gun, and without hesitation, shot, and rendered all three unconscious.

"You okay?" Burnett asked Perry.

Perry moved his trunk up and down, and shifted his weight off his right leg. "Just flesh wounds." *Oh, but they hurt like hell!*

In the next breath of silence, gunfire erupted from the house. Burnett and Chase shot back inside. In their wake were Burnett's words, "If they wake up, sit on them!"

Or had he said . . . shit? Perry surmised that either one would work.

Fifteen seconds later, Burnett stuck his head out. "Change."

Perry did, but gritted his teeth, knowing it would hurt like hell. Oh, there would be no injury, no blood. But the pain would linger for a good thirty seconds. It always did.

The second he'd morphed, Burnett was at his side.

Perry leaned forward, bracing his palms on his slightly bent knees. He breathed in, and tried not to puke.

"You okay?" Burnett asked.

"Fine," Perry gritted out. He'd barely stood up when Della, Agent Tobler, Chase, Kylie—slightly glowing—and Hayden all walked outside with four more guys who didn't look any older than Perry. But like the unconscious guys on the ground, they were all human, all with matching dragon tattoos on the sides of their necks.

This wasn't making sense. Had they gotten the wrong house? If not, what the hell was Jax doing hanging out with a human gang?

"There's bags of white powder inside," Della said.

Burnett looked at Chase and Agent Tobler. "Tranquilize 'em. I'm calling for a bus."

Miranda headed back to her cabin, not sure what scared her the most. The feeling that the trees were watching her, or the thought that it might be the ghost.

Fear of a ghost was a reasonable phobia. Her sudden paranoia of trees? Not so much. With everything going on, was she cracking under the pressure?

She remembered asking Holiday before she left. "Is the ghost here because of me?"

"I think it's the baby," Holiday had said. "But I admit it is odd that you've been present both times she's shown up."

Odd? More like freaky. Freaky scary.

Holiday's fae mental feelers must have felt Miranda's fear, because the woman offered to call someone to walk Miranda back to her cabin. Wanting to fake being brave, hoping it might actually make it so, Miranda had refused.

She hurried down the footpath through the woods, not looking at the large oaks, whose limbs appeared like arms reaching for her. She stopped once, when she heard the creek water rushing. She hurried on.

Footsteps, not her own, echoed in the distance. Faking it wasn't making it.

She told herself it was probably just another camper. Told herself she was overreacting.

She couldn't shake the feeling that she needed to run.

She started jogging, thinking only of getting back to the safety of her cabin, but rounding the bend in the path, the footsteps grew louder. Closer.

She stopped. Air caught in her lungs. She considered running back to Holiday's, but her own cabin was closer. She took off again, feet thudding against dirt, and that's when she saw a figure coming right at her.

In the back of her mind, she heard Della say, *Balls, eyes, and throat.*

Chapter Twenty-Five

"Miranda?"

Shawn's voice had her panic rolling off her but a newfound panic rolling in. She had to break up with him.

"I didn't think you'd be here until ten."

"I got off early."

"But you were walking away from my cabin," she said.

"You weren't there." He sounded guilty.

She knew why. He'd wanted to avoid seeing her. "You should have texted me."

"Probably."

She started walking. His steps moved in rhythm with hers. The sound of crickets singing filled the night air.

Her mind raced, searching for a way to tell him what needed to be said. Something that sounded right. Nothing came to her.

"How's your arm?" he asked.

"It doesn't even hurt anymore."

"That's good."

"Have you heard anything about my sister?"

"No, sorry."

They walked the rest of the way to her cabin in silence. She moved up the porch steps and on the last step she almost tripped when she saw what was left outside her door.

Flowers.

He'd bought her flowers. Now.

A spark of anger flickered inside her.

She turned. He stood there watching her.

"I . . . didn't get a chance to have any delivered to you when . . ."

He stopped talking as if just now realizing what a mistake he'd made.

She walked to the side of the porch, dropped down, and dangled her feet off the edge.

She felt him sit down beside her.

She waited to see if he'd say anything. The silence felt thick. An awkward kind of sadness filled the air. Something was about to end. She hated endings.

Even when they were right.

She pulled her up big-girl panties. "We need to talk—"

"I brought her flowers because I felt bad," he blurted out. "I was in charge of protecting her. She got shot. It was meant to be a nice gesture, not a romantic one."

Miranda looked at her flip-flops hanging from her feet. "You liked her, too. Della told me. She said that Chase and Lucas had smelled it earlier."

He exhaled with a whoosh. Frustration laced the tense sound. "She's pretty. I was attracted to her, but I wasn't acting on it. And it's not fair for you to blame me for just thinking . . . Guys can't control that especially when . . ." He pulled his lips into his mouth.

"When what?" she asked.

"When you haven't been willing to take things to the next level." He shook his head. "I'm sorry. I . . . You have all the right in the world to take as much time as you need. What's important here is that . . . I didn't do anything."

She looked right into his soft blue eyes. And she saw it.

"Then why do you feel guilty?"

He glanced off into the woods. "Maybe because I knew Della was going to blow this out of proportion."

"Or maybe . . . ," Miranda said, "you really like the girl. More than you like me."

He ran a hand over his face. "I've been crazy about you for years."

She scrunched her toes, feeling her flip-flop falling off. "I was crazy about you, too. But that's not enough, is it?"

He frowned and then looked . . . angry. "This isn't about me, is it? It's about Perry?"

Suddenly the flip-flop was on the other foot. She had the guilt now. "No." The word tasted like a lie. "Not completely."

"Define 'not completely,' " he said in a judgmental voice.

She searched for the right words.

He didn't give her enough time. "You guys are back together, aren't you?"

"Not officially."

"Define 'officially.' "

It was the first time she'd heard Shawn sound so angry. She felt terrible. Her chest felt weighty. But he deserved an answer. "I needed . . . to tell you that I didn't think—"

His frown deepened. "How dare you make me feel bad when you're already with . . ."

"I'm not with him." She wished she could say they hadn't even kissed. She couldn't. He stared at her as if it was her fault. She didn't feel at fault. But she did feel guilty. She was hurting him. She hated hurting people.

Hated.

Hated.

Hated it.

She reached deep and found the one defense she had. "When you asked me out the first time, I told you I wasn't ready. Or that I wasn't over . . . everything."

He jumped up, as if to leave. He didn't. Stopping at the other end of the porch, he stood there staring out.

After several birdcalls and a few cricket songs, he faced her. "You're right. I rushed you. I just thought . . . we were perfect for each other."

He came and dropped back down beside her. Just not as close. That little half of an inch between them said a lot. He'd accepted it.

"We're both Wiccan," he said. "Share the same moral principles. Your parents like me, and mine . . ."

His pause confirmed what she'd always known. "And your parents don't like me. Your mom doesn't."

Guilt filled his eyes again.

"Why doesn't she like me?" Were Miranda's fumbled spells common knowledge to everyone?

He finally spoke up. "She found out your parents weren't married."

"Wow," Miranda said. "I thought it was because . . . I'm a screwball. I didn't even consider that." She chuckled. "That makes me feel better."

He looked at her as if she'd lost her mind, and considering the stress she was under, it was a possibility.

Before she could stop herself, she said, "Can you imagine what your mom is going to think about you dating the Lily girl who's part human and vampire?"

He frowned. "I told you, I'm not interested in her."

Miranda looked at him and saw the truth again. "I'm not trying to be ugly. But I think you are interested. You might not have acted on it, but now that we're not . . . together, I'd like you to be happy." And she meant it, too. Angry Miranda had completely left the building.

"I'm sorry," she blurted out.

"For what?" he asked.

"For being upset about the flowers thing. I didn't have that right."

He focused on the woods again. "I was attracted to her more than I should have been."

"Then why not . . . try to make it work with her?"

He laughed. "We just broke up and already you're trying to fix me up with someone? That's just wrong."

"You're a great guy, Shawn. You deserve to be happy. Della said it wasn't just *your* pheromones polluting the air."

He seemed to consider that. Then he shook his head. "It wouldn't work."

"Why? Because she isn't all Wiccan?"

"No. Well . . . maybe."

Miranda studied him. "I didn't think you were prejudiced?"

"I'm not. I just think it would be easier to be with someone of my own kind."

"Easier isn't always the best choice." Perry wasn't easy. And he was right for her.

"My mom wouldn't . . ." He bit down on his lip again.

"I didn't see you as a mama's boy, either."

He made a scratchy disapproving sound that came from the back of his throat. "I'm not."

"Then decide what *you* want. Don't let your mother's opinions override what you feel."

While waiting for the bus to arrive to take the unconscious gang members to the Houston FRU headquarters, Perry had gotten a text from his dad informing him that tomorrow's meeting with Jax wasn't happening until four.

Why? Was Jax busy moving? He texted his dad back: *Meet you at three.*

But damn it, Perry had really hoped it would have been finished tonight. Burnett hoped to get something from the prisoners, but Perry's gut said it was a wash.

The Houston FRU headquarters wasn't that different from the one in Fallen. Except the rules. The only one allowed to watch the interviews was Agent Tobler. Hayden had left.

The rest of them were directed to the waiting room. Perry hadn't been in the mood to sit. Instead he informed them he was going to fly around to blow off steam. His gut hadn't unknotted from the whole takedown. Or maybe it wasn't just that.

Maybe it was everything.

He had a brother who excelled at murder. His mom was an evil bitch. His father . . . that's the one that hurt. He almost seemed to care.

And Perry was about to get all their asses tossed in prison.

They deserved it.

He had to do it.

Yet he still wasn't even sure what it was supposed to prove. Or was it even about proving anything? Was Burnett right? Perry sought revenge?

He found a spot in back of the building, shifted, and took flight.

The moon hung heavy in the sky. He flew high, low, darted through trees. He flew hard. He flew until he didn't think about anything but how good it felt to soar. Flew, until the weight he carried in his heart felt as light as the feathers on his back.

Landing in the same place, he shifted back, ran a hand through his windblown hair, and went to find everyone.

He walked in, nodded at Kylie, Della, and Chase, and plopped down in a chair.

"You heard anything?" he asked.

Della chuckled. "Yeah, there's been sightings of a pink polka dotted elephant in the area."

"Seriously?" Had someone besides the three perps seen him? Burnett was going to be pissed. Perry had messed up again.

"No," Della laughed. "I just think it's funnier than hell."

He sat back in the chair. "It's not funny."

"Why shift into that?" Chase asked, a smile in his voice, even when it wasn't on his face.

"Why do you care? I saved your asses, didn't I? I took the bullets instead of you or Burnett."

Chase sobered quickly. "Yeah you did. We're fast, but I'm not sure we're as fast as three AK-47s. I didn't mean to piss you off."

Silence filled the room, an uncomfortable silence that Perry had caused. He'd sounded like a jerk.

"I almost went with the purple hippo," he said in a dead serious voice. "But the elephant felt much classier." Everyone laughed. Even himself. And just like that, the chip slid off his shoulder.

He was good at that, making people laugh so he could laugh.

He recalled Miranda accusing him of joking about things to hide how he really felt. It wasn't altogether true. He didn't joke to hide the hurt. He joked so he could deal with it. Otherwise it would eat a hole through him.

"Why not a lion?" Kylie asked. "I've seen you as a lion and that was scary."

"Just following orders," Perry said.

"Orders?" Della asked. "You had orders to turn yourself into a pink elephant?"

"Burnett told me if I ever had to morph around humans to make it something no one would believe."

"Then you did a damn good job," Chase said. "I can't imagine one of those dudes telling some cell mate, 'And then a pink polka dotted elephant busted through the fence.'"

Burnett walked out right then. "That's pretty much what they said." His gaze found Perry. "Good job."

"We got anything to go on?" Perry asked.

"I'll update everyone on the ride back."

"So I got my ass shot for nothing?" *Freaking hell!*

"Not exactly." Burnett motioned to the door.

When they got outside, the big sky beckoned Perry. The last thing he wanted to do was crawl back into that van. He almost told Burnett he wouldn't be making the trip. Then he remembered he didn't have to meet his parents until three. Going back now, he might see Miranda again.

So yeah, he'd be climbing his ass back into the van. Time with Miranda would do him better than a week of flying.

Burnett got behind the wheel; Perry crawled in the front, the others in the back. Burnett pulled out of the parking lot and started talking. "The gang's called the Dragons. They've been a thorn in HPD's paw for a year. They hadn't been able to collar them. Now they have."

"So it was the wrong house?" Perry asked.

"Right house. A day late."

"What?" Della asked.

Burnett looked in the rearview mirror. "There's a Web site where people sell things under-the-table. The former owner put the house up for auction to the highest bidder. Furniture and all. Around eleven last night, the gang dropped a couple hundred thousand dollars for a house worth close to a million. All seven of the members told the same story. So it's credible."

"Why would Jax sell the house for less than it's worth?" Perry asked.

Burnett cut his eyes to Perry. "It makes sense if he's on to you and knows we were about to hit."

"No," Perry said. "I haven't even met him yet."

Burnett stopped at a light. "You said that Caleb Davidson suspected you."

"You got his full name?" Perry asked.

"I was able to run him down," Agent Tobler said from the back. "His record is almost as long as your brother's."

"You find him?" Perry asked her.

"Not yet," Burnett answered. "But let's not change the subject. If Jax knows—"

"Jax sent Caleb packing," Perry said. "Why would he do that if he bought what the guy said about me?" Perry pulled data together trying to understand. "Jax might have left because of Caleb. He wouldn't want a pissed-off ex-employee knowing his location. Or . . ."

"Or what?" Burnett asked.

"My dad said he was pissed at Caleb because the FRU was investigating Bell's murder. Maybe he's afraid that investigation could've lead you to his old address."

"Maybe," Burnett said. "The Houston FRU is investigating that angle. But I still don't think—"

"Then stop thinking." Perry inhaled. "I'm finishing this." He let the tension ease a fraction before continuing. "The meeting with Jax has been rescheduled for tomorrow at four. I'll be there."

Burnett looked at the road. The neon green eyes reflected back in the windshield said how he felt. It didn't surprise Perry that the three in back didn't speak. No one messed with a pissed-off Burnett.

Twenty minutes later, Perry muttered, "So tonight was a complete waste."

"No," Burnett answered, sounding less angry. "Catching that gang gave us some brownie points with both the Houston FRU and the police force. Both are going to assist us in the case. And we got the name of the banker who signed over the title to the house. I'm looking into it tomorrow."

"What if we can't tie Jax to this house?" Perry said. "Are we going to lack evidence?"

"There's enough evidence to convict Jaxon for ten different cases," Burnett said. "Getting info on the other underground gangs would be nice. Getting Tabitha back is our main goal."

The wheels of the van hummed against the pavement taking them back to Fallen. Back to Miranda. And yet . . . "We've got nothing to offer Miranda about her sister," Perry said.

"No news might be good news." Doubt resonated from Burnett's tone. Perry felt it echo inside his chest. If something happened to Tabitha it would break Miranda's heart.

Before he rebounded from that thought, another hit. What if they couldn't save Tabitha. His own brother might be responsible for it. Perry's gut twisted in knots, threads of fear tangled with his hopes for him and the girl he loved. Miranda hadn't completely forgiven him for his last screwups. She'd never forgive him for this.

And he couldn't blame her.

The question was, could he stop it? Or was he already too late?

Chapter Twenty-six

They arrived back at the school at eleven. Was Miranda still awake?

Burnett had given him a key to one of the empty cabins to sleep in, but Kylie and Della stopped him and asked if he wanted to stay at their cabin, because Kylie wanted to go run in the full moon with Lucas, and Della wanted to see Chase.

Perry's gut said they were playing cupid. He wanted to hug them.

He let himself into the cabin, hoping she'd be on the sofa or would come running out of her bedroom.

Neither. The kitchen light was on as if she'd been scared of the dark.

He shut the front door, not all that quietly. Then he glanced at her bedroom door. Would it be totally inappropriate to wake her up? To walk in there and climb in bed with her?

Not for sex. Not that he didn't want that. It would be heaven. But holding her while she slept would be heaven enough. For now.

He focused on the kitchen again. The light shone on the table, highlighting a bouquet of flowers.

He moved in. A plastic fork held a small scripted card: *Here's to us and our future. Shawn.*

Emotion filled Perry's chest.

Their future? They didn't have a future! Miranda was . . . his? Or was she?

Every insecurity he'd ever had about deserving her rose to the surface.

How was Miranda going to feel if they couldn't save her sister? What would she feel when she learned his own flesh and blood had caused it?

Perry knew she cared about him, but could she overlook that?

"Perry?" her soft voice echoed behind him.

He turned. She stood just outside her door.

She wore a pair of Little Mermaid pajamas. A tight tank top hugged her breasts and was paired with a loose-fitting pair of boxer-type shorts. He wanted to touch her so badly his fingers ached.

But his heart fisted. He looked back at the flowers.

"They're breakup flowers." Her bare feet padded on the wood floor as she came closer. He heard each step.

"That's not what the card says."

"He wrote that before I broke up with him. I told him he should take the flowers, but he said to keep them as . . . breakup flowers."

He swallowed. "I didn't know you were supposed to give breakup flowers." Unable to look at her, he stared at the sofa. He remembered them there—tangled in each other's arms, tasting and touching each other almost to the point of no return.

"Me, either," she said.

The lightest chuckle in her tone had him focusing on her again. "You broke up with him?"

She walked closer. Was it his imagination that he could already smell her?

"I . . . I care about someone else."

"You do?" he asked.

She stopped as if she just realized something else. "What happened tonight? Did you find Tabitha?"

The thrill, the anticipation of where her steps were leading, vanished.

"No. But we got a few more leads. And I'm supposed to meet with Jax tomorrow."

She frowned. "You keep getting leads but none of them pan out."

"I'm sorry."

"It's not your fault." Then she bolted into his arms. All that softness. All that sweetness. Against him. Heaven.

He wrapped his arms around her. She looked up, resting her chin on his chest. "Why didn't you tell me that Jax was your half brother?"

She knew? "I . . ." The question, the one gnawing at his sanity, spilled out. "What if he's behind this? What if it's him trying to hurt your sister?"

She pressed a hand to his chest. "Then you'll stop him."

He exhaled. "I will."

They stood in the middle of the room, holding on to each other. Both victims of different shipwrecks.

She eventually moved him over to the sofa and dropped down on the cushions. A soft sigh filled the room.

He sat down beside her. She pulled her knees up, curled up in a tight ball, and cuddled up next to his side. "Where are Kylie and Della?"

"Kylie went to run with Lucas, and Della's at Chase's. But I think they were playing cupid."

She smiled, not a complete smile, but enough to crinkle the corners of her eyes. "See why I love them?"

"Yeah, I see."

She blinked and the smile faded. "I don't want you hiding things from me."

He nodded. "Then I guess I need to tell you that I turned into a pink polka dotted elephant tonight and was shot." He explained. She looked worried, but then she laughed, just as he'd hoped. And it was a beautiful sound.

She looked up, the humor fading from her eyes. "About your parents?"

"Yeah."

"It hurts you." She put a hand over his heart. "I can feel it."

Not ready to talk, he said, "It hurts a lot less when I'm with you."

She nodded. "I know, I have this lump of worry over Tabitha. It throbs like a toothache when I think about it, but when I'm with you, it doesn't hurt as much."

She rested her head on his shoulder again. "Did they ever say they were sorry?"

"What?"

"You parents?"

Emotionally, he flinched. "Not really."

She looked up, her eyes bright with tears.

"Don't . . ." He brushed a finger over her cheek. "Let's not talk about—"

"No." She inhaled a shaky breath. "See, you're doing it again. Not talking to me. At least let me cry for you. Because I know you want to."

"Tears won't fix this. Not mine or yours."

She swatted at her cheeks. But the tears kept coming. "I cannot imagine how someone could . . . My mom and dad have done stupid stuff that's hurt me. Mom sometimes can't hide the fact that she's disappointed in me, and that really hurts me. She won't even talk to me right now, but . . . I know they love me. And to think your parents would . . ." A few tears slipped down her cheek. "And not even apologize . . . How can they live with themselves?"

He didn't want to spend this time with her talking about his parents, but the words spilled out. "I think my dad regrets it. He acts like he cares." He drew in a gulp of air. "I wish he didn't."

Miranda inched closer.

"My mom was the one who put him up to abandoning me." He exhaled. "I don't even think she has a heart."

"I hate her," Miranda said. "Hating people is wrong, but I hate her." She held up her pinky. "I want to put a hex on her ass!"

"Turn her into a kangaroo?" He chuckled.

"How about covering her face in pimples?" she said.

He laughed. Miranda didn't.

"What about you?" he asked. "Why isn't your mom talking to you?"

Miranda told him about their argument.

"I'm sorry," he said. "She doesn't like me."

"She doesn't dislike you. She just gets like this when she and my dad are arguing. And I apologize if she calls you Peter for the rest of your life. Because I've corrected her a dozen times and she still does it."

He chuckled. "I don't mind being Peter."

They just sat there holding on. She glanced up, a little nervous. "If I tell you something will you promise not to tell anyone?"

"Of course."

She bit down on her lip. "The armadillo showed up again the night before last."

His breath caught. "The one who was at the drug house?"

She nodded.

"Are you sure it wasn't just a regular armadillo? They live in the woods and—"

"Definitely not a regular one. It was under my bed. It talked to me."

"What did Burnett—"

"I didn't tell him. That's why you can't say anything."

Perry's mind raced. "Wait. If it's not a real armadillo, how could it be here without Burnett picking it up on the radar?"

"I don't know, but remember you promised not to say anything."

He frowned. "What if—"

"He said he wanted to help me find Tabitha. Then Della came in and he disappeared. And I've called him, looked for him, but he hasn't come back."

"He disappeared like a shifter?"

"I didn't see any bubbles."

Perry tried to wrap his head around it, and the more he thought the less he liked. "How do you know it wasn't lying?"

"Because it was the armadillo who made me leave the house before it blew up, and it woke me up when all the smoke was blowing at us. So he's practically saved my life twice. It doesn't make sense that he would try to kill me now."

"I see your logic, but—"

"No!" She put a finger to his lips. "You said you wouldn't tell." The glint of stubbornness highlighted the gold flecks in her hazel eyes.

He didn't like this. "But you'll tell me if he shows up again? Promise?"

She nodded. Then she leaned her head against him and just sat there. He rubbed his cheek against her hair.

"It doesn't feel cold in here, does it?" she asked.

He pulled the sofa throw beside him and handed it to her. "Here."

She lifted up and looked around the room. "I'm not really cold. I'm just kind of worried about the ghost."

"Bell? She came back?" he asked.

Miranda told him about the ghost showing up at Holiday's. "Holiday says she's here because of the baby, but she says it's weird that she's only shown up when I was around." Miranda let go of a deep breath.

"Has Bell said anything? There's a chance she might know where Jax is."

"No. Holiday tried to talk to her, but she just left."

"That has to be scary."

She nodded and glanced to the front window. "Do you think a ghost can possess trees?"

"What?" he asked.

She told him about her newfound phobia of trees.

"Did you tell Holiday?" he asked.

"No, it didn't occur to me that it might be the ghost then. And it makes me sound crazy."

"You're not crazy. You're smart and beautiful." And she was his now. The thought shot a wave of joy all over him.

"Don't say that, either." Her tone sounded defeated, not very Miranda-like.

"That you're beautiful?"

She sighed. "Beauty's in the eye of the beholder. But I'm not smart. I bombed the SAT test—even with someone reading me the test. I've got one week to retake it. If I don't make a good score, I won't . . ." Her voice shook. "I won't be going to college with Della and Kylie."

There was a time Perry would have been happy about her not going—wanting her all to himself. It had been thinking about her leaving for college and how he wouldn't fit into her world that had initiated him breaking up with her.

Now he knew how much Miranda wanted this. No way would he stand in the way of her dreams. Nothing should.

"Then why aren't you studying?" he asked. "I'll help you."

She looked up at him. "Not at this hour. Plus I've studied about six hours today. My brain's mush. Not to say I've given up. I almost had, but Della and Kylie knocked some sense into me. I'm going to give it my all. If I don't make it, it's not because I didn't try."

"You'll make it," he said. "I know you will."

She smiled. "If I don't, and I can learn to fight, maybe I'll work for the FRU."

"Really?" He hoped his expression didn't give him away. But he couldn't see her doing that. Miranda was just . . . soft. Softhearted. Soft spirited. He couldn't see her doing that job.

"Do you know how much I've missed this?" she asked. "Us, talking. It's as if everything bad in the world gets pushed back when I'm with you."

"I know. And I missed this." He leaned in and kissed her. It went from sweet to sweeter, from hot to hotter. They ended up stretched out, their legs tangled up. They had to work to find a way the cast didn't come between them.

He moved his hand under the back of her shirt, followed the soft curve of her waist, feeling bare skin, feeling Miranda.

His body reacted to her closeness. Their hips met. Even with their clothes on, it sent vibrations of pleasure to all the right places. Or it did, until she jerked her leg from between his.

"I'm sorry," he said without opening his eyes, knowing she'd felt his growing problem. "It just happens." The fact that it startled her, startled him. In the past, she even joked about it. She'd been happy that she had that effect on him. Maybe things between them weren't really back to normal.

He forced his eyes open. Worried he'd see anger in those beautiful eyes. She didn't look mad . . . She looked . . . tattooed. He almost said something, but didn't want to make her feel self-conscious.

"I want you to stay here." She nipped at her bottom lip. She always did that when something was hard to say. "But I don't . . . I don't want our first time to be wrapped up with my worry over Tabitha, our parents, and the stupid SAT scores." She put her palm on his chest. "Am I asking too much?"

"No," he said. "We've gone a lot further than this before. You know I wouldn't push you. Ever."

"I know. I just . . . I want it, too. I've regretted that we didn't do it earlier. I just don't think now's right. Remember the night we went skinny-dipping?"

He smiled. "Every time I close my eyes."

"Well, that's how it needs to be. No worries, no problems. Just us. Together."

He brushed her hair from her cheek. "That sounds really good." He still worried. "You know that's not all I want. This . . ." He motioned to the tent in his jeans. "Yes it means I want things, but I want more than that. And I'd never—"

She put a finger over his lips. "I trust you with my life. That's why I love you."

"I love you, too." Emotion filled his chest and he felt his eyes grow moist. Not once during all that happened with his parents had he wanted to cry. But hearing her say she loved him made him weepy.

Not wanting her to see his weakness, he pulled her against him. Every ounce of her, against him, was the sweetest weight he'd ever felt. And he'd do anything and everything to be the person she deserved.

She looked up at him. "I wish I had some ice cream to go with the birthday cake."

"Huh?" he asked.

"Every time I'm around you lately, I smell birthday cake."

"I smell like birthday cake?"

"No, the air smells like it. It's a happy smell. But it makes me want ice cream."

"Do you have some in the fridge? I'll get it for you."

"We're out."

"Zap us some," he said.

"No, I'm zapped out."

"You want me to go to the store?"

"No." She curled up against him again. "I like this better than ice cream."

A while later, looking exhausted, she fell asleep. Her tattoos faded, but then she'd snuggle a little closer and they'd come back. He couldn't help but wonder if it was them being close that brought them on. He hoped that was a good thing.

He quickly realized this wasn't the most comfortable position for his arm. Yet afraid if he moved he'd wake her, he didn't move. He didn't sleep, either. He didn't want to miss a second of this.

Chapter Twenty-seven

"Who's Peter?"

Della's voice stirred Miranda from a dead sleep. She pushed up, blinking. Why was she on the sofa?

Everything came back. Everything made sense. Except Della's question.

"Huh?" she asked.

"There's a note from a Peter?"

Miranda focused on the vampire. Sun poured through the window, telling Miranda she'd slept late. Then she noted the paper Della held out. *Peter?*

"You're not supposed to read other people's notes." Sitting up, she snatched it.

"It doesn't have your name on it."

Miranda read the note.

> *I love you more than ice cream. More than flying. And*
> *you know how much I love that.*
>
> > *Peter.*

Miranda smiled and put the note against her chest.

The vampire made a funny face. "I feel a sappy moment coming on and we have no time for sap. Get your ass up and ready. I gotta teach you to punch somebody's lights out. Come on. Chop. Chop."

"Can I pee first?" Miranda popped up.

"Full stream," Della snapped. "Because after I teach you to kick ass, we're gonna hit the books."

"Where's Kylie?"

"Sleeping in. She stayed out all night howling at the moon and getting fleas."

Ten minutes and a granola bar later, they were out by the lake. The morning sun sparkled off the water. A few cotton-like clouds hung above. The day seemed too beautiful to fight.

Her thoughts shot to Tabitha, and Miranda accepted that bad crap happened on beautiful days. She needed to learn to fight.

A breeze brushed across her skin and rustled the leaves on the trees. Until then, she'd forgotten about her weird obsession with trees. She looked at them and, oddly, she didn't feel fear, just her usual appreciation for nature. Maybe she'd gotten over whatever it was.

"Hey, we didn't come out to enjoy the view," Della said. "Do you remember how I told you to stand?"

"Yeah," Miranda copied Della's fighting stance, with her knees bent slightly for better balance, and her fists held up to protect her face. It felt unnatural, but Miranda ignored that feeling. She wanted this.

"Here's another lesson. An attacker will try to hold your hands to restrain you. That's okay. Your legs are the strongest part of your body. And if he's holding your hands, he's not protecting his boys. Wham him in the balls with your knee, or use the ball of your foot. If his boys aren't accessible, kick him in the knee to knock him off balance. And if you've got on high heels, use them. A spiky heel is as good as a knife."

For the next thirty minutes, Della kept coming at her, and Miranda showed her what she could do. Della helped her perfect her punches and her kicks, taught her a variety of maneuvers to break someone's arm or leg, and ways to deflect a blow. After a while, Miranda actually felt confident.

"If someone grabs you from behind, use your elbow to twist toward them and break their hold, then attack. You have a mean left hook, use it. If you can't break their hold, look down and start stomping their foot. Or punch the fine bones in their hand. And don't be afraid to fight dirty. Use your teeth if you have to."

"That sounds painful." Miranda caught her breath.

"Exactly."

They danced around in circles for another thirty minutes—Miranda attempting to block Della's punches and using different techniques to fight back.

Then Miranda remembered. "Perry knew you two were playing cupid last night."

"I hope so, or that'd mean he's dumber than dirt." Della chuckled.

Miranda lifted her arm to block Della's punch. "Thank you."

"You're welcome." Della stopped throwing punches.

The vamp pulled two waters out of her backpack. "What's up with the flowers from Shawn?" She handed Miranda a bottle.

Holding the cold bottle to her forehead, she told Della the breakup story. Then she told her how good it had been to spend the night with Perry.

"How good?" Della lifted a brow, leaving no doubt what she was asking.

"We didn't have sex," Miranda told her.

"Still not sure?" Della asked.

"No. I'm sure. I just want the first time to be right. I don't want to be worried about my sister, or studying." *Or my parents, or ghosts. Or most of all, her sister.*

"Makes sense," the vamp said.

Miranda pulled out her phone. Why wasn't Tabitha texting her back? "I'm so worried about Tabitha." She slumped down on the grass and eyed her phone.

Della plopped down beside her. "If it was my sister, I'd be worried sick, too. But Burnett's got everyone on the case."

Miranda nodded and checked for any messages. Not one.

Frustrated, she dropped back on the grass, and stared up at the clouds moving slowly across the sky.

Della fell back as well. "Holiday got our caps and gowns in. They're dorky looking."

"They're supposed to be dorky looking." Thoughts about graduation lead Miranda to thoughts about after graduation. She sat up. "We should go study."

"Yup." Della bounced to her feet.

They hadn't gotten to the path in the woods, when Miranda's cell dinged with a text.

She yanked it from her pocket. She didn't recognize the number. She read the text.

"It's her," Miranda yelped, and got happy tears in her eyes. "It's Tabitha. She's okay."

Miranda sent a text back, asking her sister where she was, but Tabitha hadn't answered.

Della had insisted they go tell Burnett—immediately. Not that Miranda minded, but she'd have liked a few minutes to be happy before dealing with Burnett's interrogation.

He always interrogated.

Sure, Miranda had a few questions of her own. Tabitha's message was odd.

I can hear you worrying. Stop it. I'm fine. Tabitha.

Burnett frowned, sitting on the edge of his wife's desk. "What does she mean?"

"I guess that I sent her like ten messages."

"She didn't use her phone to text you. And she said 'hear you.' " Burnett looked at Holiday, as if communicating nonverbally.

Miranda wondered about that. "What's important is that she's fine."

Burnett nodded. "I'm sending the number to my IT department to see if we can get a trace on the phone. That might tell us where she is." He frowned. "They may need your phone."

She frowned not liking the thought of surrendering her cell, but agreed if they needed it.

"Until then if you hear anything, let me know that instant." She nodded.

Burnett stood and kissed his wife. "I'll let you know what time I'll be back."

"You need some help?" Della asked.

"No, I'm assisting the Houston FRU with their search on the title of that house that was signed over."

"Are you going to check on Perry?" Miranda asked. She didn't like Perry doing this alone.

"I'm hoping to," Burnett answered and left.

Holiday, her aura suddenly going murky, looked at Della. "Can you give us a few minutes?"

"What's wrong?" Miranda asked when Della walked out.

"I heard from Ms. Wales. She thinks we might be on to something with you being related. She suggested that you do a DNA test to confirm it. Burnett agreed to run it through the agency and get it done quickly."

Why was that bad news? "Did she find the Evans name in her family tree?"

"Not exactly." Holiday's aura turned a little murkier. "The story isn't pretty."

"Okay . . . ," Miranda said. "Tell me."

Holiday picked up a pencil. "Ms. Wales was told that her grandmother Evelyn Bradley was born out of wedlock. Evelyn's mom, Mildred Bradley, was supposedly raped. After Evelyn was born, Mildred killed the man who'd raped her. She was tried by the courts and executed for the murder. Mildred's sister raised the baby. Ms. Wales has the old newspaper article that states Mildred Bradley was hung for the crime of killing an aristocrat named Rudolf Evans."

Miranda sank deeper into the chair. "So you're saying I come from a line of murderers and rapists." She suddenly laughed. "Nothing like coming from good stock."

Holiday appeared concerned at Miranda's reaction. "You know that doesn't affect who you are."

"I know." And she believed it.

"But this could mean that you actually come from a lineage of mystic witches. And . . . it might explain Tabitha's text. She heard you worrying."

Della popped in from the other room as if eavesdropping wasn't rude. "And you were talking about her just a few minutes before you got the text."

"Really?" Holiday asked.

Miranda nodded then shook her head. "I'm not even good with my normal powers. I'm dyslexic and—"

"So is Ms. Wales. Now she's wondering if the tattoo isn't somehow connected with the dyslexia. Her grandmother never learned to read, which means she could have been dyslexic. Ms. Wales's mother wasn't dyslexic and she didn't have the tattoo. And while her mom was mystic, Ms. Wales says her mom claimed she didn't have near the powers of her mom."

"But if I'm a mystic then it means Tabitha should be."

"Not really," Holiday said. "Remember Ms. Wales saying that it wasn't known to be hereditary? And your sister isn't dyslexic."

At three p.m., Perry stood outside the same diner to meet his parents.

Before walking in, he gave himself a second to remember how great it had been to hold Miranda all night, hoping that joy would help ward off the feeling that swallowed him up when he was close to his mom.

He walked in and finally spotted his dad's blond hair at a back booth.

Walking over, he noted only one plate on the table. She hadn't come. Perry smiled without meaning to.

"Hey." Perry dropped into the other side of the booth.

His father looked up as if happy to see him. "Did you have a good time with your girl?"

Perry nodded. "Yeah."

A waitress dropped off a glass of water. "Need a menu?"

"No, thank you," Perry said.

His dad moved his fork around his empty plate. "Are you ever gonna introduce us?"

Only when hell freezes over and Satan starts selling snow cones. "Maybe. Where's Mom?" He hated calling her that, but his dad had insisted.

His father dropped his fork. "She's not coming. I actually got to eat all my lunch for a change." He laughed as if it was funny.

Perry didn't laugh. He sipped his water.

His dad made a funny face. "She's embarrassed. She woke up this morning with pimples. Lots of them. Big ones, too."

Perry nearly choked on his water. The laugh slipped out before he could stop it. Had Miranda even known she'd done it? Oh, man, he was going to kiss her for this.

"It's not funny," his dad said, but he almost smiled.

His father dropped some bills on the table. "We should probably head out."

"I thought he lived around the corner." Perry hoped he sounded casual as he slid out of the booth.

"He sold that place."

"In one day?" Perry walked with his father.

"He normally doesn't trust anyone. But he's worse now. I don't know if it's Caleb that he's worried about or the FRU looking into that waitress's murder. But he's evaded trouble with the FRU for years so far, so he might be onto something."

"Do you think Caleb would go after him?" Perry asked.

"Hell, yeah. Caleb has a mean streak in him. I'm watching my back, and so should you. He liked you less than he did me. Before Jax kicked Caleb's ass out, he was chatting with your mom about you being dirty. He was trying to dig something up on you. It's the way he makes himself look good. By making others look bad. The day you left Dallas and I told him it was because you wanted to see your girlfriend, he shot out of there like a bat out of hell to find you. He obviously didn't, because he came back pretty quickly. But now he's even more pissed."

"Thanks for the warning." And Perry took that seriously, too.

"Your mom's right, though. Chances are Jax is gonna take care of him. Whatever you do, don't get on Jax's bad side."

That was gonna be hard not to do.

Ten minutes later, they were falcons flying across downtown. Perry tilted his head to the side. He realized right away that they were being followed by one, maybe two shifters. The bird in the distance didn't appear to be the same red-chested duck as before, but good shifters could morph while flying. He could do it himself.

He looked right and the same falcon trailed at about a hundred feet behind. A thought hit. Had Burnett gone against his word and sent backup?

"It's Jax's man." His father's words were snatched by the wind. "Jax's paranoid."

Perry continued to fly. Was he right that the other bird was a shifter? If so, were both Jax's men?

Later in the flight, he checked the bird on his left. Now the bird following was an eagle, but it hung about the same distance away. Definitely a shifter. A powerful one.

When his father descended, the falcon on his right did the same. The now pelican on his left kept flying, but Perry saw his speed slow down and then the bird lapped back. He didn't think the FRU had shape-shifter agents good enough to shift while flying. Perry recalled his dad saying that Caleb had bragged he could do it.

They landed in a fenced-in property out by the gulf. Galveston, he thought. Not on the beach, but close enough to taste the salty breeze.

Perry took care not to morph too quickly. No need showing Jax's guard what he could do. Right before he started his shift, he spotted a crow flying toward the back of the large white house that looked older than the palm trees surrounding it. Was it Caleb? It had to be, didn't it?

When he completed his shift, an older Italian-looking guy stood fully shifted. Forty maybe, barrel chested and looked like one of the stars that played in *The Godfather* movie.

"I was told you were good," he snickered.

Perry shrugged and noted the manicured lawn.

They walked around to the front of the three-storied house. Another guard stood at the front door that seemed built for a giant. He studied Perry oddly and then let them in.

In a room to their right were several guys holding court. There was more tension in the room than furniture. Perry couldn't help but search for his brother, hoping he couldn't recognize him. Hoping not to feel linked to him in any way.

Disappointment hit when his eyes landed on the youngest man in the room. Blond hair, blue eyes. Their body shape was slightly different, Perry was taller, buffer, but their facial features were damn near identical.

That hurt. Hurt because here was this person he should feel connected to. Hurt because he'd seen how Miranda felt about her sister. Hurt because he already knew this guy was only a step from being a monster.

Jax's gaze met Perry's. And locked.

"Eerie, isn't it?" the guard who let them in said.

Jax didn't answer. He focused back on the three men standing in front of him. Perry checked their patterns.

Two of them were warlocks. The biggest of them was vampire and looked more like a bodyguard.

Flanking his brother were two other guard-looking guys. One part shifter and vampire, one part were and shifter. At least his half sibling wasn't prejudiced.

"Look," Jax spoke to the warlock in the middle. "As you can see, I need to wrap this up. I have fifty percent of what you wanted in a secure location. As soon as I get fifty percent of what's owed me, I'll tell you where to pick it up."

Perry didn't have a clue what they were talking about. His brother seemed purposely vague. But his thoughts went to Tabitha being missing and he couldn't help but worry.

"That wasn't the deal. We wanted both," the dark-headed warlock said.

"And when things calm down here, I'll get the other half," his brother answered.

Both? Perry mulled it over.

"That wasn't the deal." The warlock's face grew red.

"Sometimes you don't get what you want. Do you need to learn that lesson?"

The threat was issued as easily as one might offer someone a glass of sweet tea.

One of the men standing beside his brother took a menacing step forward.

The warlock held out his hand. "How long before you'll finish the job?"

"A week, maybe two."

Perry stared off, pretending not to listen, but memorizing every word.

"Now, leave." His brother waved toward the door. "I have other business."

The three guys walked out. Jaxon faced Perry. "Who'd've guessed there was someone almost as good-looking as myself in the world? I'm not sure how that makes me feel."

Perry lifted his chin and spoke in the same condescending tone. "I was thinking the exact same thing."

Jax continued to stare and Perry felt the man do a complete assessment. Did it piss him off that Perry had him by a few inches and pounds?

"Caleb didn't trust you." Jax moved over and poured himself a drink from a bottle of whiskey. The man's bodyguards stood tense as if on full alert.

"Caleb was an idiot," his father spoke up. "He—"

"I got this." Perry glanced back at his half brother. "And I hear you didn't like Caleb. Odd you'd take his word."

"I didn't like his temper. He caused messes. It doesn't mean I didn't trust his judgment."

Perry moved in another foot. "You trust him enough for him to know where you live? Or is that the reason you moved?"

"What's that mean?" Jax's blue eyes brightened to gold.

"I can't swear it was Caleb, but some shifter, a powerful one, followed us here."

The mafia-looking bodyguard who'd followed them here let go with a laugh. "That was me."

"Not you," Perry said. "Someone with the ability to shift while flying. He was a falcon, an eagle, a pelican, then something else. He's good, whoever he was. He landed at the back of your property."

Jax's face hardened and he turned to the Italian bouncer. "And you didn't catch this?"

"He's making that up," the man said.

"Find out!" Jax said, looking at his two goons standing beside him. "Meter the area." He looked at the Italian-looking guy. "I warned you that I don't tolerate mistakes. If that meter reads positive, get the hell off my property. And don't stop looking over your shoulder."

"But boss, I—"

"Go!"

Footsteps thundered through the room as the three men walked out. Jaxon stood there, clenching and unclenching his fist.

They had meters? Perry thought the FRU were the only ones who had those. But they obviously didn't have the technology to build them into the security system.

Jax's cold blue eyes then focused on Perry's father.

"How about you help them, old man," Jax said. "Let me visit with my baby brother." The sinister way he said it had Perry's blood fizzing with the need to protect himself.

Chapter Twenty-eight

In an instant, Perry realized he hadn't considered Jax's motivation for allowing this meeting to happen.

What the hell did Jax want with him?

"Don't worry," Jax told Perry's father. "I'm not gonna hurt your boy. We're brothers."

Perry's father's blue eyes met Perry's, almost as if he didn't want to abandon him.

Had his father hesitated at all when he'd left him at the mall fifteen years ago?

"How endearing," Jax said after his father finally left. "I thought the only thing he loved was our mother. You've seen how whipped he is, haven't you?"

"It's just his guilt talking." The moment Perry said it, he realized how right that might be. His father might not care, guilt made people act certain ways.

"He really just left you at a mall, didn't he?" Jax laughed. Their gazes locked again. Blue on blue.

"Care for a drink?" Jax asked.

"No."

Jax walked over to the sole table in the room and poured himself a shot of the amber-colored liquid from the decanter. He put the glass to his lips and downed it in one gulp. Swallowing, he wiped his mouth with the back of his hand. The oddity of seeing someone who looked so much like him was unnerving. Like watching a mirror while your reflection was doing something different.

"So tell me, brother. Why did you hunt down your parents after all these years?"

"Curiosity," Perry answered.

"You sure you weren't just needing your mama?"

"I'd be in bad shape if I was," he said without emotion.

Jax laughed again. "She is a loveless bitch, isn't she?"

His brother walked over to the table and refilled his glass again. "And I thought I had it bad." He downed the shot. "I saw you once. I was like three, you were just born. My dad took me over for a visit. He said I should know my brother."

"A shame I don't remember," Perry said.

"Mom said you were raised in foster care?"

Perry nodded.

Jax looked down at his empty glass, when he looked up suspicion lifted his brow. "Isn't that run by the FRU?"

Make it convincing, Perry told himself. "I think their name is stamped on it somewhere. But it's just a money scheme. The FRU pockets half of the funds and places unwanted kids in homes where people don't give a shit."

Perry's words rang true, because most of it was. The system was broken, something Burnett was trying to work on as an agent. He'd made some changes, but there was a hell of a lot to do.

"Ahh, poor brother," Jax said.

"Don't pity me. I'm sure you learned just like I did. What doesn't kill you makes you stronger."

"Which brings up a really good question," Jax said. "How strong are you?"

The door swung open. The bodyguards, minus Mr. Italian, walked back in. His dad followed.

"So?" Jax snapped.

"The meter read high levels of frequency in the back of the property." The man held what looked like a cell phone in his hand.

"And Ricky?" Jax asked, his eyes almost red.

The guard smiled. "He left."

"Add the name Ricky Raco to my game list." He sounded excited.

"How much?" the guard asked.

"A hundred thousand."

Perry didn't know this game. But it seemed damn clear. Perry had pretty much signed that man's death certificate.

"Good job," Jax said to Perry.

Perry's conscience took a direct hit. It took work to hide the guilt on his face.

Jax looked at his father again. "What all have you told your boy about our operation?"

"Only what you allowed me to," his father said.

And that annoyed the hell out of Perry.

Jax met Perry's gaze as if still debating. He finally nodded. "Why don't we go into the study and I'll give you the facts."

It was nine that night when Perry spotted the large gray building that housed the Fallen FRU agency. He'd taken twice as long to fly here. Taking all different routes just to make sure he wasn't followed. He hadn't been. That said, he couldn't stop worrying that, until now, he hadn't been all that careful. What if Caleb had followed him to Shadow Falls earlier?

One more thing he needed to tell Burnett. But holy hell, he was the bearer of all kinds of bad news tonight.

Landing on the steps, he walked into the office. He'd been coming anyway, so finding Burnett's text summoning him didn't annoy Perry.

"My favorite person in the world." Mrs. Conner's voice boomed.

She stood and moved toward him. Her arms opened for a grand-motherly hug. Today she wore red and really looked like Mrs. Claus.

He obliged her with a hug, even though his heart wasn't in it.

"You should see the spoon you gave me now hanging on the wall. As a matter of fact, I insist you come see it. Wednesday you are coming to my house for dinner. I'm cooking meatballs and spa-ghetti. Mr. Conner's been asking about you."

Perry shrugged. "I'd love to, but my schedule is up in the air."

"Nonsense. You can and you will." She shook her chubby fin-ger at him. "Now, go see Burnett, before he yells at me. He's in one of his moods."

And I'm about to make it worse.

Burnett was on the phone when Perry walked into his office. The vampire motioned to the chair. "Well, keep looking. We don't know he's dead. You're jumping the gun."

The words sank into Perry like nails. How'd Burnett do this? Deal with scum, people who didn't value life. Deal with death. Perry felt dirty, tainted, just from being in the room with Jax.

His father didn't give the order, but he worked for Jax and looked the other way. That made him just as bad, didn't it?

Burnett set his phone down. "You met Jax?"

"Yeah." Perry stiffened his backbone. If Burnett knew how Perry felt right now, he'd insist he pull out. Insist that Perry wasn't ready.

Emotionally, especially after today, Perry would have to agree, but he'd be damned if he walked away now.

"What was the phone call about? Who might be dead?"

Burnett raked a hand over his face. "Anthony Bastin's cousin. We've been trying to find him. And now his father is, too. He's missing."

Perry exhaled. "Do you think he's with Anthony?"

"Maybe." Burnett leaned forward. "Good news is that Miranda got a text from Tabitha. Or at least she believes it's from her."

"You know where she is?" Perry asked. Damn his life would be easier if Jax wasn't involved with her. But his gut said that those warlocks at Jax's house might somehow be behind this. And considering what he now knew about Jax's operation . . .

"No. It was a burner phone. We got nothing. But if it was her, and Miranda believes it was, then she's alive." Burnett hesitated. "What do you have for me?"

"It's bad. Jax isn't just running a gang. It's the mafia. And my brother is the damn Godfather."

"What do you mean?" Burnett asked.

"He has his thumb on all the different supernatural underground gangs. Not just the typical rogue gangs, either. These are organized-crime kind of gangs. They pay him a percentage of what they pull in. If they want something, get in a jam, they come to him. He gets them what they want for a price. He's making money from them and his own operations. He mentioned prostitution and it sounded like human trafficking. If his own men don't meet his standards, he puts a price on their head, and it's a contest to see who kills them."

Perry told Burnett about Ricky Raco and how he'd been put on the hit list. Burnett said he'd look into it. A few minutes later, after soaking up every word that Perry said, he leaned back in his chair. "Shit."

"And," Perry added, "when I first got to his house, there were warlocks there. He's doing something for a warlock gang. It could—"

"It could be behind Tabitha's disappearance." Burnett scowled.

Perry nodded. "We don't have proof, but it's likely." He paused. "They have the meters to check for other shape-shifters. I don't know if they have it to meter other supernaturals or not. It wasn't hooked up to a security system, but the house is new so maybe they don't have it all set up yet. "

"You got the address where you met him?" Burnett asked.

Perry nodded. "I'm not finished," Perry said. "I'm worried I haven't been as careful as I should have been on all my trips back to Shadow Falls. If Caleb's shifting midflight, I may have missed him."

Burnett frowned. "I've already got everyone on guard at the camp." He leaned back in his chair. "We'll get a team together now and pick up Jax."

"He's not there." Perry ran a hand down his thigh. "The house we met in was empty. He said he was staying at another house until he gets it furnished. Following him wasn't an option. But he's bringing me into his organization. He said he's setting up a meeting to introduce me to all the leaders of the various groups. But right now he's worried about Bell's murder—and his ties to her leading you guys to him. And he's trying to come up with a plan that will throw you off his scent."

"By using you," Burnett said figuring it out. "I got his mug shot. You two could be twins."

Perry nodded.

Burnett leaned back in his chair. His posture so rock hard, he appeared chiseled out of stone. "And knowing all this, you still think you can handle it?"

"I'm your best chance of stopping this bastard. You know that."

"But at what price, Perry?"

"I can handle it."

Burnett was about to argue when his cell rang. Worry creased his brow as he answered. "Yeah? Shit. Anyone hurt?"

Pain flashed in the vampire's eyes. "Get her to Dr. Whitman's now."

Miranda dropped her phone on the bathroom counter and started the shower. She stripped down, singing while she did it. "Derivatives, derivatives. It's so fun, it's one prime two plus two prime one." Yes, she was actually in a good mood.

She'd spent a total of three hours practicing to fight. And Della couldn't deny she was learning. Miranda also spent six hours studying. And Miranda couldn't deny she was retaining information.

Her time with Perry had boosted her morale. The icing on the cake, however, was hearing from Tabitha.

She'd even talked to her dad, who'd returned back home and said her mom was better. And tomorrow her mom had plans to come see her. Not that Miranda looked forward to the visit, but . . . Miranda loved her mom. Even with her flaws.

She might not be up for the Mother-of-the-Year award, but compared to Perry's mom, she should be getting her trophy any day.

Maybe Miranda should have been more upset to learn her relatives were rapists and murderers, but it didn't sting that much. Call her crazy, but she couldn't wait to tell Perry—if for no other reason than to make him feel less self-conscious about his own family.

She'd even asked her dad about the family tree. He said he had the information on a disk at his office in Colorado. His secretary was e-mailing it tomorrow.

Thankfully, he hadn't asked why Miranda wanted it. Explaining to her parents about the weird tattoos and that it could mean she was some kind of a dyslexic mystic witch, didn't seem like a good conversation. First they'd freak out because of the tattoos. Then her mom would freak out, in a good way, that Miranda might actually be something worth bragging about.

Frankly, Miranda wasn't buying that she had any extra powers. The blood test she'd agreed to do tomorrow would give her more answers. But Holiday had insisted her mom sign a permission slip.

All Miranda had to do was come up with a good reason why she needed a blood test.

Not an easy task. She'd never excelled at lying. Thinking about what all she didn't excel at brought her back to the crazy idea that she was mystic.

Would it be cool to have amazing talents other's envied? Perhaps, but she remembered Tabitha hating her role as high priestess. Gifts sometimes brought on responsibilities. Miranda would really like to just concentrate on college and . . . Perry.

Perry and their relationship.

Perry and . . . sex.

She was ready. The fact that she'd never felt this way when thinking of Shawn confirmed what she knew. She loved Perry.

"Peter." She smiled thinking of his note.

She'd almost texted him, but remembered he was working undercover. The last thing she wanted to do was put him in any more danger than he was already in.

She worked hard not to think about that.

Sticking her cast in a plastic bag and taping the ends, she stepped into the steamy shower and closed the glass doors. Hot water hit her shoulders, and she closed her eyes and let the heat soothe her sore muscles. Learning to fight, even one-handed, was hard work. No wonder Kylie and Della always looked great in swimsuits. Miranda looked at her thighs. Hopefully she could lose a pound or so before Perry saw her naked.

Then it hit. Fast. Hard. The sense that things were going to be okay dissolved. And it had nothing to do with her thighs.

A dark feeling, a premonition, filled her chest with raw pain. Something bad was going to happen. Or had already happened.

"No." She tried to push the feeling away. But wishing it away wouldn't work. She considered calling Burnett. That thought lost momentum when she realized all she saw was gray mist. She reached out, searching for the knob to turn off the hot water. She found it. The water stopped. The mist hung on. Then fingers of cold began stroking her skin. Chill bumps chased chill bumps down her spine. Even with a chestful of doom, she recognized what this was. Death.

She covered her most private parts with her plastic wrapped casted arm and free hand.

"Go away."

The cold hung on. Got colder. Teeth chattering, she reached for the shower door, but some invisible finger started writing on the steamy glass right in front of her. Script not just written in steam, but what looked like . . . blood.

Inhaling, she felt ice crystals form in her lungs. Unable to move, to scream, she watched as what looked like an address was penned on the glass shower door. Steam made the bloody script start to run. Number by number, letter by letter, it started dripping down the glass.

Suddenly sensing it was important, Miranda repeated it inside her head as she watched the droplets of blood run down the door, onto the shower floor, and get sucked down the drain.

Now singing the address in her head so she might remember, she bolted out of the shower and screamed.

Della and Kylie were already in the bathroom. Miranda stood there naked, trembling, and singing. "One six nine zero six. One six nine zero six, Dairy Lane. Dairy Lane. Dairy Lane. Remember it," she told them, unable to catch her breath. "Remember it." She started shaking. Tears filled her eyes.

Kylie snatched a towel from the counter and wrapped it around Miranda. "It's okay. She's gone."

"Remember it." Tears ran down her face. "One six nine zero six. Dairy Lane."

"You don't have to remember it," Della said softly as if not to frighten Miranda. That's when Miranda saw the mirror behind Della. There was the same address. Penned in blood.

Chapter Twenty-nine

Perry stood in the little white room watching Burnett interrogate Chuckie and Mark. The two of them had tried to get to Lily Chambers again. Agent Tobler spotted them, and they went on full attack. They'd knifed her. Thankfully, Shawn had been there to start the next shift and he not only stopped it, but managed to take the bozos down.

"I'm gonna ask one more time!" Burnett's voice rang loud and dangerous.

Mark and Chuckie, cuffed, wearing patches preventing them from shifting, looked ready to shit their pants. Not that Perry blamed them. Burnett hadn't held back.

With his fangs out and eyes lime green, he'd broken the table in half and then tossed it around the room several times. The fact that the guys' legs were handcuffed to it made it quite difficult for the two prisoners.

"Tell me where Jaxon Bowen is or the table isn't the only thing in this room that is going to be ripped apart!"

The door behind Perry swung open. Shawn, wearing blood on his shirt just like he had the time before, started inside and came to an abrupt halt. Their eyes met. Perry didn't blink.

The warlock gave Perry a slight nod and came the rest of the way inside. Perry didn't say anything. Hell, he didn't know what to say. He wasn't going to apologize any more than Shawn was going to congratulate him.

So they both just faced the two-way mirror and watched what played out in the next room.

"The only addresses we have on him are the ones we already told you," Mark said. "Give us a break!"

"Oh, I'm going to," Burnett said. "What do you want broken first? I'm saving the neck for when you refuse to answer the third time."

Shawn chuckled. "No one interviews quite like Burnett. But if we did that—"

"They hurt a female." Perry looked at Shawn. "Is Agent Tobler okay?"

"The doctor said she'd be okay as long as she doesn't get an infection."

"Good," Perry said.

Burnett kicked a chair out from under one of the guys, then picked up an empty chair and ripped it apart and tossed it down. A clattering sound filled the room.

"Burnett gets pissed when anyone on his team gets hurt, but something about hurting girls . . . ," Perry said. "I've seen him hang a social worker from a three-story building for fifteen minutes when he slapped one of our foster sisters. And Burnett didn't even like the sister."

"I kind of feel the same way." Shawn looked at Perry. From the look in the warlock's eyes, Perry sensed they weren't talking about Burnett anymore.

"Miranda loves you," Shawn said. "I don't think I really loved her, but I could have. She's special. And if you hurt her, I'll hunt you down."

Perry's first instinct was to get mad; thankfully, his second instinct kicked in. "If I hurt her, I'll surrender my sorry ass over to you. You see, I love her. I know I do." With that said, the majority of the tension faded. They offered each other a nod, then looked back at the mirror.

After a second, Perry realized he needed to say one more thing. "Thank you. For not making this harder on her. And with things here."

"You're welcome," Shawn said.

The shrill ring of Burnett's phone brought Perry's and Shawn's attention back to the mirror.

"That's weird," Shawn said. "Burnett always turns his phone off during interviews."

"No, he blocks all calls . . . except Holiday's," Perry said. "And she doesn't call unless it's an emergency."

Perry held his breath, fearing that he'd been right earlier. Had Caleb followed him to the camp?

"What's up?" Burnett held a finger in the air at the two men as if warning them to not speak. They didn't.

Burnett's jaw tightened. "Is she hurt?"

"Okay. And the zip?" he asked.

"Zip?" Shawn asked.

Perry was too busy listening to answer.

"Text me that address." Burnett hung up and looked at Chuckie and Mark, who were lying spread out on the floor amongst the broken pieces of metal furniture. "I'll be right back, guys. Make yourselves at home."

Perry and Shawn rushed out to meet Burnett in the hall.

"What's going on?" Perry's heart drummed in his throat and ears.

"The spirit of Bell Stephens paid Miranda a visit. She wrote an address on the bathroom mirror . . . in blood."

Perry could imagine how Miranda felt. "Is she okay?"

"Spoke with Holiday, she's fine."

Perry considered the information. "Do you think Bell knows where Jax is?"

"My thoughts exactly." Burnett looked at Shawn. "I'm texting you the address. Bell neglected to give a city, so do a wide search on it. You two do that while I finish up in there. I'm gonna see if I can't break these guys."

Perry wondered if that pun wasn't intended.

"Why me?" Miranda paced in the living room, wearing only her pink fluffy robe. She kept pulling on the belt, tightening it, cinching it, knotting it. It felt as if that two-inch sash of nubby cotton was all that held her together.

If it came undone, so would Miranda.

Della, Holiday, and Kylie all sat on the sofa. Miranda couldn't sit still. Her nerves hadn't stopped buzzing, her skin crawling, or her heart pounding against her rib cage as if wanting to break free to find a needy donor. Probably one who didn't have a ghost popping in the shower.

Holiday, looking as calm as Sunday morning, leaned forward. "Did you see her?"

"No." Miranda gave the belt another yank. And her gaze went to the window. The blinds were up. A summer storm brewed outside. In the distance she saw lightning bolt across the sky. The trees swayed, back and forth. She stopped and watched them dance in the wind.

"Did she speak to you?" Holiday asked, in a normal voice, but it somehow sounded like a whisper.

"No." Miranda shook her head.

"Did you feel her?" the fae asked.

Miranda looked away from the window. "I felt the cold. Fingers of cold, touching me . . . everywhere." She looked back at Holiday and her two best friends. They'd all dealt with this. She felt like a wimp for losing it.

"Take a deep breath," Holiday said. "You're completely safe. You know that, don't you?"

Miranda nodded. But knowing it and feeling it were two different things. Fine, she'd just admit it. She was a wimp.

"Sit down and try to relax," Holiday suggested.

She yanked on the belt. "I need to move." She started walking again.

Holiday paused. "Did you pick up any emotions?"

Miranda looked at her not sure what she meant.

"Sometimes we take on the ghost's emotions and that can be a clue to what they need, or what they're trying to tell you."

"I didn't . . . Wait. I got a premonition."

"You sure that's what it was?"

"I can't be a hundred percent sure. But it felt the same." Miranda gave her belt another tug.

"What does that feel like?"

Miranda stopped by the window again. "Like someone vacuumed out all your joy. Like you got some terrible news." She turned and looked at Holiday. "Why me? Not you?"

"She somehow connected to you."

"I'm a witch. Witches don't do ghosts and I've never even been to the falls!" The waterfalls on Shadow Falls' property were known to be where the death angels hung out, and many who went there were doomed to be visited by spirits.

"Has it called you?" Kylie asked. "Like, have you heard it?"

"No." But then she remembered hearing the sound of water. Hadn't that just been the creek? Oh damn.

"You don't sound sure," Della said.

"I said no!" Miranda snapped.

"Sorry," Della said. That's when Miranda knew how bad things must be. Della seldom apologized.

Holiday stood and put her hands on Miranda's shoulders. A wave of calm had her heart slowing down. "Try sitting down."

Miranda dropped in a chair. Holiday sat on the arm, as if she might need to be close.

And maybe she did. Miranda's insides hadn't stopped trembling.

Right then she heard the wind outside. She heard trees lashing in the air. She heard sadness, pain, and grief.

"Two things could be happening here," Holiday said. "Ghosts with strong motivation can attach themselves to anyone—even someone without the gift of spirit communication. Bell probably followed Perry when he picked up her baby. She knew Perry. So chances are, she trusted him. Then he gave you the baby. For a mom to see a stranger take her infant, it might have given her the energy to attach herself to you."

"I didn't have the baby when she came here. I was butt naked in the shower."

"The spirit of Lucas's grandmother came to me in the shower. Talk about an awkward way to visit with his family." Kylie half grinned as if trying to throw some humor in the thick tension. The tension sucked it up and tossed it out into the storm.

Holiday continued. "If Bell is simply attached to you, and she needed to communicate with someone, she'd choose you. But the likelihood of it happening again would be rare."

Miranda took a deep breath. That didn't sound bad. For all she knew, Bell could be done communicating. Then she remembered. "What's the other thing? You said it could be two things."

Holiday put her hand on Miranda's shoulder. "I did some research on mystic witches."

"Don't tell me they deal with ghosts. Please."

Holiday gave her shoulder a squeeze. "It's not common, but not unheard of."

"Oh, mother cracker!" Miranda took a deep breath. She popped up and went to the window again. It was as if the trees performed for her. They dipped, swayed, and leaned side to side. Their limbs reached up, down, then toward her.

Something about it was . . . oddly comforting. She inhaled deeply, her lungs now open, and she took the air. With oxygen, she found a little clarity—enough to realize she was being a self-centered little witch. Her fear over a ghost was the least important thing happening right now.

The ghost had given her that address for a reason. And the

doom . . . ? Premonition or not, it had felt like a message. And not a good one.

Could it be about Tabitha? She tied another knot in the robe's sash. If this was about Tabitha . . . was the blood a sign?

Fear for her sister had a chemical reaction erupting in her body and made the air taste bitter.

"Have you heard back from Burnett yet?" she asked, looking away from the window.

"They are on their way to the address now."

"I'm scared what they are going to find. " Miranda looked up at Holiday, and then Kylie and Della. She waited for them to assure her that it wasn't going to be bad. That she was overreacting. How much harm could a little blood bring?

They didn't say a word.

Perry, Burnett, and Chase flew to the address penned in blood on Miranda's bathroom mirror. Perry had wanted to call her so badly, but time hadn't allowed it.

The only Dairy Lane they found was one in Tomball, Texas, about forty miles from Fallen. The house, a run-down home built up on blocks, stood on about ten acres all to itself. If not for the lights on in the front of the house, and one old Chevy pickup truck with a couple of hay bales in the bed, he'd've assumed it was abandoned.

They landed in the back of the house in a patch of trees near a broken down Ford Falcon. They faced the wind, so hopefully it would whisk their scents away.

Perry morphed into human form. Burnett and Chase were crouched down behind the old car that vines had smothered. Perry moved in. Their eyes grew brighter by the second. He'd been around Burnett enough to recognize the different shades of color. This shade screamed blood.

Someone in that house was bleeding.

They both lifted their noses in the air.

"Vampire, shape-shifter, and Wiccan," Chase whispered so low Perry almost missed it. The younger vamp took in another noseful of air. "Shit."

Burnett nodded and his eyes lit up with anger. "Tabitha and Anthony." He tilted his head to the side as if listening. "Three, maybe four." He stared at the house as if pulling together a plan. "We might need—"

"Let me shift and go in," Perry whispered.

Burnett looked at him. "They might have meters checking for shifters."

Perry inched closer. "I don't think so. Not here. Jax wouldn't live in a place like this. This might be where his men stay, but he wouldn't supply security."

Burnett nodded. "In and out. Tell me what we've got. I'm coming in in five minutes."

Perry considered his shift and went with a rattlesnake. Not his favorite, but one that wouldn't look out of place.

He slithered through the overgrown brush and slipped under the house. A mouse squeaked and scurried off, not wanting to be dinner. Spiders scattered and some pulled their webs up into the dank corners of the house's foundation. Others ignored him, too busy sucking the blood out of their latest kill.

In the far corner of the front of the house he saw some rotted wood that could allow entry into the home. He inched that way, his scaly underbelly rolled over gravel.

He slowed down when voices echoed. Footsteps pounded the floor above him, flakes of old wood and dirt showered down. The scales over his eyes protected him from the specks of dirt.

He listened, hoping to make out what was being said. Hoping to hear Tabitha's voice. Needing to believe she was alive.

Muffled voices continued—he counted three different ones— coming from the front room of the house.

Fitting his triangular-shaped head in the hole, his underbelly muscles pulsed and contracted to pull himself up. Once inside the house, he slithered beneath an old cabinet. Curling up to make himself smaller, he eased his head out to see two men sitting on a sagging sofa. A third was in an old recliner eating chips. A gun rested on the side table.

Perry checked their patterns. Mixed-breeds. Not that it meant they weren't dangerous, but it definitely made them less concerning.

"Someone needs to bury the first body," one of them said. "He's starting to smell."

Perry's scales crawled.

"I don't want to dig two holes," the bigger one on the sofa said. "Did Jax give us the go ahead to finish the other one?" the guy in the chair asked.

"He said he'd send someone over tomorrow to try to get more information out of him."

"That French bastard doesn't know shit," the other guy on the sofa said. "I beat the crap out of him. If he knew where she was he'd have told me."

She? French? Anthony? Was Tabitha not here? But wasn't Tabitha's scent here?

Perry slithered from under the cabinet and headed to the back room. He stayed as close as he could to the dirty corner molding, hoping not to be seen. Once out of sight, he let his tongue out, flickering it up and down to catch the scents.

Immediately he wished he hadn't. The stench of blood and death flavored his tongue.

He eased down the hall. The door was shut, but it had a hole in it that looked as if someone had kicked it in.

He eased through it, and a piece of wood splintered off and clattered to the wood floor.

One of the goons must have sensitive hearing because the floor creaked with heavy weight.

"Where you going?" a voice boomed.

"I heard something."

Perry shot the rest of the way through the hole, ending up in a dark room.

Footsteps echoed down the hall.

His snake heart pounded. He searched in the darkness for something to hide under. He spotted bars, separating the room. No furniture offered cover.

He slid through the cold metal poles that made up one jail cell. He saw it. The only thing that offered him any cover was a body.

One as cold as, if not colder than, the reptile form he'd taken on. The door to the room swung open. Light flooded the room.

With no choice, he eased into the ripped and bloody shirt worn by a corpse.

But he hadn't made it in time.

The man screamed. Bullets started exploding.

Chapter Thirty

Holiday had left to take care of Hannah and the baby. Miranda, Kylie, and Della all piled into Della's bed. They didn't sleep, but they didn't talk much, either. They waited.

Waited to hear from Burnett.

Della shot upright. Miranda knew what that meant. She bolted up and ran into the living room.

She'd opened the door when Perry stepped onto the porch.

One look at his face, at his eyes, and she knew . . . knew he had bad news.

"Don't tell me she's dead!" Miranda started backing into the cabin. "Don't you dare tell me she's dead!"

Perry moved in. To hold her. To comfort her. She didn't want comfort. She wanted her sister to be alive.

He started talking, but she refused to hear it. She jerked loose and put her hands over her ears.

"No," she screamed.

"Miranda stop. Listen to me." He pulled her against him. "We didn't find Tabitha."

Miranda caught her breath. "Then what's the terrible news that you have to tell me. And don't say you don't have any. I can see it."

He nodded. "I'm not going to lie to you." He moved her back

until she hit the sofa and she dropped down. He sat beside her. So close his thigh pressed against her leg.

"The address . . . there were three of Jax's men there and some of their victims." He took her hand. "Anthony is hurt, pretty badly, but he's in our care. One of Jax's men confessed. Tabitha was handed over to an underground gang of Wiccans."

"Why would they want her?"

"We don't know. But we're almost certain that it's not just her they want. They want you, too."

She heard him. It should scare her, but all she could think about was how scared Tabitha must be. The last time they were in trouble in Paris, they had each other. Now her sister was alone.

"I don't understand. What have we done to them? What do they want with us?"

"Burnett and Shawn are looking into it."

Emotionally spent and exhausted, they sat there on the sofa. Kylie and Della went to bed. Miranda asked Perry to stay the rest of the night. Or maybe she begged. She didn't care. She didn't want to be alone.

She changed into a pair of light blue pajamas. He came in later and took off his shirt and crawled into her twin-size bed with her. They didn't make out, didn't kiss. It wasn't that kind of night.

They lay close, holding on to each other like two people needing something. Needing each other.

She rested her head against his bare shoulder. His hand rested on the curve of her waist. In his arms she finally felt safe. In his arms she finally fell asleep.

"How's Anthony?" Perry dropped into the chair across from Holiday's desk. Burnett had his own office, but if Holiday wasn't there, he'd use his wife's. Her office was bigger, but Perry suspected it wasn't the space that the vampire cared about. The essence of his wife was in this room. Color, crystals, family photos, and live plants.

The room even smelled like Holiday. Like love. Everyone loved Holiday. But no one more than Burnett.

Burnett frowned. "His heart stopped beating last night, but they were able to pull him back. Doctor said his blood pressure looks better this morning."

"Good." Perry had told Burnett he'd meet him at the office before he took off. The sun hadn't risen when he left Miranda's. Perry would have given anything to stay there. To feel her sleeping on his chest. To be the one to make sure she was safe.

But he knew the best way to help Miranda was to find her sister. Last night, Perry had remembered again the conversation he'd heard at Jax's house. The warlock had said he'd only gotten 50 percent of what Jax was supposed to deliver. Miranda must be the other 50 percent.

How Perry was going to keep from ripping out his brother's heart and feeding it to him was a mystery.

"Holiday spoke with Ms. Wales late last night," Burnett said.

"Ms. Wales?" Perry didn't recognize the name.

"Holiday's old professor with the same tattoo as Miranda."

Perry leaned forward. "Yeah, Miranda mentioned her. Does she know something?"

"Not exactly, but something she said might shed some light on things—if she's correct. Holiday admits she's an eccentric."

"What did she say?" Perry asked.

"Holiday had never mentioned anything to the woman about Tabitha being missing. When Holiday told her, she remembered her mom warned her to never show her tattoo, because according to her grandmother there were a gang of evil Wiccans in the world who would try to take her. Ms. Wales thought her mom was just being overprotective. But she now wonders if perhaps she was never in danger because she was only half Wiccan."

"But Tabitha doesn't have the tattoo," Perry said, thinking aloud.

"She did when the fortune-teller read her palm the first time.

Tabitha told me that Miranda's tattoo was bigger than hers. But she said her tattoo had been a lot bigger than that of her friends when they went."

"So the fortune reader was just a ruse to find girls with power?"

"It's a theory."

"So the tattoo could be the reason they want them, but to do what? Did Shawn come up with anything?"

Burnett's expression went grave. So grave Perry's gut did another twist.

"Nothing definite. But a couple of old cases in the eighties offered two possible motives. Both equally disgusting. You sure you want to hear them?"

"No," Perry said. "But I probably need to know."

"One rogue Wiccan gang was kidnapping young witches of child-bearing age. The plan had been for their leaders, the strongest of the warlocks, to impregnate them so he could produce powerful heirs to build an army."

Perry clenched his fists resting in his lap.

"Another gang who practiced black magic were believed to want the witches to sacrifice, believing their powers would be transferred to the one who wielded the knife."

Perry closed his eyes. "Shit."

"I know." Burnett twisted in Holiday's chair. It squeaked. Perry's desire to run back to Miranda to stay with her grew stronger. His gut still said it wasn't right. "You have to make sure Miranda is safe."

"I'm putting a shadow on her, even in the camp." Burnett picked up a pencil and twirled it in his hand. "Do you think Jax will really trust you with information about the Wiccan gang that has Tabitha?"

Perry looked up. "I sure as hell hope so. I'm the only chance we've got."

Burnett frowned. "Do you have a meeting set up with him today?"

"He said he'd call my mom and tell us where and when to meet him."

"Why doesn't he call you directly?"

"He said he doesn't trust me enough yet."

Burnett slammed back in the chair. It sounded like a couple of screws popped off.

"If he discovers you are working with the FRU . . ." His gaze met Perry's. "You'd better make it out of this unscathed."

"You awake?" Miranda stormed into Della's room.

Miranda had woken up when Perry had left. Without his arms around her, her concern for her sister threatened to consume her and pull her into a dark mental place where everything felt hopeless.

Instead of letting depression swallow her, Miranda chose to get mad. Mad at whoever had taken her sister. She paced around her bedroom thinking about how she'd like to kick their ass.

Thoughts of kicking someone's ass had driven her to wake up Della.

Della lay there, eyes open, a cranky lump under her covers. "I am since you started stomping around your bedroom."

"Good, can we go practice fighting?"

Kylie had also been training her, but Della's methods stuck better.

Della lifted her head an inch and glanced at the window. "It's not even six."

"Please."

Della rose up on her elbow. "Fine. You head that way. I'll pee and brush the crud off my teeth and be there waiting for you."

Miranda started out.

"Wait," Della said.

"What?" Miranda looked back. Della held her phone in her hand.

"Give me a minute and I'll walk you."

"Why?"

Della frowned. "Burnett wants you shadowed."

Miranda's eyes widened. "Here? He's overreacting."

Della popped up. "Yeah, that means he cares about you. Don't you hate it when people do that?" She snagged clothes from her closet and shot over to the bathroom.

Ten minutes later they stood by the lake, the eastern sky a rainbow of colors. Della was showing her how to flip someone over her shoulder. Miranda listened, soaking in every word, and tried really hard not to think about the sound of rushing water. Nope, she didn't want to think about that.

Instead she thought about using each and every attack move Della showed her on her sister's kidnappers.

"I'm going to pull you over my shoulder this time," Della said. "I won't do it hard, but I think you'll understand more what I mean. Come at me from behind like I showed you." Miranda did and air whooshed out of her when Della effortlessly grabbed her upper arm, tossed her over her shoulder, then set her—gently—on the ground.

Miranda popped up. "Do you think I could do that? Even without your strength?" She inhaled again thinking about Tabitha, wishing her sister knew how to protect herself. Wishing Miranda was there to protect her.

"Yeah. Humans do it."

"Can I try?" Miranda asked.

Della took a small step back, motioning with her hand up and down. "You're getting your tattoo groove on."

Miranda looked at the pattern spidering down her legs. "I think Ms. Wales was right. They come when I get emotional."

"You're emotional?" Della asked.

"Mad as hell," Miranda admitted, and saying it out loud felt good. "Someone took my sister, killed Anthony's brother, and almost killed Anthony."

"Yeah, pisses me off, too," Della admitted. Then she smiled. "Does it work when you feel pleasssurre?"

It did. Miranda had woken up last night in Perry's arms, aware of his naked chest, and saw herself all painted up. Not that she cared to share that with Della.

"Forget the tattoos. Let me try to throw you," Miranda said.

"You aren't able to use your arm."

"I can move it some." Miranda showed her how she could reach up to her shoulder with the cast on.

"Yeah but . . ."

"You scared?" she taunted, knowing it would convince the vamp.

"Don't hurt yourself. And if you do, you can't cry."

Miranda turned, remembering the instructions. "I'm ready."

She felt Della approaching. Her arm went around Miranda's neck in a fake chokehold. Miranda caught Della's forearm with her right hand, bent slightly over, and gave it all she had.

It happened fast. Miranda gasped when Della went flying. High, like thirty-feet high. A squeal left Miranda's lips, and she worried Della would get hurt when she landed.

Not to worry.

Della came down on the balls of her feet. Then Miranda realized how stupid she was. She hadn't done that. Della had. "Not funny," she muttered.

Then she noticed Della's wide dark eyes filled with serious shock. "Holy crap cakes!" the vamp yelled. "Am I a good teacher or what?"

Miranda stood there, letting it soak in. If she could throw a reborn vampire into the air, think what she could do to her sister's kidnappers.

In that moment, Miranda resolved to do just that . . . go after the kidnappers. And an instinct—or premonition—washed over her confirming she would do just that. Somehow, someway, she was going to save Tabitha.

. . .

Miranda waited in the conference room at the back of the school's office as Holiday met her parents in the front. Ms. Wales and Burnett sat at the other end of the table.

Nerves buzzed around Miranda's stomach like bees on a witch hunt. And they'd found their witch.

Her palms sweated, her arm under her cast sweated. She had boob sweat. She hated boob sweat.

Footsteps came down the hall announcing the disaster about to happen. Miranda stood and met her parents' confused gazes.

"What's going on?" her father asked. "Did Anthony wake up?" Burnett had informed him about last night's finding. "No, not yet."

"Let's sit down and I'll explain," Holiday said.

Holiday and Burnett had concluded that Miranda should tell her parents everything. About the tattoos, the whole mystic connection, and the real reason she wanted them to sign a consent form to get her blood drawn. Well, not everything. Not about the fact that she'd thrown Della about thirty feet in the air. Not once, but five times. Holiday and Burnett didn't know about that.

Miranda had sworn Della to secrecy. The vamp didn't like it, but Miranda had pulled every girlfriend card she had, pointed out every favor she'd done, every blood donation she'd made. Della relented, with one condition. They tell Kylie. They had, and Miranda had to pull a few more girlfriend cards.

Miranda's mom dashed over to hug her. Sitting beside Miranda, she took her hand, squeezed, and leaned close. "We'll talk in a few minutes. I love you. And I'm sorry."

"I love you, too," Miranda said and she did. She might have said it with more conviction if she wasn't plum terrified about what was about to go down.

Once settled in, both her parents started eyeing Ms. Wales as if wondering why a stranger had been asked to join them.

Holiday, positioned at the head of the table, sat silently as if now trying to figure out where to begin.

Holiday readjusted in her chair and started the conversation by introducing Ms. Wales—by name, not by purpose for her attendance—then she glanced at Miranda's father. "The reason Miranda asked about the family tree is that we suspect that Ms. Wales may be a distant relative of yours."

"Why would you think that?" her mother asked.

"Why, the tattoo, of course," Ms. Wales said.

"What tattoo?" Her mom's tightened eyes shot to Miranda. "Tell me you didn't get a tattoo, young lady? You know how I feel about them."

Yup. Miranda knew. Another reason she didn't think this was a good idea. "I didn't. It just . . ." She glanced at Holiday for help.

"Miranda didn't get a tattoo," Holiday spoke up. "We're getting ahead of ourselves. Let me continue."

Holiday explained about the tattoo Miranda had gotten from the fortune reader.

"Why didn't you tell us this?" her mom asked.

Caught in her mom's gaze, Miranda blurted out. "It went away. I thought it would stay away."

"Where is it?" Her mom eyed Miranda. "I want to see it."

"It's not here now," Miranda said.

"So you don't have it anymore?" Her mom looked puzzled.

"It comes and goes," Miranda said.

"Wait," her father finally spoke up. "What does this tattoo have to do with Ms. Wales being a relative?"

Her mom looked at Holiday for an answer.

Ms. Wales pipped up. "Let me show you."

Miranda nearly freaked thinking the woman was about to disrobe down to her leopard skinned skivvies again. Instead, she pulled something out of her large brown manila envelope.

She pushed something across the table to Miranda's father. "Here is the image of your daughter's tattoo. Here is mine."

He looked at it. Her mom did the same then looked at Miranda. "It's on your arm? High or low? Can it be covered up with a short sleeve?"

Miranda almost moaned at how insignificant her mother's concerns were.

"Dare I say," Ms. Wales spoke up, "that the tattoo's location isn't the point, Mrs. Evans."

Evans! Oh, mother crackers! Miranda knew that wasn't going to go over well.

Holiday recognized disaster as well. "Kane. They go by Kane."

Fire lit in her mother's eyes and her pinky twitched.

"Odd," the old woman said, either blind to Miranda's mom's glare, or choosing not to see it.

Holiday opened her mouth to speak again and was cut off by Ms. Wales. "We didn't even consider we might be related until Holiday pointed out that we are also both dyslexic."

Her mom shook her head. "What? Are you aware how many people suffer from this affliction?"

"'Suffer' is a strong word, don't you think?" The woman looked at Miranda.

Miranda literally sank into her chair. Burnett did the same.

"Please," Holiday said. "Can I explain—"

"Oh, dear," Ms. Wales said. "I've got this. You see, Mr. Evans, the moment I heard the name Evans I knew we were related."

Her father put his hand on top of her mom's and spoke up. "I brought the family tree with me. Miranda requested it. What was the family name?"

Holiday stood up. "I really don't think—"

Ms. Wales piped up again. "You won't find it there," Ms. Wales said. "Your great great grandfather forced himself on my ancestor."

"What?" Miranda's mom asked.

Miranda sank deeper in her chair.

"I have the proof. Here's an article of her execution. She killed the bugger. His name is here." She pulled the article back and began to read. "Mildred Bradley was hanged to death, accused of striking Rudolf Evans, whom she accused of sexual assault, forty-six times with an ax."

Everyone sat there speechless then.

"Wait," her father said. "Are you saying that my great, great grandfather raped your great, great, grandmother then she killed him?"

"See," Ms. Wales said to Holiday. "I told you I could explain this."

Chapter Thirty-one

Miranda held her breath. The explosion she predicted in the room was going to be far worse than the one at the drug house.

Ms. Wales looked back at Miranda's father. "It's all right here." She pushed the article back over.

Miranda's butt slipped lower in her chair.

When a cloud of befuddlement settled around them, Ms. Wales spoke up again. "Oh dear, don't misunderstand. I hold you at no fault. You cannot help it if your ancestor was a bloody bastard."

"That's it." Burnett stood up. "I really think we should call it a day."

"No." Her father started flipping pages, looking at his own documents. "I remember . . ." He stopped. Read. Then looked up. "I have a copy of the same newspaper clipping."

Burnett sat back down but looked worried. Miranda shared his concern.

"We don't know if the accusation is true," her mom spoke up.

"Which is why I've asked Miranda to do a blood test," Ms. Wales said. "I had mine drawn at the FRU agency. Thanks to Mr. James, here."

Her father shot out of his chair so fast his chair hit the floor. He directed his comments to Burnett. "This is ludicrous. My daughter is kidnapped, you bring me in here to talk about a distant relative?"

Burnett stood up to explain, but once again, Ms. Wales, with her English-accented, commanding voice, intervened. "Please calm down, Mr. Evans. As far-fetched as it may sound, our relations may have something to do with your daughter's abduction."

Burnett nodded. Her father yanked his chair up and dropped back down. Holiday finished the story. No one interrupted for a good five minutes.

Until . . . "What!" her mom asked, smiling. "Are you saying my daughter is mystic?"

"No," Holiday said. "I'm saying that Ms. Wales's mother and grandmother were mystic. I'm saying that Ms. Wales's grandmother was and Ms. Wales is dyslexic like Miranda. And then there's the tattoo. It may or may not have anything to do with being mystic."

"But are there any signs that it may be true?" Her mom directed that question to Miranda.

"A few." Miranda explained about Perry hearing her voice and she his, and about Tabitha's text. While talking about hearing things, Miranda started hearing things again. Not just things. But the sound of cascading water. *Shit!*

A short time later, Ms. Wales announced she had to get back to Houston. Her mom went to the restroom, Burnett walked out with her father to stretch their legs.

Holiday let go of a deep sigh and rested back in the chair. "That went tons better than I expected."

Miranda and her mom walked out to the front porch of the office to have their "talk." Holiday went to check in on Hannah and the baby. Burnett and her father sat in Holiday's office to discuss the case.

Miranda's nerves hadn't calmed down from the meeting they'd just had, and now she was having another one.

Yes, she wanted to clear the air with her mom.

Yes, she loved her with all her heart.

Yes, she wanted to just run back to her bed and cover her head. She couldn't.

Instead, she mentally reached down and yanked up her big-girl panties so hard she got a wedgie. Then she dropped down in one of the rocking chairs and prepared herself for yet another difficult talk.

The sound of rushing water in her ears made this hard. The devastating feeling she got every time she thought about Tabitha, made it harder. Tears started welling up in her eyes. She blinked them away.

Her mom scooted the second chair closer to the one Miranda occupied and sat down. Then she reached for Miranda's hand.

"Aren't you the least bit excited about being a mystic witch?"

Several choice replies danced on her tongue. She swallowed the more offensive ones. "Right now I don't give a son of a monkey spank about being mystic." She wasn't sure what it meant. She'd probably heard it from Della, but it felt appropriate.

Her mom's eyes widened. "Oh, I shouldn't have . . . I'm sorry. I know you're worried about Tabitha. I am, too."

Miranda looked at her mom, her anger too close to the surface. "You don't even like her."

Her mom exhaled. "I don't dislike Tabitha." The tears in her mother's eyes caught Miranda's attention. She'd seen her father cry more than she had her mom. And her mom wasn't one to fake anything. So those tears were . . . real.

Her mom blinked. Tears fell. "After our argument, I went to see a therapist."

"You did?" Just like her mom didn't cry, she wasn't the type to go talk to therapists. That would imply she had problems. And her mom, of course, was perfect. Just ask her.

Her mom inhaled. "What you said . . ."

Guilt rose above Miranda's anger. "I was wrong to say . . ."

"No. I needed to hear it. I've been terrible since . . . since you learned the truth and Tabitha came into your life." Fresh tears filled her eyes. "No, I've been terrible long before that, since I found out about Mary Esther and her pregnancy. I didn't know your father was married, Miranda. But I was pretty sure there was another woman. His pager went off way too much. And he'd never make a call in front of me. I let . . . things happen quicker because . . . I thought he'd forget about whomever it was paging him if we slept together."

She sat up straighter. "When he told me he was married, I was meeting him to tell him that I was pregnant. He told me about his wife and her pregnancy. I told him I never wanted to see him again. I left."

She inhaled then continued, "He came to see me the next week. He told me his marriage was basically over and that . . . he loved me. But he couldn't divorce her because of his inheritance and because of Ireland's no-divorce rules. He said he wanted to be with me and our child, but he couldn't turn his back on Mary Esther or their child. He swore he'd never touch her as a wife again. He offered to change his name, and I could take that name and we'd live as husband and wife. We could even say we were married."

Her voice shook. "I accepted it because I loved him and I wanted you to know your father. But every time he left to go to Ireland, every time I knew he was with Mary Esther and Tabitha, I was petrified that he would decide that he loved them more. When she moved to the States so they could be closer, I almost lost it."

Her mom stopped rocking. "Over time that hurt, that fear, grew. I couldn't blame him, because I accepted his deal. I refused to take any blame—refused to acknowledge that if I'd just asked questions about his damn pager none of this would have happened. Instead, I blamed Mary Esther and Tabitha."

She sat silent for a few minutes, her tears still falling. Miranda felt her mom's pain. She couldn't imagine how hard it would be to see the man you loved leave to take care of someone he'd once loved.

Her mom must've felt so insecure. And while the thought sliced into Miranda's heart like a paper cut, Miranda knew that while her mom would never admit it, this was the reason she wanted Miranda to be perfect, the reason she hadn't been able to accept Miranda's dyslexia. For if Tabitha proved to be the better daughter, her father might have left them.

"The therapist says it will take time to completely let go of what I feel, but I'm working on it. Already I can honestly say that I don't hate Mary Esther or Tabitha. I don't think I ever hated them. I hated the part of your father that he gave them—the time, the consideration, the money. I felt it belonged to you and me."

Her mom took Miranda's hand again. "I'm not proud of how this has . . . I'm not proud of the type of mom I've been."

Wow, her mom was going to admit it.

Now, Miranda's tears almost equaled her mom's. Feelings, old resentments, hurts rose to the surface, and her love for her mom, love that meant everything, kicked the resentments' asses. Forgiveness was bliss.

Her mom started talking again. "I'm going to change, Miranda. I promise. Forgive me, please?"

Miranda stood and pulled her mom into a tight embrace. It was a good one. A healing one. "I forgive you. Maybe you haven't been perfect, but you told me you loved me every day. You taught me to be kind and not to be prejudiced against any race or species. You hugged me every day. You never left me at a mall and let total strangers raise me."

That last statement required some explanation, but what was important was that Miranda not only had made peace with her mom, but some old grudges she hadn't even admitted having were gone.

Before her parents left, Miranda felt her skin tickling, her tattoo wanting to come out and play. She put her hand around her cast and whispered, "Not now."

Her mom and dad had enough shock for one day. They didn't need to see their daughter covered in tattoos.

. . .

Perry took a deep breath and walked up to Jax's house. He'd flown back to Houston early, expecting his dad to set up a time to meet and leave together. He hadn't texted until almost five, giving Jax's address and telling him to meet there directly. The same house he'd shown up to yesterday.

He realized what this meant. Jax trusted him.

Keep that up, brother.

A guard pushed the door open.

Perry's mind went straight to the Italian guard he'd gotten placed on Jax's hit list. Burnett still hadn't gotten anything on him but wasn't giving up. Perry didn't like knowing he might've gotten the man killed.

Entering the hall, he saw three guards standing court in the corner of the room. Then he saw Jax. He breathed through his right nostril, letting it out his left. He couldn't lose it now.

His gaze shifted. He spotted his mom and dad seated on a sofa. Yesterday the room had been empty, now it held furniture, the kind that came with price tags that Perry knew he could never afford.

He nodded a greeting and eased into the room.

He settled into one of those French-looking chairs with embroidered cushions. A glance at his mom showed she still had pimples. She'd tried to hide them under her bangs.

Was he wrong to find joy from that? Hell no.

He realized he hadn't told Miranda thank you. Maybe tonight. If he returned.

Honestly, he was exhausted. Holding her was heaven, but not conducive to sleep, and the trips back and forth were draining him. But he'd use his last little bit of energy to do it. As long as he wasn't being followed. And he'd been more careful than ever.

Jax spoke up. "Mom and your dad were telling me you have a girlfriend."

"I do." He glanced at his mom. "What's wrong with your fore-head?"

She scowled at him.

Jax laughed.

Her father just looked at him. Odd-like.

"I'm seeing a dermatologist tomorrow," she answered.

"Tell me about your girl." Jax went to pour himself a drink.

Perry had hoped to derail the whole girlfriend subject. It hadn't worked. He needed another angle.

He shouldered back into the chair, which wasn't at all comfortable. "Tell me about yours?"

Jax laughed. "She's built like a brick shit house. Tits out to here." He held out his palms. "And screws like a rabbit. Your turn?"

Perry noticed one of the guards was vampire. He'd bet his front teeth Jax had him checking Perry for any mistruths.

Maybe Jax didn't trust him all that much after all.

"She's soft. Pretty. And I like her enough that I don't talk vulgar about her."

Jax laughed harder. "She's got you whipped." He pretended to snap a whip in the air. "You take after your dad."

Perry flinched at the insult.

A guy wearing a white apron walked into the room. "Dinner is ready, sir."

Jax waved for everyone to stand up. "I had my chef prepare something extra special."

Perry's stomach grumbled at the thought of food. He'd grabbed a breakfast around eleven, yet missed lunch. Even so, with the knot of hate filling his belly, he didn't think he could eat.

The dining room table could sit twelve. It looked empty, lonely, with just the four of them there. Jax was presented a wine cork to smell. Perry had heard they did that in fancy restaurants. This wasn't a restaurant.

When the chef got to Perry to pour the wine, Perry covered his glass. "Just water."

Plates of food were set in front of each of them. Perry's appetite waned even more.

The chef standing to the side of Jax took the cloth napkin off the table in front of his half brother and placed it in his lap. He did the same for his mom and dad.

He moved to Perry. "Got this." He tucked it between his legs.

"Enjoy." Jax waved his hands.

Perry forced himself to eat a few bites of food. But the prime rib practically mooed when pierced by his fork. The mashed potatoes? He liked mashed potatoes—they were his favorite food. But these had garlic in them? Perhaps he'd gotten his tastes from Burnett, but someone had just ruined his favorite food.

"You eat like a bird, brother," Jax said when everyone was finishing up.

"I wasn't aware we were doing dinner. I grabbed a Big Mac on the way here." He flinched realizing he'd lied.

The vampire in the corner smiled. "That was a lie."

Perry set his fork down. "Okay, I was trying to be polite. I actually don't like my meat bleeding and someone should be shot for adding garlic to mashed potatoes. And the green beans? I heard that people call these al dente or some crap like that, but I like mine cooked."

Jax laughed. "I like your sense of humor. But you don't know shit about fine food."

"Not my fault." Perry glanced at his mother. "We didn't have chefs in foster care."

Jax laughed again. Perry knew then that the humor, the humor he sometimes hid behind, was going to come in handy.

Now if he could stop imagining how much damage he could do to Jax with the steak knife, he might be okay.

"What's your excuse, Paul?" he asked Perry's father.

"Not hungry."

Perry noted something off with his dad, but that would have to wait.

After dessert—strawberries with some kind of sweet rum-flavored white sauce, which Perry did eat—Jax asked Mom and Dad to leave so he could . . . get to know Perry.

"I thought we were going to discuss our next job." His father looked nervous.

"Not now," Jax said. "Something's happening. I got men dropping like flies. Even Chuckie and Mark haven't gotten back with me." He grimaced when he said it.

Perry watched his parents leave, hoping the vampire guard would also retire. No such luck.

Perry turned down Jax's offer for a beer or whiskey. He had to stay on his game. Thankfully, he'd watched Burnett dodge truths for years when talking to their vampire foster parents. The trick was to be the one asking more questions, so you weren't dancing around the truth the whole time.

Before he could come up with a question, Jax did. "Tell me something, brother. You aren't staying with mama dearest. Where have you been hanging your hat?"

Chapter Thirty-two

The question ran laps around Perry's head. He sought for an acceptable answer. Finally he relied on his humor to give him a few more seconds.

"I don't wear hats. But if you're asking where I was, I was at my girlfriend's place."

"Where's that?" Jax sipped his drink.

"A nice place. Not this nice."

"You avoiding my question?" Suspicion sparked in his eyes.

Keep it honest. "Let's just say I'm keeping her to myself for right now."

Jax grinned. "You afraid I might . . . try something?"

Perry knew what Jax meant, but yeah, he was afraid Jax would try something. "Yeah, I am."

"Can't say I blame you. I am the better-looking brother."

Perry forced himself to smile. "I don't agree, but you do have a hell of a lot more money."

"Whoever said money doesn't buy happiness was a poor man," Jax said. "So you've decided to work for me?"

"I think you knew I'd say yes. But first I was hoping you'd tell me a little more about how all this works."

"I told you. I run a few operations myself, like what you and your dad were doing. Then the different gangs pay me protection fees. When they need something, they come to me. I'm not cheap."

"Exactly what do you do for them?"

"Anything," Jax said. "Anything they want."

Perry folded his arms over his chest. "Exactly what would I be doing for you?"

"Anything and everything I want."

Before Perry could toss out another question, Jax got one in. "You have restrictions? You worried you don't have the stomach for it?"

"Depends," Perry said. "If you're asking me to put a damn napkin in your lap, then you're right, I don't have the stomach for that."

Jax laughed, but sobered quickly. "You ever kill anyone, brother?"

He thought of Jax's guard. "It's possible. But for sure, I've come close several times."

"Would you have a problem doing it?"

Perry let the rage he felt for his brother simmer in his empty stomach. "Honestly, I might even enjoy it."

"We're more alike than I thought."

Perry still wasn't getting anything useful. "I'm not getting a clear picture about the job. Take that warlock who was here yesterday trying to get out of paying you. What did he want from you?"

Jax chuckled. "He wasn't trying to get out of paying me. He'd be dead, if he did. I was only able to get him half of what he wanted."

Perry's stomach cramped. "You going to finish the job?"

"When it's right, I'll do it." He got up and poured himself another drink. "Like I said, some of my men are dropping like flies. I don't take chances."

Perry stretched out his legs and crossed them at the ankles. "Then why don't you let me take the chances for you? Tell me what they want, where to hand over the goods, and I'll do it."

Jax swirled the whiskey in his glass then stared right at Perry.

Had Perry pushed too hard, showed too much interest?

"I like that you're eager. But you need to prove yourself before I give you my big cases."

"How do I prove myself?"

Miranda had eaten pizza with Holiday and Burnett. When she asked about Anthony, Burnett gave her the good news. Anthony appeared to be coming out of his coma. He wasn't lucid, but close.

It was after seven when Burnett walked Miranda to her cabin. It was still light outside, hazy, but not dark. The trees did their crazy stirring in the non-stirring air. She almost asked Burnett about it, but felt stupid. So they didn't talk. Instead she worked on convincing herself that the plan she'd conjured up over dinner was a good one.

When she walked in, Della and Kylie were at the table, their noses in books. They'd gone to the FRU library and checked out books looking for information on tattooed powerful witches. Kylie must've been in vampire mode, not that Miranda checked, but both of them had glasses of blood.

"Anything?" Miranda asked.

"Zilch." Della frowned.

"We haven't gone through them all," Kylie said, always the optimist. "How did things go?"

"Bat-shit crazy, but good." She told them about her mom.

"About time," Della said.

Miranda waited to make sure Burnett had gotten far enough away before getting down to business. "I need a favor."

"What?" Kylie asked.

"Go to the falls with me."

"I knew it. You were called, right?" Della asked.

"Should we tell Holiday?" Kylie stood up.

"She's caring for Hannah and the baby. Can't we just go?"

"We can," Della said.

Ten minutes later, facing the falls, Miranda, flip-flops off, took her first step into the water.

She looked back at Kylie and Della. The two of them were exchanging curious glances. "Come on."

"We can't," Della said.

"They don't want us to go in." Puzzlement filled Kylie's tone.

If it didn't feel so peaceful here—Miranda might have been afraid. But this place was like a paradise, flowers of all different kinds, aromas of sweet herbs. The tree limbs hung low as if embracing this little bit of heaven. She'd never known places could have auras, but this one did. And it was amazing.

"Will you wait here?" she asked.

They nodded.

Moving through the water was like walking through liquid glass. It didn't move. She did. The rush of water rang loud. But a pleasant kind of loud. Like church bells in a small southern town.

She ducked her head and moved through the cascading wall of water. Chills ran down her spine. The kind of chills you got when good things were about to happen.

Perry hadn't been surprised when Jax had the vampire follow him. He'd debated flying to a hotel and calling it a night. But then Jax would assume Perry hadn't known he was being tailed.

No, Perry needed Jax to respect his powers. He just had to make sure that Jax didn't feel threatened by him. Which was why when he'd shifted for Jax, he'd held back. And when Jax decided to make it a game of who could shift faster, Perry had let him win. Not by much. But enough.

So instead of finding a room and calling it a night, he'd dived into a patch of trees, scared off another falcon, and waited until the vampire had followed the wrong bird. Before he took off, he texted his dad. *Tell Jax, better luck next time.* He figured making light of it would be less likely to piss the guy off.

Even as he started out, he backtracked, and never stopped checking if someone followed.

As he neared Shadow Falls, thoughts of seeing Miranda pushed him to fly faster. But he needed to see Burnett first.

He landed, shifted, and walked straight for the office. The light in Holiday's office told him someone was there.

"Hey." Burnett sat in Holiday's chair again.

Perry dropped the two files on the desk.

"What's this?"

"Info on Ricky Raco and Caleb Davidson."

Burnett reached for the papers. "How did you get this?"

Perry dropped down in the chair. "Jax."

"You stole them?" Burnett asked.

"No, he gave them to me."

Burnett's brow creased. "Why would he do that?"

Perry's stomach turned just saying it. "Because I'm supposed to hunt them down and kill them."

"Will it ever stop raining shit?" Burnett asked, but after blowing steam he came up with a plan. "I'll put some men on finding Caleb and Ricky, let's stay focused on finding Tabitha."

Perry remembered Bell, and how Caleb had taken her life as if she meant nothing. "I'd like to help to find Caleb. He killed Bell." Perry owed the girl that much. "And my gut says he might know more about Jax's operation."

Burnett wavered, but finally agreed. "But we'll do it together."

Miranda walked through the lagoon of water into the cave behind the falls and sat down on the rock floor. The same aura that was outside followed her inside. Tranquility, peace. Miranda had never felt anything like it.

A scratchy noise sounded behind her. She turned. Not out of fear, curiosity. The armadillo moved from behind a rock.

He scuffled over beside her.

She didn't say anything for several seconds. "Are you a death angel?"

"Oh no."

"Then what?" Not that Miranda was afraid. He wasn't evil. Evil couldn't exist here.

"Think of me as your fairy godfather."

She studied him. "That doesn't work. You don't look like a fairy godfather. What are you?" Then another question hit. "Did the witch, the one at the drug house, curse you?"

"No, I was cursed a long time ago. Zander just . . . imprisoned me. I was trying to help her, but she was too scared. Then she was too scared to let me go."

"What was she scared of?"

"The bad ones."

"What did they do that was bad?" Miranda stared into the water, iridescent circles danced on the surface.

"They took her, took her power, took her memories, took her babies, took her self-will. Finally they didn't have to take it. She just gave it to them. Hoping they wouldn't take her life until the point came when she hoped they would."

Miranda considered that. It was ugly, but the essence of this place kept it from hurting too much. "Did she get injured in the explosion?"

"No, she caused it. To stop the others from coming for you and your sister."

"Why? What did they want with . . . us?"

"The same as they took from Zander. You are powerful, they wanted their sons to be just as strong."

"But . . ." If not for the peace of this place, she'd be freaking out. "How did they know we'd be there?"

"Zander's magic. They forced her to put magic spells on all young witches. They were looking for the powerful ones. Those like you and your sister."

"And the drug house?" Miranda asked, confused. "How is that connected to the warlocks?"

"The drug house belonged to another gang leader. One who is

even more powerful than the warlocks. They went to this leader to help them find new breeders for their younger warlocks. He set up Zander there to read the fortunes of young witches so she could find the girls the warlock gang needed."

Miranda's mind swam. "So my sister's sudden need to see Zander was because of a spell?"

"Yes, I am afraid so. But Zander couldn't carry through with it." The creature came to the witch's defense. "Because of you and your sister, she found some self-will. She couldn't let happen to you and your sister what happened to her and her sister."

His words sent the tiniest wave of worry her way. "Do you, or does Zander, know where my sister is? Do they have her?"

Fear pushed back some of the calm she felt. The creature's snout bobbed up and down. "That's why I'm here."

"Tell me and my friends and I will go get her. Then I'll do everything I can to wipe away your curse." The second part was a bribe, but Miranda didn't care.

He shook his head. "No. Zander has looked into the future. There is only one way to free Tabitha." He put his paw, claws and all, on Miranda's leg. "And only one way to free myself."

Miranda's heart started to race. The peacefulness was still present, but the tension built inside herself. "How can I free my sister?"

"You must take her place."

Miranda swallowed. It wasn't that she wouldn't do it, but she'd been hoping for a slightly better plan.

"Okay." But then she had to ask. "What are they going to do to me?"

"No, you misunderstand. You aren't merely taking her place. You have what it takes to fight them. Your sister, she has some of the magic, but not enough. It has to be you. Zander's seen it. She had an image."

"So I'm mystic?"

"You share many traits with mystics, but your gifts are unique."

"Because I'm dyslexic?" she asked. He looked puzzled, so she clarified. "My disability?"

"You mean your gift? Your brain works differently. Yes, it makes some things harder, but the gifts more than make up for it. You see life, you experience life, in ways others can't. You think, you feel through emotion, not through whims. You empathize with others, their pain, their struggles—even the creatures. You released me, didn't you?"

"What does that make me?"

"Some refer to your kind as a forest mystic. You also share traits with the forest witch."

"The trees?" Miranda said. "They frightened me."

"Don't be afraid. They are there to protect you. You draw strength from them, and them from you."

Miranda had so many questions she didn't know where to start. "Why didn't my gifts show up earlier?"

"The magic in you is not released until you find another . . . magic."

"What?"

He stared at her as if she should figure it out. Then suddenly she knew. "True love."

He nodded.

A warm swirl of emotion curled up in her chest like a happy kitten, knowing Perry was her true love.

Then a shimmering light, colors unlike any she'd ever seen, appeared before her. Miranda gasped, not from fear, but awe.

The armadillo looked up. "I must go now."

"No! How do I get to my sister?"

"Your chance will come soon. I will be there to guide you. But when I say it's time, do not hesitate. And you must not, under any circumstance, tell anyone. They will try to help, but people you love will be sacrificed."

The armadillo faded. The light vanished. Then Holiday walked through the wall of water.

"Are you okay?" The fae's wide eyes told Miranda her tattoos were back.

Miranda stood. "I'm fine."

"They're beautiful."

"Thanks."

"Would you like to talk—"

"Not now," Miranda blurted out. She didn't like keeping secrets, but she knew as clear as she knew her name, the armadillo hadn't been lying. If she told anyone, people she loved would die. "I asked Kyle and Della not to bother you."

"They didn't. I just came down for a visit." Holiday hugged her. "Did you learn anything here?"

Miranda couldn't lie. "Yes. But I'm still digesting it."

After a few minutes, Miranda left. Her two best friends, like Holiday, respected Miranda's requests not to talk. As they walked back, she attempted to cling to the peace she'd found. Unfortunately, all but a little of it slipped away like an old memory fading with time.

However, she drew some peace by focusing on the trees. *You draw strength from them, and them from you.*

But she couldn't lie to herself. The thought of leaving Shadow Falls, without telling anyone, already felt like a betrayal.

When they rounded the turn to their cabin, she saw Perry on their porch.

Her true love.

She took off running. She ran right into his arms. He must have showered, because he smelled of man's soap, of wind. But he felt like pain.

For two hours, Perry helped Miranda study. She'd tried asking him about his day—his pain—he'd avoided answering. As much as she resented it, she couldn't fuss. She wasn't talking about everything, either.

He'd asked her why she was wet. She told him about the falls, she'd told him how beautiful it was, and how she'd sensed Tabitha would be okay.

Later that night, her pajamas on, his shirt off, they resumed their position in bed. She felt his heart beating against her ear. With every thu-thump she felt his pain. She remembered what the armadillo had said about her feeling other's emotions.

"Are you okay?" She lifted her head.

He shot her a smile, one that wasn't a complete lie, but he used his smiles to cover his pain.

"Hard day," he said. "But now I'm good."

"You want to talk about it?"

He spoke quickly. "No. It's not that I don't want to share, Miranda, but I don't want to go back there right now. I don't want that here."

She placed her hand on his chest, knowing his heart hurt. "We don't have to tell each other everything. Not right away. We can tell each other later."

He kissed her. It was the first real kiss he'd given her in a few days. It felt good, so good she shifted, rested on top of him, and let the kiss deepen. She ran her fingers over his abs, loving the ripples. He slipped his hand under her pajama top, touching her naked back.

Loving it. Needing more. She sat up and pulled her top off.

They touched, they tasted, they kissed. They'd set these rules and abided by them in the past. Anything above the belt. Lost in the magic and the delicious feeling, she wanted more. She started to slip off her pajama bottoms.

He caught her hand, broke the kiss, but leaned in so close they breathed the same birthday-cake scented air. "No. Not like this. Soon though."

He smiled then. A real smile. One that reached down inside her and made her happy. Hopeful.

"I love you," he whispered as he slid her top over her head. When he did, she noticed—as Della had put it—she had her tattoo groove on. But she wasn't the least bit self-conscious. She saw the way his eyes watched the shirt lower over her breasts. He didn't seem to mind.

"I love you, too," she said, then giggled. "More than ice cream."

He countered. "More than flying."

She brushed her finger over his smile. "My Peter."

He lifted up on his elbow. "That reminds me. How did things go with your mom?"

She told him about the conversation with her mom, and even got teary-eyed. "But the good news is, you're not the only one who comes from rough stock." She told him about the rape and the murder.

Afterward, he told her about his mom's pimples.

"I didn't do that. I swear."

"Yes you did." He kissed again. It got hot again. Hands went back to touching. But her shirt stayed on.

He finally pulled away, breathing hard. Everything about him . . . hard.

"We need to sleep," he said, his voice deep and husky.

Coming back down from that high, and staying down, was hard. Especially with him, still shirtless, pressed against her.

As she lay there listening to him breathe, she couldn't help but think about what the armadillo had said and worry about how it would go down.

Chapter Thirty-three

On Tuesday before lunch, Shawn walked into the hospital. This could be a big mistake. But damn it, he kept hearing Miranda. *Then decide what you want. Don't let your mother's opinions override what you feel.*

Was his reluctance to get involved with anyone other than a Wiccan because of his mother? She'd certainly preached it to him all his life. So yeah, maybe it was?

He didn't like that answer, so he decided to play with fire. He'd decided to stop avoiding Lily. See what happened.

He'd even asked Burnett for this assignment. Mr. Crow had gotten out of the hospital a couple of days ago. And now Lily was being discharged, too. Burnett had put a guard 24-7 on the house.

They'd told the Crows the truth. Or part of the truth. They suspected it was Lily's family behind the robbery. Until they were caught, a guard would be watching them. Since the two goons Jax had hired to kill her had been caught, some of the pressure was off. But not completely. Jax could send someone else.

When he got to her door, Lucas was standing guard.

The were nodded. "They're bringing her walking papers any minute. You got it from here?"

"Yeah. Thanks." Shawn had noticed a little awkwardness from

both Lucas and Chase as if they worried he might somehow blame them for not warning him about Perry and Miranda. Yeah, it dinged Shawn's ego a bit, but he wasn't going to let it affect their friendship. Or work relationship.

Taking a deep breath, he pushed the door open.

Lily sat in the bed dressed to go. When her gaze found him, her eyes widened. He couldn't tell if it was from anger or surprise.

"Well, look who the dog dragged up." Her words came off angry, but her tone wasn't. Color him confused.

"I've been putting in a lot of work hours." It wasn't a lie.

"I bet."

Her backpack, opened, was beside her. He remembered when it had been full of money. Remembered he'd been responsible for a lot of her pain since.

"Need help packing?"

"Nope. It's done." She studied him. "You the one giving me a lift home?"

He nodded, prepared to be slammed with insults.

She smiled. "Should I go ahead and take a pain pill now?"

He bit back a smile. "I know you don't believe this, but I'm really a good agent. When I'm around you I . . ." He paused, unsure how to say it. "I end up thinking more about you than what I need to be doing."

Her eyes widened. "So I should take the pill now?"

He laughed. "I think I've learned my lesson."

They left the hospital, and while he never stopped checking their surroundings, they made small talk. Weather. Where she'd traveled. Their favorite restaurants.

Right before he turned down her street, she asked, "Did your girlfriend love the bracelet?"

He pulled into her driveway. A black sedan sat outside the house—the agent on duty. Shawn ran his hand over his steering wheel.

"We broke up."

The tension in the car rose.

Then she chuckled. "Why? Did you put her in the hospital, too?"

He laughed. "No. I think I was a rebound relationship for her. The guy came back and she bounded right back to him."

Lily made a sad face. "Sorry."

"I'm okay with it. There was something missing between us."

She tilted her head to the side a little as if listening to his heart. Then she met his gaze. "Maybe we'll see each other later." She got out of the car before he could say anything.

Shawn watched her until she got in the house and knew she was safe. "Yeah." Smiling, he pulled away. "Maybe we will."

Wednesday evening, Perry drove Burnett's new car to Mrs. Conner's. He'd seen her yesterday at the agency and she'd all but threatened to neuter him if he didn't show up for dinner. Then today, during lunch, she'd called to remind him. He'd gone to her house before, but to make sure, he'd taken down her address.

He hoped she didn't plan on a late evening. He missed Miranda so badly his toenails hurt. They'd spoken on the phone for two hours last night, but he hadn't gone to her place—hadn't slept with her in his arms. Not just because he'd been exhausted from running down leads but because of how hard it had been to hold back with her the night before.

She'd asked him to wait until this was over, and by damn he was going to wait. Tonight he hoped she'd be wearing something really ugly to sleep in.

Glancing down at the files on the passenger seat, Perry's hands on the steering wheel tightened. All of his leads on Caleb and the warlock gang had been a wash. They had a few more addresses to check tomorrow before Perry would admit failure.

And his dad had texted to say Jax wanted to meet tomorrow night.

The thought of turning up empty-handed at Jax's hurt like a

toothache. Not because he gave a damn what his asshole half brother thought, but because he needed to win his trust so he'd hand over information about the warlock gang.

The plan was if they didn't get anything in the next two days, they'd storm Jax's house and hope like hell Jax, or one of his men, would turn over the information on the gang that held Tabitha. His worry was that Jax or his men wouldn't turn over anything. Perry had to find something out and fast. But how? How could he get his brother to trust him enough to tell him things?

Perry reached into the backseat for the flowers he'd bought for Mrs. Conner. When he told Miranda about his dinner tonight, she'd suggested he bring flowers. Call it silly, but he liked her making sure he did the right thing. It made them feel like . . . a real couple again. Probably because he'd heard Holiday tell Burnett things like that.

Getting out of the car, Perry went around and checked all the locks. The fact that Burnett had offered to let him use his classic Mustang said a lot. The man loved his cars.

At times Perry wondered how he could tell an undemonstrative vamp how much he cared without sounding mushy. Maybe he should ask Miranda.

He rang the doorbell.

Mr. Conner, also a were, greeted Perry at the door. "I'm glad you came. She was going to send me after your butt if you didn't. She purposely left out garlic from the meatballs just for you."

Perry laughed. Mr. Conner still had a couple of inches on Perry. Everyone described the couple as Mutt and Jeff. He was a gentle giant, his wife was a tiny spitfire.

"I wouldn't miss it," Perry said. "She threatened to have me neutered if I did."

"And she'd probably do it, too," the old man said. "She got me neutered after our fourth kid."

"Is it Perry?" Mrs. Conner called from the kitchen.

"Yup," Perry answered.

"Come and let me show you my spoon collection now that I've got them all up!"

After oohing and aahing over the spoons and the photos of her grandkids, she found a vase for the flowers, and they sat down for dinner. Her table was set with expensive-looking white plates and cloth napkins, but Perry would bet no one tried to put the napkin in his lap. Mrs. Conner told a few stories about when she worked the field as an FRU agent. The woman might stand less than five feet, but Perry didn't doubt she'd been good at the job.

They had finished eating salad when the doorbell rang. Mrs. Conner stood up. "I hate it when my dinner parties are interrupted. But it's probably another Girl Scout selling cookies. And I can't say no." She grabbed her purse on the way out of the kitchen.

Voices came from the other room. Perry couldn't distinguish what was being said.

Mr. Conner suddenly dropped his fork and shot out of his chair. He hadn't gotten around the table when he stopped and gasped.

Perry looked up. His breath caught, and he gripped the edge of the table. Caleb had Mrs. Conner and was shoving her into the kitchen. He didn't hold a weapon, but with his arm around her neck and a hand on the opposite side of her head, it was evident how he planned to kill her. One jerk could break the elderly woman's neck.

"Fancy seeing you here." Caleb tightened his arm around Mrs. Conner's neck. Her face reddened from the lack of air flow.

"What do you want?" Perry asked, feeling his pulse thump against his tonsils.

"To prove to Jax that he's wrong about you and that ass of a father you've got. And now I've got the proof. He'll make me his top man. And he'll make you . . . dead."

Perry wasn't sure what proof Caleb meant, but now wasn't the time to worry about that. It wasn't even himself he was concerned about, it was Mrs. Conner.

Mr. Conner leered at the man, his gaze bright orange.

Perry stood up, slowly. "Let her go," he seethed. "She's not part of whatever proof you need. Let's you and I go outside and play."

"But it's dinnertime." Caleb's eyes zeroed in on Perry as he pushed Mrs. Conner to move in a few more feet.

Fear filled Perry. Caleb was going to kill her. Kill her right in front of Perry. No.

He hadn't decided his next move, when Mrs. Conner extended her hand out, snagged a knife from the counter, and drove it into Caleb's stomach.

She cleared her throat, yanked the blade out, then glared up at Caleb now leaning against the wall. "No one interrupts my dinner parties! Except Girl Scouts."

Hatred filled Caleb's eyes. An iridescent bubble floated up.

"Back up!" Perry flew across the table. Knowing he had only a fraction of a second to strike—the word "strike" giving him the idea—he morphed into a red spitting cobra.

The venom hit Caleb's face. Blinded, he shifted slower. Perry sank his teeth into the man's arm, but too late to stop the morph. Caleb in Big Foot form rose to eight feet.

Perry, knowing the stab wound and venom would at the least slow the beast down, tried to strike again. The beast dodged him, then, accepting his weakened state, turned and shot out the door.

Perry gave chase, slithering through the living room at top speed.

Caleb crashed through the closed door, sending wood splintering, but wavered as he ran. The venom must have done more damage than Perry realized.

Darting forward, Perry hoped to bring the beast down with another bite, but the damn creature leapt off the porch. Perry slithered after him. Caleb made it to the road, then reached for . . .

Not Burnett's Mustang!

Too late. Caleb picked up the car and tossed it. Perry raced through the grass, barely escaping the car. The sound of metal crunching rang loud as the car rolled forward and landed upside down.

Caleb turned to run. Perry rose up and threw himself, hoping to sink his fangs into the beast's shoulder. Right before he made contact, Caleb swung around and caught Perry around his upper body. The beast squeezed, his fat fingers sinking, damaging the snake's vital internal organs. The beast won. Perry could morph back to human, unharmed, but that would be when Caleb would come in for the real kill. Perry would die.

Knowing he had seconds of snake life left, he lunged his head forward and sank his fangs into Caleb's neck, sending venom into his carotid artery.

The beast dropped to his knees. Bubbles started popping off of him.

Perry clung to stay alive, the pain almost unbearable, hoping he had enough venom to stop Caleb if he came out of the shift unharmed.

One, two seconds later, the beast disappeared and Caleb lay there. His breathing was shallow, his eyes closed. Blood oozed from his gut where he'd been knifed.

Perry, unable to hold back any longer, shifted. The pain in his ribs made breathing impossible, but he managed to grab his phone and dial Burnett.

Two hours later, Perry sat in Holiday's office across from Burnett. Help had been sent to try and save Caleb. He died as they rushed him to Dr. Whitman's office. Dr. Whitman concluded the cause of death had been the snake bite—the one Perry had given right before Caleb had shifted.

"Maybe we should reinstate Mrs. Conner," Burnett said.

Perry forced a grin. He knew what he'd done was right. Caleb would've killed him and the Conners, and he'd already killed Bell. Still, knowing he'd taken a life didn't sit well on his empty stomach.

He gripped his hands in his lap. "My dad said Caleb had wanted to follow me to have a reason to turn me over to Jax. He must have followed me there. But how . . . Shit. Mrs. Conner made me repeat her address back to her today. Caleb must have been around. I never even sensed I was being followed."

"I didn't sense him, either," Burnett said.

Perry looked up. "I'm sorry."

"For what?" Burnett asked.

For killing someone. "Your car?" He tried to make light of things. Change the subject.

"At least it wasn't your Ferrari," Perry said.

"Sold it."

"You loved that car."

"Yeah, I did."

"Maybe you'll start driving the Porsche now," Perry said.

"Sold it, too." Burnett glanced at him as if he sensed what Perry was doing, but he obviously decided to let it ride. "Holiday and I bought twenty-five acres next to the camp. We want to expand to take in more students. There're thirty chameleons applying this fall. We still had to apply for a loan to finance the cabin construction. We're hoping it clears and we can get everything up and running before September."

"Now I feel really bad about your car."

"Don't. I was going to sell it, too, and the insurance paid more than I could have gotten for it. It's a piece of metal. Nothing more," Burnett said.

"It was a classic. You loved it." *It was a life.*

"And right now you're sitting here, not a scratch on you, Mr. and Mrs. Conner are at home probably watching *The Bachelor*— she loves that show—and that car doesn't mean shit." He half-smiled.

When Perry didn't smile back, the humor in Burnett's eyes vanished. "It's tough, I know."

"I'm a wimp for letting it get to me, aren't I?"

Burnett stood and put his hand on Perry's shoulder. "If it didn't bother you, I'd be worried."

"How do you do it?" Perry asked, for the first time questioning if he had what it took to be an agent.

"You put it in perspective. There are good people in this world and there're bad ones. The bad ones rape, kill, and torture the good ones. There's no telling how many people Caleb's already killed, but think about how many more innocent people who'd have suffered at his hands if you hadn't stopped him."

Perry nodded. His mind raced, guilt coated his soul like an emotional stain, but then it hit—one good thing that might come out of this. "He might trust me now." When Burnett looked confused about the statement, Perry elaborated. "Jax's game. He wanted Caleb dead. He might trust me enough to tell me what's going on."

Burnett nodded. "Now all we need to do is figure out how to play this."

After Burnett and Perry made plans, Perry went to Miranda. He didn't tell her anything, but just being with Miranda had helped bring home Burnett's point. He'd taken a life and nothing was going to change that, but Caleb had brought this on himself. The next morning, the dark spot on Perry's soul wasn't completely gone, but he could deal with it.

Leaving Shadow Falls, he called his dad and requested a two p.m. meet with Jax. Burnett had Caleb buried on an empty lot in what had been dubbed the Killing Fields under the only oak tree on some property just a mile from where Jax lived.

This went against Jax's rules, but if his brother wanted proof of Caleb's demise, he'd have to get it himself.

When it was show time, Perry walked up to the front door. The goon standing guard let him in. Perry grimaced when he saw his parents. He didn't know why, but the idea of them thinking of him as a murderer stung. Perhaps it was because he knew they were sick enough to be proud of him for it.

It felt so screwed up that it reminded him of the unresolved issues. He'd been so worried about Miranda and Tabitha, he hadn't dwelt on his own problems. They were still there, like a forgotten to-go box of food in the fridge that would start stinking soon.

"Ah, little brother, come in," Jax said. He held a glass that looked like whiskey.

Did his brother always drink? Maybe he needed it to be able to live with himself.

"I'm told you come bearing good news." Jax stood up and downed the rest of the liquid from his glass. Perry noticed the slight slur in his voice.

Perry had been around enough drunks to know that some got happier, some got meaner. A meaner Jax could be dangerous.

Perry sat down in the same straight chair. It was uncomfortable as hell, but the last thing he wanted to feel here was comfortable.

"Do I need to cut you a check for taking care of Ricky?" Jax asked.

"I haven't found Ricky yet," Perry said.

His brother frowned. "Then why are we meeting?"

"Caleb." Perry pulled air through his nose. He saw his mom smile. His father didn't. Did that mean anything?

Jax, eyes wide, just stared. "Where's the proof?"

"I buried him."

"I told you that you're required to bring the head to me."

"I let him keep it." The thought of removing a head from a body turned Perry's stomach.

"So I'm just supposed to believe you." Jax poured himself another shot. "Perry, Perry, Perry. I've got three of my best men after Caleb, they haven't gotten shit. You waltz in here, a greenhorn, and expect me to believe you've done it."

"I figured you'd send someone for the proof. I don't particularly like toting around body parts."

"Yeah, and now you're going to tell us his body is halfway across Texas."

"No. It's less than a mile away." He recited the address and mentioned the oak tree. Jax appeared doubtful. "If I send my man over there and it's gone, I'm gonna be pissed. If it's not Caleb and you messed his face up just to try to fool me, I'm gonna be furious. You'll end up with a price on your head." His smile was a threat.

Perry leaned back. "And if it's there, and it's him. What are you going to be?"

Jax stared. "I'll be impressed. Then I'll put you in charge of another job."

Thursday evening Miranda sat at the kitchen table with Kylie and Della. She'd spent the last few days studying and learning to fight— without her tattoo groove on—and clinging to the inner peace she'd found at the falls. She'd considered going back, but she hadn't been called. So she waited, albeit impatiently—with a mix of dread and anticipation—for the armadillo's words to come true.

She would be told when to run.

Run away from everyone who made her feel safe. At times, she wanted to question this. Really, really wanted to question it.

She looked up. While she studied, her friends went through the books searching for a clue about tattooed witches with "mojo" as Della described it.

Miranda considered how they'd feel when she ran away. They were going to be so mad. And Burnett. She didn't even want to think about him. Or Perry. He'd be devastated.

Her sinuses stung. Swallowing the need to cry, she spoke up. "I've finished the math section." She nudged the SAT study guide away. Right now she wished they offered one on faith, because she felt weak on it.

"You want me to question you over it?" Della asked.

"No. I'm done." Miranda hesitated. "Can I ask something?"

"I've already explained this. A boy has a ding-a-ling, the girl a vajayjay," Della teased.

Miranda rolled her eyes, not in the mood for humor. She had to find a way to ask it vaguely without saying too much. "If you get a message, or a feeling, from the falls, could it be bad?"

"Sometimes what they tell you hurts," Kylie said. "But generally it's—"

"No, I don't mean bad like sad. I mean bad advice."

"No," Kylie said, empathy painting her words. "You ready to talk about what happened in the falls?"

"No. Still mulling things over."

"If that was me mulling, you'd get pissed," Della said.

"Sorry." Miranda stood. "I should get ready."

"For what?" Della asked. "Is Perry coming again?"

"Yeah. I want to shower." *And talk to Tabitha.*

The armadillo hadn't defined which talents she got from the mystic side. But since Tabitha's text seemed to imply she could hear her, Miranda, counting on it, had been talking to her every thirty minutes or so.

Miranda spoke to her sister as if she were sitting beside her. Promising that she would come there soon.

As she stepped into the shower, a wisp of steam rose, and Miranda couldn't help but think of the ghost and bloody messages. Fear traveled up her spine like a spider. She stood naked and determined, holding on to her last bit of courage. The last message had saved Anthony. If the ghost needed Miranda to help save anyone else, she'd hear her out.

At six o'clock on Thursday evening, Perry walked through the Shadow Falls gate. Burnett and Holiday were both there in her office.

"What happened?" Burnett asked, already waiting for him.

Nodding at Holiday, who was positioned behind her desk while

Burnett sat on the edge of it, Perry walked into the office and shut the door.

They both stared with eyes round with worry.

"Did something go wrong?" Burnett spoke first.

"Not really," he said. But then there was the fact that he'd had to see Caleb's severed head tossed on Jax's table. And in Perry's mind, the image kept appearing. He looked at the dirty pillowcase he held, not knowing where to start.

"Then what is it?" Holiday asked. "You're upset, I can feel it."

"Two things," Perry said. "Jax gave me another job."

Burnett stood up from the desk. "You got Tabitha's whereabouts?"

"No, I tried. He wasn't opening up about that. He wants me to find his son."

"He's not getting him!" Holiday seethed.

Perry looked at her. "I'd die before letting that happen. But just because he put me on this case, doesn't mean he won't put others on it. This could be dangerous."

"You said the babysitter left the country," Burnett said.

Perry nodded. "He suspects the babysitter took him. He's found some info on her family in Mexico. He has contacts checking if she's there. If he thinks she is, he's sending me and another guard there."

"I don't care." Holiday looked at Burnett. "He stays here." Then she exhaled, still looking at Burnett. "Can I ask now?"

Ask what?

Burnett nodded and Holiday refocused on Perry. "We wanted to ask if you'd mind if Burnett and I adopted your nephew. We've fallen in love with him."

Perry's chest tightened, leaking out some of the bad he had dwelling there. "You have no idea how much that'd mean to me." He looked at Burnett.

Worry wrinkled the vampire's brow. "We need to contact the babysitter. If one of Caleb's men catches her . . ."

"I already called her. The only family she has in Mexico died a few months ago, but she's scared. I told her if she'd come back to the States we'd make sure she's safe."

"Does she have tickets yet?" Burnett asked.

"No, I said I'd let her know as soon as I spoke with you."

Burnett did a short lap around the office then stopped. "Give me her information. I'll have someone make her a ticket under an alias. They'll meet her at the airport with a fake passport and fly back with her."

Perry nodded. "Thank you."

"Now, what's the other thing?" Burnett asked.

Perry hesitated then dropped the heavy, dirty pillowcase on Holiday's desk. It landed with a dead thump.

Chapter Thirty-four

"What's this?" Burnett asked.

"Seven hundred thousand dollars," Perry answered. "Payment for taking care of Caleb. I didn't want to take it, but it would've been suspicious if I didn't."

Perry sat down. "I figured we'd turn it over. For evidence. Then I remembered what you said. That the FRU already had enough evidence to bury Jax from his previous crimes. I considered dropping it by a homeless shelter. But I didn't know who'd find it."

Burnett looked puzzled.

"I don't want a dollar of this money, and if you need it to make a case, by all means, take it. But if not, maybe it could go to some good use. Maybe half of it to help straighten out the FRU's foster program." He looked at Holiday. "Burnett told me that you two bought the property next door and were trying to get a loan to build cabins. Why not use this?"

Burnett sat back down on the edge of his wife's desk and looked at her as if asking for advice. She shrugged.

He looked back at Perry. "Because you aren't officially working for the FRU right now, you aren't required to turn it over. But . . ."

"No buts then," Perry said. "Jax would have a shitfit if he knew his money was going to some common good. That makes it all that sweeter."

Perry stood there, still feeling emotionally numb. "I guess it's time to go to plan B."

"What's plan B?" Holiday asked frowning.

"Arrest Jax," Burnett answered and looked back at Perry. "The Galveston FRU is lead agency because it's their territory, but our Fallen team and the Houston team are all in. They'll call when they have everything in place. It will probably be tomorrow."

"I don't like this," Holiday said, and Perry agreed with her. He could not let his half brother, whom he shared no love with, hurt anyone at Shadow Falls, who had become the family of his heart.

Miranda rested back on the blanket and stared through the trees to the stars twinkling in the sky. The weight of the cast rested on her abdomen, the weight of her worries were lighter. Being with Perry and being amongst the trees was like an emotional hug.

Perry shifted. "Why did you want to come out here?"

"I like the trees," she said.

"Didn't you tell me you were afraid of them?"

"Not anymore." She slipped her hand in his. She could feel his pain, but she also felt the healing properties the trees offered her. She wished she could share that with him.

Tightening her grip, she said, "Are you ever going to tell me what's happening? What's hurting you?"

He dropped his right arm over his eyes. "Not now. It's so ugly."

She leaned up and looked down at him. He moved his arm. Their gazes met. He was her true love. He was hurting. Not being able to console him was like not breathing.

She swallowed. "Yeah, but when you share things like that sometimes it lightens the load on you."

He caught a strand of her hair in his hand. "The last thing I want to do is put these things in your head just to make me feel better. You've got enough crap on you already."

"I can handle it. I feel better about things."

"How about I promise that when it's done, I'll tell you everything."

She frowned, but nodded.

"Now, let's talk about good things." He sat up, looking down at her.

"You know something good?" she asked.

He smiled—a real one. "I'm with you, aren't I?" He ran a finger from the middle of her forehead to her nose. Then slowly he traced her lips. "Don't get any ideas, but I don't deserve you."

She gave his finger a playful bite. "You're the one getting a bad deal. I'm dyslexic . . ." She stopped, remembering what the armadillo had told her about it being a gift. If she was so upset with Perry for thinking little of himself, maybe it was time she stop doing it.

"Neither of us are getting a bad deal," she spit out. "You're amazing. You're funny, sensitive, powerful, and you're so hot you could do commercials for men's cologne. And I'm . . . I'm okay, too."

"Okay? Now there's the understatement of the century. You're freaking amazing."

"But you're too sexy for your shirt." She started unbuttoning it.

"And you're better than eating ice cream while flying."

They rolled around on the blanket, laughing, kissing, and tossing out silly compliments. While he didn't share what was hurting him, Miranda felt his pain fading. And that wasn't the trees doing it. That was nothing more than the power of love.

Burnett's text woke Perry up Friday morning at six a.m. Three words: *My office now.*

Miranda was still sleeping. He'd allowed himself one quick glance back before walking out. She looked like an angel. His an-

gel. What had he ever done to deserve her? With no time to waste
he flew off to meet Burnett.

The vampire waited on the office porch.

"Is it time?" Perry morphed as he landed. Burnett wore his stoic
expression. He looked wrinkled and tired as if he'd been up all
night. "Guess who walked into the FRU headquarters about two
a.m. this morning?"

"Who?"

"Ricky Raco. He wanted our protection for the exchange of information."

"Does he know anything about Tabitha?" Perry asked.

"Not where she is. He's not even sure that Jax knows where
they've taken her. He said they're very secretive about that, but . . ."
Burnett swallowed. "He knows why they wanted her and Miranda."
He frowned. "They need powerful witches to produce heirs."

The thought made Perry sick.

Burnett continued. "At least that means that they don't have
plans to kill her." He shook his head as if the thought hurt him.
"The drug house was Jax's operation. He said they were using the
witch as a front and also to draw in potential young witches. But
he claims they weren't behind the explosion. He also gave details
of how many guards and what kind of firepower Jax has at his
place."

"How bad is it?" Perry asked.

"Not good, but at least we're going in prepared. Considering
what Tabitha might be going through, I don't want to wait any longer." Burnett paused as if needing to say something else. "I know
you wanted to go, but—"

"No," Perry bit out. "I'm going!"

Burnett met his gaze and probably didn't like the determination he saw in Perry's eyes. The vamp growled. "Only if you agree
to stay in the van."

"Damn it!" Perry snapped. "Would you please stop treating me
like I'm six."

"Listen to me!" Burnett got in Perry's face. "There's only a small chance that Jax will tell us where Tabitha is, but if he sees you, he'll know it matters to you. And he won't give us shit."

"You just don't think I can handle it!" Perry's voice deepened, emotion rattled his chest.

"That's not true. Do I worry that you could get hurt? Hell yeah. But it's not because I don't think you can handle it. It's 'cause . . ."

He squeezed the back of his neck. "I taught you to ride a bike. I was the one who taught you how to treat a girl. You are my family. But that's not why I'm asking you to stay back. It's because you could ruin any chance we have of learning something from Jax."

"But—"

"Say you will stay in the van, and you can go with us. Say it, and swear to it," Burnett insisted.

"I could morph," Perry offered. "He would never know it was me."

"He has the alarm for shifters," Burnett reminded Perry.

"Then I can't go in until after you've made the first move. And I'll go in morphed."

"We're using gas to prevent any shifts."

"I'll shift before I go in," Perry countered.

Burnett looked prepared to argue, but instead he let out a string of curse words and motioned for Perry to follow him.

Miranda, Della, Kylie, and Chase crawled into the school's silver Toyota Corolla at eight that morning. Chase had been given the duty of taking Miranda to get her cast off. When Holiday had told her this yesterday, Miranda pleaded with Burnett to let them make one other stop. To see Anthony.

He was conscious, and they'd moved him from Dr. Whitman's office to a safe house. They'd had to put extra guards to keep the injured vampire from leaving to search for Tabitha.

The story Anthony had given had gotten him mostly out of hot water with the FRU. He'd explained that he'd gone to the drug house before the explosion with his cousin Frank to pick something up. Anthony hadn't known his cousin was dealing drugs, but he'd gotten suspicious.

When the FRU started questioning Anthony, he hadn't wanted to turn his cousin in. Instead Anthony planned to talk Frank into turning himself in, hoping it would lighten his cousin's sentence. But then the FRU threatened to deport Anthony.

When he told Tabitha, she'd concocted a plan for them to run away. Told she needed a second MRI, she texted Anthony and told him to meet her on the sixth floor. Only when Anthony arrived thinking he and Tabitha were going to try to make a run for it, he found Agent Farrell unconscious. A shape-shifter, one who happened to be one of the guys Anthony met at the drug house earlier, had Tabitha. Anthony fought him, grabbed Tabitha, and took off.

On the run, not knowing who they could trust, Anthony got a text from his cousin offering a safe place for them to hide. When they got there, Frank was dead. While he didn't know why, they took Tabitha and were trying to get Anthony to give up Miranda's whereabouts.

When Miranda walked into the hospital room and saw Anthony, she almost cried. He looked terrible, and he'd gotten that way trying to protect her. She went over to his bedside to hug him but was afraid it might hurt him.

The guy's eyes were almost swollen shut. Because he'd lost so much blood, his healing process was slower than normal vampires'. "I'm sorry," he said. "I should have protected her."

Knowing the person who did that to Anthony had her sister sent fear banging against her ribs, but she dug deep to find a little faith and then told him her secret.

"Don't worry, I've had a . . . a premonition. Things are going to be okay."

Problem was, Anthony wasn't the only one to hear it. As soon as they walked out of the hospital room, the questions began.

"What premonition?" Kylie asked.

"You had it while you were in the falls, didn't you?" Della asked.

"If you know something you need to tell us!" Chase added.

Miranda hedged. "I don't have specific details."

They knew she was holding back. But she offered nothing else, especially because she had a sneaking suspicion that today might be the day she'd make a run for it. It would be easier to get away outside the school's alarm system.

Miranda hoped it was so, because her gut said that Chase would waste no time telling Burnett about her non-specific premonition. And . . . mother crackers, she didn't think she could hold out being interrogated by that man.

Burnett had driven a less expensive Mustang to the Galveston FRU agency. Perry hadn't even noticed the scenery, he'd been too busy chewing on what was about to go down. And what would go down after that. His parents. They hadn't talked about it, but he knew it was just left unsaid.

A mix of different supernaturals were gathered in a room with about twenty agents. The plan was explained. They had at least twenty men going in on all sides. Twenty-one after the first agent made it into the house, Perry had thought. Armed with gas grenades with a chemical to prevent shifts, and guns—guns loaded with both more anti-shifting drugs, and bullets that would kill a mad hippo—the agents seemed ready.

They would first toss in the grenades to prevent shifting, then there would be one warning shout out for Jax to come out and surrender. If unanswered, they would hit all four sides. It pissed Perry off that he wouldn't be included in the original surge that would overtake the house. But part of what Burnett had said was the truth. If Jax knew Perry was behind this, the chances of him cooperating would be zilch.

And more important than Perry's ego was finding Tabitha and

keeping Miranda safe. Not that Perry thought Jax would offer up anything to help. His half brother didn't have any feelings. He used people and then he killed them.

But Perry would do what Burnett requested. He wouldn't go in until they had made their entrance. If he was already shifted, the smoke bombs shouldn't harm him, but it would make shifting back slower, which, if fatally wounded, might be bad news. Not that he planned being fatally wounded.

They pulled up to the house in four vans. The large century-old home looked more like a fortress than ever before. Probably because he'd never stood outside the gate. The thought of any of these men losing their life from his half brother's hand made this hard, the thought of Jax hurting the man who'd taken the role of big brother, made Perry uncomfortable in his own skin.

Perry sat in the back of the van, ringing his hands. Burnett, poised to follow the others out, glanced back at Perry. He wore the protective vest and a look of determination. "Not until they are in, and don't let him know it's you." Their eyes met, and as always Perry felt Burnett's affection.

As soon as the door closed, Perry moved forward. He opened the door a bit so he could make a quick escape as soon as he knew the agent had made his entrance. He shifted into an extra-large silver wolf. Burnett had made him tell everyone what he'd be shifting into, to prevent anyone from confusing him with any of the other shifters. He sat on the seat on his haunches, waiting, ready to run like the wind.

It happened so fast. The sound of glass breaking as the agents tossed in the gas bombs. The call for Jax to come out and surrender. The fireworks of guns exploding. The sound of doors being ripped off hinges and windows shattering as the agents made entry.

Perry leapt out of the van, his front paws hitting the ground with force. Before he even got to the fence he could smell the smoke bombs.

He heard screams. "Agent down! Agent down!"

More gunfire exploded, loud pops sounded all around the house.

Growling, thinking of Burnett, he took a flying leap over the seven-foot fence. The front door was ajar, he darted inside, knowing Burnett's orders had been to enter the front.

The drapes were all pulled. Darkness and smoke from the grenades hung heavy in the house. He ducked his head lower to breathe clearer air, and kept going.

One agent heard him and swung his gun around. Perry saw the vamp's finger twitch on the trigger, then relax.

More gunfire exploded in the back of the house. The agent and he ran at the same time. A female agent, a witch, lay on the wood floor, pain in her eyes, blood oozing from her shoulder.

A low growl built in Perry's chest. While the vampire agent knelt to check on his fellow agent, Perry shot into the next room. He heard breathing—tight, nervous breathing. His powerful gift of scent put the guy on the other side of the door.

Right then footsteps sounded behind him. Perry looked back. Burnett stepped into the doorway. And that's when the perp in the bathroom shot out, and bullets started spraying.

Perry dove in front of the man who'd been his mentor, friend, and brother. But as Perry took his own bullet in the side, he saw Burnett hit the ground.

Miranda sat silent in the backseat. Chase pulled up at Dr. Whitman's office, Tension rode shotgun in the car. Miranda wanted to tell her friends she was sorry, but they'd know she was hiding something for sure.

Walking into the office, she smelled animals. Dr. Whitman was one of the best doctors in the supernatural community. But by all appearances, he was a vet in the human world, where he also had a thriving practice. Supposedly, Dr. Whitman tried to never schedule a supernatural case when his human clients showed up with their pets. To prove her point, there were two half shape-shifer-half-warlocks flipping through dog magazines in the waiting room.

"You must be new," Della asked the man at the counter.

"Yup," the sandy haired half-warlock half-vampire said. He looked at Miranda. "You must be our patient? Let me show you to the room."

"Aren't they first?" Miranda pointed back at the two guys.

"They didn't have an appointment," the man said.

Miranda felt a bit bad, but started following him back. Chase moved with her.

The employee frowned at Chase. "Sorry, we just let the patients go in the back."

Miranda spoke up. "It wasn't like that—" Della cleared her throat. And somehow that scratchy sound seemed to mean something.

That's when all hell broke loose.

Chase pulled out a gun, but before he got off one shot, popping sounds started firing off.

Voices started yelling from the back room.

Chase gave Miranda a forceful push, landing her behind the counter. Not willing to cower, she popped back up. The first thing she saw was Chase going down. Face down. Then Kylie dropped.

"No!" Miranda screamed.

Chapter Thirty-five

Della, in full vamp mode, kicked ass. She had one guy down. The attackers were now unarmed, but still coming at her hard. Then they morphed into lions.

The downed half-vamp got up and aimed his gun at Della. Miranda shot across the counter and tackled him. He jumped back up. "Come with us and no one else has to die."

Fear shot bolts inside Miranda's heart. Were Chase and Kylie . . . ?

Della kicked one lion in his nose. He backed off and roared. She shot a glance back at Miranda. "Get your tattoo mojo on!"

Miranda didn't know how, but then she felt it, her skin tingling. The half-vampire came at her. Miranda caught him by his upper arm and tossed him at one of the lions charging at Della.

Suddenly angrier than she was scared, Miranda dove right into the mix of things. The lions stopped when they saw her covered in tattoos. It gave Miranda and Della just enough time to grab the lions by their manes and throw them hard across the room.

Della dove for the gun Chase had dropped and shot all three of the attackers.

Miranda dropped to her knees beside Kylie. Hands trembling, Miranda touched the chameleon's neck praying she'd find a pulse.

Before she even felt it, she saw Kylie's chest move, drawing in precious air. "She's breathing," Miranda said.

Screams rang out from the back room.

"It's Dr. Whitman and his daughter," Della yelled. "Go check on them." With tears running down her cheeks, the vampire dropped down beside Chase.

Tears of empathy, of fear, ran down Miranda's cheeks. Her heart felt like it would explode as she waited to see if Della found Chase alive.

But then she heard it. The voice. Not Dr. Whitman or his daughter. A voice in her head. *It's time. Go through the back. The door's unlocked. Run. Now!*

Miranda felt her pulse flutter at the base of her neck and on both wrists. How could she leave now when . . . when . . .

Everyone is okay. We switched the death darts in their guns with tranquilizers. You have to go, Miranda. Now, or people will die. Your sister, Perry, and others!

Miranda blinked the tears from her vision. Chase shifted as if coming to. Then Kylie started stirring.

The armadillo wasn't lying about them just being tranquilized. Which meant he probably wasn't lying about the others dying.

She did it then. She sped off.

She stopped when she saw Dr. Whitman and his daughter tied together on the floor, squirming to get free. Dr. Whitman's face was bleeding. "Is anyone hurt? Cut us loose," he said.

She almost did, but then the armadillo spoke again. *Now!*

"I'm sorry," Miranda told the good doctor and bolted out holding on by the thinnest thread of faith she'd done the right thing.

One bullet wasn't enough to stop a gray wolf. Especially a flesh wound. Perry charged, he buried his teeth into the guy's face, felt the flesh tearing, and he tasted blood. The shifter fell to the ground screaming. Perry pushed the gun away with his snout and then turned to see Burnett.

He was back on his feet. Blood oozed out of his arm, he looked madder than a trapped rabid raccoon. His eyes glowed, his fangs were fully lowered. It obviously took more than one bullet to stop Burnett as well.

"We got Jax!" someone yelled from inside the house.

Burnett moved in and turned the guy over who had his cheek hanging open, and cuffed him.

"You okay?" Burnett asked.

Perry bobbed his snout up and down. He felt blood ooze from his side and he tasted blood oozing from his jowls. Thankfully that wasn't his. "You?" Perry asked.

"Fine." Burnett pulled up his sleeve. "Barely a scratch. The vest and you saved me." He inhaled. "Get out of the house before you get more of that chemical in your system."

Perry did as told.

There were twelve guards, plus Jax. Three of the guards were dead, four more injuried. Two agents had been shot, and were already being driven by ambulance to see doctors. Jax, wearing three patches to prevent him from shifting, had been driven away. As Jax had walked past, he'd eyed Perry in wolf form. He glared, but there didn't seem to be any recognition.

Perry waited until they took Jax away before turning. Either this bullet wasn't as bad as the others he'd gotten recently, or he was getting used to being shot, because it didn't hurt as bad.

"Good job," Burnett said to Perry, as they loaded the last of the healthy guards into a van. "You are going to make a fine agent."

"I've been trained by the best," Perry said.

Burnett almost smiled and watched the vans pull away. "The bullet you took would have gotten me in the head." He ran a hand through his hair. "It's the second time in a week that you've saved my life."

Perry nodded. "You saved mine every day you were there for me when I was in foster care." Emotion tightened Perry's voice.

Burnett reached over and gave Perry's shoulder a squeeze. After a heartfelt second, Burnett spoke again. "If they know something they'll tell us."

"I sure as hell hope so." Perry imagined Miranda sleeping again. More than he wanted air, he wanted to find her sister, wanted to wipe away every worry and concern she had. He wanted the whole thing with his parents behind him. He wanted to move forward with his life, with their life together.

For the first time in his eighteen years, he got a glimpse at his and Miranda's future. Before, when he couldn't control his powers, he'd been scared to imagine it. Now he saw it. Working beside Burnett. Waking up with Miranda every day.

Burnett's phone rang. "Yeah?" he answered.

Perry couldn't hear what was being said, but Burnett's eyes turned neon green, and his fangs started to come out, telling Perry it wasn't good.

"Call the office. Every agent is on this now. Set up roadblocks. I'm on my way," Burnett ground out. He shoved his keys and phone back into his pocket and locked his car.

"What?" Perry asked.

"Trouble. Follow me!"

"What kind . . ."

Burnett didn't answer, he took off in flight. Perry morphed into a falcon, and took after him. Burnett seldom broke the rule of flying during the day, where he could be seen by humans. This had to be bad.

When Burnett's speed left Perry behind, he morphed into a prehistoric bird to catch up. Something told him getting spotted was the least of their problems right now. Fear of what that problem was had Perry forcing his wings harder, faster.

After a long and hard flight, Perry spotted Dr. Whitman's

office below and saw Burnett going down. His heart knotted in fear. Miranda was supposed to get her cast off today. Descending, Perry saw the school's car parked in the front.

He morphed right before he hit the ground behind the office and ran to catch up with Burnett, who'd went right for the door.

"Dr. Whitman is checking Chase and Kylie now," Della said, her eyes neon bright, her canines partially out. "But they looked fine."

Perry's gaze shot around the room. Three males lay on the tile floor. Perry didn't recognize them. But he recognized death. They weren't breathing.

"Where's Miranda?" Perry asked, his tone tight.

Della looked at him, her face bruised, and the look of failure in her eyes sent pain shooting through him.

"Is she hurt? Is she with Dr. Whitman?"

Della still didn't answer. The now deeper emotion flashing in her eyes sent raw panic into Perry's bloodstream. He felt himself losing it. Felt his blood on fire, felt his soul start to shift. Felt his future—the little bit of future he'd allowed himself to believe in—crumble.

Burnett put his hand on Perry's shoulder and squeezed. "Miranda left. As far as we know she's okay. Let me hear the rest of this."

The cells in his body stopped fizzing. His skin stopped crawling, but he couldn't remain silent. "Left? Left for where?"

"I don't know." Della looked defeated and the same feeling raged inside him.

"They took her?" His blood started fizzing again.

"I don't think so," Della said.

Burnett's hand, still clasped on his shoulder, squeezed harder. "Let her talk. We need to hear what happened so we can look for Miranda. Pull yourself together."

Perry nodded, fighting with every beast inside him wanting to come out, as Della told the story. When she finished by saying Miranda had apologized to Dr. Whitman and ran out the door, Perry snapped.

"Miranda wouldn't leave on her own." He clenched his fists, digging his nails into his palms to keep from shifting.

"What happened here?" Burnett waved at the three dead men.

Guilt filled Della's eyes. "The gun was set on stun, I shot them so they wouldn't give me trouble. They were coming to, when I was cuffing them."

"It appears that their hearts just stopped." Dr. Whitman, his face swollen, walked out. "I can't swear it yet, but I don't think it was the stun gun."

"One of them started chanting while I was putting on his cuffs," Della said as if she just remembered it. "Like a prayer or something."

"It could have been a suicide pact," Shawn said walking in with Agent Tobler. "Some of the rogue gangs believe failure equals death. There's a curse that could do it."

Shawn met Perry's gaze. Worry filled the warlock's eyes. He'd given Miranda up, but he still cared.

Then Shawn met Burnett's gaze. "The roadblocks are set up."

"Why roadblocks?" Perry asked.

"Dr. Whitman heard someone call Miranda's name and a car take off as soon as Miranda ran out."

The pressure in Perry's chest threatened to crack his ribs. "She wouldn't have left on her own. They took her."

"They may have blackmailed her into going," Dr. Whitman said, "but no one forced her to walk out that door."

Kylie and Chase stepped out then. Dark rings circled both their eyes, but they were alive, and they were here. Miranda wasn't. And he didn't even know if she was alive. "I don't understand," Perry demanded.

"She had a premonition," Kylie said, looking teary-eyed. "I think it was when she went to the falls."

"What kind of premonition?" Burnett snapped. "And why the hell am I just hearing about all this now!"

"We just found out right before we came here," Chase answered.

"All she said was that her sister was going to be okay," Della added. "We tried to get her to tell us about it. She wouldn't talk."

Burnett looked at Kylie.

Kylie must have understood his question, because she spoke up. "I've asked the death angels. They haven't answered so far."

"Damn!" Burnett looked at Agent Tobler, who seemed to know what he wanted to hear.

"I have the shifters and the other vampires checking outside the roadblocks in case they already passed them," Agent Tobler said. "Everyone is on this."

The old witch from the drug house, Zander, was covered in dirt, driving the light green Volkswagen Bug like a bat out of hell. Every question Miranda spat out from the backseat received the same one-word answer. "Later."

Miranda finally quit asking.

"Damn!" Zander snapped. "There are vamps flying around. In broad daylight."

"They're looking for me." Miranda's heart fell to the pit of her stomach. She couldn't imagine what Della and Kylie thought. And Burnett. He was going to hate her.

"And if they find us, it's over. I won't be able to stop this. I'm gonna need your help. And fast." She peered back at Miranda for the first time and frowned. "Oh, your hair."

Considering Zander's hair looked as if it hadn't been combed since the last blue moon, Miranda found that quite insulting.

"But first thing's first." Zander faced forward, dipped her head down and gazed up through the windshield. "Ask the trees to help us," she ordered.

"Huh?" Miranda asked.

"Jeremiah," the witch yelled.

The armadillo materialized in the backseat.

"What?" he asked.

"I thought you told her about the trees," Zander snapped.

"I did."

"Then tell her to ask the trees for help. I've spotted three vampires flying and sooner or later they're gonna spot us."

Jeremiah looked at Miranda. "Ask the trees for help."

Miranda sat there, feeling pretty dumb. "How?"

"Just ask. That's all it takes."

Miranda swallowed. "They aren't going to hurt the vampires, are they?"

"No," Zander said. "Ask them to hide us."

Miranda looked out at the trees. "Can you hide us? Please."

The trees lining the street started folding in on them. "Whoa." Miranda looked back at Jeremiah. "Where are we going? What's the plan?"

Before Jeremiah could answer, Zander bit out, "Have her change her hair. I didn't realize hers was a different color from Tabitha's. And get rid of the cast." The witch tossed a box in the backseat. "Put that on." Glaring at Miranda in the rearview mirror, the witch stomped on the gas. The car hit a bump in the road and almost knocked Miranda into Jeremiah. "Now! We're already three minutes late."

Miranda flinched at her tone. "I might be a lot more cooperative if you'd explain what's going on. And say 'please,' it's polite."

Zander's faded gray eyes zapped to the rearview mirror and turned red. Blood red. "Do you want to save your sister or not?"

Throwing modesty to the wind, Miranda started disrobing. She tossed her shirt on the seat and her jean skirt on the floorboard. Jeremiah knocked the top of the box, and light baby blue silk almost spilled out.

"The hair," Zander screeched. "Don't forget the hair."

The car came to a sudden stop. Jeremiah pushed the box closer. Miranda lifted her butt off the seat to slide into the layers of soft silk. She started trying to think of a spell for her hair and her cast.

When the dress fell softly to her shoulders, she saw her hair against the blue material. Red like her sister's. And the cast was gone.

Had she done all that without a spell?

She puffed out a breath. Zander was already out of the front seat and opening Miranda's car door. She offered her hand.

"We must run or we won't make it."

Zander didn't run like an old witch. She moved quickly, deftly, one bare foot in front of the other. Miranda held her dress up and ran beside her. Her heart rocked in her chest.

All of a sudden Miranda realized the woman running beside her was not so old anymore. Her wrinkles were gone, her dark hair showed only a few silver strands flowing behind her.

"How much farther?" Miranda asked.

"Don't think about it. Just run. We are late. We have to hurry."

Miranda kept going and going.

Just when she didn't think she could go any farther, Zander stopped suddenly. "No," she moaned and turned in a circle.

"What?" Miranda said, barely able to breathe.

"We're too late." She collapsed on the ground.

Chapter Thirty-six

"We can't be too late!" Miranda said. "We have to get Tabitha!"

Jeremiah appeared at Miranda's side. "Zander, you can open it. You can do it."

Zander shook her head, but when she looked up she was old again. Ragged, defeated, lost. "How many times have I told you they've taken my power? I have none."

"They haven't taken it all. Believe in yourself."

"What do you need?" Miranda asked. "Maybe I can help you."

Zander shook her head. "Only those who've been there can open it."

"Then get up off your ass and open whatever needs to open. Now!" Miranda yelled.

Tears filled Zander's eyes. "You are so much like my sister. They took her, too."

"Then help save *my* sister," Miranda pleaded. "Please."

Zander looked at Jeremiah. "You think I can do this?"

The armadillo moved closer. "I've been telling you all along that they haven't taken it all away."

She stood up, and before Miranda's eyes she became beautiful again. Not young. But beautiful. Miranda realized how important one's belief in oneself was. It not only changed how they saw them-selves, but how others saw them.

The witch held out her pinky. The ground started shaking. Then it split open and a cavern appeared.

"I told you," Jeremiah said, staring at Zander with pride and . . . love. "Now go, you still have to hurry. I'll wait for Tabitha here."

Miranda, holding the folds of the dress in her hands, had to work to keep up with Zander. The older witch now carried a flashlight, illu-minating the way. The cavern walls seemed to get smaller and smaller.

Miranda started to feel isolated, shut off from everything and everyone she knew and loved. Their footfalls echoed. The damp, dank smell of darkness filled the air.

"Be careful of the snakes," Zander said.

Miranda looked down and saw a big fat one slithering away. She wanted to scream but was afraid she might alert someone they were here. Did she need to be quiet? Questions filled her head as she ran.

"Where are we going?" she asked in a low out-of-breath voice. She glanced at her feet, glad she'd worn her tennis shoes instead of flip-flops. "Where's Tabitha?"

"If she did as I told her, we should be close to her now." Zan-der's voice sounded less breathless than Miranda's. Did the witch always run this path?

"I still don't understand," Miranda said. "If we find her, why can't we just all three leave?"

Still running, Zander looked at her. Miranda saw the empathy in the witch's eyes. "If things work out you'll have plenty of time with her later."

If? Miranda's heart skipped a beat, her feet pounded the rock floor. "Damn it, Zander, I need answers!" She stopped.

Zander stopped and held her stomach. "The guards, they do hourly checks," Zander said. "They have guards set up in various stations in the woods. If we are not there, they release the guards. They will catch us in the woods. Do you think others have not tried? They have and all have died."

"Then why didn't you just bring her with you?" Miranda asked.

"I clean the guard's houses. That's the only way I could get you in time. I could not have gotten and taken her with me. I tried to find another way, there was none. I even asked the Goddesses, there is no other way. Now, we must go. Or we all die."

Frustration rose in Miranda's chest. But she commenced to running. She recalled her talk with Jeremiah in the falls. "Jeremiah said you had a plan that with my power we could escape."

"Yes. We'll talk when we get to the cell."

Cell? Mother crackers!

Miranda picked up the pace, concentrating on the sound of their feet hitting the rock floor. She tried to keep her breath even. She'd taken up running once, for about a month. This reminded her why she'd hated it.

Zander looked at her again. "You are brave and courageous. I admire you for that."

"No I'm not. I'm scared shitless," Miranda said. "I'm not doing this because I'm brave. I'm doing it because I don't want anyone I love to die."

"And that's what courage is. Doing something in spite of fear."

All of a sudden a small light appeared farther down the cavern. It waved like a flashlight.

"It's your sister," Zander said.

Miranda ran harder, hoping to earn herself another second with Tabitha.

"Remember no time . . . to waste," Zander said behind her.

As the light drew closer, Miranda could make her sister out. She wore the same blue dress as Miranda. They ran right into each other's arms. "Zander says we don't have much time," Miranda said, still in the embrace. She pulled back. Air hung in her lungs, her sides ached, but she forced the words out. "You okay?"

"Yes. Because of Zander and you. I heard you comforting me. Thank you."

Zander caught up. Tabitha turned to her. "Are you sure I can't stay and help? Maybe we should all run."

"No. Go! Jeremiah is waiting. If the gate is closed . . . Hide where I showed you. I have it set to open again in a few hours." Zander grabbed Miranda's arm.

"Go," Miranda told Tabitha, and with tears in her throat, Miranda took off running again. Every few minutes, Miranda would glance over her shoulder to check on Tabitha.

"You sure she'll be okay?" Miranda asked, her air coming out in short gasps.

"Her odds are good."

Miranda almost asked about her own odds. But decided not knowing might be better. The sound of their breathing echoed. The cavern seemed to get smaller still.

Tears ran down Miranda's face, her sides hurt from running, her heart hurt from thinking of Perry, Kylie, and Della. They were going to hate her. She might not even blame them. Then her thoughts shifted to Tabitha and fear kept her moving. "Ask the trees to help your sister," Zander said.

After another few minutes, Zander came to an abrupt stop. "From here on out, no talking. Remove your shoes, throw them there."

"What about the snakes?" Miranda whispered, but she kicked off her shoes, and tossed them.

"They are as scared of you as you are of them." Zander caught Miranda's hand. "Now let's go, and no more light." Miranda let Zander lead her, straight into the darkness, straight into the unknown.

An hour had passed. They had nothing. Perry couldn't think straight. He sat in Burnett's office going through everything he knew, hoping to offer something helpful.

Burnett was interviewing some of the guards to see if they knew anything that could help. They didn't, but several of them jumped at the chance to confess and get off easy, eager to restart their lives.

Perry just wanted his one chance at life, but she was missing. What would have made Miranda take off? Blackmail, Dr. Whitman had said. Kylie thought it had to do with a premonition. His mind raced. His heart ached. Why would Miranda do this to him and everyone else? That wasn't like her.

Burnett walked in. "You okay?"

Tears suddenly filled his eyes. "She looked so damn innocent this morning." Perry raked his hands through his hair. Then he kicked a chair and knocked it across the room. "Why would Miranda do this to me? To all of us?"

"I don't know." Burnett put his hand on Perry's shoulder.

Then Perry remembered. "What about my parents?" Damn, he didn't think he could deal with all of this at the same time. Then he realized in an instant how unimportant dealing with his past was, when his future stood in crisis. All this time he'd spent looking in the rearview mirror, he should've been focusing on the damn windshield.

"You said they weren't supposed to see Jax until Sunday."

"Right," Perry said.

"Then let's worry about that tomorrow."

"Yeah." Perry inhaled and tried to control the panic clawing at his insides. "Let me at Jax. I'll make him talk. I will."

"No," Burnett said. "They are interviewing him now."

"But . . ." Perry drew his fist and slammed it into the plastered walls. "Where is she? Damn it, I can't just sit here and do nothing."

"Then do something," Burnett said. "Go soar the sky, look for Miranda and Tabitha. I've got six other shape-shifters doing that right now, too. Go help them."

. . .

Miranda followed Zander's order. She didn't say another word the rest of the way. Finally they got to a turn in the cavern, a few feet in she saw where the rock wall appeared to have been dug out, and bars had been placed in front to create a cell. Oddly enough, Zander had a key and locked them inside.

Miranda couldn't help but wonder how long Zander had had the key to her own prison.

Zander had literally just pushed Miranda inside when footsteps sounded. Zander motioned for Miranda to sit on the cot.

An extension cord running through the bars gave power to one small lamp on the floor. The footsteps echoed closer. Voices rose. Miranda's heart thumped faster.

"Slow your breath. Do as they say. Don't talk unless spoken to," Zander whispered. "Don't let them see your tattoo. Keep your hand and arm covered."

What about my face? Miranda wanted to ask. But fear washed over her and threatened to drown her. She caught the air in her lungs and held it, slowly letting out her next breath.

Three men approached the bars. Two wore white robes. "Stand up!" the taller man ordered.

Sensing the order was for her, Miranda stood. Her pulse raced, and the sound of blood rushed in her ears. Her lungs begged for more air. She took in a mouthful. Then she noticed Zander, huddled on the cold floor, her shoulders hunched over in terror. And just like that, Miranda's fear turned to rage.

"You are right," the older robed man said. "She is fine. When will we have her sister?" he asked the unrobed man.

You already have her, idiot. She felt her arm begin to itch. Her tattoo wanted to come out and play. *Not now. Not now.*

"I am told soon," the man answered.

The younger man wearing a robe neared the bars and leered at her.

"Then why not wait until you have both?" the older man said.

"Why wait when we can start building our army now," the younger man answered. "She'll make fine soldiers for us."

Balls, eyes, and throat. The words ran through her head. No holding back. She stared at the men and made herself a promise. *No one would ever get close enough to make anything with her.*

Just their words made her feel dirty. She looked at Zander staring at nothing. Miranda's heart hurt for what this woman had endured.

The men walked away. Hugging herself because she needed a hug so bad she wanted to cry, she stood silently. Her heart still raced from the run. Only when Miranda could no longer hear their footsteps did she speak.

"What's the plan, Zander? How are we going to stop these assholes!" Miranda felt her arms tingling, the tattoos racing across her skin.

Zander didn't move. Finally she spoke in a low whisper. "When the sun goes down they will take you outside for the ceremony. I will follow as soon as they pass the first bend, so they will not hear me. I will shut down the lights and lock the gates. The guards in the east will not get there. There will be less to fight."

"What about the guards in the woods?" Miranda asked.

"They will all be here for the ceremony."

"Wait. If the guards are in the woods now, how do you know they won't catch Tabitha?"

"The guards never go into the woods unless there is a reason. That property does not belong to them."

Miranda prayed Zander knew what she was talking about.

"What about their powers?" Miranda asked. "How strong are they?"

Miranda saw Zander shift slightly. "Before a ceremony they celebrate. Jeremiah put a potion in the wine. If it works, their powers will be diminished. You will have the authority of the trees on our side. I will stand in the mouth of the cavern. I will attempt to help you bring a storm." She drew quiet. "They fear storms, they think it is the Salem witches, returning to punish them."

"Good." Miranda knew Zander could do a pretty powerful storm.

"As soon as you can, run west. There's a path in the woods, the trees will guide you. I will hold the storm here as long as I can. If you run fast, you can escape before the guards get to the woods."

"Two things," Miranda said. "When I run, you're coming with me, and two: I thought we were stopping them."

"The bad ones have existed since Salem, stopping them may be impossible. And someone must close the gates so they can't follow you. I will do that. They will open it, but it will give you time to escape."

Zander finally looked back. A gasp left her lips. "Your markings! I knew you held great power, but I never guessed . . . you were this . . ." She motioned to her tattoos.

"What I am is furious." Miranda watched as Zander's wrinkles began to fade, her hair turned brown and unmatted. "We can stop this. And I'm not leaving you."

Zander smiled. "With your strength, you may be able to stop them."

"No," Miranda snapped. "You're not putting this all on me. Jeremiah said you still had strength. We both need to do this."

"I will try." She waved to the cot. "Rest now. We will need our strength."

Time passed. Zander slept, but Miranda couldn't. The guards came past several times.

Miranda wasn't sure how much time had passed when she saw the witch, still curled up against the rock wall, lift her eyes.

Miranda stood from the cot and dropped on the floor to sit beside her. "I have some more questions."

"I hope I have answers."

"Who are these jerks?"

"They are a clan of warlocks. A gang, you'd call them in today's terms. Legend has it they were Salem warlocks who turned their wives in to save their own skins. They told themselves they'd done it to stop the persecution of all witches. They were shunned by the Wiccan society. So they turned to black magic and created their own beliefs. Ones that devalued women and saw them as property."

"They've survived all these years?" Miranda asked.

"And grown more powerful by capturing the most potent witches and producing heirs with them." Tears filled her eyes and Miranda suspected she thought of her own children.

"My powers, what can you tell me about them that might help me?"

"They come when you find and accept your true love. They are at their strongest now. You will never lose them completely. When needed you will be able to call upon them. They are the same as your regular powers. Just faster and more potent. And now you have the ability to command the trees."

"And Jeremiah? Where did he—"

She sighed. "He was a guard, over forty years ago. His job was to watch over a powerful witch's daughter. The girl was taken by the bad ones. The witch was so angry, she cursed him. He would remain a creature of scales until he stopped it from happening."

Miranda inhaled. "So what happened to the girl?"

"She died. He didn't. He continued on his mission to save the forest mystics." She paused. "He came to help me. I was too afraid to fight, but I wouldn't let him leave. I imprisoned him, like they did me, but he still came back to help."

"Maybe helping you is what will free him." And somehow Miranda sensed it was true.

"Helping us," Zander corrected.

"Yes." But Miranda sensed there was something special between Zander and Jeremiah.

"Can I really communicate telepathically?" Miranda asked.

"Tabitha said she heard me. I've been trying again, but I don't know if it's getting through. Does it work with anyone?"

"It varies with each witch. Normally, you must be connected to someone to speak."

Miranda remembered she'd communicated with Perry.

The witch touched her arm. "Do not tell anyone where we are. If they come too soon, it will lead to death for many of those you love."

"But could I just let them know I'm okay?"

She nodded.

"How?" Miranda asked, still unsure.

"Through your heart, the same way you connected with Tabitha."

Footsteps came hammering down the hall. "Witch, what have you done?"

Zander looked at her. Fear rounded the woman's eyes, and she began to age. "Something's wrong. I'm sorry."

"For what?"

Zander never answered. A bearded man with gray hair, wearing a robe, came rushing toward the cell. He latched on to the bars and stared in. Evil shone in his eyes.

"What have you done?" he yelled at Zander.

"Who left from our gates just now?"

Chapter Thirty-seven

Perry had spent over six hours soaring, searching, hoping for anything that would lead him to Miranda. He knew Burnett wanted him back, but to stop meant failure.

I love you. He could hear Miranda saying it. She'd told him that last night, right before they'd gone to sleep.

I love you.

The memory echoed louder, but as good as it had felt then, it hurt now. "If you loved me why would you leave? That's not love."

Bitterness, anger, and fear all gave his wings strength.

He started to turn around when he caught something under the trees. Something moving through the woods. Moving fast. Something blue.

He descended to try to see what it was.

I'm sorry.

He ignored the voice and flew downward to peek through the trees. But the branches appeared to shift, blocking his view. He started down, shocked when the vines and limbs laced together, preventing his entry.

This wasn't normal. This wasn't natural.

It had to be magic.

To hell with that.

He shot up, straight up. Flew hard and high. Only when the air thinned, did he start back down. Tucking his wings, molding into a teardrop shape, he dive-bombed downward. Fast, faster, his speed over two hundred miles an hour. His third eyelid moistened his eyes to keep debris out. The fine bones in his nostrils kept his lungs from exploding.

Nothing protected his heart. His heart was already broken.

He shot through the interlocked vines, the limbs ripping his feathers hurt like hell, but his next impact with the hard earth, would be worse. It would kill the bird, but ultimately Perry would survive.

He felt each bone crush. Felt the heart of the bird stop beating. Felt the life as he lived it now end. Then he started to shift.

Pain. Raw agony like he'd never felt tugged at his sanity. He fought the pain pulsing through him, needing answers. He tried to get up but lost consciousness instead. The pain that took him away now brought him back. Opening his eyes, he saw the tree limbs moving toward him. "No."

He forced himself to stand on legs still broken. Then he saw her. Dressed in light blue, red hair flying in the wind. Tabitha. Her feet pelted the ground as if running from the devil himself.

"Open your cell, old woman!" the man screamed.

"Don't do it!" Miranda said under her breath. "Just because he asks it—"

Zander's eyes met Miranda's. She heard the woman's words in her head. *I'm sorry. Don't argue or fight them now. Wait until you are outside. Ask the trees for help. You still may make it. If not. Death is better than this.*

"Now!" the man screamed and wrapped his fist around the bars.

Zander winced but moved to unlock the prison door.

Miranda saw the fury in the man's eyes and knew he intended to cause Zander pain.

No. Miranda pleaded in her head. But Zander didn't listen. She unlocked the gate.

The older of the men grabbed Zander by her hair and pulled hard. She cried out. "Who did you let out of that gate?"

"No one." Her voice trembled.

In her head Miranda heard Zander. *Don't show your tattoos. Wait.*

Miranda felt a storm brewing inside her. Felt her skin tingling and crawling.

"It's time." The two robed men from earlier walked up. "What are you doing?"

"I was walking along the north side, I heard the gate open. I went there, but the corridor was empty. No one came in. So someone must have left. We need to send someone."

Had Tabitha just gotten out? Don't let them go after her.

The younger one moved in. "But Zander's here. So is the girl. Who would have left?"

The old man wearing a robe, who still held Zander by the hair, yanked harder. "She's up to something. I feel it."

The younger man spoke up. "I told you she's outlived her usefulness. Leave her here and we'll take care of her later."

"No!" Miranda shot forward.

All three men looked shocked that she dared to speak.

"See!" the older guard said and slapped Zander across the face. "You have failed to teach this one the rules. What good are you?" He reached back as if to strike her again.

"I will follow the rules." Miranda squared her shoulders, struggling to keep her voice meek. "I'll do what you ask," Miranda said, "but only if she comes with us. To the ceremony."

The younger man stared at Miranda. Or rather leered. "Give her what she wants."

"I think it's dangerous," the older one said.

"I said give her what she wants. Come. We have a ceremony to perform."

. . .

"Where is she?" Perry pleaded again.

In spite of his injuries, Perry had morphed into a large bird. He snatched Tabitha, found a small opening in the trees, and flew straight to FRU headquarters.

Tabitha now sat in a straight chair, looking afraid. But something told Perry she wasn't just afraid of Burnett. "I told you, I don't know."

"You're lying!" Burnett slammed his fist down so hard it rattled the table.

Tabitha flinched. "Yes I am. But I can't tell you. Not until sunset."

"Why?" Burnett roared.

She lifted her chin and in that moment she looked so much like Miranda, Perry wanted to cry. "Because if I do, you'll die." She looked at Perry. "And you, too. And a bunch of my sister's friends."

"What about Miranda?" Perry raged, unable to speak calmly anymore. "Are you going to let her die?"

"If things go the way they are supposed to, she'll be okay."

"And if they don't?" Burnett seethed.

Tears fell from Tabitha's eyes. "They have to. Zander said as long as everything went as planned, she'd get away."

They paraded Miranda through the caverns. They came out into a patch of woods, most of which had been cleared. About twenty-five guests mingled under a large tent. Mostly men.

Miranda prayed that Jeremiah had indeed spiked the wine, because no way could she take on this many.

The older guard dragged Zander under the tent and forcibly pushed her down into a chair. Miranda met her eyes. But Zander could barely raise them. The power that man had over Zander made Miranda sick. No telling what he'd done to her in the past.

Two other men, also warlocks, but not in robes, came over, each took her arm. She almost started fighting then, but her gut said wait. They walked her up to the front to a platform.

All eyes turned to her.

A bell rang. Everyone moved to their seats. About ten robed men stood at the bottom of the platform.

Tell me when, Miranda said in her mind, praying Zander could hear her. *And the sooner the better.*

No answer came back. Miranda felt herself start to sweat. Boob sweat. Her biggest pet peeve. She hated this.

A guy walked up on the platform. He started to chant, like some scriptures, but nothing she recognized.

Chills ran up one side of Miranda's spine and down the other. Everyone stood and repeated some verse. Miranda tried to make it out, but her heart pumped so loudly in her ears, it was all she could hear. Some man in the audience stood and shouted out something about making their army strong. It was getting creepier and creepier.

Air felt trapped in her lungs. She saw a tree to her right stir and forced herself to calm down enough to ask. *Help us.* She looked at Zander who appeared so submissive, a slave to the man who sat beside her. *Help us escape.*

Words suddenly filled her head. Zander's words: *Think wind. Think hurricane. Think if you don't get out of this you'll end up like me.*

Miranda had never conjured up a storm, but she called upon every Goddess she knew, even some she didn't know, to conjure up a storm. An epic storm.

At first she heard nothing. Then a crackling came. Wind followed.

A roaring sound suddenly hit.

The two guards holding her elbows looked up. The sky opened and rain poured. The drops hit so hard they stung. Chills brushed against her skin like wind. Unwilling to have the guards on each side of her touch her any longer, she jerked free. They turned to grab her. Their mistake.

Balls. Eyes. Throat.

The guy on the left got the ball technique. She went for the eyes on the guy on the right.

Another guard charged. Miranda kicked. Her foot hit his larynx.

The youngest robed guy who'd leered at her earlier moved in. Miranda went all out on this one. She gave him the trifecta. *Balls. Eyes. Throat.*

Then grabbing his arm, she tossed him over her shoulder. Like Della, he flew up in the air.

But unlike Della, he didn't come down.

A tree limb reached out, wrapped around his middle and held him there.

Miranda, now soaked from the rain, looked back out at the audience. The cowards were running. Lightning crackled and popped. Men screamed. She saw several raise their hands to use their powers. She prepared herself for disaster. Nothing happened. *Thank you, Jeremiah!*

She thought cages and at least four fell from the sky, capturing men. She needed more. She saw the tent swell up like a parachute. She flicked her pinky, and the metal pipes that held it to the ground came up and struck the warlocks left and right.

Then through the wind that was lifting trees and chairs in the air, Miranda saw the old warlock dragging Zander back toward the cavern.

Fight him! Miranda said to Zander but it appeared she couldn't hear. The roar of storm echoed, the trees stirred. Dark clouds rolled in.

Miranda held out her pinky and a bolt of lightning shot out. It missed, but hit the two warlocks beside them running to the cavern.

Realizing the cavern might mean their escape. Miranda took one second to envision it collapsing in on itself.

A rumble sounded, louder than the storm. The ground shook like an earthquake. A chair came thrashing through the air right at Miranda, and she ducked. She shot back up, searching for Zander. She couldn't find her. Miranda bolted off the platform and took off. The wind flung her hair around; her dress, now heavy with rain, whipped in the air. Several robed men charged her.

One grabbed her. He went flying with the wind. Then two more came, each latching on to her arms.

"Help me." She looked at the trees. A limb, driven by wind, swept forward, loose vines tangled around one of the guy's legs and yanked him up. But just as quickly another man took his place.

With both arms restrained, Miranda started to panic then she heard Della: *An attacker will try to hold your hands to restrain you. That's okay. Your legs are the strongest part of your body. And if he's holding your hands, he's not protecting his boys.*

She took down the old fart to her right first. The second fart to her left came next. They dropped, screaming. But the wind yanked their screams away.

Running, she went in search of Zander. Then it stopped. The rain. The wind. The storm.

"Where's Zander?" Miranda yelled.

The trees opened up and Miranda saw the old man dragging Zander by her hair.

She almost took after them, but Zander's hair started to change from gray to brown.

Miranda stood still, poised to run if needed, but she sensed how important it was for Zander to do this.

Miranda spoke from the heart. *Jeremiah says you have the power.*

Zander's arm reached out and she latched on to the small tree. The old man lost his footing and let go of her hair. But Zander didn't get to her feet, didn't fight.

The old man, still on the ground, gave Zander an order.

The witch, no longer old, feeble, or anyone's slave, stood up. She kicked the warlock. He curled up in a ball. She kicked him again. Then she looked up and yelled something out, like a warrior claiming victory. Miranda couldn't make out her words, but she watched as a limb from a nearby tree swept down, wrapped around the man's torso and carried him up, trapping him in the tree.

Miranda gasped when she saw that dozens of men were ensnared in the vines.

And that's when a vampire swept in. No, not one, but three, four, five.

Burnett, Della, Kylie, and then at least a dozen more, all the Shadow Falls camp vampires, landed and circled her. Then a large bird descended. Perry.

Tears filled her eyes. She ached for him.

He morphed. She waited for him to run to her, to pull her into his arms. She needed to feel safe. To feel loved.

He didn't come. He stood there, staring at her with anger and disappointment.

Burnett, his eyes bright and wide, looked around, nodding as he moved—as if counting the downed warlocks.

"You okay?" the vampire asked.

Tears filled her eyes. She nodded. Her gaze went to Perry.

"Is this everyone?" Burnett asked, looking at a guy sprawled out on the ground.

She pointed up. Burnett and all the vampires looked up. Murmurs of surprise echoed as they saw the men caught in the trees.

Burnett looked back at her. "How . . . ?" He shook his head. "Later." He turned back to his crew. "Cuff the ones on the ground first. Then"—he pointed up—"get the ones up there."

Miranda walked toward Perry. He held his hand to stop her. She did, but it hurt.

"Perry," she said and took another step.

He took one back. His eyes turned a bright yellow. His aura was both dark, bright, and angry. She'd never seen him like this.

"I'm sorry."

"No." He shook his head. "Do you have any idea the hell I've been through the last eight hours?"

He shifted and before she could say anything, he took flight. Tears filled her eyes. Kylie swooped in. She wrapped her arms around Miranda.

Then she spoke. "I'm gonna hug you, because you look as if you really need one. But we're all pretty pissed at you right now."

Kylie wasn't joking. Everyone was angry. Her parents were waiting at the FRU station. Her dad yelled at her. Her mother wouldn't talk to her. Then a very irritated Burnett made her go over everything a dozen times. It didn't help that Zander hadn't been found. Miranda would have worried, but a feeling said she'd be okay.

She explained why the warlock gang wanted her and Tabitha, and how they had gone to Jax and his gang to find and kidnap them. It didn't seem to matter too much. They were still angry. The two to forgive Miranda the quickest were Kylie and Della. But only after Miranda pointed out that they'd both, at one time, left to take care of something on their own. Della still couldn't look at her without growling.

Miranda could take the vamp's attitude. Perry's not so much. Didn't he know how much she needed him?

Back at the cabin, Holiday came to see her. Teary-eyed, Miranda soothed Holiday's ire by telling her about how she'd gotten this message at the falls and considered it blessed by the death angels.

Holiday hugged her. "You did the right thing. It's just hard to be on this side of it. We thought we'd lost you."

Miranda dropped down on her bed. "I know, but if I'd told Burnett, what were the odds he'd have let me go?"

"Negative zero." Holiday smiled with empathy.

Miranda felt a little bit validated. "Have you seen Perry?"

"No." She sat down beside Miranda. "Burnett told me he's upset. Don't worry. He'll come around."

Miranda inhaled, wishing it was birthday cake she smelled instead of everyone's anger. "I've never seen him so mad."

"I know exactly how he feels," Holiday said.

Miranda looked at the fae. Hadn't she been on Miranda's side?

Holiday continued. "I feel it every time my husband runs off and puts himself in danger. I told him once that if he died I wouldn't attend his funeral." Holiday's eyes got misty. "I was lying. He knew it. The thought of losing someone you love this much . . . It's devastating. You get scared and mad."

"I know," Miranda said. "But he put me through it when he was off working undercover with his brother."

Holiday chuckled. "I've had a very similar conversation with Burnett when he gets bent out of shape about my need to help a spirit. There's something about the male psyche that can't see that the danger they put themselves in as being in any way related to the dangers we might face. I mean, Burnett's a smart man, and I've explained it to him in a logical manner. He doesn't see it."

Miranda gave her pillow a punch. "Now I'm getting mad. I need him."

Holiday squeezed her hand. "I don't blame you, but give him some time. On top of being upset that you put yourself in danger, Burnett called a few minutes ago and said the Galveston FRU brought Perry's brother to the Houston facility. Burnett and Perry are headed there now. That can't be easy for Perry."

Holiday went to leave, then turned back. "Oh, good news. Bell crossed over. She knows we'll take care of her son."

"Good."

Miranda curled up in bed. Her pillow smelled like Perry. Her heart ached for him dealing with his family, but she was still pissed. And if he thought he could waltz back here and expect her not to give him some hell, he'd better think again.

Chapter Thirty-eight

"I'm telling you, you got the wrong guy. My name is Perry Gomez. I was visiting my brother."

Perry watched through the two-way mirror as his brother threw him into the fire. Jax wore the special shape-shifter cuffs and a patch with a potent drug that kept him from shifting.

Burnett sat across from him. "You've got about ten minutes to write down all of your gang contacts. Your cooperation will decide what prison you go to while awaiting trial."

"You are sending the wrong brother to jail!"

Burnett smiled. "You're really sticking with that story?"

"It's true. Call my mom. You took my phone. Her number's there. She'll tell you who I am."

Perry exhaled. Jax was right. She'd lie for him. Not that it hurt Perry. That wasn't the parent who pulled on his heartstrings.

As if he had any heartstrings left to pull. Miranda had snapped them in two. But goddamn it! How could she think what she'd done was okay?

"Hell, you have records on me. I lived most of my miserable life in the FRU foster home. Check your own damn records."

Perry decided it was time.

He walked out of one door and in through another. Shock then fury tightened the skin around his brother's skull.

"You . . . ? You helped them. You turned on your own blood! How can you live with yourself?"

Perry chuckled at the irony of Jax saying that after trying to do the same. "And you were selling girls as broodmares. How much were they paying you for their lives?"

Jax looked back at Burnett. "He killed a man. I'll tell you where his body is."

Burnett leaned back. "You mean the body I buried and you dug up?" He glanced at the clock. "Now you've got seven minutes."

The cold look in Jax's eyes said he knew it was over. He finally understood how hopeless his case was. "I ain't giving you shit. I pray one of those gangs kills every last one of you! And you," he glared at Perry, "I hope they gut you like a pig. Slowly. Mama was smart to get your daddy to abandon your ass."

Burnett kicked Jax's chair and he went down. "I tried to make it easier on him," Burnett said.

"I knew he wouldn't work with you," Perry said. They started toward the door. Then Perry turned around and went to stand where Jax could see him. "When I showed you how fast I could shift, I held back. And seriously, I'm much better looking than you are."

Once in the hall, Burnett looked at Perry with concern. "You okay?"

"Yeah, I am." And he meant it.

Sunday morning, Miranda lounged in bed, her nose in a book, because tomorrow morning was test day.

She was checking her phone again for a text when it dinged with a message. Perry? Her heart soared, but crashed when she saw it was Holiday telling her she had a visitor at the office. She texted back: *Perry?*

It seemed unlikely, practically impossible, because Holiday would never call Perry a visitor, but damn it, she could hope.

That hope died with the next ding. *No.*

Miranda had even texted Perry, told him she was angry—because she was—but then insisted they needed to talk. He hadn't even texted back!

The pain was so déjà vu. Him walking away from her. Hurting her, yet again.

How many times was she going to let him do this?

Pinning her hair up, she took off to see who was visiting. Wouldn't Holiday have said if it was Tabitha or her parents?

Walking through the door, she moved into Holiday's office. A man, maybe in his fifties, sat in a chair. Dressed in a suit and tie, he wore his hair flipped back, like an old movie star—or Elvis.

She didn't have a clue who he was.

Glancing at Holiday, who looked puzzled herself, Miranda waited for her to say something.

"This gentleman says he knows you," Holiday said.

"From where?" Miranda asked.

He stood up. "I'm Jeremiah Makepeace."

"Jeremiah." Miranda went right in for a hug. "Wow. Now you'd pass for a fairy godfather."

"So how do you know each other?" Holiday asked.

Miranda looked at Jeremiah, seeking permission to tell her. He nodded.

Miranda leaned in. "He was the armadillo."

Holiday's eyes opened. "Oh."

Miranda focused on the man again. "The curse . . . ? How did you break it?"

"Helping you and Zander stop the evil ones," he said.

"And Zander?" Miranda asked.

"She's at the FRU agency speaking with your friend, Burnett James."

"Is she okay?" Miranda asked.

"It will take time, but I think she'll heal. I'll see to it."

"You love her, don't you?" Miranda's heart went to Perry. She pushed the pain away.

He blushed. "Was it that obvious?"

"Pretty much." Miranda smiled. "You didn't abandon her."

"Neither did you. You helped save her. Thank you."

"Will you two be okay?" Miranda asked. "Do you have a place to live?"

"Zander still has family and I've managed to bury a few keepsakes over the years that will pay my way."

Miranda imagined him as an armadillo stealing from the warlocks all those years, burying his loot in a hole in the ground. She hoped he had enough to live well.

Sunday afternoon Perry stood outside of the interrogation room. He couldn't remember the last time he'd eaten, or gotten a full night's sleep. But last night he hadn't slept a wink, going over in his mind what he'd say to his parents. Or rather to his dad.

Seeing Jax yesterday hadn't hurt. He doubted he'd be hurt by his mom, either. He'd known she hadn't loved him from the beginning.

His dad had been different.

"You don't have to do this," Burnett said to Perry.

"Yes, I do." Even as raw as Perry felt on the inside, he knew this was right. This was putting his past behind him. This was hoping for a future.

He'd agreed to just let Burnett bring his parents in. While the arrest had taken place in Houston, Burnett had managed for them brought directly to the Fallen FRU headquarters. No doubt so Perry would have privacy.

Burnett held out the envelope they'd found stuffed in his dad's suitcase. Part of him wished they hadn't found it. Part of him wished it changed things. And maybe it had, but not enough.

"I got this." Perry took the envelope, then said, "Thank you."
Burnett nodded.

He walked in. His mom gasped. His dad didn't look surprised.
He wouldn't.

Like Jax yesterday, their hands were cuffed and they wore
patches on the sides of their necks.

"I told you he was behind this!" His mom seethed. "How could
you do this to us?"

"Shut up, Sophie," Perry's father said.

"Our own son!" she screeched.

"I said shut up!" his father ordered. Then he met Perry's gaze.
"Why, son?"

Perry found his voice. "Why turn you in?"

"No," his father said. "Why did you find us?"

"Because he's evil! I told you this when he was born," his mom
yelled.

Perry's father turned and stared at his mom. It was as if he saw
her for the first time. "Can someone take her out of here! Please!"

Perry swallowed.

The door opened. Burnett looked at him. Perry nodded. Burnett took his mom by the elbow. His mom glared at him, but she
somehow knew not to mess with Burnett.

When the door closed his father confronted him again. "Why
did you find us?"

Perry tried to lean back in the chair, but he was too tense. "I
didn't know at first."

"Revenge?" his father asked.

Perry ran a hand over his face. "No. When I was young, I
dreamed of finding you. You'd give me a good reason for why you
left me. Maybe someone was trying to kill me and you left me at
that damn mall to protect me." He waited for the knot of pain to
lessen in his throat.

"Yeah, there were a few times I got mad. I thought about revenge, but that's not it. When I started looking for you, I thought

it was just to ask you why." He inhaled. Perry saw pain and tears in his dad's eyes.

Perry had to take a deep breath to continue. "For years, I lacked any kind of self-worth. If your parents didn't even want you, or love you, who would? But thanks to some people, one being the man who put those cuffs on you, I moved past that. So for a while I thought I just wanted *you* to see *me*. To see I turned out okay. But that wasn't it, either." He swallowed.

His father leaned in. "Perry—"

"No, you asked a question and I'm going to answer it." He raked a hand through his hair. "I found you because as a kid, the only damn thing I could remember you doing wrong was leaving me. Before that, I remember wanting to be just like you. And I needed to see your flaws, your mistakes, because I wanted to make sure I turned out to be a better man than you."

"It wouldn't take much." His father pushed a hand over his face. "I—"

"The thing I've learned is that it's not our parents or DNA that defines us. It's not our mistakes, our powers, or our handicaps. It's the choices we make. And the little ones are just as important as the big ones." His throat tightened to the point of pain. "But even the right choices we make don't always correct the wrong ones."

Perry pulled out the photos from the envelope. Photos of him walking in and out of the FRU building. "When did you get these?"

His father looked away. "Tuesday morning. Caleb brought them for your mom. She was in the shower, so I kept them."

Perry swallowed. "Why didn't you give them to her, or give them to Jax?"

He looked at Perry. "Because whatever you did to us, we deserved."

"So it was just to relieve your conscience?"

His father shook his head. "I carried guilt around for so long, I don't remember what it feels like not to have it." His voice shook. "It might not matter to you now. But I did love you. My mistake was loving your mother more. I'm not asking for forgiveness, but I thought you may want to know that."

Perry stood. It hadn't stopped hurting, but now it was a different kind of hurt. One he could move past. "Burnett's fair. He's only charging you for the robberies, and he's going to make sure you're sent to a decent prison."

"And your mom?" his father asked.

"Same thing." Perry picked up the envelope and started out. He told himself he didn't owe his dad anything, but then damn it, he realized he did. He turned and held out the envelope. "Like I said, this choice doesn't make up for your earlier ones, but . . . thank you."

A few hours later Burnett pulled up at the one hotel in Fallen and glanced at Perry.

"You don't have to stay here," Burnett said. "It's summer. There's plenty of empty cabins."

"I know." He exhaled and then needed to know. "Is she doing okay?"

Burnett cut the engine off. "Yeah. She asked about you."

Perry clenched his fist. "I'm still so pissed at her. I love her so damn much, but the thought of her putting herself and me through what she did . . . it infuriates me."

"I know. I feel the same way, and I don't know if it makes any difference but she was warned in the falls that if she told anyone, people would die. I think you were on that list. She said it was . . . something she just had to do, even if it was dangerous."

"It doesn't matter. Do you know what they were going to do to her?"

"I know, but . . . truth is I felt the same way about you getting mixed up in this."

"That's different. I'm a guy."

He kind of chuckled. "I have this same argument with Holiday when she does something dangerous for a ghost. But there's something about a woman's psyche that doesn't understand that. I'll bet Miranda thinks the same way. Now, I'm not saying they're right, but there is just a tiny bit of logic to it."

Miranda had felt pretty good about her test after she'd taken it. Most of the answers came to her with a little happy feeling in her chest that said, "You got this one." But now, three hours later she was back to having boob sweat.

Holiday, Kylie, Della, and Miranda were all sitting in Holiday's office. Mr. Garcia, the dean of the school, who was doing this as a favor for Holiday, had told her he would call with the results at two.

That was five minutes away. Anticipation danced on Miranda's shoulder.

"Everyone breathe," Holiday said. "There's so much anxiety in this room, it's fogging up my windows."

"I did the best I could," Miranda said, now fearing it hadn't been enough.

"Let's not start thinking negative thoughts," Kylie said. "You're going to make the score."

"Right!" Della said.

"Have you seen the caps and gowns?" Holiday asked.

"They're dorky looking," Della said.

Holiday frowned. "I'm still not sure what we're having for snacks."

"Just have pizza," Kylie said. "It doesn't have to be fancy. It's going to be midnight."

Holiday frowned. "You guys didn't have a prom, I just want it to be nice."

"It will be," Kylie said.

The phone rang. Everyone held their breath. Even Holiday.

She picked up the phone. "Shadow Falls Academy . . . Hello Mr. Garcia," she said.

Miranda wished she had sensitive hearing like Della and Kylie.

Miranda bit down on her lip, looking to Kylie, Della, and back to Holiday. What was he saying? Was it good news?

Then Della let out a big cheerful whoop!

Holiday motioned for silence, but was smiling. "Thank you," Holiday said and hung up.

"So I did it. I did it? I'm in?" Miranda asked.

Della and Kylie jumped up, grabbed her arm, and started twirling around.

"No one breaks up the three musketeers!" Kylie said.

Miranda took in a big gulp of air, then suddenly started crying. And they weren't happy tears. "I want to tell Perry."

"Then why don't you?" his voice came from the door.

Miranda swung around. Exhilarated she'd confirmed her place in the college with a solid score, exhilarated Perry was here. But damn if she wasn't still madder than a wet hen who'd been shampooed, blow-dried, and permed.

"Let's take a walk," Holiday said and started out.

"But I want to see Miranda kick his ass," Della said. Kylie got her by the elbow and pulled her out. As Della passed Perry, she growled, "You're lucky I like you."

Holiday shut the door as she exited.

Miranda stared at him. "I'm not sure I can forgive you."

"Good," he said. "Because that makes two of us."

"I needed you," she spit out.

"And I needed you. But for eight hours I was almost certain I'd lost you." He raked a hand through his hair. "I've never loved anything as much as I love you. And you willingly risked your life and put me through hell."

"You think I don't know how that feels?" she countered. "You left me for nine freaking months! I never heard from you."

"You had my number," he tossed out.

"And you had mine," she tossed back.

"You had Shawn," he countered.

"That's not fair. We weren't together—and I broke it off with Shawn so we could be together."

The emotions crowding the air space made the room feel small. But the emotion making it hard for Miranda to breathe wasn't anger, but . . .

"I still love you," he said.

"Me, too." A lump rose in her throat.

"How about we apologize?" he offered.

She nodded. "I'm sorry I scared you."

"I'm sorry, too," he answered.

He took a slow step closer. "Can I kiss you now?"

"Maybe," she teased.

He smiled. "Then I'll wait until you decide, because from what I hear, you can really kick ass now."

She rolled her eyes.

"Oh, I got something for you." He turned and walked out of the office, but in seconds he walked right back. He carried an ice cooler.

He set it on the sofa and opened it up. "Breakup flowers." He handed her a bouquet of bright yellow daisies. "And make-up flowers." He reached back in and handed her a bunch of red roses. "And . . ." he reached back in. "Congratulation flowers for scoring so high on your test. I knew you'd do it."

She couldn't hold them all so he put the daisies down. "And"— he picked up the cooler, and held it so she could see inside—"three gallons of ice cream. Because you said I smell like birthday cake and it made you want ice cream. And since I plan on sticking to you like glue until you have to go to college, I figured we should have lots of ice cream on hand."

She dropped her flowers. He dropped the cooler. She ran into his arms. "Now you can kiss me!"

Chapter Thirty-nine

Class of 2016

...•◆•...

Every yesterday is a memory of dreams.
Every tomorrow is a vision of hopes.
Together we unite
To accept our differences
To appreciate our uniqueness
To make our world a just and fair place

Join us at the midnight hour
June 16th
for the Shadow Falls Academy Graduation

At eleven p.m. on June 16th, Miranda kept putting her hair up, then down. She pushed a strand behind her ear. Then just for grins, she added her old streaks. Pink, black, and green. Turning her head, she stared at herself in the mirror.

It felt right. It felt wrong.

Everything was changing. Things were coming to an end.

It both exhilarated her. And scared the crap out of her.

She wanted to cling to the way things were. She wanted to rush out and stake her claim on the world.

She supposed most graduates felt this way. Growing up was scary business.

Not that she'd be doing it alone. College would be with Kylie and Della.

Perry was staying at Shadow Falls, taking a few classes at the local junior college and working for the FRU. He, Lucas, and Chase were going to share a cabin here on school property. School was less than an hour away. They'd see each other three or four times a week.

"Miranda, we're gonna be late to our own graduation," Kylie called out.

"Coming." She glanced at the mirror again. She so wasn't the same girl who'd come here two years ago. She'd accomplished some amazing things. She'd made some bad mistakes. But she'd learned from each one.

Twitching her pinky, she changed her hair back to just her normal color. Her hair didn't define her. It was as Perry said, her choices did. He'd told her about his talk with his parents. He'd cried. She'd held him. She told him how scared she'd been when she'd been kidnapped. She'd cried. He'd held her. They had each other.

She knew in her heart, they'd always be there for one another.

And tonight they'd take that step. Perry had rented a cabin about ten miles from here. It was on five acres. It had a lake, a hot tub, and a king-size bed.

Her bag was packed. Not a lot of clothes. She figured they wouldn't need them.

Tugging up her green strapless dress, not wanting her girls to fall out, she gave herself one last glance in the mirror. They had decided not to wear prom dresses, but something just a little fancy. The emerald-colored silk hung in layers, giving her what her mom would have called the flapper look. Realizing her parents and Tabitha might already be here, she walked out of the bathroom.

"You two look wonderful," Miranda sighed.

Kylie wore a dusty blue dress that matched her eyes. It was simple, loose-fitting with a scooped neck, and sleeveless. Della wore black. No surprise there. But the front crisscrossed and hugged her body and came off a little more feminine than Della regularly chose.

"We look like Charlie's Angels," Miranda sighed.

"I thought we were the three musketeers?" Della said.

"Before we go." Kylie held out a beautifully wrapped package. "Della and I got you something."

Miranda frowned. "We said no gifts, guys. This isn't fair."

"This isn't for graduation," Della said. "Besides, Kylie and I had a blast picking them out."

Miranda rattled the package. "What is it?"

Della laughed and looked at Kylie. "Can I just tell her?"

Kylie giggled. "Yes."

Della faced Miranda. "It's love socks. Often referred to as love gloves."

"Huh?" Miranda asked.

Kylie laughed again. "What was the other name you called them?"

"You mean weenie beanies?" Della answered.

Miranda finally got it. "You two bought me condoms? How sweet."

"They aren't condoms," Della said, "they're woodie hoodies or willie warmers. And not just regular ones. We got French ticklers, ribbed, and flavored."

Miranda put the present to her chest. "Only really good friends would do this." They all started laughing and then they latched arms and went to start the next phase of their lives.

Wearing caps and gowns over their dresses, each and every one of the 2016 graduates walked up and collected their diplomas from

Burnett. Holiday gave a talk about spreading their wings. About finding their places in life. Miranda cried all the way through it. Not that she was alone. Even Della got misty-eyed.

Everyone was there. Tabitha and Anthony, Miranda's parents, Della's parents, her uncle, and Natasha and Liam. Kylie's parents, as well as all her grandparents. Fredericka had shown up with Brandon, her artist boyfriend. Jenny's parents came. Derek's mom. Jonathon and Helen's parents. There were sixteen of them graduating. Afterwards, when the parents and grandparents had gone home, and Burnett and Holiday retired to their cabin, they all congregated in the dining hall.

It turned into a game of remember when.

Remember when Kylie first came to camp and saw Perry turn into a unicorn.

Remember when Miranda caught Tabitha and put her in a cage.

Remember when Fredericka got sprayed by Socks in skunk form.

Remember when Della had to help deliver Holiday's baby, Hannah.

Remember when Kylie's boobs grew overnight.

Remember when Kylie accidently cut Lucas with a sword.

Remember when Perry mooned everyone.

Remember when Miranda turned Burnett into a kangaroo.

There was a lot of laughter. A lot of memories.

It was almost two in the morning when Miranda collected her bags and walked to the school's car. She turned around and looked at the gate as they walked out.

As sad as it was to know that in a few weeks she wouldn't call Shadow Falls her home, she knew change was inevitable. And while this address wouldn't be listed on forms, it would always be listed in her heart. She took with her the life lessons she'd learned. Here, she'd found self-confidence. She'd learned how to dream, how to never turn away from a leap of faith.

She learned the value of friendships. Of laughter during hard times. Of love.

"You okay?" Perry asked.

She looked up, tears in her eyes, and nodded. She slipped her hand in his. "Come on. Let's go make some more memories."

Read the series that started it all.

Available now

St. Martin's Griffin

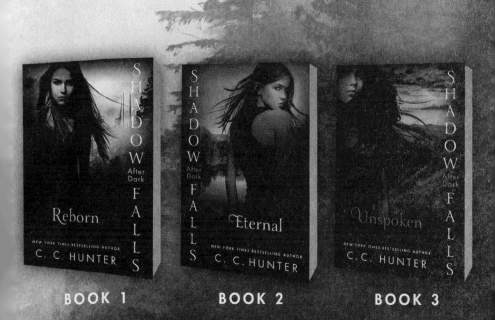